Transportaling

Adventures in a (Nearly) Parallel Universe

Robert Milks

Robert Milks Books

Robert Milks Books LLC

www.robertmilksbooks.com

ISBN 979-8-9914322-1-4 (pbk.)

ISBN 979-8-9914322-0-7 (e-book)

For Frances, of course

BORDERLANDS
LANDS BEYOND
Darksome Wood
Mines
Mines
GREAT CLEFT
Carcella
Kondora
NORTHERN HILLS
Barella
Kascara
Karament
Pantera
Mersala
Pelora
Lentala
Buscara
Velera
Kerela
Buzakor
Cantorba
Dilabel River
HAZY MOUNTAINS
MELENCA
Penrala
Mencara
East Highway
Mountain Trail
Calabra
Kedera
Remora
RESEMU TRACKLESS WASTE
Rushing River
Delfera
Candola
Clinging Road
Lingora
Hills
Bancara
Secora
BOUNDLESS SEA

Contents

1

— ◆ —

WHISKED AWAY

As the plane droned on steadily in a cloudless blue sky, Sam Tolliver was finally relaxing. He had been dubious when he first saw the old seaplane by the dock, even more so when the man who showed up in a blue and white Hawaiian shirt and jeans, with dark, longish hair and a dark mustache, whom Sam figured for a maintenance worker, turned out to be the pilot. Sam glanced at the four other passengers, all strangers, his gaze lingering momentarily on the young woman across the aisle from him, Allie Siddell. Should he strike up a conversation with her? *Don't get too interested,* he told himself. *You'll most likely never see her again after we reach Cabo Sereno.*

Sam looked out the window again and was startled to see an overcast sky around him where there had been no clouds a moment before. The plane shook for a moment, then steadied. *Wind,* he thought, *out of nowhere.* The sky was darker, too. Suddenly, the plane shook violently and dropped, throwing him forward, and almost immediately it plunged in a spiral toward the sea. He was tossed around. Someone cried out. Sam gripped the arms of his seat tightly. Out the window he could see only a swirling gray as the plane spun around and around.

"Brace yourself!" cried the pilot, Eddie Fortune, from the open cockpit. "I'm fighting it, but I can't pull out—we're heading toward the water!" Sam leaned forward and crossed his arms against the seat back in front of him. Just as suddenly, the plane was out of the wind and the sky was blue again, but they were not far above the water. Eddie kept it level for a minute or two and cut the speed, but then the plane plunged again, and with a tremendous jolt bounced on the water and up again, two times, three times. Sam's seat belt kept him from hitting the ceiling, but he banged his knee into the seat ahead. The plane jerked down and then back up and then sideways, and then it was floating in the sea, rocking gently. Sam caught his breath and after a few seconds loosened his grip on the armrests. He could see out the window the same cloudless blue sky, with no sign of the gray whirlwind that had plunged them into the water. The sea was calm.

"Is everyone OK?" said Eddie, standing in the doorframe. Sam's knee ached. He had played high school football and injured that knee badly. It had long since healed. He hoped the pain would resolve once he walked on it. He didn't say anything.

"I think she hurt her shoulder," said Allie Siddell, pointing to the older woman next to her. Winnie Smithers winced, but said she would be OK. Eddie told her he had a first-aid kit but couldn't do much for a bruised shoulder—or worse.

"What the hell happened?" she said.

"Don't ask me," replied Eddie. "Some kind of whirlwind, but I've been flying for a long time, and I've never seen anything like it." He looked out a window. "I *didn't* see it—that's the problem—there was no sign of any bad weather. It just materialized."

Peter Morey, sitting in front of Sam, cleared his throat. "I, ah, I've never encountered such a phenomenon. And I've done fieldwork for years in the Caribbean."

"That's what I just said. I've flown for years in the Caribbean. It happened. I think we're all aware of that." Eddie returned to his seat and fiddled with the instrument panel. They could hear him speaking but couldn't make out what he said. Sam leaned over closer to the window. The water lapped against the plane, and judging from the waterline, a good bit of the bottom of the plane appeared to be submerged. The wing was warped at the end.

"That wing looks pretty banged up," he called to Eddie. "Are we going to be able to lift off again?"

Eddie stared out the port window in the cockpit. "No. If we stay in the plane we can chance someone spotting us. But I don't know how stable the plane's going to be. Who knows how long it's going to stay afloat?"

"You said if we stay in the plane. Is there any other choice?"

"Yes, we can—"

"I'm not going to start swimming," cut in Rafe Thomas.

Eddie glared at him. "Did I say anything about swimming? You want to listen? We've got a raft. We'd be OK in this calm sea."

"What if it doesn't stay calm?" said Allie anxiously. "Wouldn't we be better off in the plane then?"

"Not if it sinks."

"Won't they send out a search plane when we don't show up? Won't the plane be easier to spot?"

"The raft is bright yellow. The plane's bigger, but the raft's more noticeable."

"They *will* send a plane, right?" said Winnie. "You radioed for help?"

"You think I'm clueless? I sent out a mayday—but I didn't get any response." He paused for a few seconds. "That's another strange thing. There's nothing on the radio at all—no chatter from anywhere, just noise."

Rafe broke in again. "Try your cell phone. You do have a cell phone?"

"You think I didn't try? No service."

"You probably forgot to charge it."

"I did not forget to charge it. Since you're so smart, try yours."

Rafe pulled his out. "Hmm. Can't get a signal."

"What do you think we should do, then?" Allie asked Eddie.

He glanced out the window. "Get in the raft."

"Are you sure it's better to get off the plane?" said Peter. "Shouldn't we stay inside and wait for help?"

"You can stay here if you want. I'm going."

Peter looked at the others. "What about the rest of you?"

After a few seconds, Sam responded first. "I'll go along with Eddie. He knows a lot more about this than I do. Than I'm guessing any of you do."

"Ditto," said Winnie.

"I'll go too," said Allie.

Peter hesitated, looked out the window, then back at the others. "All right, I'm not staying here by myself."

Eddie opened the door to the cargo hold in the rear. They could hear him rummage around, then open a hatch, and then there was a splash. Then he reappeared. "Let's go."

"What about our bags?" said Rafe.

"Sorry. No room in the raft."

"But I have stuff in there I need!"

"Forget it," said Winnie. "I'm not giving up a shot at rescue for your fucking bag."

"Can't we just get a few things out?"

"We can replace things," said Allie. "Not lives." Rafe looked at her sullenly but didn't say anything.

Eddie ushered them to the hatch, where a rope ladder swayed. The raft below was bobbing gently in the swells. Eddie turned back to Sam. "You go first. Make sure everyone gets in OK. I'll come last." Sam climbed down the ladder and stepped into the raft, which tipped a little, then stabilized. Winnie followed him, then Allie, each with her purse strapped over a shoulder. Sam gave each a hand to steady them as they stepped into the raft. Winnie grimaced as he took her right hand—the same side as her injured shoulder. Peter accepted Sam's hand; Rafe grabbed his shoulder. Eddie closed the hatch and clambered down into the stern, moving aside a large bag with his foot. He gazed at the horizon on all sides.

"Which way is land?" said Allie.

"That's the big question, isn't it?" Eddie glanced around. "We got spun around coming down, so it's hard to know which way to head. No cell service, so no compass or GPS. The GPS on the instrument panel isn't working either."

Sam squinted at the open water in the bright sunlight. The green sea was calm, the raft wafting slightly back and forth. It was tranquil, but his stomach churned. Getting lost at sea was not a fate he had ever imagined could happen to him. "Lamora and Cabo Sereno are in opposite directions," he said. "If we get to either one we'd be safe."

"And how do we know which direction to go?" said Winnie, wincing again.

Eddie nodded. "She's right. Even if we headed just a little oblique, we might miss land."

"Would we hit an island around here?" asked Allie.

"There are a lot of islands, but there's a lot more water."

"What's that over there?" said Rafe.

"Where?"

Rafe pointed to the horizon behind Eddie. "There. Some sort of dark thing way out there." Sam shaded his eyes with his hand and after a couple of seconds made out an indistinct shape low on the horizon. Eddie pulled a pair of binoculars from the bag. He surveyed the horizon from side to side.

"It's land. And it extends a long way—it's not just a small island." He took another look. "That's not possible."

"How the fuck is it not possible?" said Winnie. "Is it there or not?"

"It's there, but it can't be. There's no land between Lamora and Cabo Sereno, maybe a small islet—certainly not a mass like that."

"We must have been blown way off course, then," said Rafe.

"We weren't in that whirlwind but a couple of minutes, tops, and it took us down, it didn't blow us out. It doesn't make any sense."

After a moment, Sam said, "Maybe it's a mirage. But if it looks like land, we ought to head for it, don't you think?"

When he had discovered on Lamora that the ferry to Cabo Sereno was out of service for repairs, Sam had also learned that FortuneAir Charters was the only alternative. The small waiting area for FortuneAir was in a corner of the ferry terminal, in front of a door that opened onto the docks. The only person waiting was a middle-aged man wearing a long-sleeved oxford shirt, blue blazer, and khaki slacks, with neatly combed gray-streaked blond hair. The only furniture was a small table with a sign for FortuneAir. On a small blackboard on the wall behind the table was chalked "Next flight Cabo Sereno around 11:00, cost TBD from no. of passengers."

"I assume you're not with FortuneAir," said Sam.

"Are you a passenger too? Hopefully more will show up to split the cost."

A minute or two later, a short, stocky, sixtyish woman with short gray hair, wearing loose-fitting slacks and blouse, joined them. "Hell of a way to get somewhere," she said. "If they want this paradise-in-the-making to work, they better damn well make it easier to get there."

"There is a ferry," said Sam.

"Yeah, a broken down one. Let's hope that piece of junk out there works better." She glanced at the blackboard. "I've got to have a smoke. Don't let them take off without me." She walked through the outside door.

She'd just returned a few minutes later when a young woman with chocolate-colored, shoulder-length hair joined them. Sam noticed at once her luminous brown eyes. The rest of her didn't disappoint either.

"Good, someone else to chip in," said the older woman. "It's getting crowded. If we're going to be elbowing each other on that contraption, we'd better get acquainted. I'm Winnie Smithers." She was a longtime newspaper reporter who had retired a few years before to freelance, producing articles and a couple of books on different regions in North America and the Caribbean. She looked at the others expectantly.

"I'm Peter Morey," said blue blazer. "I'm an anthropologist. I'm looking at Cabo Sereno as a site for fieldwork."

"Studying the fascinating communal rituals of resort developers?"

He laughed. "The transition from traditional culture to tourist destination. It's a golden opportunity—no one's done work on the island." He turned to Sam.

"I'm Sam Tolliver. I'm here for my family's business."

"What sort of business?" said Winnie.

Reporter, she said, thought Sam—*nosy.* "We import craft objects you'd find in upscale shops." He didn't want to go into more detail. His new title sounded impressive, but he hadn't wanted to take the job and didn't think he was the right one for it—and that was before the worrisome situation in Cabo Sereno. The board had sent him to find out what was going on and deal with it. He had no idea where to start. *"We're sure you can handle it,"* his mother had told him when he left. *"You've always handled your roles competently—you'll grow into this one. We wouldn't send you if we didn't think you could take care of this one. We have confidence in you, Sam. I have confidence in you."* He wished he shared it. His last job, now, managing the section, software work that he'd done himself for years and had been trained for, that was different. He was happy. But this, something he had no experience at. . . .

He was spared further questioning when a young man approached the group. He was a little taller than Sam, about six feet. With his curly light brown hair, he reminded Sam of busts of ancient Greeks.

"Yes, this is where you queue up for Cabo," said Winnie before he could say anything. She looked at the young woman. "You were about to say?"

"Allie Siddell. Just a tourist—a friend rented a bungalow at one of the new resorts. She invited me for the week."

"Do you do anything in real life?"

"Actually, I do. In marketing, copywriting. For a small corporation you probably never heard of."

Winnie turned to the latecomer. "Your turn."

"What is this, twenty questions?"

"Are you antisocial? Since we're chartering that antique out there together, we're introducing ourselves. You got a problem with that?"

"Who said I did? I'm Rafe Thomas. I'm an entrepreneur."

"Entrepreneur at what?"

"A startup."

"On Cabo Sereno? You're joking."

"I don't joke about my business. It's video production, virtual reality stuff. Settings here are great, costs are low—especially labor."

Just then the outside door opened and a late-thirtyish man emerged. Eddie Fortune, it turned out, was owner, proprietor, and pilot of FortuneAir Charters, which consisted of the one old seaplane floating beside a dock. To Sam, both the plane and the pilot were unsettling. Eddie looked more like a daredevil stunt pilot, or maybe a drug smuggler, than a commercial charter pilot. Still, the plane appeared to be the only way Sam was going to get to Cabo Sereno anytime soon, and if they split the cost, it wasn't prohibitive. So they all went out to the dock and climbed aboard the plane.

Eddie started the small motor on the raft and turned the raft toward the dark shape. The sea remained calm, so the raft didn't rock much, and it fit six comfortably enough. As Eddie kept a steady course toward the shape, slowly it grew larger and more defined. Eventually they could make out a shoreline. Gradually it resolved into a wide, sandy beach. At the back of the beach they could now see trees, and beyond them in the distance some low hills. Soon they could make out individual trees.

"That's bizarre," said Eddie. "Look at the trees."

"I see oak and hickory," said Sam. "And some others I don't recognize." Striking among the unfamiliar ones were slender trees with shiny, silvery bark and thicker-trunked trees with spreading branches with blue-tinted leaves.

"But there aren't any palm trees," observed Winnie.

"No there aren't," said Eddie. "It doesn't look like the Caribbean,"

Eventually they drew up into shallow water. Eddie directed Sam and Peter to get out in the small breakers and pull the raft onto the beach. Sam took off his boat shoes and socks and rolled his trousers up to his knees. Peter followed suit. Pulling the raft wasn't difficult in the surf, and they had to strain only over the last three or four feet until it was out of the surf.

The beach was deserted. They could see no buildings or other signs of civilization. The others climbed out of the raft onto the beach and stretched. Eddie pointed to the trees. "Let's pull the raft up there." After they dragged it a short way among the trees, he found a fallen branch and stuck it into the ground as a marker.

"Now what?" said Winnie, pulling out a cigarette from a pack in her purse and lighting it. She tried to hold the hand on her injured arm steady.

Eddie glanced around. "Walk inland, I think. We might run into a settlement. Or at least a higher point in those hills where we can see farther."

Peter frowned. "What if we get lost? These woods look pretty thick. I think we'd be better off staying on the beach—surely there's a town along it somewhere."

Sam slipped back into his boat shoes, cramming his socks into his pockets. He studied the landscape ahead. "We saw openings in the woods from the raft. I don't think the woods are all that thick, at least not everywhere."

Winnie took a drag on her cigarette, then nodded. "Let's not stand here and jabber. Let's see if we can find out where the hell we are."

"At least stay on the beach until we see an opening," Allie suggested. "It will be easier than going through woods."

"But which way?" said Rafe.

"You do understand we don't know where we are?" said Eddie. "It doesn't matter which way." He set off to the left from the sea. The others followed. Pain shot through Sam's knee with each step, and he limped, but he was determined not to let it slow him down. They walked about two hundred yards on the hard-packed sand near the water before they came upon a clearing in the trees. Ahead through the clearing the land sloped upward gradually until it abruptly rose forty or fifty feet. They moved into the clearing. After twenty yards or so, trees and underbrush—small shrubs with prickly, dark green leaves—closed in on both sides. From there, the woods looked thicker than from the beach. A narrow way through the trees remained open, however, and Sam realized they were walking on a path. After fifteen minutes, they reached the foot of the hill. The trees stopped. The grade steepened, but not enough to be challenging, not even to the cigarette-puffing, sixty-something Winnie.

At the top, a broad vista suddenly opened before them. Fields spread out, interspersed with small stands of trees. Here and there were stone houses that Sam guessed were farmhouses. A river glinted in the distance as it wound across the landscape, and off to the left a town sprawled back toward the sea and ended in a harbor, where a few boats lay at anchor. Scattered along a line parallel to them were other hills in both directions, none of them any higher than this one. The ridge wasn't very broad, and the slope plunged down the other side. At the bottom, parallel to the hills, ran a paved road.

"Where to now?" said Rafe.

"The town—duh," said Eddie. They'd taken only a few steps when they spotted two men walking on the road below, coming from the direction of the town. As the group descended the hill the men saw them and stopped, talked for a moment, then kept walking. They wore tunics of a rough, drab cloth that ended at the waist, one beige, the other gray, and navy trousers that narrowed until they were drawn tight at the ankles, below which were low-cut shoes without laces. The group reached the road just as the two men drew even with them.

The men stopped again and spoke in low voices. Then one, a stocky fellow with an unruly mop of graying hair, addressed the group in a gravelly voice. "Who are you? Where are you from?" Both men stared intently at Sam and his companions.

"We're a group of stranded tourists," replied Winnie, "trying to figure out where the hell we are."

"Where you are?" He pointed back toward the town. "That's Secora."

"I mean which island. This obviously isn't Lamora or Cabo Sereno."

"Island?" said the man. "Do you mean which district? This is Dolobar District."

"The whole place—the country."

The man looked puzzled. "Which land, is that what you mean?" said his companion, a tall, thin man with a high-pitched voice. "You are in Melenca."

Winnie looked at Eddie. "Ever heard of it?" He shook his head.

The second man looked at the first. "They're obviously not Newcomers."

"Newcomers don't dress like that—I've never seen outfits like these."

Suddenly there was a buzzing from behind Sam and his companions. They turned and saw approaching them a man standing on a contraption like a skateboard, only longer and wider, about the size of a surfboard, made of metal with sides that curved up slightly to even with the knees of the man, who stood at what appeared to be a steering column. The machine had four wheels and was self-propelled in some way, rolling along at a fairly fast clip.

"What's that?" exclaimed Rafe, pointing to the vehicle, which rapidly distanced itself from them.

"The skimmer?" said the first man. "It's . . . well, it's just a skimmer." He looked curiously at Rafe. "You don't know?" He looked at the second man. "If they were from the Lands Beyond, they would know what a skimmer is, wouldn't they?"

"I guess they would." He looked them over again. "Maybe they're Outbounders"

"Outbounders? That's just an old legend."

"It's not—they're real. My uncle knew one."

"Your uncle tells many tales."

"I'll wager Beldan would know if they're real."

"Maybe, maybe not." He paused for a few seconds, then continued. "Beldan might know what sort of folk these are, though. He travels widely around Melenca."

The conversation between these two may as well have been in Greek, thought Sam.

What's happened to us?

"We should take them to him," said the nephew. "And find out I'm right." He pointed back toward the town. "Come with us."

Sam and the others stood there, hesitating, looking at each other. Finally, Sam spoke up. "We don't know what you're talking about, but if this Beldan can tell us where we are, and maybe how to get where we're going, I'd say we should go with you. What do the rest of you think?"

"May as well see if we can find out anything," said Eddie.

"We're just going to go off with these guys?" said Rafe. "We don't know anything about them, or this guy they're taking us to. They could be setting us up."

"OK, hotshot, what's your plan?" said Eddie.

"I didn't say I had a plan. You don't either."

"Yes I do—follow them and see what we can learn."

"Cut the squabbling—let's go," said Winnie, and she gestured to the men and started walking toward the town. Sam and Eddie followed and then so did the others.

To their left as they walked toward the town were more woods, hickory trees and oaks again and the silver-barked and blue-leaved trees. No palm trees. To their right were mostly fields, pastures and croplands—wheat in some fields, but a low-lying yellow plant Sam didn't recognize in others—and they passed an occasional stone farmhouse, with a shimmering roof apparently made from silver-barked wood. After ten minutes houses began to cluster together and side streets branched off. They walked at the edge of the road—there weren't any sidewalks. More skimmers buzzed past them in both directions, and people walked along the road on both sides. Everyone they passed stared at Sam and his companions, some stopping while they looked. The men wore similar clothing to that of the two men, but most of the women wore skirts that fell to mid-calf. Many of the clothes were in the same drab colors, some in brighter hues.

"This is inexplicable," said Peter, who had caught up to Sam. "Is this a private island? Is this some kind of cult? If so, they've gone to a lot of trouble developing these 'skimmers.'"

"It's more bizarre than that. Eddie said there shouldn't be any land here. But there is. And nothing looks tropical."

"He was right—it doesn't make any sense."

The side streets widened. Some of the buildings appeared to be houses, but as they paraded along, some displayed objects in windows or had signs above the doors, which Sam guessed were stores or offices. Soon they glimpsed the harbor ahead, but their guides turned onto a side street before they reached the waterfront. Ten minutes later, they entered a more affluent neighborhood, the houses bigger and spaced farther apart, with large, well-kept lawns. Finally, the men turned into a drive leading up beside a large two-story house of white stone. The drive led to an outbuilding behind the house, and a path branched off to the front of the house. The men turned onto the path. The nephew knocked on the door. When no one had come within a minute or so, he knocked again.

A moment later the door opened, and a young blonde woman, probably in her early twenties, smiled at them. She wore a white blouse and navy slacks that flared slightly where they ended midcalf, with the same sort of slip-on shoes as the two men wore.

"Is your father in, Elja?" said the nephew.

"He's in his study."

"We encountered this group out on the north ridge. We think they're Outbounders. Your father can confirm that."

"Or not," said his skeptical companion.

"They *are* dressed outlandishly," said Elja. She stepped back. "Please, come in. I will tell my father." They entered a large foyer. Elja followed a corridor past a couple of doorways, then disappeared into a room on the left. Other doors opened on the right side, and at the end of the hall, a staircase led off the hall on that side. The floor in both the foyer and the hall was dark hardwood. A large rug with geometric patterns lay in the middle of the foyer. On the wall to the right of the hall hung a large, skillfully painted landscape of a scenic lake surrounded by forest and meadows.

After a few minutes, Elja emerged from the room and beckoned. "He'll see you. This way." They entered a spacious room, with a lighter brown hardwood floor, another large rug, bookcases, a large desk, and several comfortable-looking chairs scattered around. Another landscape painting hung on one wall, and a painting of a convivial pub scene on another. A wiry, middle-aged man stood in front of the desk. He was a little shorter than Sam, with light brown hair flecked with gray. His pale-green tunic resembled those the men wore, but was of a finer cloth, as were his azure-blue trousers, the colors of both contrasting with the dull neutral colors of the two men's clothes.

He looked the group over for a moment, then turned to the two men. "These people may well be Outbounders," he said. "You did right to bring them here. You can go now."

"Told you," said the nephew to his companion as the men left the room. "Just think—we've seen real Outbounders! Wait until I tell people."

Beldan looked after them, rubbing his chin. "I wonder . . ." he mused.

"You called us 'outbounders,'" said Winnie. "So did they. But we don't know what you mean."

"People from beyond the Boundless Sea. They never do seem to be able to explain how they got here—not that there are many in Melenca. I've only met a few in all my years."

"We had to crash-land our plane in the water off the beach near here," said Eddie. "Is that the Boundless Sea."

"The sea is off the beach—the rest of your explanation is mysterious to me."

"We're trying to get to the island of Cabo Sereno," said Sam. "Can you tell us how we might get there?"

Beldan shook his head. "I know nothing of lands beyond the Boundless Sea. But I know someone who does. He is himself an Outbounder, though he has lived in this area for many years. Perhaps he can help you."

"How do we find him?" said Winnie, wincing as she spoke.

"Wooden's house is outside Secora, not far." He paused. "You appear to have an injury. We should take you to our healer."

"She banged it up when we crash-landed," said Allie.

At that moment, a middle-aged woman entered the room. "Beldan, have you heard yet from Katera—oh, I did not know you had company. Forgive me." She was striking, not beautiful but graceful and poised, a little taller than Beldan. Her gray hair was swept back in a bun and she wore a full-length gown of a shimmering blue cloth.

"This is my wife, Silenda," he said. "These people have just arrived in Secora—have just come to Melenca, in fact. I think they're Outbounders, Silenda. "

"That would explain their outfits." She paused, then said, "Wooden's the only Outbounder I've known."

"I told them Wooden might be able to help them." He looked at Winnie. "Since you don't know the area and are on foot, it will be best for us to take you to him. But perhaps you should visit the healer first."

She shook her head. "No. I want to find out where we are—and how we get home."

"Before you take them," said Silenda, "is there anything further from Katera?"

"Not today. Don't worry—things are chaotic. She probably hasn't had time to write again." He turned back to the group. "Our daughter is with a group up north, near the crystal mines, assessing the damage—cracks, rockslides, maybe worse. Her letter hinted that it's spreading quickly."

"Beldan, I *am* worried. It appears she dashed that letter off in a hurry."

"She most likely had to rush to get it off—I suspect message delivery is erratic in the chaos."

"Not just chaos—buildings hit by rockslides, lives lost."

"Those are just rumors. We don't know for sure. The *Current* and the *Vantage* have sent reporters, so there should be accurate reports soon." He looked back at the group. "I realize all this means nothing to you. But it's probably best to let Wooden explain it to you—he likely knows the land you come from."

"But we do gather your daughter is in danger," said Allie.

"Yes," answered Elja, "my sister's life is at risk thanks to Flammer, who pulled the monitors out."

"We don't know for sure she's at risk," said Beldan, glancing at Silenda. "Let's wait to get more information. Meanwhile, we need to go to Wooden's."

"Wait, Beldan," said Silenda. "Have they eaten lunch?" Sam realized now that he had in fact not eaten anything since a hurried bagel and coffee early that morning. After all the turmoil of their journey, he wasn't sure how much time had elapsed, but he was hungry.

"I think our guests are anxious to meet Wooden," said Beldan. "Time for eating afterward. Am I right?"

"Yes," said Allie. No one contradicted her.

"Not even time for a chicken sandwich?" persisted Silenda.

"When we return," said Beldan. "First, though, it's past time for proper introductions—my apology. Beldan Falembo, at your service." The members of the "Outbounder" group introduced themselves one by one. "Odd names," said Beldan. "But of course our names will be odd to you."

Just then they heard the front door open and soon a young man joined them. He looked a little older than Elja, maybe mid-twenties, an inch or two taller than Beldan, with the same wiry frame and light brown hair.

"This is my son Dalbin," Beldan said. They introduced themselves a second time. "They're Outbounders, we believe. We're going to take them to see Wooden."

"That's sensible."

"Of course. You can take them."

"As you can see, we're eager to volunteer around here," Dalbin told the group. "All right, follow me." As they followed him to the outbuilding, a yellow dog the size of a Labrador retriever but more resembling a shaggy Irish setter approached them wagging its tail. After stooping to pet the dog, Dalbin lifted a garage-type door, revealing a couple of skimmers and a larger vehicle the size of a van, with sides that came up about shoulder height and with two metal frames, in the front and the back, that rose from the sides and curved across the width, then back down to the other side. On the back frame, a roll of cloth was furled up and tied. Two wide doors in the side were open. Behind the driving column were several large metal boxes bolted to the floor, then two wooden benches with wooden back supports running across the vehicle's width, with a narrow aisle next to the doorways. Behind the back bench was a storage space. The vehicle had four wheels, bigger than skimmer wheels.

Dalbin pointed to the large vehicle. "Make yourselves comfortable in the hauler." Winnie, Peter, and Eddie climbed through the back doorway onto the back bench. Allie scooted along the front bench, followed by Sam and then Rafe. Dalbin started the engine—or whatever powered the hauler—and it moved out into the street they'd walked on, turning in the opposite direction.

The bench was plenty roomy for the three of them, and they weren't physically touching, but Sam could feel Allie's presence next to him. *Maybe I was wrong on the plane. We've been thrown together for more than an hour. A chance to get to know her better?*

"I didn't even think about my family," she said.

"Your family?"

"After we crashed, all I've thought about was where are we? What's happened to us? I was going to call my parents when I got to Cabo Sereno. They'll be worried."

"I didn't think about that either." He paused, then said, "So you don't have a husband, then? Or a partner?"

She looked at him as though sizing him up. "No." She started to say something else, then stopped. After a moment, she asked, "And you—what about your family?"

"I'm not married." *And no prospects, either. Not since Sylvia, but. . . .* "I was going to call home too, pretty soon after I got to Cabo."

"So your parents will worry too."

"My mom, yes, I guess when I don't check in fairly soon." He hesitated. "My dad . . . passed away a few months ago."

"I'm so sorry. That was clumsy of me."

"No, you couldn't know. You get through it the best you can. You carry on."

At that moment, they felt a few rain drops. Sam wondered about riding in the open like this—what did Melencans do? Dalbin answered his unspoken question: "Someone in back, unfurl the roof and bring it forward."

Eddie stood up and untied the stiff cloth, then stretched it toward the front of the hauler.

"I can attach it up front if you want," said Sam.

Eddie glanced at him, his eyebrows arched. "You're kidding, right? I'm an engineer." And indeed, he quickly hooked the cloth to a small projection on the front frame. The rain pattered pleasantly on the roof.

Soon they had clearly reached the outskirts of Secora. The wood houses here were smaller, and looked weather-beaten. A large sign appeared in the small yard of one house. "Restore Melenca to Glory," it read. A few houses later, another large sign appeared. "Flammer" ran across the top, and there was a drawing of a large, scowling man beneath it. Written below it was "Follow the Supreme Leader!"

"Flammer," said Winnie. "Wasn't that the name Elja mentioned?"

"Not favorably, I'm sure," said Dalbin.

Outside Secora they turned onto a broad highway. The terrain resembled what they had seen from the hilltop: mostly flat, with fields of wheat, now some corn, and the yellow plant they had seen earlier; patches of the same familiar and novel trees that had lined the back of the beach; farmhouses.

After a few minutes, Dalbin swung the hauler down a lane to the side, which led into a grove of oak trees and then a clearing, where a one-story, rambling, wood-frame house stood in the center. It had dark siding and a lighter wooden roof, though not silvery, with some carved curlicues where the roof peaked. A porch ran along the front, with several rocking chairs in a couple of small clusters. When Dalbin knocked on the door, a fiftyish man soon opened it. His blondish hair was cut short and streaked with gray.

"I'll be damned!" he said. "Outbounders—or should I say Americans?"

2

— • —

GETTING BEARINGS

Eddie stared at him. "How'd you know?"

"Your outfits," said the man, eyeing his Hawaiian shirt and jeans. "It's been a long time since I saw any like those—another Outbounder shows up here every once in a while."

"You're Wooden, I presume?" said Winnie.

"Timothy Wooden, in full—you can call me Tim. Since Dalbin brought you here, you must have met Beldan."

"He told us to see you," said Sam. "You're American too?"

"Originally. I've lived here for thirty years now."

"Where the hell is 'here,' exactly?" asked Winnie. "We can't figure it out."

"I'll leave you to talk," said Dalbin. "I'll return for you later."

"Let's go inside," said Wooden. He led them down a long hallway to a large room to the right, with cozy-looking upholstered chairs spaced around and several small tables. On one sat a wood carving of a moose, about eight inches long and six high. It was skillfully carved, detailed and lifelike. Other carvings perched on tables and on the shelves of a small bookcase against one wall.

Wooden gestured for them to sit. "No doubt you've observed that things are strange."

"Beyond strange," replied Winnie. "Weird. Bizarre."

Eddie nodded. "For starters, this land mass we came upon after my seaplane crash-landed in the sea shouldn't be here."

"Let me guess," said Wooden. "You were in the Bermuda Triangle and you ran into a whirlwind."

"How'd you know that?"

"It happened to me—it's how I got here. I was on a fishing trip with a couple of buddies. It was calm, then suddenly there was the whirlwind, and our boat capsized. I saw the land not far off—which wasn't there a few minutes before—and I didn't see my buddies, so I made for it—I'm a pretty good swimmer."

"What does it mean?" said Allie. "What is the whirlwind?"

"It was a while before I found out—almost a year. I couldn't figure out what had happened, why everything was so strange."

"But you did find out," said Winnie.

"You better sit down. You're going to have trouble believing it."

"Believing what?"

"Some things are beyond what we can grasp, what our science knows. The best way to explain it—as far as I *can* explain it—is that the whirlwind is a portal, a doorway. You entered it in the Caribbean. You passed through it into a parallel universe."

They all stared at Wooden. Then Sam said, "You're saying we're. . . ."

"I'm saying you're not on Earth anymore."

"Not on Earth!" exclaimed Rafe. "But they're all human beings."

"They said they had chicken sandwiches!" said Allie.

"Everyone speaks English!" said Winnie.

"It's parallel," Wooden replied. "It's not identical. It's sort of a replica Earth, in a different universe, or maybe a different dimension. I don't know the techne—science—of it. As for English, I'm not sure about that. There's no England here, at least in the lands around Melenca, though no one knows what lies beyond the Boundless Sea. I think we just understand them—that's part of the parallel thing."

"But a lot about it is different," said Peter.

"Like I said, it's not identical. Some things are the same or very similar, others are different."

"There's got to be some other explanation."

"Maybe it's a wormhole to another part of the universe," said Eddie, "our universe."

"With a replica Earth with human beings just like us, who we understand?" replied Wooden. "That seems even more far-fetched." He thought for a moment. "Did you get here today?"

"As far as we know. We took off this morning, and everything still seems the same day, just in the afternoon."

"So you haven't spent the night here. Tonight, look at the sky. The constellations are different, not anything recognizable from Earth." Everyone fell silent again.

After a moment, Allie broke the silence. "But . . . but what do we do now?"

"I suggest you adapt to life here. That's what I did."

"Isn't there a way back?"

"No." He hesitated, then said, "I, uh—no."

"If it's a doorway," said Sam, "shouldn't it work both ways?"

"The whirlwind deposited you in the sea. It did me too. Hunting for a whirlwind in the sea would be futile. And if there is one, who knows if it would take you back? Maybe it would take you somewhere even worse, from your perspective." He shook his head. "You'll be better off if you accept that you're here to stay and adapt to Melenca. I can advise you."

"But there's got to be some way back," said Allie.

"What Sam said makes sense," added Peter. "If there's a portal in one direction, it stands to reason there would be one in the reverse direction."

"I'm not sure the universe runs on reason—any universe," said Wooden.

"You started to say something,'" said Sam. "You seemed to be thinking of something."

"No. It was nothing."

"Are you sure? No possibility, no matter how remote?"

"Look, I don't want to give you false hopes. Like I said, the sooner you learn to accept what happened and adapt, the better off you'll be—especially mentally."

"There is something, isn't there."

Wooden sighed and hesitated, then he said, "There's a sort of spiritual leader in Melenca. Mentor Perroso, he's called. His real name is Miles Perroso, but he's widely known as Mentor Perroso. He was an Air Force pilot whose plane got sucked into the whirlwind. He's lived here a lot longer than me—around sixty years. He's in his eighties now."

"What about him? Does he know a way back?"

"The first time I met him was when I found out where I was. And he asked me if I was interested in returning to Earth. I'd settled in by that time, and I said no. He said, 'Then I'll say no more.'"

"That's all?"

"Years later I met a couple of other Outbounders, separately. They both wanted to go back, just like you. I mentioned what Mentor Perroso had said. I saw them again later, and they had both talked with him. They both were sure there was a way. One I met again later, though. He was bitter, said it didn't work out."

"Why not?" said Allie.

"He wouldn't elaborate when I asked, just repeated that it didn't work out, that was it."

"What about the other?"

"I never saw him again. I passed through the town where he lived later and asked about him. He'd gone away and never come back. So . . . who knows?"

"So if we're to have any hope we need to talk to Mentor Perroso."

"I suppose so. But I'm sure you'd be wasting time—just putting off the inevitable. And even assuming there is a portal that would take you back, and Perroso knows about it, there's no guarantee the whirlwind happens regularly. It might be months before it came—or years."

Once more everyone was quiet. Then Winnie said, "You said you were settled in after a year. Didn't you miss your family? Wasn't there anything you wanted to get back to?"

"Not really. I hadn't had that great a life."

"Why not?"

"My father died in a wreck when I was eleven. My mother died of cancer when I was eighteen. My older brother and I never got along, and we stopped speaking to each other when my mom died. I went to college for a year, helped by my uncle, but I didn't like it. So I quit and took menial jobs, whatever I could find. Didn't like them either.

"My mom worked two jobs after my dad died, and my brother and I had to work hard too. So I didn't have anyone to go back to, or any prospects. When I found success here, and made money, I liked it."

"Adapt, you said," said Rafe. "How did you adapt, get settled in?"

"I didn't have time to dwell on what had happened—I had to survive. No money, no job, no contacts. I grew up in Minnesota, and spent a lot of time on the lakes near our town, so I was able at first to catch some fish and sleep in the woods, wandering from place to place.

"I had a fishing knife strapped to my leg when the boat capsized. I learned to carve wood when I was a kid. One day I was feeling sorry for myself, and homesick, so I sat down and carved a moose." He pointed to the carving on the table. "Like that one. I took it to a craft fair. Right away, two people got into a bidding war, so I ended up with a tidy profit—the first money I made in Melenca.

"So I carved other objects, familiar to me, but they were exotic to Melencans, and they became popular." He laughed, then walked to a table at the back of the room, picked up an object, and brought it back. "Do you recognize that?"

"Is that a coffeemaker?" said Peter.

"'A fascinating example of his inventive imagination,' one critic wrote." He returned the carving to its table, and sat back down. "I was doing pretty well selling these at craft fairs and the like. Did you meet Silenda?" Several nodded. "She's a talented artist. She'd come to the area as Beldan's bride a year or so before that, and she spotted my work and we became friends. She introduced me into some art circles she was part of. My work really took off then, considered real art—which gave me a kick."

"We saw some paintings at Beldan's," said Allie. "Did she do those?"

He nodded. "Then I met a Melencan woman. I fell in love and got married. We had kids. So pretty soon I was happy here."

"What about the friends with you in the boat?" said Winnie. "What happened to them?"

"I assumed they drowned. Then, several years later, I thought I spotted one of them in a crowd, from a distance. By the time I got to where he'd been, he was gone. I'm not sure it was him, but it looked like him. I never saw any more signs of either after that."

At that moment, they heard the front door open, then a middle-aged woman carrying a cloth bag walked past. She glanced at them and stopped. "You didn't tell me we were having guests, Tim."

"I didn't know until just a short while ago. This is my wife, Marella. Beldan sent these people to me for advice—they're Outbounders, Marella, just arrived in Melenca."

"I might have guessed from the outfits. Welcome to our land. I know many things here will seem strange to you, but you'll get used to it." She nodded toward Wooden. "He likes it here." She held up the bag. "Let me put the groceries up, and then I can fix tea if anyone would like some."

"Yes, please," said Allie.

After Marella left, Peter looked at Wooden. "When you showed us the carving of the coffeemaker—they thought that was exotic? Does that mean they don't have coffee here?"

"Afraid not. That was hard to get used to. But they do have several very good varieties of tea."

"What? No coffee?" exclaimed Winnie. "Holy shit! That's awful." Then she looked alarmed. "Wait a minute—do they have cigarettes here?"

"Sorry, tobacco is unknown here." He smiled. "You better prepare for nicotine withdrawal."

"Son of a bitch—I'm down to my last pack. How the hell am I supposed to adapt?"

"You'll get used to it, after a while."

"Let's get back to the portal," said Sam. "How do we find Mentor Perroso?"

"It's not easy these days. He has a home base in the Hazy Mountains, but he's always traveled around too, teaching small groups of followers, spiritual seekers. Lately he's been focusing on the looming catastrophe from the mine collapse technists have been warning about." He paused. "Sorry, that must be Greek to you."

"Beldan mentioned something about crystal mines and rockslides," said Peter. "Is that what you're referring to?"

"You came in a hauler, and you no doubt saw skimmers. They're powered by crystals that are found in the high ridge on the Melencan side of a feature called the Great Cleft."

"And that's where the mines are?"

"Right. About a century or so ago someone discovered that if you pulverize those crystals and mix the residue with powdered leaves from a certain plant and ignite them, the resulting burst could power vehicles, so we now have skimmers and haulers, and other vehicles."

"Like gas in cars," said Allie.

"And that's not all. Mix a different kind of crystal with a different type of powdered plant and you can power lights and heat." He gestured around the room.

"And these mines are collapsing?" said Winnie. "Causing rockslides?"

"Overworked after a century, so the land around the mines has become unstable. And there are signs of other problems elsewhere that technists have warned about as well."

"Not from collapsing mines, you mean."

"Once it's used, the crystalline fuel leaves a toxic residue. Disposing of it safely is a concern. We've learned over recent decades it poisons land and water where it's been buried or dumped. That affects people and animals, and crops."

"I can see how these problems are serious for people here," said Sam, "but what do they have to do with finding Perroso?"

"He's traveling most of the time now, moving quickly, covering a lot of ground, speaking to larger groups than in the past—mostly young people, they've become enthusiastic followers. So he can be hard to locate." He paused for a moment, then said, "Not all who seek him have a benevolent motive."

"What's that mean?" said Winnie.

"There's been a push to develop alternate fuels that don't use crystals, and new vehicles using such fuel are just reaching the production stage. Beldan has his hand in that movement. There are powerful interests that oppose it."

"Because of their vested interests? Money?"

"Precisely. In preaching respect for the land, Perroso is promoting the alternate move-ment. He has growing influence. Some are not pleased by his message."

"Those mines—Beldan and Silenda were worried about their daughter being near them," said Allie.

"Katera's organization has been monitoring the changes in the land for some time. Now that the damage has started spreading, they're documenting it."

"Does that have something to do with monitors being withdrawn?" said Winnie. "Elja said her sister is in danger because of it."

"Those are from the Secretariat of Land and Water—or they were, technists who for years have been measuring changes in the land around the mines. That's where the warnings started coming from, because of the changes they've seen. But six months ago, the chief administrator, Flimsel Flammer, ordered the monitors withdrawn."

"Elja mentioned that name. I gather she was not a supporter."

"But why?" said Allie. "Don't people want to know when disasters are a threat?"

"This is getting into Melencan politics. The mine owners and other great merchants don't—they don't want people to think there is any threat. So they call the warnings exaggerated and dismiss the reports of the technists. They control most of the Com-pactors—that's one of the two main political parties— in the Grand Council, so those do the same. So does Flammer."

"So Beldan's daughter's group has taken over for what the official researchers—tech-nists?—had been doing," said Peter.

"Now that the predicted damage has actually started, they're sending their documents to the digests—like newspapers—to try to drum up more public awareness. Their work is even more important now because Flammer has ordered the Secretariat to stop issuing statistical reports on the changes they've published for years, based not only on their own research but that of outside technists as well. So it will be even harder for people to know."

Sam was growing impatient. "It may not be easy to find Mentor Perroso, but we have to look. Where do we start?"

Wooden thought for a moment. "I'd ask Beldan."

"Why Beldan?"

"His concern—company—has projects going on throughout Melenca. He travels widely and has many contacts. And since he's involved in the new techne, he may be able to find out something about Perroso's whereabouts."

"These newspapers—digests?—you mentioned," said Winnie. "Have they been reporting on this damage?"

"They're starting to—at least the *Current* and the *Vantage*. They're two of the main ones. They're reliable. The *Weasel* . . . well, you have to be careful what you read there. It's downplaying the risk, and starting to attack those who warn about it."

They were interrupted by Marella, who brought in a tray with several teapots and ceramic cups. "There are different types of tea here for different tastes," she said, and she pointed to each pot as she spoke: "Somewhat sweet, mildly spicy, and quite tangy." Sam chose the "quite tangy," which it was, and flavorful.

As Allie poured a cup, Marella stared at her. "You never told me there were brown-eyes among Outbounders, Tim."

"It never came up."

"I don't mean anything offensive, I assure you, miss. Well, I'll leave you to talk with Tim."

After she left, Allie said, "What did she mean by that, Tim, not being offensive?"

"There's a lot of prejudice in Melenca against a certain group, 'brown-eyes.'"

"Prejudice against people who happen to have brown eyes, you mean? Like me?"

"Like you. Most Melencans have blue eyes, some green or gray. Those who have brown eyes are descended from war captives who were brought here as indentured laborers, supposedly for a set term—but that supposed term was often ignored. The practice was banned, eventually, but many Melencans are still prejudiced against them. Not everyone."

"So I may run into trouble?"

"You'll likely encounter bigoted attitudes, hear some insulting comments."

Allie shook her head. "Well, thanks for the warning."

There was silence. As Sam sipped his tea, he thought, *We should all be. Maybe focusing on these questions helps us avoid thinking about what's happened.*

"So we're stuck here," said Rafe finally. "Now we seize the opportunity."

"What opportunity?" said Allie

"To make a fortune in a new world. Build a company on something we know but they don't."

"Were you not listening? We've got to find Mentor Perroso."

"Didn't you hear what he said? Like finding a needle in a haystack. You need to get real—you all do. This is a once-in-a-lifetime chance."

"How do you figure that?" said Winnie.

"Simple. People here didn't know about ordinary things. And look how Tim worked that. All the things we know on Earth they don't know about here—introduce them and there are fortunes to be made."

Allie frowned. "Fine—you stay here and make your fortune. I'm not giving up on going home just to make money."

"I'm not either," said Sam.

"Rafe's got a point, though, at least partly," said Peter. "If we can't find a way back, then we have to consider how to survive—adapt, just as Tim said."

"I can sure do it," said Rafe. "I'm an entrepreneur. There was nothing on the radio when we crashed. They don't have it, Tim?"

"No TV, either, nothing of that sort."

"See—a broadcast empire waiting to happen."

"And you're going to reinvent radio, hotshot?" said Eddie.

"You're an engineer—do you know how?"

"I built a radio in my garage when I was a kid. But I don't come cheap."

"These are pipe dreams," said Winnie. "We need to focus our energy on finding if there's a way back."

Everyone was quiet for a moment. Then Eddie asked, "Tim, do you know if time flows in parallel here and on Earth?"

"I never really thought about it. But there's no way to know—short of going back, that is."

"What are you driving at, Eddie?" said Peter.

"If we went back through the portal—assuming there is one and we can find it—would we come out at the same time we left, or a few seconds later? Or would the same amount of time have passed back on Earth as we had just spent here?"

Wooden shrugged. "Without going back, it's just speculation."

"So let's say Perroso does know about a portal. Maybe he knows if it's regular. If it is, if it's predictable, then we'd have time to explore here."

"You don't want to go home either, Eddie?" said Allie.

"Sure I do. But if we knew we could get back whenever we wanted, how many people have the opportunity to explore an alternate world? We're voyagers, like the pioneers in the New World."

"That's a lot of ifs," said Sam.

Before Eddie could respond, Peter cut in. "I certainly want to go back home—I have a wife and two children, a good career. At the same time, if there was a regular way back, this *would* be a terrific opportunity to study a fascinating new culture. It would be virgin scholarly territory."

"Yeah, I'd ditch the Caribbean island culture and write my next book on living it up in another universe," said Winnie.

"And do without cigarettes and coffee while you're researching," said Allie.

Winnie gestured toward Allie. "She's right—we need to find Perroso, pronto."

"The bottom line is we don't know," said Sam. "You said yourself time might flow differently, Eddie. Suppose it's not the same as what we spent here. What if it's months later? A year later?"

"What's your point?"

"My point is we need to find a portal, if there is one, as quickly as we can. The longer we stay here, maybe the time that passes back home is longer still."

There was another pause. Then Wooden shook his head. "If you're determined to hunt for Perroso, I think you're making a mistake. But I wish you luck." He glanced at Eddie. "You can't avoid exploring Melenca while you do."

"Thanks for letting us know where we are and what we're up against," said Winnie. "Now I need a smoke." She pulled out her pack of cigarettes and walked out of the room. They heard the front door open, then Winnie greeting someone. A moment later, Dalbin entered the room.

"Has Mentor Wooden filled you in?" he said. Wooden laughed.

"We know what we need to do now," said Sam.

"Ready to go back, then?" Several of them nodded.

Wooden shook hands all around. "Keep in mind what I said. I've made a good life here. I'm here to help if you decide to stay."

3

SETTING OFF

They were gathered in Beldan's study. "Was Wooden helpful?" he said.

"We need to ask you something," said Sam.

"I'll answer, if I can."

"We want to return home—to our land. Wooden said Mentor Perroso might know how."

"Perroso—ah yes, I remember, he's an Outbounder too."

"Wooden said he can be hard to track down. You have contacts, he said, and might be able to help us find him."

"Wooden's right—where he is these days is hard to know." He thought for a moment. "Well, I'll put out word in my stores and among my contacts. But even if we learn where he'll be at some point, he's likely to be gone by the time you get there."

"Ravinn might know something about Perroso's comings and goings, if anyone outside his immediate circle does," said Dalbin.

"He might, true."

"Ravinn?" said Winnie.

"Ravinn Navaeto," said Beldan. "He's an inventor. The large concern he founded develops products from his inventions. He's the leading force behind the alternate fuel source for the new engines and other devices."

"Why would he know about Perroso's whereabouts?"

"Years ago, when Ravinn was a youth, Perroso was teaching in the Hazy Mountains, where Ravinn grew up. They became friends. They still are."

"So Ravinn is spiritualist as well as inventor, a disciple of Perroso," said Peter.

"Ravinn is too independent minded to be anyone's disciple. And I certainly wouldn't call him a spiritualist. But Perroso proclaims respect for the land, and Ravinn is a leader in the alternate-sources movement, so I wouldn't be surprised if they're in contact."

"How do we find *him*?" said Sam.

"That's easier. Ravinn's headquarters are in the north, at Pelora in the foothills not far from the mines."

Sam looked at the others. "Should we go there?"

"It seems better to do that than wait for some word about Perroso's whereabouts," said Allie. "Who knows how long we might have to wait."

"It would at least be doing something," said Winnie. "How about it? Rafe?"

"Ravinn started his own company, and turned it into a big one? Sure I'd like to talk to him."

Eddie and Peter both nodded.

"If you're going to set off for Pelora, you could travel by transport," said Beldan. "But in these times, I think by skimmer would be better. Less interaction with people on the way."

"Why does that matter?" said Dalbin.

"Those two men who brought them here are going to talk. And Flammer has followers around here. . . .'"

"No one has said anything about Outbounders."

"No—not yet."

"How are we going to go by skimmer?" said Winnie.

"We can lend them to you."

"We don't know how to operate them," said Allie.

"It's not hard. We can give you a lesson. Dalbin will be happy to."

"Once again, eager to volunteer," said Dalbin, rolling his eyes.

"It's a good day's journey to Pelora, and it's late afternoon now. So it's best to wait until the morning to set off. We're happy to put you up for the night, if that suits you." It did. He looked at Winnie. "Now, we need to have our healer look at your injury." She nodded in acquiescence. "Dalbin, summon Elja. She can accompany Winnie—is that the right name?"

Passers-by stared as Winnie as Elja led her to the healer's office. So did the three waiting patients and receptionist inside. *I've never been noticed for my clothes before,* she thought. *Not exactly the right reason now.* Elja spoke to the receptionist as a woman called one of the patients into an interior room. The woman, presumably a nurse, stared too.

After a moment, one of the two patients, a woman, said to Winnie, "You're dressed very strangely. Not like a Newcomer. Are you from the Lands Beyond?"

"I believe I'm an outbounder," answered Winnie.

There was a sharp intake of breath from the other patient, a man, and he stared hard at her.

"I didn't think they existed," said the woman.

"Oh yes they do," said the receptionist. "I met one once, several years ago."

"Does the MNAA know there are Outbounders around here?" said the man to the receptionist.

"Why should they care?" she said. He started to respond, then just shook his head.

After a few minutes, the nurse reappeared and called Winnie in. The healer was a young man. He questioned Winnie about her injury, which she said simply had happened when the vehicle she was traveling in had wrecked. He had her lower her blouse on her shoulder and probed it. After a moment he applied pressure on where it ached most, manipulating it. Then he picked out a jar from several on a shelf and spread ointment on the shoulder. Winnie felt a warm sensation spread throughout her shoulder and upper arm. He told her the pain should gradually ease.

As Winnie and Elja left the office, Winnie asked her about payment. "It's covered by a program of the Secretariat of Good Health, for all Melencans." She frowned. "Of course, the Flammer regime is trying to kill the program, so everyone will have to pay for their own care. So far, Unifiers in the Grand Council have staved that off—Compactors don't have the votes, at least not yet. But people fear Flammer will just try to kill it on his own, even though the chief administrator doesn't have authority to do so."

Winnie started to ask Elja for more details on Melencan politics, but decided a lesson in it could wait. And as they walked, she noticed the pain in her shoulder was subsiding.

Winnie hadn't been seated long back in Beldan's study when Silenda entered. "Would anyone care for ale or wine before dinner?" she asked.

"Thank God!" said Winnie. "After no tobacco or coffee, this is a gift from the gods."

Silenda led them into a larger room, a living room, with comfortable chairs spaced in clusters and bookcases lining one long wall, several large rugs with geometric patterns on the dark oak floors, and more landscape and abstract geometric paintings on the opposite wall. A couple of wood sculptures stood on tables—Wooden originals, Sam guessed. They'd just seated themselves when Beldan and Dalbin brought in pitchers of beer and red and white wine, along with ceramic mugs and glasslike goblets. Allie poured herself white wine, Peter red, while the others all poured themselves beer. Sam took a swig. The beer was as good as a craft beer at home.

"Now, if you'll excuse us, we have preparations to make for dinner," said Beldan.

Sam realized this was the first time he and his companions, his fellow "voyagers," had been alone since they walked down the hill off the beach hours before.

"It's strange," said Allie. "It feels like we've been together for weeks, but we just met this morning. I hardly know anything about any of you."

"We all know what we do for a living, and why we're going to Cabo Sereno—or were," said Winnie. "I suspect we'll be thrown together for some time. So I think we'll have plenty of time to get acquainted."

Peter shook his head. "First, we haven't really mapped out any strategy for how to get back. Are we doing the right thing going to meet this Ravinn person? Or should we analyze this more deliberately?"

"How, Professor?" said Eddie. "How are we going to analyze anything when we don't know squat about the situation we're in?"

"You can call me Peter. I don't know, maybe find out more without running all over."

"How are we going to find out more without pursuing leads?" said Sam. "I think going to meet Ravinn is the right first step. Wooden said those other two Outbounders who knew something about a portal had both met with Perroso. Until we learn different, we have to assume he's the only one who knows—and if meeting Ravinn is a chance to learn how we can find Perroso, then we need to do it."

"Maybe so," said Rafe, "but if Ravinn doesn't know where Perroso is, then it doesn't make sense to keep chasing where he might be—or might not. If we can't find out anything about him, then we need to start working on how to fit in here—and take advantage."

"You don't have a family, do you, Rafe?" said Allie.

"Of course I do—I've got parents. And a brother."

"I've got parents too, and a sister, and I want to see them again—you don't seem to care all that much. I want to return to my world, and my life. And I'm going to hunt all over if I have to, if there's a chance of that."

Gathered in the dining room, Beldan's family included a couple they hadn't met yet. A young blonde woman was with Dalbin, Galena, his wife of a year, a teacher. They lived in a small house nearby. A teenager was also there, Relko, Beldan and Silenda's youngest son. Unlike the rest of his family, he had dark hair. He had been working in the main family store that afternoon.

"He's on break now," said Silenda. "He's finished senior school and will be attending the Academy next semester. Elja is already a student there—also on break." Elja helped out with the family business affairs there at the house, in Beldan's study.

The chicken sandwiches they'd finally had for lunch had been similar to those at home, but dinner consisted of an unfamiliar sweet fish fillet in a creamy sauce, roast potatoes—those were familiar—a vegetable that looked like a green bulb of garlic but tasted somewhat like broccoli with a pungent edge, and a crusty loaf of bread. It was all delicious. There was more wine and beer and a couple of varieties of tea. As they sat around the dinner table, Sam wondered if the conversation would be awkward. *What do you say to people in a different world?* But it soon took an unexpected turn.

Beldan was telling Galena and Relko about the voyagers' visit to Wooden, and how they needed to find Perroso when Relko interrupted him. "I hear the mentor is headed to Kascara, where the worst damage is."

"Who told you that?" said Beldan.

"Word gets around, among those of us who pay attention to what he says." He looked from his father to their guests. "Many of us younger people are worried about what's happening—the problems from using crystal techne over years. We're frustrated—no one in power wants to deal with them."

"Especially among Compactors," added Elja.

"Mentor Perroso is telling people we need to act, to protect our land. We keep up with what he says."

"Relko has had an interest in his teachings, Beldan," said Silenda.

Beldan laughed. "I'm putting out word among my contacts, and here's a source I didn't know about in my own house."

"Should we go to Kascara, then?" asked Sam. "Before we try Ravinn?"

"Yes," said Allie. "This appears to be the chance to find him."

"Even if he's there now," said Rafe, "how do we know he'll be there when we get there? Wooden said he moves fast. Going to Ravinn's is smarter—he probably knows more about his schedule, more than just the next place. We should stick to the plan."

"Relko said he's headed to Kascara," said Eddie. "If we head there now, we'll probably overlap. I say we go."

Before Rafe could respond, Winnie cleared her throat. "Where the damage is, Relko said. Isn't that near where your daughter is, Beldan?"

"Not just near—at Kascara." He looked at Silenda. "I've decided to send Dalbin there, to check on the situation—and on Katera. To reassure her mother."

"If you all want to go to Kascara, you're welcome to accompany me," Dalbin told the voyagers. "I leave tomorrow."

"It could be dangerous," said Beldan. "We don't know how bad the damage is. So you need to understand that before you decide to go."

"In spite of what you told me earlier," said Silenda.

"We just don't know—that's why I'm sending Dalbin. Reports will be out in the digests in a day or so, but I want to know now."

"I'd like to go," said Allie. "I understand there could be risk."

"I'm going too," said Sam.

"Count me in," said Winnie.

"What's the danger, again?" asked Peter. "You said rockslides?"

"There could be quakes too, splits in the ground," replied Beldan. "At least that's what technists project. We can't assure you it'll be safe."

"Are you a chickenshit, Professor?" said Eddie.

"I'm not afraid! I didn't say I wouldn't go."

"So Rafe's the only one who wants to head off on his own," said Allie. "Good luck wandering through a strange land on your own."

"How do you know what I'm going to do? I didn't say." He paused, then continued, "I'll go this time. But if we don't find Perroso there, I'm going to Pelora. I want to talk to Ravinn."

Winnie rose from the table. "I'm going outside for a smoke."

"For a what?" said Beldan.

"It involves . . . it's a habit in our land."

"Not of everyone," said Allie.

"No, not everyone."

"Look at the constellations while you're out there," said Peter.

"What the hell do I know about constellations? I'm a city girl."

"I'll go look," said Eddie. After a few minutes, he returned. "Wooden was right," he said. "Nothing familiar in the sky—except the moon. It looks the same."

Back in the living room, Sam's concern about conversation vanished. Beldan and his family told them about their lives and their history. The voyagers reciprocated. Both groups kept what they said as general as they could for people from different "lands." At one point, Beldan asked if any of them worked for their family concerns.

"Sam does," said Winnie.

"What is your role?"

Sam blushed. "Well, I'm the president." When Beldan looked puzzled, Sam added, "The chief executive—the leader."

"You're young for that role."

Sam had already mentioned his father's passing. "My mother and the directors wanted me to take over. I finally agreed." Not before a lot of convincing—aside from his doubts about handling this responsibility, he hadn't wanted to work for the business, and hadn't wanted to leave his job, and the work he knew. *"We need you, not someone from outside the family who's not invested in it as a family business,"* his mother had said. *"You're managing your unit in your job now—they thought you were the best for the job. We think you're the right person for this one."* That was different, he'd told her. *Managing a handful of people doing the same thing I'd been doing for years, something I liked—that was different. "You can handle any new challenge if you put your mind to it,"* she'd said. And she persisted.

The night ended early. The voyagers were exhausted after everything that had happened. Sharing a room with Peter, Sam collapsed into his bed and quickly fell asleep.

Sunlight filtered into the bedroom through a crack in the curtains when Sam awoke. For a split second, as he took in the unfamiliar surroundings, he wondered where he was. Then he remembered. *So I guess it wasn't a dream.* The other bed was empty. He washed the sleep out of his eyes in one of two bathrooms on the hall—he found the plumbing about the same—and made his way downstairs. He could hear conversation from the dining room. Beldan and Silenda sat at the ends of the table. On the sides were Winnie, Peter, and Eddie, as well as Elja and Relko.

"You'll find the serving platters in the kitchen," said Silenda. The platters were heaped with scrambled eggs, ham, and bread, and a pale green fruit he didn't recognize. He filled a plate and poured a cup of tea from one of two pots. Once again, the food was tasty and the tea even smoother and milder than the variety he'd had at Wooden's.

"How're your driving skills?" said Eddie to Sam.

"What?"

"The skimmer lessons start after breakfast," said Winnie.

As she spoke, Allie joined them. Beldan held up what looked like a tabloid and said, "There's a short piece in the *Weasel* about Outbounders being sighted in Secora."

"What do you know—we made the news," said Winnie.

"The two men who brought you to my house must have talked to their friends, and word must have reached local Compactor leaders. They'd be the likely ones to contact the *Weasel*. It makes me very uneasy."

"Why? You said Outbounders arrive from time to time."

"Occasionally. But Flammer and his regime are always looking for enemies they can use to divide people and to rile up his followers."

"There wasn't any of that in the article," said Relko. But Elja mentioned the suspicious reaction of the man in the waiting room.

"We need to be alert to where this goes—and so do our friends," said Beldan. Winnie asked him what the man had meant by whether the "MNAA" knew about them. "The Melencan Native Authentication Agency used to make sure Newcomers coming here weren't criminals. Under Flammer, it has aggressively rounded up Newcomers, whether they're criminal or not."

"Those two men yesterday used that term," said Peter. "Is that a specific group, then?"

"People from the Borderlands. They've come into Melenca for years, mainly because there isn't a lot of work for them in the Borderlands. And Melencan concerns have hired them for years."

"They compete for jobs?" said Winnie. "Is that why Flammer's followers don't want them here?"

"Mostly they do menial work for low pay that not enough Melencans want to do. If you want my opinion, they don't like the Newcomers because they look different from us."

"How?" said Peter.

"Ruddy complexions, reddish hair."

"What happens to them when they're rounded up?" asked Allie.

"Some get dropped back in the Borderlands. Others get put in camps. It wouldn't surprise me if the MNAA became interested in Outbounders as well. So some precautions are in order. First, your outfits. You're conspicuous in them."

"Everyone stared at us yesterday," agreed Allie.

"You have to avoid calling attention to yourselves. Dalbin will take you to a store."

"We don't have outfits here to fit all of you," said Silenda.

"We'll have to hope you don't draw too much interest after that article." Beldan was interrupted by the arrival of Rafe; once he sat down, Beldan continued. "Second, you should not identify yourselves as Outbounders—and neither should we. We will say you are from the Lands Beyond."

"Keeping it as vague as we can," said Silenda.

"What do you call yourselves in your land beyond the Boundless Sea?"

"Earthlings," said Winnie promptly. Allie started to laugh, and then cut it off.

"All right then. From now on, we have as guests the Earthlings, from an obscure place in the Lands Beyond."

"Beldan, we've heard several references to Compactors, not positive ones," said Peter. "Can you explain to us who they are?"

"There are two main groups of politicos—Compactors and Unifiers. Compactors have a majority in the Grand Council now, and they support anything Flimsel Flammer does—he's one of them—whether it's good for Melenca and Melencans, or not. The other main group is Unifiers—they oppose Compactors, and Flammer."

"Why those names, Compactors and Unifiers?"

"A few centuries ago, the different districts in Melenca were unified. The founding document was the Compact of Unification. In recent history, at least, Compactors' central principle has been keeping to the Compact." He frowned. "Lately, in my view, they've abandoned that role—Flammer doesn't pay any attention to what the Compact requires."

"And Unifiers?"

"Their guiding idea was Melenca as a united land, not just a collection of individual districts. In recent decades they've been playing up the welfare of all Melencans, not just the great merchants." He laughed. "They're called Unifiers, but there's a group among them who want more radical change faster than many Unifiers support and who attack Unifiers who don't agree with them."

As he was speaking, Dalbin joined them. Soon they were riding in the hauler. In the town center, Dalbin parked outside a building with clothes displayed in two windows, larger than the windows in the homes they'd been in, but not as wide or tall as display windows in stores back home. Inside, Dalbin had the couple of clerks who greeted them measure them. They soon returned with armfuls of clothes, which they distributed to the group to try on in fitting rooms. They each received three outfits, made of the fine cloth and bright colors Beldan and his family sported. Sam wore a bright-blue tunic and beige trousers. He glanced at Allie, who had on a pale-green blouse and a pale-blue skirt. *She looks stylish. Not so sure about me.*

The clerks also brought out some toiletries and a large duffel bag for each one. They stashed the clothes in the duffels. Sam hoisted his bag over his shoulder. As he stood there waiting for the rest to pick up their bags, Winnie laughed. "Going to sea, sailor?"

"Not on your life," said Allie. "We've had enough of the sea for a while—unless we spot a whirlwind."

They stowed the duffel bags in the back of the hauler, and Dalbin drove away. But he kept on going past Beldan's street, through a residential area with smaller houses. At the front of one they passed, a large sign bore the message "Melenca for Real Melencans" in large letters.

"What does that sign mean?" asked Winnie.

"A slogan of Flimsel Flammer and his followers," said Dalbin. "They don't think anyone not born here should be allowed to settle in Melenca."

"Including Outbounders, I presume?"

"Not enough people know much about Outbounders, or even know any. No, it's aimed primarily at Newcomers."

They soon reached the outskirts of Secora. A minute later, Dalbin turned onto a lane between two fields, along one side of which ran a ditch. He unloaded a skimmer from the rear of the hauler. He gave the group some brief instructions on how to start a skimmer, how to use the steering column, how to speed up or slow down, and how to stop. Eddie volunteered to go first and quickly got the knack of it. So did Allie. The skimmer was a bit wobbly under Rafe's steering at first, before he got the hang of it. Sam stepped between the steering column and the power boxes and set off. He had to get used to steering and accelerating and decelerating, but soon managed to handle the skimmer tolerably well. Peter did similarly. Winnie ran into the ditch.

She leaped off the skimmer as it headed into the ditch. After she retrieved the skimmer and Dalbin inspected it, she tried again. This time she plowed into the field of the yellow plants on the opposite side. "Shit! This thing's impossible," she cried. On the third try the skimmer wobbled down the lane a short distance before heading toward the ditch, but she brought it to a stop and dismounted. "Maybe I'll just walk."

"Have you ever driven a car?" said Eddie.

"I've been driving a goddamned car since before you were born."

"Then you ought to be able to master this. It ain't that hard."

She glared at him. Dalbin more tactfully gave her other pointers, had her start the skimmer at a low speed, and trotted next to her, reaching down to hold the side and balancing the vehicle. After they moved this way for a short distance, Dalbin let go, and Winnie steered it more or less straight for a fair distance, increasing the speed gradually as Dalbin coached her, until he fell behind, and finally she brought it to a stop without crashing it.

"You did great!" said Allie.

"I'm not a three-year-old," snapped Winnie.

"I'm serious—you did well there on that last run."

"I opt for going in the hauler as long as we can."

They had planned to leave for Kascara after lunch, but when they returned to Beldan's house he told them they would need to leave immediately. "MNAA agents came to the house while you were gone," he said. "They were looking for Outbounders they'd heard were seen in Secora and had been brought here. I told them you'd gone and I didn't know where you were headed. From their questions, I fear they may be suspicious and may return."

"But there's no official campaign against Outbounders?" asked Sam.

"Not yet. But as I said, Flammer and his regime may well exploit your presence. And if the MNAA interviews those two men who brought you here, and the man at the healer—if he's not the one who contacted them already—they may have general descriptions of you." He picked up a folded piece of thick paper. "You'll ride with Dalbin to Kascara, but after that, you'll be on your own. Here's a map, so you'll have at least a basic guide to Melenca's geography." He unfolded it, and after indicating where Secora was on the coast, he pointed to the region to the north they were about to head to, the hills leading up to the mines, which were dug into the side of a rocky, rising landform, which then fell away from the ridge at the top into a deep, wide valley, the Great Cleft.

On the other side was a parallel rising landform that was not part of Melenca, Beldan told them, but of "the Borderlands" and "the Lands Beyond." He moved his finger not far to the east, and they could see Pelora labeled. Beldan then pointed to the Hazy Mountains in the east, and to Remora, home base of Mentor Prossero. At least on the map, it looked a long way from Secora and from the Northern Hills.

4

— · —

THE NORTHERN HILLS

Their journey to Kascara would take that afternoon and well into the next day. As Allie climbed into the hauler, Rafe elbowed past Sam and climbed in next to her. Sam sat down beside Rafe. The hauler drove north on the highway, past the lane to Wooden's house, through countryside much like that the day before and several small towns.

"I didn't mean to be short with you yesterday, Rafe," said Allie.

"Apology accepted," said Rafe.

Sam felt himself tense up. *That wasn't exactly an apology. And she didn't have anything to apologize for.*

"If we're going to be together for a while, we all need to get along," she said.

"More than a while. That's what I'm trying to get the rest of you to understand, Allie—we're stuck here. Face it."

"I'm not just giving up. I want to go home—I told you."

"You'll change your tune eventually. When you do, stick with me. You'll see, it's a real opportunity to start a new life here."

"I'm not interested in a new 'opportunity,' Rafe."

Good, shoot him down, Allie, thought Sam.

"Good answer, hotsicle," said Eddie from the back bench. "Ask him why he has to keep trying new startups. What happened to the old ones? If we're going to be here for a while, I'm the one you want to stick with."

"I said all of us need to get along, Eddie," she said, "not just a couple of us."

Rafe glared at Eddie but said nothing.

In early evening, they reached a larger town. In the town center the hauler turned into a drive leading behind a building with a sign reading "Wayside Stop." A number of skimmers and a few haulers were parked behind it. They entered a large room with a counter against one wall and large chairs scattered around, some occupied. A few people looked up and glanced at them, then went back to reading or talking. Clearly this was a lobby, not so different from a hotel back home. A broad staircase farther down the room led upward. A tall, thin man behind the counter checked them in, handing Dalbin several keys.

They left their duffels in their rooms on the third floor, and were soon back downstairs. Beyond the staircase, a sign over a door read "Wayside Tavern." There was a hubbub of conversation and bursts of laughter from the people filling most of the tables in the large room.

The thin man from the reception counter soon appeared at their table. "Traveling far?"

"Up in the hills," said Dalbin. "Kascara."

"You hear a lot from travelers in the inn. You never know what's true or not. But I will say I've heard talk of rockslides and unstable land up that way—and serious damage, even casualties."

"That's why we're going there, to check on those reports. My sister is there with a group. We haven't heard from her in a while."

"Folks around here haven't put much stock in what technists have been predicting. Nothing's happened here. But who knows what's going on in the hills? I'd be careful if I were you." He took their orders.

Two men were seated at the next table. One leaned toward them. "I heard what the landlord said. Tremors and damage around Kascara. I hope it's just rumor, or at least exaggerated."

The other man snorted. "Rumor nothing—it's phony reports. I read all about it in the *Weasel*. It's part of a plot to discredit the Supreme Leader. Pay no attention to those reports."

Dalbin said, "I think I'll take sensible precautions rather than trust my fate to the *Weasel*, if it's all the same to you."

"Oh, so you're one of *them*."

"If you mean someone who prefers facts to fanciful yarns, yes, I am."

The man looked at his companion and pointed to Dalbin and the others. "They're deluded. Ignore them." As the men turned back to their meal, Sam noticed that the second man's gaze lingered on Allie—a hostile stare. The two men stood up and left as the landlord brought tankards of ale and goblets of wine to Dalbin's table.

"Wow," said Winnie. "That guy's a fanatic."

"Unfortunately, there are many more like him," said Dalbin. "We call them 'right-cakes.' They believe anything Flammer tells them, or the *Weasel*. Flammer has convinced them that factual accounts in reputable digests—like the *Current* and the *Vantage*—aren't true. When we're facing a crisis like that spreading from the mines and people don't believe it . . . and you heard the landlord—even sensible people haven't paid attention to the technists' warnings."

The landlord soon reappeared, along with a young helper, carrying plates heaped with steaming food, and the conversation lagged as they turned their attention to their plates.

Dalbin paid their tab. "Thank you, Dalbin," said Allie. "We should contribute, but we don't have any Melencan money."

"I don't mind paying while I'm ferrying you. But once you are traveling on your own, you'll need money."

"That's a problem," said Winnie. "How are we going to earn it?"

"Rafe's the hotshot entrepreneur," said Eddie. "Let him make us a quick bucketful of cash."

"You think you're funny," replied Rafe, "but no one's laughing."

"Knock it off, you two," said Allie. "We've got enough problems—we don't need to be quarrelling among ourselves."

"But we will need to determine how to finance our travels," said Peter.

They rose early the next morning and after a light breakfast stowed their bags aboard the hauler. Allie slipped to the side and climbed onto the back bench, and Sam followed her before Rafe noticed. Winnie had just come back from a smoking break and climbed in beside Sam.

"Shit!" she exclaimed, shaking her pack and examining it. "These are my last few. Adventure is well enough, but we're running out of time."

Sam and Allie laughed. "Cheer up," he said. "Maybe we'll be talking to Mentor Perroso this afternoon."

Allie asked Winnie how her shoulder felt.

"It throbs some from time to time, but it's not really painful. Whatever that doc—healer—did seems to have worked."

At first, the countryside remained the same as the day before. Gradually, the terrain became hillier, with grassy meadows and wooded slopes and valleys with narrow, swift-flowing streams. They stopped for lunch at a tavern in a small town. When they tried to pay, Dalbin wouldn't let them. "You need to save your coins for when you set off on your own."

Back on the road, they twice passed a stream tumbling down from a height into a valley. "This is lovely," said Allie. "I hope the rockslides don't happen around here. It would be a shame to spoil this beauty."

They'd been traveling another couple of hours when Eddie cried, "Look! Up there!" He pointed at a slope on their right. Sam saw a crack in the rock face, fairly wide near the top, and beyond it, a jumble of boulders clustered at the bottom of a hill. They were soon forced to stop by water flowing across the road. Several people stood on the road near a makeshift bridge of wooden planks lashed together. Dalbin got out and asked a man what had happened.

"Sinkhole," he said, gesturing to Dalbin's left, "over there, a small one, but there must be a spring or underground creek, because the water came spurting up."

"Sinkhole! Technists projected those farther south—not around here."

"They can project all they want—this one is here. We put up this bridge. I think it should bear the weight of your hauler. Maybe your passengers should walk across, though."

"I don't know—that bridge looks pretty rickety to me," Peter said as they stood behind the hauler and waited.

Dalbin said to the man, "You don't look like officials."

"EmRes is tied up in the Kascara area—no one to spare. Constables too. We're just townsfolk, from over there, not far."

"Things are pretty bad in Kascara?"

"So I heard. I haven't been there."

"Can we get there—is the road clear?"

"Far as I know. I wouldn't be going there, though."

"We'll be careful." Dalbin drove the hauler on across the bridge, which held, and the others followed cautiously on foot.

As they drove on, Winnie called to Dalbin, "What did he mean, 'EmRes'?"

"Emergency Response Agency—the administration group that handles things like this—not that we've had things like this before."

Soon more cracks appeared in the hillsides. They made slower time, maneuvering around rocks in the roadway. But they came at last to the outskirts of Kascara.

"Look at that!" cried Rafe suddenly, pointing. A house leaned on its side like a sinking ship, half submerged in the ground.

"That's a really big crack," said Dalbin. "Or maybe a sinkhole." Down another side street, a wide crevasse in the pavement made it impassable. A couple of streets farther, a couple of houses against a hillside had roofs bashed in.

Downtown, a crowd milled about. Some people hurried purposefully between buildings. Several hopped onto skimmers and drove off. Dalbin parked in front of a four-story stone building, with a sign reading "District Administration," and as he climbed out told them, "I'll see if I can find out where Katera's group is."

They waited, and waited. Finally, Dalbin emerged. "It's chaos in there," he said as he climbed into the hauler. "I finally found someone who could tell me something. We have to follow that street across the square to the edge of town."

A few minutes later, they reached a vacant area between a couple of houses where a small group of people stood talking, most of them young. The women in the group wore gowns of a rougher, plainer material than Silenda's, and tighter, cinched at the waist with belts. Dalbin stopped the hauler and got out. "Come on," he said.

Several in the group looked up as they approached. "Dalbin!" gasped one young woman. "What are you doing here?"

"Since you wouldn't write, Pop sent me to see just what you were up to. Seriously, I'm glad to see you're safe and well. We were all worried when we didn't hear."

"I'm sorry—it's been turmoil around here and we've been tied up night and day." She was almost the same height as Dalbin, but unlike him, Elja, and their parents, she had dark hair, darker than Relko's. She had blue eyes like the rest of her family, though.

Odd how I noticed that first thing, Sam thought.

Katera looked curiously at the strangers with her brother. "Who are your friends?"

"Come over here," he said, and he led her a short distance away from her group, followed by his companions, then explained their situation in a lower voice. "This is my sister Katera," he told the others.

"We had worked that out," said Winnie. "But we're happy to meet you and to see that you're well. Dalbin's right that your parents were worried."

"As you see, I'm quite well. I'm pleased to meet you." She turned to Dalbin. "But why did you bring them here?" He told her what Relko had told them. "I haven't heard anything about Mentor Perroso being here," she said. "I can ask Ralbo Jasko if he knows—he's the *Current* reporter here."

"Is he around?"

"He might be where we're going now, the village of Pantera, a couple of miles from here." She paused. "Something has happened there, we heard. Worse than in Kascara."

"If Jasko is there, I think our friends want to talk to him."

"Yes," said Allie.

"We're not to refer to them as Outbounders, by the way. That's Pop's advice. They're Earthlings—their name for themselves."

"Look, Pantera could be unsafe," Katera warned them.

"We don't care, right, Professor?" said Eddie. "We'll go, whatever the conditions are." Peter frowned at him but kept quiet.

On the way, they passed more houses with collapsed roofs, and one where a couple of large boulders sat amid the remains of what had been a wall. Farther along, a house tilted at an angle precariously straddled a large split in the ground. Then they were in open country. Before long the two haulers in front of them pulled off the road to the edge of a lake. Haulers and other, larger vehicles spread along the shore. People stood among them. The lake was perhaps two hundred yards wide. On the far side stood a few houses, and near the other shore, the top of a roof jutted out of the water, and Sam spotted another half-submerged roof some distance to the left of it. They gazed at the scene for a moment silently.

Finally, Katera said, "I'd hoped the reports were exaggerated. This sinkhole has swallowed most of the village." She glanced at the people among the large vehicles. "I need to talk to the EmRes staffers." She went up to a man at the edge of the crowd, not far away. He wore a white armband with "EmRes" in large red print. "Was there much warning?" she said.

"Some people managed to flee when the cracks started. We had organized an evacuation of nearby houses when the ground suddenly gave way. It spread quickly. I was lucky to reach solid ground."

"Casualties, then. A lot?"

"It happened so quickly. We're not sure how many, but you can see there's not much left of the village. We're trying to determine who is missing."

"Have you seen Ralbo Jasko around here?"

"He was here earlier. I think he's gone back to Kascara. There's Devis Belbar of the *Vantage*, if you need a reporter."

Katera led them to a slender blond man standing not far away. She introduced herself. "I'm with Rally Round. We heard that Mentor Perroso was coming to Kascara. Do you know if he's in the area?"

"How'd you hear that? It wasn't publicized."

"My brother is one of the youngsters following him."

"I've been keeping track of him myself, what with him injecting himself more prominently into the controversy over the technists' projections and the alternate techne. He was supposed to come here, that's true. But apparently that plan changed. What I'm hearing lately from my sources is that he's on his way to Mersala."

Sam groaned. He glanced at Allie, who caught his eye and frowned.

"I guess we go back to Kascara and regroup," said Dalbin.

"You'll need to spend the night there regardless," said Katera. "There's probably room in the inn where we're staying."

"Lead on."

As they walked back toward the hauler, Winnie asked the others, "What now? Do we go to Mersala, hoping this tip pans out? Or just go on to Pelora?"

"Obviously go on to Pelora," said Rafe. "Quit chasing rumors and talk to Ravinn. If he knows anything, fine. But if he doesn't, then we accept reality."

"And suppose Perroso is in Mersala?" said Allie. "Suppose we miss our best chance for now?" No one else said anything. She was a couple of steps ahead of Sam. She slowed down and put her hand on his arm, inclining her head slightly toward the others. Her touch thrilled him. He slowed to match her pace.

"Someone's got to take charge here," she said in a low voice. "You're the natural one—you're a CEO."

"What do you mean take charge?"

"Make what seems the best decision, then tell the others, forcefully. Say here's what we need to do, and here's why. Otherwise we'll just dither."

"I can't just tell everyone what to do. As for me being a CEO, it's a very small company. I haven't been president for long. Besides, these people don't work for me. And I don't know what we should do."

"Can't you assess options and choose what seems best?"

"You seem pretty self-assured. Why don't you take charge?"

"Oh, I won't be shy about giving my opinion. But I'm not in a position of authority. You are. You've got credibility. They'll listen."

Before he could say anything else they reached their hauler and followed the Rally Round haulers back to Kascara, past the District Administration building and into a side street, where the buildings were undamaged. Soon they turned into a drive around a building with a sign reading in faded letters "Peaceful Rest." This inn was not as large as the one the previous night, nor as cozily furnished: straight wooden chairs lined the walls of the lobby.

"Rally Round must not have much pull if you're billeted here," Dalbin said to Katera.

"The two better inns in the town center are full. Evacuees, mostly, and some of the EmRes officials. This is what we could get."

They dropped their duffels in their rooms, then rejoined Katera outside the "Cozy Tavern." It was mostly full, including many people with the white armbands on. Laughter broke out from a table on the far side of the room. "Ralbo's there," said Katera. She led them to the empty table closest to Ralbo's. As she stood at a seat between Dalbin and Sam, she gestured to the table of laughter. A burly man with dark hair and a bushy beard nodded, got up, and walked to their table, carrying a mug of beer. "Ralbo," said Katera. "You've seen Pantera, I heard."

Blue eyes, Sam noticed.

Ralbo grabbed an unused chair nearby and slid it between Dalbin and Katera, who moved her chair closer to Sam's. "I just dispatched a story on it," he said.

"We've just been there." She introduced her companions. "I wanted to ask you something. My father's concern is interested in meeting with Mentor Perroso about alternate power sources. My youngest brother had heard he was coming here, but Devis Belbar of the *Vantage* said he heard Perroso is going to Mersala—we ran into Devis in Pantera, or what's left of it. Have you heard anything about the mentor's whereabouts?"

"Odd that you should mention Perroso. His name popped up today. I was interviewing a couple of townfolk about the rockslides and the damage. This was in a part of town that hasn't been hit yet. They denied there was any problem."

"Rightcakes, sounds like," said Dalbin. "If they were just ordinary people who haven't paid attention to technists' warnings, the damage in their own town would open their eyes."

"That did occur to me. Then one said he heard Mentor Perroso was headed to Kascara to push the alternate techne—brought it up out of the blue. His pal said, 'If he shows up here, we'll know how to deal with him. People are looking for him. We're not going to sit by and let a meddler like him threaten our way of life.'"

"That's alarming," said Katera.

"I pressed him on what he meant, more detail, but he clammed up."

"Would they actually harm him?" said Winnie.

"With rightcakes, violence isn't out of the question."

"He needs to be warned," said Katera, "and protected. So do you know anything about where he's going?"

"Devis is more interested in Perroso's movements than I am—but I talked to one of my colleagues who's been keeping up with him. His information has been reliable so far. He's been told he's headed for Lentala."

"He seems to be everywhere," said Winnie.

Ralbo laughed. "He has charisma, but not superpowers. He'll be in one place—depends whose word you believe on where." He took a swig from his mug. "I heard something else alarming, from an EmRes official—wait, there he is, over there. He can tell you himself." He signaled to a man with a white EmRes armband, who came over and stood beside Ralbo. "Tell them what you told me," Ralbo said. The man hesitated and looked around at them uncertainly. "You can trust them," Ralbo added. "Katera works for Rally Round. This is her brother—their father is Beldan Falembo, one of the leaders in the alternative techne."

"We're under pressure from above, new appointees from the Flammer regime," the man said in a low voice, looking around beyond the table as he spoke. "We're supposed to downplay the seriousness of what's going on here, not acknowledge the damage and the casualties."

"Why?" said Katera.

The man shrugged. "They're more interested in maintaining the profits of the mining concerns than protecting people's property—or lives. That's what many of us in the agency think, anyway."

"Maintaining Flammer's image, too," said Ralbo. "It won't do to admit that something bad is happening on his watch—something the technists he canned predicted. It won't work. We're getting the news out anyway."

"A lot of people read the *Weasel*."

"And no doubt will be believing the *Weasel* when the ground disappears beneath their feet, or a boulder drops on their heads." He gestured to his right. "See the blond man three tables over? He's Axo Saltar, the *Weasel* reporter here. Wait and see how he spins this."

Katera mentioned the places where Rally Round had witnessed damage.

"We've documented all those," the official said. "What will happen to our reports when they go up the chain—well, that's anyone's guess now. But we'll keep filing them." He moved on then.

"You're not going to mention the poor man by name, are you, Ralbo?" said Katera.

"Anonymous but reliable source. Now I need to rejoin my colleagues—I need a refill."

After he left, Winnie said, "Now we've got two possible landing spots for Perroso—not to mention Pelora. What do we do?"

"Why Pelora?" said Katera.

"We thought Ravinn might know something about Mentor Perroso's whereabouts, if anyone does," said Dalbin. "That was before Relko set us off this way."

"Ravinn—possibly. As good a starting point as any, I suppose."

"Three choices, then, for our next direction," said Peter. "How do we choose?"

"You know what I think," said Rafe.

"I thought Mersala earlier," said Allie. "Now I'm not sure." She glanced at Sam.

He took the hint. "If rightcakes are hunting Perroso, we have to find him before any of them do. It's imperative. So don't put all our eggs in one basket."

"Just what does that mean?" said Eddie.

"It means we split up—some of us go to Mersala, the others to Lentala. Then we all rendezvous in Pelora. If one group finds him, we ask him what we need to know, and go from there once we get to Pelora. If neither group finds him, we see what we can learn from Ravinn."

"That makes sense to me," said Allie. She looked at Sam and smiled slightly.

"How are we going to do that?" asked Peter. "All set off on skimmers?"

"Does that make you nervous, Professor?" said Eddie. "We knew we'd have to eventually—may as well start now."

"No need to get snippy, Eddie," said Winnie. "I don't like the idea of heading off on skimmers either, but Sam's right. Do any of you have a better idea?" No one said anything, then Katera spoke up.

"I might be able to help. I've got to go to Pelora now myself, to our office at Ravinn's concern. Mersala is on the way. I could take several of you there, as long as I don't have to stop for long."

"Since it was my idea," said Sam, "I'll volunteer to go to Lentala on a skimmer."

"I'll volunteer to hitch a ride with Katera," said Winnie.

"I'll go to Lentala too," said Allie.

"I'll go with Allie," said Rafe.

"Well, you're in luck, Professor," said Eddie. "Looks like you and me in the hauler."

"Is Rally Round part of Ravinn's concern, Katera?" asked Allie.

"Oh no. We're a public organization. But Ravinn's concern promotes alternate power sources, so our interests align. Ravinn does have the public interest in mind, right after his interest in making money. Anyway, he offered us the office space—we compile the results there from our monitoring teams."

"You yourself put those two interests in reverse order, then?" Winnie asked her. "And though your father's concern makes money, it serves the public interest too, right?"

Before Katera could respond, Dalbin answered Winnie. "We do, but we never forget the making money part."

"You had no interest in joining the concern, Katera? Everyone else in the family seems involved."

"Not me—I wanted a job that serves a high purpose practically. And I found one. I studied techne and public policy at the Academy, and it combines both."

"I don't think Pop has recovered yet from her decision, poor man," said Dalbin.

Katera laughed. "My father let all of us choose for ourselves. I was fortunate in finding this job."

"I'm a reporter," said Winnie. "I'm always skeptical when I hear talk about working for a high purpose. But after what we saw today, I believe you."

"We all have a duty to protect the land and water—not to mention people's lives. That's what I believe."

"Me too," said Dalbin, "but let's turn a profit while we're at it."

As they dined, the conversation drifted, sometimes different topics on opposite sides of the table. In a lull on their side, Katera turned to Sam. "How can Mentor Perroso help you?"

"Maybe you don't know—Perroso is an Outbounder. He's from our land."

"So? That's beyond the Boundless Sea, right? Presumably you came in a boat. Did it sink?"

No one's asked me that here. How do you explain airplanes, portals, and alternate universes to Melencans? "Our vessel was badly damaged."

"Can Mentor Perroso build you a new one?" She laughed. "That conjures up quite an image."

Sam was silent for a moment, unsure how to respond. "We can get a boat, I assume. No, the tools we use to navigate were badly damaged too. Wooden said Perroso was a skilled technist in our land." *Not sure if that's true, but. . . .* "He might be able to help us, uh, build new ones."

"He's a skilled technist here too—he tinkers with things. Maybe he *can* help."

As they talked at close quarters, and he looked into her blue eyes, Sam noticed something he hadn't paid attention to in all the hectic events in Kascara: Katera was really attractive—in fact, lovely.

5

PURSUING PERROSO

Sam's sleep was troubled: dreams of houses teetering on the edge of a cliff, then falling; people flailing in rising waters; a steep hillside splitting and sending boulders tumbling toward houses full of sleeping residents. When he woke, Eddie was still asleep. Sam dressed and made his way to the Cozy Tavern, where he found Winnie, Allie, and Dalbin at a table. The room was not as crowded as at dinner.

"Katera must be a late riser," Allie said to Dalbin.

"She's out tying up loose ends with her group. She should be back soon, then we can prepare to leave—when your late risers are finally up." He gestured to a gemstone on a necklace Allie wore. "That's a beautiful stone. I've never seen anything like it."

"It's just carnelian," she said.

"Where'd you stash that?" asked Winnie. "We lost our bags."

"I had put it in my purse before we got on the seaplane."

Someone dropped a couple of digests in front of Sam. "I knew you'd want to read my account," Ralbo Jasko said. "I throw in the *Weasel*, for comic relief." As Ralbo pulled up a chair and poured himself a mug of tea, Winnie picked up the *Current* and perused the front page. Dalbin looked through the *Weasel*, shook his head, and placed it in front of Winnie. She picked it up, read for a moment, and snorted.

"Listen to this. 'As I stood on Borgal Street, I could see no signs of damage, as some rumors have had it.'"

"That's the street we're on right now," said Dalbin, looking up from the *Current*. "One of the few without much damage."

"Translation: he sat in the tavern here, quaffing beers and dreaming up his yarn," said Ralbo.

Winnie continued, "'Dagor Malpen, a supervisor with the Emergency Response Agency, denied that there had been widespread damage, as some have reported.'"

"He's one of the Flammer flunkies, lately installed in a supervisory role in EmRes."

"'Malpen said there had been a slight tremor,'" read Winnie, "'which caused minor damage. "It's purely natural," he said, "not resulting from any mine activity." He did confirm there had been a few minor injuries from the tremor.'"

"It gets better."

"'I did hear reports that the tremor had caused a small creek to widen into a picturesque lake near the village of Pantera. If so, it will create a pleasant spot for picnickers in the Kascara area. I plan to check on these reports today.'"

"Maybe we should offer to pack him a lunch," said Dalbin.

"At least your report gives a true account," said Winnie to Ralbo.

"The account in the *Vantage* corroborates mine. As I said, the truth will get out—to those who can distinguish legitimate reporting from propaganda." He frowned. "When Flammer disparages reporting like mine as 'phony stories,' and the True Believers in his cult swallow what he feeds them, so that they believe only what the *Weasel* tells them, that's the worse disaster." He got up. "Enough chitchat. I need to go gather more material for incisive accounts." He laughed.

Dalbin said, "I waited until Ralbo was gone, but there's something else in the *Weasel* that's disturbing."

"There's a lot disturbing in it," said Winnie.

"I mean specific to you. The MNAA is looking for a group of Outbounders for questioning."

"But you said Flammer's supporters didn't care about Outbounders," said Winnie.

"I said they don't know about them. Now they do. It looks like Pop was right—the Flammer regime is going to use this. You're more at risk now."

"Does it just say a group of Outbounders?" said Sam. "That's pretty vague."

"It says a group of four or five, possibly a woman and several men, in bizarre outfits. But it says people should be alert to strangers asking unusual questions. And report them to local constables, or the MNAA."

As they mulled the implications, Peter joined them. "When do we leave?" he asked.

"We were waiting for you," said Winnie. "Now we can go." Peter looked flustered.

"We're waiting for Katera to return, and for Eddie and Rafe," Allie told him.

"The good news is none of you will have to take a skimmer," said Dalbin.

"Why not? I thought the three of us would need to."

"After I report on what's happening here, I suspect Pop will want to consult with

Ravinn. I'm going to follow Katera to Pelora and await further instructions. Lentala isn't too much of a detour—as long as you make it snappy."

An hour later, they gathered in the parking area behind the inn. Boxes of paper were piled on the back bench of Katera's Rally Round hauler, reports she was taking to the office at Ravinn's headquarters. Katera glanced at Allie. "That's a lovely necklace. Is that stone found in your land?" When Allie nodded, Katera added, "We don't have anything like it here."

As Dalbin's riders prepared to climb into his hauler, Allie motioned for Rafe to get in first. He started to object, but she shooed him in. She sat next to him, between him and Sam. Just beyond the outskirts, Katera's hauler turned onto an intersecting road, while Dalbin's continued straight. A few miles past Kascara they couldn't see any damage. The countryside, like that of the day before, was scenic, or it should have been. But Sam couldn't appreciate it. He couldn't shake the image of this beautiful landscape with wide cracks in the hillsides and valleys, boulders and debris lying at the foot of slopes, sinkholes and water flooding.

"I knew you could take charge," Allie said to Sam, keeping her voice low.

"No one was sure what to do. You were right—someone needed to."

"No one put you in charge," said Rafe.

"You think you should be in charge?" said Allie. "You're not exactly hot to find Perroso."

"I'm a realist. And the reality, Allie, is we're here to stay. Stick with someone who's going to make the best of it—me."

"Stick with someone who wants to just give up?" said Sam. "*We're* the ones on the right path. We want to go home. Maybe Perroso holds the key to getting us there."

"That's not what the other two from Earth found."

"One of them disappeared—I think maybe he got home."

"I think he died trying."

"I'm optimistic, Rafe," said Allie. She sighed. "It is discouraging, though, all these reports that have Perroso in different places. What if we can't find him?"

"We keep looking," said Sam. "We'll find him at some point. We just have to before rightcakes do."

"And be on guard against them yourselves," said Dalbin.

For an hour the countryside remained unmarred. Then Dalbin said, "Uh oh, more damage, ahead to the left." Sam spotted a large crack in a hillside. A few minutes later, they saw boulders at the bottom of a slope. "I'm surprised the damage has already spread this far," said Dalbin. "Concerned, too." They saw more of it as they continued. Before long, they reached the outskirts of Lentala.

"Exactly where in Lentala do you propose to look?" said Dalbin as they drove ahead. That stumped them. "I have a suggestion—whoa, look there!" Down a side street, the scene resembled Kascara: collapsed roofs and walls.

A couple of minutes later, not far down another street, a house perched precariously on the edge of a large crevasse. Dalbin stopped the hauler, and they followed him on foot to the house next to the one at the crack. Several people, including a couple of EmRes workers, stood watching as two men wearing blue uniforms shouted to a man standing on the front stoop of the precarious house.

"What's going on?" said Dalbin to the onlookers.

"Won't leave," a woman said. "The constables are trying to convince him to evacuate, but he claims Unifiers are trying to steal his house."

"I know my rights!" the man screamed.

"We're trying to save you, you ninny!" yelled one of the constables.

"It's a plot, I tell you! This is all phony, a bunch of exaggerated reports to fool us into giving up our property."

"Look out the back window, you nincompoop," the second constable said in an exasperated tone.

"You're not fooling me!" the man yelled. "I have rights!"

"This is crazy," said Dalbin.

"As if we didn't have enough problems, just dealing with the damage," said one of the EmRes workers.

"We heard Mentor Perroso was coming to Lentala," said Sam. "Do you know if he did? Where he might be?"

"I haven't heard anything about Mentor Perroso being here."

"Try the Town Administration building," said the woman. "Maybe they know something there."

They drove farther into town but soon saw down another street a wider crack and other crevasses beyond it and empty spaces where there should have been houses. Dalbin stopped the hauler again and they approached the larger crowd gathered near one house swaying on the edge of the crack, the back half hanging over a void. Several EmRes personnel were among the crowd. A few constables stood near the house calling to a woman whose head stuck out a second-story window.

"You need to leave now!" yelled a constable.

"I'm not listening to your phony stories. We have rights! We own this house, and you're not taking it."

A man poked his head out next to her. "We've been warned about the Unifiers' schemes," he yelled. "You're not going to cheat us!"

"I'm not a Unifier!" shouted another constable. "Your house is doomed. We're trying to save you. You're acting—" His voice was drowned by a loud crashing sound as the land remaining under the front half of the house crumbled. The house toppled into the enlarging split in the ground.

The woman's voice followed the house as it disappeared, "It's phony reports, I tell you!" The crowd quickly drew away from the advancing crack and dispersed.

"Let's go!" Dalbin shouted, and they ran to the hauler and he quickly accelerated away from the widening schism. Another house teetered and then toppled as they drove away.

But soon they saw water ahead stretching across the road. A couple of rooftops floated on the surface. A lone house remained set back about thirty yards from the water. A crowd had gathered along the water's edge, including EmRes personnel and constables. When Dalbin and the others joined the crowd, they spotted Ralbo Jasko and Devis Belbar.

"What about Mentor Perroso?" said Sam as they drew up to the reporters. "Is he here?"

"Looks like my source turned out not to be correct," said Ralbo, "or else Perroso changed his plans."

"Should have listened to me," said Devis. "Mersala's the place."

"We didn't take any chances," said Allie. "Some of our companions went there."

"A sinkhole?" asked Dalbin.

"It took houses to the end of the street," said Ralbo. "We're trying to pin down casualty figures from the EmRes people, but they're still working on that." He nodded toward the stoop of the remaining house. "Look over there." Axo Saltar sat talking with a man. "It will be interesting to see how the *Weasel* spins this. No denying those houses are gone."

"Is that house in danger?" said Allie.

"The water's stopped—for now. There's no telling when the ground around the house may give and it spreads again. EmRes officials and constables have tried to convince that homeowner to evacuate. But he refuses, says no one is going to force him to leave his home, especially not administrators."

"What's all this nonsense about Unifiers trying to steal their houses?" said Dalbin.

"Flammer has got them riled up," said Devis. "Quoted in the *Weasel*, saying Unifiers were trying to force them to leave their homes under false threats, so they can take their property." He pulled out a notebook. "Then he says, and I quote, emphasizing Flammer's all caps: 'Don't let them take away YOUR RIGHTS!'" He glanced at an EmRes man standing nearby listening. "And it gets worse. Listen to this: 'And EmRes workers say they're there to help you, but THEY'RE THERE TO HELP UNIFIERS TAKE YOUR PROPERTY! RESIST THEM!'"

The EmRes worker shook his head. "We're working in an agency in his administration, which he's supposed to lead, which is supposed to help people. And he's making our job impossible—maybe dangerous." He sounded weary and discouraged.

Dalbin looked at the others. "On to Pelora, then?"

"Yes," said Sam, and Allie agreed.

After a couple of hours back on the road, they stopped at a tavern in a small town for lunch. It wasn't crowded. As they ate, five or six people took a large table near theirs and proceeded to talk loudly. Sam wasn't paying attention until he heard someone say "Mentor Perroso."

A man said, "He's just an old crank philosopher. How much harm could he cause?"

"A lot," said a woman. "He's spreading these dangerous ideas about banning crystals." Dalbin and the others had heard as well and were listening.

"It's deeper than that," said another man. "He's one of the main secret conspirators behind this movement to overthrow the Supreme Leader and cripple the economy."

"How do you know that, Tanco?" asked another woman. "He seems just like what Bordo said, a crank philosopher."

"It's common knowledge, obvious to those who pay attention, who can read the signs."

"What signs? Tell us examples."

"They're everywhere, for those who know how to look."

"The *Weasel* has an exposé in today's issue," said another man. "And it identifies the driving force behind this movement—Outbounders."

"Isn't the *Weasel* owned by Margan Anthrite?" said the skeptic. "And isn't he one of the biggest mine owners?"

"So what?" replied Tanco. "Margan's not going to let his own interests get in the way of spreading the truth, instead of the phony stories you see in the *Current* and others."

"You can trust the *Weasel*," added the first woman. "That's the only place you need to get your news."

"I'll tell you what we need to do," said another man. "We need to mobilize, to protect our way of life."

"What do you mean, 'mobilize'?" said the skeptic.

"Organize armed groups. Go find Perroso and make sure he doesn't keep spreading these ideas."

"And Outbounders too," said the first woman.

"How do you find Outbounders?" said Bordo. "What do they look like?" That seemed to stump the others.

Finally, the first woman said, "Well, you just have to look at actions—anything that seems suspicious. Then you question them about their background—then I bet you have them."

"We need to mobilize as well against those others who are trying to cripple our economy, those people trying to replace crystals," said the mobilizer.

"You mean like Ravinn Novaeto?" said the skeptic.

"Yes, and the others like him."

"And I'll tell you who else," said Tanco. "Those public employees who are thwarting the will of the Supreme Leader, that opposition movement among the career officials in the secretariats."

"Like the EmRes workers who are helping Unifier tyrants confiscate people's property in their towns up north, where they're spreading the phony stories about rockslides and such," added the first woman.

"You're talking about violence," said the skeptic.

"We're talking about protecting our rights," said the mobilizer. Several of the others chimed in, agreeing with him, and the skeptic was silent.

"Say, did you see about the Champions' League nudgeball match?" said Bordo, and their conversation veered into sports.

Winnie came back from a smoking break as Eddie and Peter were boarding the hauler. She had just sat down next to them on the front passenger bench when Katera set off. Once they turned off the main road, their route was north of Dalbin's, and the countryside remained marred by cracks, the debris from rockslides, and the other signs of the spreading damage. Occasional piles of rocks lay partly across the road, and they had to maneuver around them, sometimes onto rough ground to the side of the road.

They'd been driving for about two hours when they approached a cluster of large tents off to one side of the road. A hauler was parked not far off the road with "EmRes" painted on the side. A wooden barricade blocked the road ahead. Katera parked near the EmRes hauler.

"Something has happened here," she said. "There's a healing house over there, and from the size of it, there have been a lot of injuries." She pointed to a particularly large tent at one end of the encampment, with a sign depicting someone lying in a bed and an attendant with arm extended toward the patient. A man nearby wore an EmRes armband. "I'm with Rally Round," Katera told him, "just come from Kascara. There are a large number of injured being treated? From rockslides?"

He shook his head and glanced into the distance, as though watching for something, then looked back at her. "Not rockslides. This is something new." He gestured toward a group sitting on the ground not far away, a man and two women and a boy and girl. "See how they are?" They were listless, glassy-eyed. "This group just came in. They're waiting for beds. There are many more in the healing house—it's full." He pointed to an area beyond the small group. "And worse." A number of forms lay motionless on the ground, white blankets draped over them. "They may not have long to wait."

Katera inhaled sharply. "What is it?"

"We're not exactly sure. There's a large sinkhole—our guess is that a giant crack in land closer to the mines created it."

"And it's spread this far? But what's causing the injuries? They can't all be from the water."

"There must be something in the groundwater that filled the sinkhole. Some of the victims who could talk and some of our workers who reached the area said the air grew hazy. Fumes caused people to cough and have trouble breathing. We had to withdraw our workers. Some are in the healing house." His voice broke. "We lost a couple."

"Can the healers do anything?"

"They're trying. Some people have improved in the fresh air here." He looked toward the healing tent. "Here's one of the healers. You can ask him." A man with a green armband approached the listless group. The EmRes man called him over.

Katera introduced herself. "This illness—it seems clearly to come from the fumes?"

"So we assume. We've never seen anything like it. We're trying various treatments, to see if any will work."

"Could it be different types of crystals crushed by the rocks in the quakes mingling and producing an uncontrolled reaction?"

"That seems plausible. Or maybe crystals reacting with underground gases released when the sinkhole was created. It's all guesswork at this point. So are treatments." He went over to the patients and began talking with them.

"The road's blocked ahead," Katera said to the EmRes man. "We're trying to get to Mersala. I guess we'll have to backtrack and take alternate roads?"

"You can't go there at all. Mersala's one of the affected towns."

"We heard Mentor Pessoro was coming to Mersala," said Winnie. "Do you know if he did?"

"Ask Dogar. He's one of those who reached Mersala before he had to evacuate." He nodded toward another EmRes man a short way off.

When Winnie asked him, Dogar said, "He did come this morning. When the water and the fumes spread, he left, along with everyone else."

"Is he here?"

"No reason. He wasn't harmed."

"And you don't know where he headed?"

"He didn't say. Odd thing though—he collected some of the air in a jar and sealed it. We told him it was risky staying near the fumes too long. I don't know what he thinks he can do with that."

Katera looked at her passengers. "We'll have to go back and detour to get to Pelora." Once they were all aboard, she turned the hauler around and went back toward Kascara, but turned off before long and drove south until they reached another road to the east. After another couple of hours they began to pass through the outskirts of a town. Soon they saw a sign: "Pelora." Instead of turning toward denser development, Katera kept going straight through more widely spaced houses and shops and after another ten minutes passed into countryside again.

"I thought Ravinn's headquarters were in Pelora," said Winnie.

"Outside Pelora," said Katera. "Not far now." Soon she turned onto a road leading up the slope of one of the hills on that side, and a few minutes later turned into a driveway and through a gate and into a compound. A couple of buildings appeared to be warehouses. In the center was a rambling structure that looked like a large house, with two stories in the middle and one-story wings. Katera pulled up beside a few other haulers and several skimmers in front of the house. She lifted a couple of boxes from the back bench. Eddie picked up a couple more. Peter and Winnie each lifted one. They followed Katera through the closest door, into a small foyer from which several corridors branched off.

Down one corridor in a room that was clearly an office a middle-aged man with closely cropped gray hair looked up from behind a desk and greeted Katera.

"I'll be tied up here for a moment," she said to the others. "Wait for me back in the foyer."

When Dalbin and the others walked into the house they entered a small foyer. There stood Winnie, Eddie, and Peter.

"You took your sweet time," said Winnie.

"A lot happened," said Sam. "Did you find Mentor Perroso in Mersela?"

"I guess you didn't find him in Lentala, then. We just missed him."

"Katera can find us later," said Dalbin. "Let's go see Ravinn." He led them into a large room in the center. Big upholstered chairs were scattered around and a few small square tables with straight chairs. Ten or twelve people sat or stood talking or reading. Dalbin crossed to the far side of the room, where one man stood. "Hello, Miraban," he said.

"Dalbin. It's been a while since we've seen you here." He looked at Dalbin's companions. "And you come with an entourage."

"We came to consult with Ravinn. Is he around?"

"Consult about what?"

"My friends need advice from Ravinn. It's a private matter, nothing to do with my father's concern or the monitoring."

"That's mysterious. I'll see if he's available." He went through a door behind him. After a few minutes, he returned. "Go ahead. He'll talk with you now. You know the way."

Dalbin nodded and gestured for the others to follow him.

6

— · —

RAVINN

Down the corridor, Dalbin passed through a doorway into a large room. Several tables were covered with devices. A man stood in front of a large desk a few feet out from the far wall—a tall, broad man, with an ample stomach. He was maybe sixty, with thinning gray hair that bristled from his head. A couple of other men stood facing him.

"Those officials at the Secretariat of Public Works are going to need more than just a demonstration to be convinced," one of the men said.

"Bah! Those officials are simpletons," the large man said, in a voice as big as the rest of him.

"They're not keen on having that pointed out," said the second man, in the more measured tone of the first. "That's why you pay us to be go-betweens, Ravinn. We're more tactful than you."

"Drawing out implications is beyond them." Ravinn glanced at Dalbin and the others, then back at the two men. "All right, go play their game. But speed it up as much as you can." The men turned and on their way out nodded at Dalbin. Ravinn turned to a keg on a table behind him and poured himself what appeared to be a large mug of ale. Then he turned back to them, took a sip, gave a satisfied sigh, and said, "So, young Dalbin, you bring strangers who wish to consult with me."

"They've just arrived in Secora. They're looking for Mentor Perroso—it's important, Ravinn. We thought you might be able to help them."

"Just arrived in Secora, have they?" He stared at them for a moment, a penetrating gaze. "Are you Outbounders?"

"Well, yes, we are," said Sam.

"And you think Perroso can help you find your way back whence you came."

Sam nodded, and Dalbin said, "Beyond the Boundless Sea, yes."

"Or wherever it is you come from, like Perroso."

After a moment, Sam said, "Yes, like Perroso."

"The mentor moves around. He's hard to pin down."

"We've found that out. We heard rumors he might be in several places at the same time, but we didn't find him in any of them."

"That's why we came to you," said Dalbin. "We thought you might know something about his whereabouts in coming weeks."

"No more than anyone else," said Ravinn. He chugged more ale. "Even if you could find out where he plans to be a few days hence, he's diverging from his plans more often lately, since Flammer's toadies have started paying attention to his movements." Dalbin told him what they'd heard from Ralbo and overheard from rightcakes. "Doesn't surprise me," said Ravinn. "Flammer will stir them up." He glanced at the voyagers. "And now, rightcakes and the *Weasel* have fixed on Outbounders as a convenient target. Flammer will exploit that—sowing division is what he thrives on. The more you move about searching for Perroso, the riskier it will be."

"What about Margan?" asked Dalbin. "And the other mine owners?"

"They won't do anything overt. But Margan will manipulate rightcakes through the *Weasel*. Protecting his profits is what drives Margan on." He snorted. "That, and trying to crush me. But he won't."

"We have to look for him whatever the risk," said Sam. "We have no choice."

"I didn't sign on for that," said Rafe. "You say that, but the rest of us didn't agree."

"I do," said Allie heatedly.

"Me too," added Winnie.

"If it's risky, maybe we'd be better off waiting somewhere safe," said Peter, "until we learn something definite."

"You can argue about this elsewhere, on your own time," said Ravinn. He took another gulp, and appraised Sam. "You could go to Perroso's home base in Remora—he returns there periodically."

"The problem with that is they might have to wait a while," said Dalbin.

"I didn't say it was a guarantee. The risks would increase too. Sooner or later rightcakes will decide to go there, even if he doesn't go there often these days."

"Perroso might go back even less frequently when he gets wind of what they intend."

"Why do you think he's putting out contrasting stories about where he's headed? He's no fool."

"We're back to square one," said Winnie. "What do we do now?" She glanced at Ravinn. "Not to drag you into our deliberations—we can continue this discussion later."

Ravinn scratched his chin. ""What I can do is send a message to his associates in Remora. Ask them to get word to him that I want to meet. If I hear back with a date, I'll send a message to you—if I know where *you* are." He took another swig.

"Thank you, Ravinn," said Dalbin. "You can send one to Pop if need be. As you said, my friends can discuss their options somewhere else. I'll take them to the Silken Slumber in Pelora for the present."

"Bah. You'll do no such thing. We have plenty of room here, Dalbin, as you well know, and this house is renowned for its hospitality, which you are well acquainted with."

"I didn't want to presume."

"Now that that's settled, have you had lunch?"

"My group has. The other group—"

"Has not," said Winnie. "And we're famished. So hearing of your renowned hospitality, we accept your kind invitation."

Ravinn laughed. "Well played. You heard the lady, Dalbin. Don't just stand there."

A handful of people sat eating a late lunch in a large room with a number of long tables. Katera waved to them and they joined her. Winnie, Peter, and Eddie helped themselves from an ample spread on a buffet table. Among the choices was a roast fowl Dalbin called galupa, which Winnie pronounced delicious. Each group filled the other in on the morning's events.

Then Winnie asked, "Is Margan really out to crush Ravinn?"

"The big mining concerns see him as a threat," replied Katera.

"Alternative power might just be a minor nuisance to them without Ravinn's presence," said Dalbin. "That's how they see it, anyway. I like to think our concern makes a notable contribution to the field."

"Ravinn said they won't do anything openly," said Allie.

"They'll use rightcakes," said Katera. "But violence isn't the only worry. Compactor politicos—who are owned by the mining concerns—and Flammer's regime, egged on by the mining magnates, will do whatever it takes to stop the alternate techne."

"Besides violence?" said Winnie. "Like what?"

"New acts in the Grand Council and new regulations in the secretariats that make it harder to get vehicles and devices into production," said Dalbin. "Those affect not just Ravinn's enterprises but Pop's as well. But we won't quit."

"This looks like a big operation. The mining concerns and the politicos may be out to stop Ravinn, but from what I've seen of him, that may not be so easy."

"He's formidable," said Katera. "You don't want to cross him. He has little patience with anyone he regards as a fool. Best to stay on his good side."

"We'll be sure to stay there," said Sam. "But getting back to Winnie's question: what next?"

"Wait here?" asked Allie.

"Either that or go to Remora. If we do that, we ought to leave as soon as possible."

"You heard Ravinn and Dalbin," said Winnie. "That's uncertain, and risky. Maybe it's better to wait here for a response to Ravinn's message."

"One story we heard was correct," said Allie. "Perroso *was* in Mersala."

"If we hear something that sounds credible, then one or two of us could go check it out," said Sam. "From what we've learned, my guess is Perroso will go to an area where there's damage."

"That may be a bigger area than you think," said Dalbin. "The damage is spreading. And it's going to occur in the south as well, where it's flatter, if the technists are right."

"Still, if it seems likely, one or two going to check is better than doing nothing. The rest can stay here to see if Ravinn's message gets a response."

By the time they finished lunch it was mid-afternoon. Dalbin excused himself to send his message to Beldan. He offered to show them Ravinn's operation when he returned. Eddie and Rafe said they'd like to see it. The rest demurred.

In early evening they gathered again in the dining hall. It was more crowded than at lunch, and others trickled in in twos and threes. Katera told them Ravinn had invited them to dine at his table. So they found themselves seated around one of the long tables, at first by themselves. In a few minutes, Miraban joined them, accompanied by another man, whom Miraban introduced as Jalno, an employee of Ravinn's just returned from the capital, Calabra. Five minutes later, Ravinn barged into the room and plopped down at the head of their table.

"Another setback for our side," said Jalno. "Carno has a column in today's *Vantage*, on the projected cost of replacing crystals in our society."

"I saw it," said Ravinn.

"Carno is one of the leading moneysayers," Dalbin told the voyagers.

"Enormous sums, he says it will cost," said Jalno. "Like most moneysayers, he gets specific as to amounts. He questions how we can afford them."

"Bah!" said Ravinn, his voice booming over the hubbub. "The same noise has been coming from other moneysayers."

"You don't think they have a point?" asked Miraban. "Granted, we need to proceed—we can't afford not to. But we can't disregard the cost."

"They ignore one inconvenient fact: the history of techne—especially in the past couple of centuries. Namely, every innovation in techne has led to whole new fields and many new kinds of jobs. They're not predictable. Moneysayers should be tutored that these happen to produce a great deal of money—which they don't include in their projections."

"True," said Dalbin. "It is a branching-off effect that can't be foreseen."

"Obviously—if anyone could foresee those branches, they wouldn't be innovations. So predictions of this sort by moneysayers are useless. They can't in fact account for those innovations—and the profits they lead to for those who exploit them."

"Such as you, Ravinn?" said Miraban.

"Naturally. I shall be at the crest of the wave of exploiters making money from innovations." He looked at Katera. "While serving society as well."

Katera laughed. "I'd be skeptical, Ravinn, if I didn't know you, that you do in fact have a soft spot for serving the general well-being."

"Don't let it get out." He poured himself a tankard of ale from a large pitcher.

"Carno does at least acknowledge the cost of not doing so will be increasingly steep as well," said Jalno.

"Still, he's giving fuel to Compactors," said Miraban.

"Compactors don't need any more fuel," said Katera. "The most determined Unifiers won't be discouraged, either. It's the undecided and uninformed people in the middle we need to worry about—and persuade."

"Changing the subject," said Jalno, "Flammer posted a note on the bulletin board today about the reports coming out about cracks in the land and so on."

"Oh?" said Ravinn. "And what does the Illusionist bluster on about today?"

Jalno repeated the statement that Devis had read them that morning.

"We ran into the effects of that in Lentala," said Dalbin. He told them of the exchanges they had witnessed with rightcakes.

"The True Believers in Flammer's cult follow whatever he tells them to do," said Miraban. "Even if they follow it to their own doom."

"Don't shed any tears for rightcakes who take a ride on their houses down into new ravines," said Ravinn. He took a swig.

The conversation then veered from ecological threats and politics and the economics of Ravinn's innovations to sports and the arts, both of which Ravinn professed to have little interest in. The other Melencans, though, engaged in a lively discussion. Sam listened attentively, wanting to learn all he could about Melencan culture. *You never know when that might come in handy, particularly when people are suspicious of us.* The food was plentiful, and excellent. Ravinn's appetite was prodigious. After everyone finished eating, the conversation continued without flagging. So did the ale and wine. Ravinn refilled his tankard often but seemed little affected. Eddie kept up the pace as well, and so did Winnie. After a couple of hours, Allie, then Peter, then Rafe excused themselves. Sam too had had enough and, feeling lightheaded, headed to his assigned room.

The next morning at breakfast, as she sipped a mug of tea, Winnie said, "Now I really miss some coffee. That was enjoyable last night, though. It's been a long time since I've been in a drinking bout like last night—too damn long. It took me back to my reporting days."

"That's what you get at dinner with Ravinn," said Dalbin. "He likes to hold court, even when he's not taking part in the conversation."

"The drinking didn't seem to affect him," said Allie.

"Or the eating. He never appears to gain weight—or at least more than his already considerable girth. And no, the beer doesn't slow him down." He glanced at Eddie and Winnie. "Not many can keep up with him."

"I've had a lot of experience," said Eddie, as he picked up his mug of tea. He appeared no worse for the wear.

They hadn't been at the table long when Miraban walked up to them and dropped several digests on the table. "I thought you might want to see these," he said. He looked at Kateia. "We've had reports of damage spreading east from the mines, directly north of here. I'm going there to assess."

"That's fast," she replied, "faster than the technists thought it would spread. I'd better go too. Rally Round needs to be there."

"I need to wait for word from Pop," said Dalbin. "Anyone want to go with her?"

"No need," she said. "It could be dangerous, and there's nothing anyone can do."

"Do you suppose I could borrow a skimmer?" Eddie asked Miraban. "I'd like to look around Pelora." Miraban said they could provide one.

"Don't get lost," said Sam. "We need to stick together. There's no telling when we might hear something about Perroso and have to leave."

"I wasn't aware I report to you."

"Just be careful, Eddie," said Allie. "People are suspicious."

Peter told Miraban he'd like to interview some Melencans about their culture, and Miraban said he'd round up some volunteers. Rafe asked if he could meet with Ravinn to discuss how he started his concern, and how it ran.

"Ravinn is busy, I'm afraid. But I'm sure we can find someone you can meet with."

Winnie had picked up one of the digests and scanned the front page. "Listen to this. It's by our friend Axo Saltar in the *Weasel*, from Lentala."

"We saw him there," said Allie. "Ralbo Jasko wondered how he would report what happened there."

"In a glaring example of agency overreach," Winnie read, "EmRes officials, abetted by local authorities, tried to force a homeowner here to move out of his house just when it and his land have become waterfront property. 'They're trying to rob me,' Rinko Vorpol charged. A small pond developed next to his house, which a techne adviser to the Supreme Leader confirmed is a natural development in the landscape. The local authorities insisted the man's house was in danger from the gentle pond, but the house is perfectly intact. The scenic view and proximity to water have no doubt increased the value of Vorpol's house and land, and the agency is trying to confiscate that property."

"Ralbo should have known the *Weasel* can twist anything," said Dalbin. "Just ignore the houses that are no longer there."

After Miraban left and they finished eating, Winnie said, "I need to go outside for a smoke. I've been rationing, which is killing me, but I'm almost out."

"There's a lovely garden back beyond the complex, and some wooded area beyond that," said Katera. "It's a pleasant walk."

"Maybe I'll go too," said Allie. "I could use some tranquility."

"So could I," said Sam.

Outside they strolled past the outbuildings, at first through well-tended lawns interspersed with trees and shrubs, and then among yellow and red tulips, daffodils, and pink and red azaleas. To their right were rows of flowers they didn't recognize, brilliant scarlet and bright blue. More trees rose beyond the garden, and in the distance, they could see hills rising. Barely visible on the horizon was a dark indiscernible shape.

"Is that where the Great Cleft is, I wonder?" said Allie.

"Yes it is," said a voice. They turned in its direction, and a middle-aged man of medium height and build stepped out from behind a tall bank of azaleas. He glanced at Winnie, who by now had dangled a lit cigarette from her mouth. "You must be some of the notorious Outbounders. You're being sought, you know."

"We're not dangerous," said Sam.

The man laughed. "I know how to ferret out truth from lies, especially preposterous ones coming from the Flammer regime. I'm a reporter. Arban Melroc of the *Current* at your service."

"We've just been around Ralbo Jasko over the past couple of days," said Allie.

"No doubt he impressed upon you how incisive his reporting is."

"Maybe in a self-mocking way."

"I'm sure."

"Why are you here?" said Winnie.

"I've been covering the alternate techne—and the attempts to thwart it. I check in with Ravinn and his people from time to time."

"You haven't heard anything about Mentor Perroso's movements in the near future, have you?" said Sam

"You hear various rumors. Why are you interested?"

"It's a personal matter, but we need to see him—it's important. We've heard rightcakes talking about going after him—so it's urgent we find him, before they do."

"I keep pretty close tabs on rightcakes' opposition to the new techne and to technists in general. Yes, I've heard their talking lately about hunting Perroso and taking down Ravinn and others. It's not just rhetoric." He looked toward the Cleft. "What are you Outbounders doing here?"

"Ravinn didn't know any more than you do about Perroso's movements. But he's sent a message to his base in Remora, trying to get through to him and arrange a meeting with us."

"Ravinn agreed to do that much for you? I'm impressed. If he trusts you. . . ." He hesitated a moment, looked them over, then said, "I have a source in Flammer's inner circle. They're talking about pushing rightcakes toward violence against his opponents.

But that's not all—they're also going to use you—a growing threat, Outbounders, calling for stronger measures."

"Such as?"

"Outright arrest, not just questioning. And the rightcakes are going to listen, and lump you in with Ravinn and the technists. So you'd better watch your step, and keep your guard up." He paused. "Some might have firetubes."

"Firetubes?" said Allie.

"You don't have them in your land? They're metal tubes that use crystal powder to shoot a projectile. Deadly."

They were silent for a moment, then Winnie said, "You really have a source in Flammer's circle? That's quite a coup."

"I have to be careful how I use that source. Obviously I can't quote the person, or make anything too specific that might identify him—or her."

Early in the lunch hour, people straggled in at a more leisurely pace than at dinner. Eddie had made it back safely. So had Katera. Rafe had talked with an employee, and Peter with several. Before long, Dalbin joined them.

"I've heard from Pop," he said. "He's going to Kerela. That's our first big contract for our alternate lighting, in all the municipal buildings in the district. It's a huge deal—the first one in all Melenca. He wants me there."

"Why?" said Katera. "He's got people to install them, right?"

"I've got contacts there—that's one of the places I travel to for the concern."

"You've already got the contract. Why would Pop need you and your contacts?"

"We suspect the district administrators are on the verge of reneging. That would be a huge setback."

"Why do you suspect that?"

"They keep putting us off—vague excuses, not convincing. And Pop has just learned that the Bureau of Power is pressuring them to pull out."

"That's one of the agencies where Flammer has managed to get his cronies into the top spots."

"The top dog came straight from Margan's concern."

"Then what good will your contacts do you? How can Pop fight this?"

"The administrators won't say what's behind this. I can try to find out. Then we'll figure something out from there.”

"You're leaving us here?" said Allie. "Right away?"

"Pop will get there in two days. So I'll leave tomorrow."

"I'm afraid I'm leaving too," said Katera. "We got word this morning that there's new damage—in the lowlands, not damage from the mines."

"Where?" asked Dalbin. "What kind of damage, if not from the mines?"

"Out past Buscara. The ground has collapsed where crystal residue has been buried for years. Technists warned it could be eating away the subsoil. They were right."

"So sinkholes?"

"Those, and just big gaps in the ground. Buildings collapsing—same depressing story. Rally Round is sending my group to assess."

"We'll be on our own, then," said Sam.

"I think you can manage," said Dalbin. "You've traveled some already, and you know to be careful."

"We need to decide," Allie told her companions, glancing at Sam. "Go somewhere? Or stay here?"

"Got new orders for us, Captain?" said Eddie.

Just ignore him. Sam thought for a moment. "I suggest we talk with Ravinn at dinner. Then discuss our options and pick out what seems the best chance to find Perroso." Sam asked Dalbin if the facility had a library in the afternoon, and spent the afternoon learning all he could about Melencan culture before they set off on their own.

At dinner they had just sat down at the same long table as the night before when Miraban came up with another man. "I think you know Caldan Gandoro, Dalbin, Katera," said Miraban. "He's a leading Wayfarer," he added, looking at the others. Caldan was probably over sixty. Katera and Dalbin greeted him.

"We were in the garden this morning, Miraban, and we could see the Cleft in the distance," said Winnie. "Not close, but not terribly far either. Is the damage from the mines likely to reach here?"

"Certainly. In a few months, we calculate—but that's only an estimate, because we haven't dealt with this sort of destructive force before." He shook his head. "We're hoping it won't be weeks."

"Then all this complex, these beautiful grounds—they'll just be swallowed up, or crushed by rockslides?" said Allie.

"I'm afraid so."

"What then for Ravinn?" said Peter. "Rebuild?"

Miraban shook his head. "Too unstable here at that point. Relocate—we'll have to."

"What a shame, to have to just abandon all of this," said Allie.

"Ravinn isn't sentimental—he's pragmatic. Even so, it's a short-term solution. The damage will continue to spread, to the south, rifts in the land, sinkholes—it's already started, as you may have heard. Melenca's only hope is to make a large-scale transition to the alternate techne, and quickly."

"Fortunately, Melenca has us—and we're working on doing just that," boomed a voice. Ravinn took the chair at the head of the table.

"So are those who oppose us," said Dalbin. He told Ravinn what Beldan had discovered.

"Bah! Not surprising, coming from Flammer." Ravinn filled his tankard with ale.

"They're not sitting idly by in the Grand Council either," said Miraban. "There's a rumor Compactors are going to formulate an act prohibiting harvesting the sap from silverbarks—and they have a majority."

"And we'll respond—we'll fight it in the magistrates' chambers. For those Compactor buffoons in the Council to interfere with the operations of a private concern would clearly violate the codes. So far the Illusionist hasn't managed to fill the courts with enough flunkies to erode the rule of law, not entirely, anyway."

"The mining magnates and Flammer's regime will use other means against us."

"Let them try. We have other ways to resist." He paused to fill his tankard with ale. After a prodigious swallow, he said, "But we're forgetting one factor, aren't we? Is the Essence going to save us, Caldan?"

Caldan smiled. "The Essence gives us the ability to fend for ourselves. And we've proven many times we have the ability to foul things up." He took a sip of beer. "But we also have the wherewithal to act intelligently. At times, we have. Will we now?"

"It's touch and go which way we'll choose," said Katera.

"You're doing all you can to help make the right choice. That's all you can do. That, and pray to the Essence."

"I think I'll keep working at it, if it's all the same to you," said Ravinn.

"You don't believe in the Essence, do you, Ravinn?"

Ravinn took another mighty pull at his tankard. "I reserve judgment—I don't know if the Essence exists or not. I recognize that it's an important question, but I don't spend time worrying about it. I focus on my work."

"It's interesting that you don't ponder philosophical questions, yet you maintain a good relationship with Mentor Perroso," said Peter. "I understand that's exactly what he does."

"I respect Perroso. Have done ever since I was a youth. Our conversations are more practical. He's interested in practical matters, as well."

"This whole question of switching to the alternate techne, for instance," said Caldan. "As you know, Mentor Perroso has become involved. He's speaking on the matter at my meeting house in three days."

"You may be disappointed," said Dalbin. "We've learned rightcakes are searching for him—and not up to any good."

Sam glanced at Allie. "Ravinn said he was putting out multiple stories to keep rightcakes off his trail. My friends and I want to meet with him. But we've heard he was supposed to be in several places, and when we got there he wasn't."

"That explains something he told me when I saw him recently," said Caldan. "He said he's not publicizing his visit. I wasn't sure why. But I am sure he'll come."

"Then it's worth me taking a chance. Where do you live?"

"Buscara."

"That's on my way," said Katera. "I can give you a lift."

"The rest of you stay here," said Sam. "Like we said—one goes out if we hear anything solid."

"One or two, we said," Eddie said. "And after Katera drops you off, we're supposed to believe you can find your way back? Not without a navigator."

"Like you, for instance?"

"Like me. And someone to keep you out of trouble."

"That does make sense, Sam," said Allie. "You can look out for each other."

"I don't need a babysitter, or a bodyguard—and I can find my way around just fine, Eddie. But I'm not going to sit here and argue—two of us, then."

After dinner the evening played out much as on the previous night. Ravinn set the pace on drinking, and talking. Eddie and Winnie kept up, at least with the drinking. Miraban and Caldan did too, though at a more measured pace than Ravinn. The hubbub of conversation from tables throughout the dining hall, punctuated with laughter, was steady. After a while, Peter left for the night, soon followed by Rafe. Sam decided he would go too.

"Wait," said Allie, as he got up. "I'll go too." As they walked out of the dining hall, she said, "I'd like to talk to you. Do you want to walk outside?"

"Sure. It should be pleasant."

It was. They strolled toward the garden. Outside lights were placed throughout the grounds. The moon was full and bright. They could make out flowers and bushes, though not the bright colors.

"What's up?" he said.

"I wanted to say. . . ." She hesitated for a moment. "I guess it's just I'm concerned about you and Eddie having to come back on your own. We've been escorted until now. And you don't have any money."

"We knew this day would come, when we'd set out on our own. And Eddie I can manage—camp in the woods if we have to. I don't know how many more chances we'll have to find Mentor Perroso before—well, you know."

She sighed, and nodded. "But it's hard for the rest of us, just sitting here doing nothing. I want to do something."

"You'll have Rafe's advances to ward off—that will keep you busy."

"I've had plenty of practice." She turned and looked at him. "But I wish. . . ."

"What?"

"Nothing. It can wait."

I wish I was sure what she's thinking, or feeling. What does she want from me? And what does she feel about me?

Allie took hold of his arm. "Just be careful, please. Take care of yourself."

7

— • —

THE ROAD TO KERELA

At breakfast the next morning, Peter looked at Katera. "Caldan is a Wayfarer leader, Miraban said last night. That apparently is some kind of religious role, but it didn't come up in my interviews yesterday."

"Religious?"

"Spiritual, maybe?"

"Ah. Wayfarers believe in the Essence, who created Melenca and all the other lands, the stars, all that is, and still rules it all. Others believe in the Essence as well, but Wayfarers—and another group, Proclaimers—believe also that the Essence was born in human form centuries ago as the One, Essence and human in one, and lived in Melenca before returning to the Essence."

"Sounds familiar," said Winnie.

"We—my family—are Wayfarers." She glanced at Dalbin. "Some of us go to meetings more regularly than others. Not as often as my mother would wish, in certain cases."

"Nor even in certain somewhat more regular cases as my mother—our mother—would wish," said Dalbin.

"But not everyone believes in the Essence, or so I gather from Caldan and Ravinn's conversation," said Peter.

"Some, mainly technists, are Technians, who worship techne itself—an idol, in our view," said Katera. "Then there are some who don't believe in anything."

"You mentioned another group who believe as you do. If you both worship the same things, why are there two groups?"

"Proclaimers split away from Wayfarers a century ago. The two groups argued—and still argue—over how to interpret the sacred writings, particularly stories about the creation, but others as well."

"Argue? Over what?"

"Wayfarers believe some of the sacred writings are cast in story form, not literal history—though that does not make them any less true, if not literal fact. Proclaimers do not accept that stories can convey truth and insist everything in the sacred writings is actual history."

"What do those names mean?" said Winnie.

"Proclaimers believe the main task is to tell as many people as they can—especially those who don't believe—about the Essence and the One. Wayfarers—most, anyway—don't deny the importance of that, but believe following the One's teachings in our actions is of prime importance."

"And of great importance now," said Dalbin, "many Proclaimers are True Believers in Flammer's cult. In fact, they may form the majority of his cult."

"So Proclaimers are rightcakes?" said Sam.

"Not all of them, but many—maybe most."

"Then they disagree on everything except the Essence and the One?" said Peter.

"Both sides do also agree that when the One returned to the Essence, he secured the same good fortune, ultimately, for us," replied Katera. "This was through his act—"

"That may be more detail than they want to hear right now," said Dalbin. "I suspect they may want to finish their breakfast."

"The professor can dig into this more if he wants on his own time," said Eddie. "I'd rather dig into my breakfast."

Katera left with Sam and Eddie soon after breakfast. By lunchtime, Allie, Winnie, and Peter had plied Dalbin with everything they could think to ask about Melenca and its culture. Rafe had borrowed a skimmer to scout out stores and other concerns in Pelora.

"With all the fieldwork you're doing, you'll be able to publish a paper when we get back, Peter," said Winnie as the three sat at a table in the dining hall. "You'll be the world's leading expert on Melenca—think of that!"

"He'll be the only expert," said Allie.

Peter didn't respond for a moment. Then he said, "It's not just academic interest."

"What else is there?" asked Winnie. "Getting us ready to go out on our own, is that what you mean?"

"If we're stranded here, I'm going to have to decide what to do with my life."

"Don't say that," said Allie. "I feel strongly Sam is right—we can find Perroso, and he can guide us to a portal."

"That may just be wishful thinking. We have to face the possibility that we're stuck here."

"So you're joining Rafe as a naysayer."

"I agree we should look for Perroso—indeed, I hope we find him, and that there is a way back. But I'm being honest with myself. We can only look so long."

Allie started to respond, but someone said, "May I join you?" Arban Melroc, the reporter they'd met in the garden, stood there. They hadn't seen him at dinner the night before. Within a few minutes, Rafe and Dalbin came in as well. "I've learned something that might interest you," said Arban. "At his meeting house in Buzakor, a prominent Proclaimer will give instructions tonight on where they can find Perroso next week."

"Does that mean there's a spy in Mentor Perroso's inner circle?" said Winnie.

"That's no surprise," said Dalbin. "As many followers as he has and as open as his organization is, anyone can show up, and gain access. Perroso's well aware of that possibility, I'm sure—as Ravinn says, that's why he's putting out conflicting messages."

"Be that as it may, this tip is based on inside info," said Arban. "I'm headed to Buzakor myself to hear what he says."

"Can you get word to us about what this leader says?" said Winnie.

"What if Sam and Eddie find out something and we have to leave?" said Allie. "We need to go to Buzakor—act instead of just sitting here."

"Find out what rightcakes are plotting, and where Perroso will be? OK, I'm on board with that. But not all of us—Peter and Rafe need to stay here in case Sam sends word. And we can get a message to Caldan through Ravinn, to let Sam and Eddie know where we've gone."

"I don't have any intention of going," said Rafe.

"I'm happy to stay here too," said Peter.

"You're in luck," said Dalbin. "Buzakor is on the way to Kerela. I plan to stop there for the night. I'll give you a lift—provided you go on with me to Kerela for a day or so. Or else you'll have to come back here on your own."

"It depends on what we find out," said Allie. "We might go from Buzakor to wherever Perroso is. We'll go with you, then decide what to do next when we know more."

"I'll meet you in Buzakor, then," said Arban. He arranged to rendezvous at a park near the meeting house.

Allie and Winnie left with Dalbin soon after lunch. The hauler soon reached flatter land, undamaged so far, which resembled the country they'd passed through between Secora and the northern hills.

They hadn't traveled far when Winnie said in a low voice, "I wonder about something, Allie. Here we are, six strangers thrown together by some quirk of the cosmos, or fate, take your pick, including three young men you can have your pick from."

"You make it sound like a reality show."

"They're all interested in you. Surely it's obvious."

"Eddie just wants a good time. Rafe wants a helpmate for his big business plans here—no thanks."

"What about Sam?"

Allie waited a moment before responding. "I'm fond of Sam." She paused. "It's kind of like being attracted to someone you meet on a cruise—though this is the ultimate cruise. How do you know a relationship would work with someone you've known for only a week?"

"How do you know it wouldn't? We are in close contact with each other in a serious business. This isn't a pleasure cruise."

"I don't know that it wouldn't. But we live in different states, both have jobs we like—or at least will stay in, in Sam's case. That makes a relationship complicated."

"You think living in two different states is a problem, compared to living in two different universes?"

Allie laughed. "When you put it that way, it doesn't seem so complicated. I guess I better not fall for a Melencan guy."

"I gather there's no one back home."

"I'm not involved with anyone."

"It's none of my business, but that's never stopped me. How come someone as good looking as you, with a pleasant personality like yours, doesn't have someone?"

Allie looked away for a few seconds, then back at Winnie. "I was married, Winnie."

"Past tense."

"I met someone in the first job I had, after I graduated from college. By the end of that year, we were married."

"It didn't work?"

"It did for three years. I thought it was good. Brad was nice looking and charming—and that was the problem. There were other women who thought he was nice looking and charming, and he indulged them.”

“Ah, I get it.”

“When I found out, that was the end.”

“How old are you, Allie?”

“Thirty-four—why? What does that have to do with anything?”

“If you got married a year out of college and were married three years, you’re going on a decade since your divorce. And you’ve never found anyone since?”

“Maybe it’s my fault, partly. Maybe I’ve held back some—I don’t want to get burned again.” She looked out at the landscape. “But I don’t want to end up alone, either. I’d like to have a family. But it has to be with the right person. I need to be sure I’m making the right choice this time.”

“And you don’t feel that with Sam?”

“I don’t know. I need to give it more time.” She looked back at Winnie. “What about you, Winnie? You’ve been married a long time, right?”

“You’ve got time. I didn’t get married until I was in my mid-thirties. And I’ve been married twenty-eight years. Even had a kid. And by the way, sometimes either Paul or I would commute to a job in another city. We made it work.”

They reached Buzakor in late afternoon. They were approaching the town center when Dalbin suddenly exclaimed, “What in the—what is that?!” He was looking ahead on the left. A large, ornate building loomed, looking something like a nineteenth-century European opera house. Next to it were two other buildings, not as grand or as large, but still big. A small crowd of people mingled outside the ornate building, and others were walking in and out of the two other buildings. A large statue of a burly man posed in a patch of lawn in front of the opera house. One of the man’s arms pointed upward, while the other hovered close to his chest, his thumb pointing inward. Dalbin slowed down the hauler and peered at the buildings as they drove past, glancing back quickly at times at the street ahead.

“What is that complex, Dalbin?” said Winnie.

“No idea—it wasn’t there when I was last here, a couple of years ago. There was an agency building there, as I recall.” He sped the hauler back up as they passed the complex. “But I don’t have a good feeling about this. I recognize the statue. It’s Flammer.”

Within a few minutes they turned into a drive around a modest two-story building, the

Weary Traveler's Rest. The lobby was relatively compact.

"Welcome!" said the short, plump man behind the counter. He squinted at Dalbin. "You've been here before. Dalvin, is it?"

"Close—Dalbin. And you have a good head for faces."

The innkeeper grinned and shrugged. "You develop a knack for it when you run an inn in a town where people have mostly passed through over the years." He glanced at the group. "How many rooms?"

After sorting out the arrangements, Dalbin said, "I wondered about the big complex of buildings on the edge of town. That wasn't here last time I passed this way."

"It's why people aren't just passing through anymore—they're staying a few days. You recognize the statue?"

"Of course."

"The complex is operated by Flammer Enterprises. The fancy big building is a casino. The one on the end is a large and expensive inn." He lowered his voice. "Frankly, I was worried about the competition at first. But my humble little establishment has survived. Enough travelers know about it from experience."

"And the building in the middle?"

"Its official name is the Skills Training Center, but only women need apply, and only young and attractive women, if you catch my drift."

"A choice house! I knew Flammer frequented them, but I didn't know he operated one."

"It turns a large profit."

"Wasn't there an agency building there before?"

"The district relief agency for the poor."

"What happened to it?"

The innkeeper lowered his voice again. "It was supposed to be slated for renovations. They moved all the staff out—temporary, they said, until the building was ready again. Then the 'renovations' commenced—it was torn down. Before you knew it, they started work on the complex."

"And the agency staff?"

"Dispersed to other agencies."

"So there's no longer a central place for poor relief in this district?"

"There's no longer any poor relief period. The staffers were reassigned to other duties."

"And the district council just went along with this?"

"Compactors have a majority on the council. They'll do whatever the Flammer administration wants. And they don't care about—well, I shouldn't get into politics with a guest."

"Don't worry, I understand." He turned back to his companions. "Let's get checked into our rooms, then we'll go to the common room for dinner—and perhaps some ale."

"You've come to the right place! Our supply is unsurpassed in these parts." And he laughed at his own exuberance.

Half an hour later they were gathered at a table in the Travelers' Tavern. The innkeeper delivered mugs of ale for Dalbin and Winnie and a goblet of wine for Allie. "You travelers must be weary from your arduous journey." He recited the dinner choices. "What'll it be? Whatever your pleasure is, it will be a meal that will refresh your bodies and lift your spirits."

"That would certainly be welcome," said Winnie.

After they gave their orders, Allie asked Dalbin, "What's a choice house?"

"You take your choice of the young women available."

"And pay for the privilege, presumably," said Winnie.

"Pay handsomely."

"Are these choice houses everywhere?" said Allie.

"It depends on the district. Some permit them, some don't." He took a sip of his ale. "It's worrisome how brash Flammer has become, closing down a local agency and then putting up buildings for his own concern."

"You don't know the half of it," said a nearby voice, startling them. A sixtyish man, with longish light brown hair and a wrinkled face, sat alone at a table. "If you'll pardon the intrusion, I couldn't help but overhear your conversation. I take it you're traveling through. The Flammer regime not only closed down the agency, it built the new complex using funds allocated for renovation as well as other funds designated for relief."

"Isn't that against the codes?"

"Of course."

"And the revenue coming from the new complex goes to Flammer's enterprise—that compounds the offense."

"Not only that, the regime is hosting official events at the complex, requiring participants—agency personnel, representatives from concerns, and so on—to stay at the complex, and pocketing the proceeds. These events have always been held in administration buildings before." He paused to take a sip from his mug. "Flammer pushes against the bounds of what the codes permit, and then beyond, and as long as the Compactors are in charge, he's allowed to get away with it. So he pushes more."

"And more." Dalbin took a sip from his own mug. "Thanks for the information."

"Always happy to enlighten," said their new friend, smiling. "The more people become aware, perhaps the more momentum will build." He finished his beer and then, bidding them farewell, arose and left.

Arban Melroc was waiting for them in the park with another man, a reporter for the *Vantage* who covered Proclaimers and Wayfarers and their differences in these turbulent times. Arban introduced him as Felbin Roponar. Dalbin had led them to the park.

"I'll meet you back at the inn afterward," Dalbin told them.

"You don't want to go to the meeting?" said Winnie.

"It would just get my ill temper up."

"There will be some Proclaimers from out of town," said Arban. "Still, rather than go in as a group, it will be more prudent for each of you to accompany one of us and sit separately." So when they reached the meeting house, Winnie and Felbin entered first, followed shortly by Arban and Allie. Glancing back, Winnie noticed a number of people turning and staring at Allie. As Winnie sat, she saw on the front wall a portrait of a man she recognized as Flimsel Flammer.

"Why is there a picture of Flammer?" she whispered to her companion.

"Proclaimer houses all used to have pictures of the One hanging there. But they've replaced them with pictures of Flammer. They relegated the pictures of the One to their storage rooms."

A few feet from the portrait was a long metal tube, propped up on a stand on top of a small table. Winnie started to ask what it was, but then thought she didn't want to appear too ignorant of Melencan culture. "Why is that there?" she said.

"The firetube? It's become an object of veneration in Proclaimer meeting houses."

"An idol."

"You might say that."

Just then a man entered the room from a side door, carrying a thin book. After bowing down before the firetube, he turned to the gathered worshippers and held up the book.

"Hear now the Sayings of the Anointed One."

"Let me guess," said Winnie, "Flammer." Felbin nodded, a slight smile on his face. "Do they have a book of sacred writings as well?"

"That's it. They did have the ancient writings, the Chronicles, but they've replaced it with the Sayings. The ancient books are in their storage rooms now."

The speaker opened the book and began to read: "There's no need to gather so-called information before acting, you only need to follow your instincts. And I will tell you what the instincts say—listen only to me.'" He looked up from the book. "Listen only to him."

"Let it be so," the crowd recited in unison.

"And the Anointed One says, 'The Essence has sent me here to lead you to truth and to free you. Listen only to me.' Listen only to him."

"Let it be so."

"And the Anointed One says, 'Wayfarers and Unifiers tell you to welcome strangers, like Newcomers, but I tell you don't let them overrun our beautiful land—repel them!' Listen only to him."

"Let it be so."

He turned a few pages in the book. "Next I will read from the Anointed One's Central Truths: 'Wayfarers and Unifiers tell you to coddle those who are grieving, but I tell you that's the time to take advantage of the suckers, while they are vulnerable. They tell you to protect the weak, but I tell you now is the time to get ahead of those losers and stomp them into their place. They tell you to honor those who don't retaliate, but I tell you that just gives you the chance to finish those fools off.' Listen only to him."

"Let it be so."

He closed the book. "We need to face the hard truth: we are in a holy war for the soul of our land. The Unifiers are trying to sabotage our economy by disrupting the flow of crystals, by spreading lies about harm to the land supposedly caused by the mining of crystals, by spreading lies about how the residue of crystals is supposedly toxic to our water and our soil. We know the truth, that the Anointed One and the Compactors are protecting our water, our soil, and our supply of crystals."

"This is the truth!" shouted someone.

"And now, my friends, we must mobilize to join the crusade of the Anointed One, the courageous Compactors, and the mining concerns to thwart these evildoers who would destroy us."

"Let it be so!" several people called out.

"Join the crusade!"

"Crush the evildoers!"

The speaker swept his hand over the gathered congregation. "We have friends from other parts of Melenca here this evening. They are here to learn some vital intelligence we have gathered. Mentor Perroso plans to address a small group in Penrala in three days." He mentioned a specific location in Penrala. "He and his followers believe the event will be kept secret until the last minute. They are wrong. We will be there, in force. Tell your friends and prepare to march. Mentor Perroso will find out just what happens to meddling old fools who oppose the Anointed One's will." The assembled congregants roared their approval.

"Now we will close with a prayer," he said. "We call on the Essence to defeat the enemies of your Anointed One, the Unifiers and Wayfarers, who seek to destroy him. Protect him and bring to ruin his adversaries, the Unifiers and Wayfarers, who strive to abolish the beautiful trade in crystals you have favored our glorious land with. We pledge ourselves to his lasting rule and we beseech you to cast his opponents, the Unifiers and Wayfarers, into permanent wilderness."

"Let it be so!" rang out the worshippers.

"What do you know—he did mention the Essence, finally," said Winnie to Felbin.

"When the Essence fits their purposes."

As they filed out, Winnie noticed that the people around them avoided getting near Allie. When the four of them came together on the way back toward the park, Allie burst out, "That was appalling!"

"Not like any goddamn church service I've ever attended," said Winnie. "Are they all like that?"

"I don't know that every single Proclaimer service in Melenca is the same as that one," said Felbin, "but it's like many I've seen—most, I would say."

"Somebody's got to get word to Perroso," said Allie, "but we don't know how to."

"A story in the *Current*?" said Winnie.

"We'll see," said Arban. "I have to be careful. I can't compromise my source."

"What about the *Vantage*?" asked Allie. "You're going to Proclaimer meetings. It wouldn't be surprising if you happened on this one."

"Maybe. I don't want to alienate all Proclaimers. I still need access to them."

"This is a fucking crisis," said Winnie. "And your digests can help defuse it."

After a moment, Arban said, "We'll try to figure something out."

8

SHENANIGANS IN KERELA

They left early the next morning, fortified by the substantial and satisfying breakfast the Travelers' Tavern provided. After several hours, they came to a town. Dalbin stopped the hauler in front of a store on the main street and told them he needed to replenish the hauler's crystals. Winnie and Allie followed him in. The woman behind the counter nodded to Dalbin, then stared hard at Allie.

The shop appeared to be a general goods store. Dalbin asked the woman at the counter where crystals were and started to head for the appropriate section when he turned back to the woman and asked about one of the alternate-power devices Beldan's stores were now selling.

"We don't stock any of that stuff," she said.

"You don't want to take advantage of the growing market for it, especially in light of the growing crisis near the mines?"

She snorted. "Those are phony stories. They're just made up to try to hurt the mining concerns and the Supreme Leader."

"But we've just come from that area," said Allie. "We've seen the damage."

"You think I'm going to believe a brown-eye? You're lucky you're even allowed in here."

"That attitude went out of fashion a good while ago," said Dalbin.

"Well, the Supreme Leader is going to make sure brown-eyes and Newcomers don't lord it over us blue-eyes—he'll make sure they know their place."

Dalbin turned to the others. "I think we've seen enough here. Let's go." As they left, he looked at Allie and said, "Sorry for that behavior."

"Wooden warned me, but still, to experience it . . . it's jarring. Someone you don't know dislikes you just because of the color of your eyes."

"What I said was accurate mostly, about not being fashionable, but unfortunately there are still far too many who share that woman's attitude."

"And Flammer encourages it, it appears?" said Winnie.

"The better to divide us."

"Don't you need crystals, Dalbin?"

"We have enough to get to the next town. I wasn't going to buy anything from that woman if I could help it."

Returning to the hauler, Winnie noticed a crowd in a small square off the other side of the street near the end of the long block. A man stood above the crowd on a small platform, and she made out a voice dimly, though not what it was saying. "What's going on there?" she said.

Dalbin looked down the street. "It's the shouter."

"Shouter?"

"It's traditional, centuries old. Every town had a shouter to read off official information, things going on in town. They still do, though larger towns do it by neighborhood."

"Why do they shout?"

"That's just the title. They've always picked someone with a loud voice who could project. Do you want to hear what he's saying?"

They both did, so they strolled over to the square. Closer, they noticed some of the people holding signs with a drawing of a thick-necked man's head, with a scowl on his face. Under the face, signs had different words: "Supreme Leader" on some, "Anointed One" on others, "Melenca for Real Melencans" on others.

"Flammer?" Winnie said.

"Of course," replied Dalbin.

"You might have heard claims that there are problems happening near the mines, cracks in the land and such," yelled the shouter. "The Supreme Leader has assured us this is not true, and the *Weasel* has confirmed that nothing of the sort is going on. If you want to know about real news from across Melenca, read the *Weasel*—not the phony stories in the *Current* and the *Vantage*." The crowd murmured in acknowledgment. "Moving on, the Supreme Leader has kept rivers flowing down from the hills. He discovered plots by Unifiers to dam the rivers upstream, flood farmlands, and dry the rivers up downstream."

"They are evil!" one man shouted.

"The Supreme Leader has thwarted those plans. He told us all about it." The crowd roared its approval. "Not only that, the Supreme Leader has kept the sun rising in the morning and shining down on us throughout the day. Unifiers tried to erect giant mirrors to reflect sunlight away from the land, causing perpetual darkness to descend upon us."

"They are monsters!" a woman shouted.

"The Supreme Leader once again stopped them and saved us."

"He is our savior!" a man yelled.

"Dalbin, how could anyone believe such bullshit?" said Winnie.

"They're gullible. They believe what they want to believe. It doesn't matter whether it reflects reality."

"I thought you said they announced official information and news about events in the town," said Allie.

"They always have done that, and many still do. But in towns where Flammer is especially popular, the shouter's role has been corrupted into just spreading propaganda for the Illusionist, as Ravinn calls him." The shouter had continued in the same vein as they spoke. "Are you ready to go?" Dalbin asked them.

"We've certainly heard enough," said Winnie.

As they turned away, the shouter yelled, "It's been revealed who is behind the Unifiers' plots. A group of Outbounders has infiltrated Melenca and is bent on destroying our society. Be on the alert for these foreigners—we need to smash them."

"Let's get out of here," Winnie said. "Arban Melroc warned us they were going to step up the campaign against Outbounders."

"He's right," said Dalbin. "If the MNAA is involved, and Flammer and the *Weasel* are inflaming rightcakes, the threat is serious."

As Dalbin had said, they reached the next town, and they found a similar store where he could replenish his crystal supply. As they approached the entrance after he parked, Dalbin said, "Now that's interesting," pointing to a large sign over the door. "Crystals and products for vehicles and homes," it read.

"That they sell crystals?" said Winnie. "I thought that's what this kind of store did."

"Look at the fine print below," he said. "Alternate power sources available," it read. "I need to check on this. If a traditional crystal store—and not a small one at that—is starting to branch into alternatives, that could be a hopeful sign."

Inside, where rows of shelves holding various products stretched the length of the building, a few customers wandered among the shelves. As Dalbin engaged the proprietor, the two women drifted apart examining the merchandise. Toward the back of the store, Winnie was halfway attentive to the objects on the shelves as she waited for Dalbin to finish. Power sources were not a subject of great interest to her. No one else occupied the area she was in.

Suddenly, she was startled by voices coming from behind the shelf. "I can't believe they're selling this crap," said a male voice. "If they're making inroads in places like this, that means trouble. I've distributed products to this store for years—I never dreamed they'd offer that stuff."

"I've seen the same in a couple of stores in my territory too," said a second male.

"I need to report it to my concern—though you know they'll blame me for letting this happen."

"I don't know—when I reported it, I was just questioned intensely by some of the higher-ups. They wanted to know about it. And from what I hear, there's bigger fears."

"What do you mean? Hear where?"

"Just picked up scraps of talk around the concern, from people in the know. Apparently Margan and some of the other great merchants have got wind of some powerful force that Mentor Perroso has discovered, and might have figured out how to harness."

"Perroso? He's a harmless old crank. How would he know how to harness some force?"

"He may not be as harmless as you think. Margan and the others don't think so. Apparently he knows a lot about techne, and nature. It wouldn't surprise me if he'd discovered how to manipulate some natural force. Anyway, word is this force might boost some of Ravinn Novaeto's inventions, or even be something entirely new."

"Sounds farfetched to me. Though if Margan and the others are concerned, maybe there is something to it. I grant you, it would be a real blow if it was real, maybe more than Ravinn's crap."

"Obviously. So Margan and the others aren't sitting still. They've got people out looking for Perroso. He moves around, you know—hard to catch."

"And if they find him?"

"When. Not if. Find out what this force is, and then learn how to control it—or at least keep anyone else from harnessing it. Especially Perroso."

At that moment, Winnie heard Allie calling her from a couple of rows over. The two male voices broke off. Winnie hurried away and found Allie, then gestured toward the front. Dalbin was waiting for them there, holding a bag. "I've seen all I need to," he said. As the women climbed aboard the hauler, Dalbin opened two of the boxes behind the steering column and emptied the contents of a pouch from the bag into one box, then another pouch into the second box.

As they drove away, Winnie told Allie in a low voice what she overheard. "That's concerning, for sure," said Allie, "but we already know rightcakes are looking for Perroso.

This just makes more of them."

"They may have better intelligence and more sophisticated methods of looking. I don't know where they got this force of nature idea, but if that refers to the whirlwind, we need to know about it."

"You're not seriously thinking that Mentor Perroso could control a bizarre force of nature that I doubt even our own scientists back home would understand, are you? Or worried these people could interfere with the whirlwind?"

"Of course not. But suppose the whirlwind shows up in a specific location—like it does in the Bermuda Triangle on the other end—or under specific conditions. Or suppose it can even be triggered. Then suppose they force that information out of Perroso—they might conceivably make where it occurs inaccessible."

Allie thought for a moment. "Even if they just find Perroso and hide him away somewhere, if the whirlwind only shows up at certain times, we might have to stay in Melenca a lot longer than we hoped."

They reached Kerela in late afternoon. It was a district capital, bigger than Buzakor. They passed a complex of official buildings in the center of town and reached a large inn, the Placid Glade. After checking them in and handing out keys, Dalbin told them to put their bags in their room and then meet him in the common room and await Beldan.

The Placid Repast was bigger than the Buzakor inn's tavern. When they were seated, they ordered a round of ale and wine. They were on the second round when Winnie spotted Beldan at the entrance. She waved, and he nodded and joined them. He greeted them all warmly and ordered a beer. Dalbin said, "What's next, Pop?"

"The latest stonewalling is suddenly a need to inspect the buildings for suitability. A survey that will take six months."

"You know what the result will be—they'll claim they're unsuitable and cancel."

"Of course. There is no issue with suitability. They saw our design with details on building modification, and they approved it. I'm meeting with our advocate here tomorrow to go over our options when they do back out. See what you can find out—any more insight on this will be useful."

"I'll ask around."

Beldan looked at Winnie and Allie. "Now, tell me about your adventures in the northern hills and beyond."

Dalbin left after breakfast the next morning to meet an administrator he knew. Meanwhile, Beldan gave Winnie and Allie a tour of his concern's Kerela store. Dalbin returned to the inn in the late morning.

"Well?" said Beldan.

"Nothing. He was vague, evasive. He wouldn't admit they were planning to back out. I asked him point-blank."

"Not surprising. You're going to have to go further up the bureaucracy."

"First I sent a message to another contact I think will be more forthcoming. I just heard back. He'll meet me, but not at his office—in a small tavern a bit out of the way. I'm going there after lunch." He looked at Winnie. "You were a digest reporter, right, Winnie? Will you go as a witness? If I use an anonymous tip with other officials, I'd like it to be more than just my word."

"In a tavern? Sure. I've gone to plenty like that—I'm your girl."

"Good point—it will look like a get-together for drinks."

The tavern was in an area of small and dingy stores and workshops. The building needed a coat of fresh paint and new boards here and there. A few people sat at the bar and among the few tables. A man sat at a table in the back corner, away from everyone. As they joined him, Dalbin introduced Winnie as a family friend, then mentioned that she was a retired reporter for a digest. The man just nodded. Dalbin didn't introduce him by name.

After they ordered beers, Dalbin got to the point. "We've got a contract. Why all the evasion and delays? We can't get an answer."

"No one wants to stick their neck out."

"We suspect the district administration is getting ready to cancel the deal."

"Not an illogical thought."

"We wonder why."

"Pressure from the Flammer regime."

"Pop knows the Bureau of Power is leaning on them."

"It's more than bureaucratic pressure. I don't know for sure what form it's taking—only a few people do, and they're tight-lipped. But it's enough to bring things to a halt."

"But the agreement is signed and recorded. It's a done deal. Flammer hasn't gone to the magistrates' chambers to challenge it."

"You didn't hear this from me."

"Understood. I won't use your name."

"Whatever the regime is doing is against the codes. I don't know what exactly, but that's the only explanation that makes sense."

Dalbin thought for a moment. "So we need to find out what they're up to—that might give us a lever."

"No one's going to tell you."

"Pop might have some thoughts on how to use this."

When Beldan heard what Dalbin and Winnie had learned, he nodded. "That fits," he said.

"How do we find out what exactly?" said Dalbin. "I can keep asking people up the chain, but I'd bet our informant is right."

"Perhaps we don't need to. Maybe we don't need to know any more than we do now to use it against the district administration. Let's talk with Barji Corsano when he comes. Then I think we'll meet with the administrator."

They didn't have long to wait for the advocate. They met with him in the Placid Repast in mid-afternoon. Corsano was a short, stout man, neatly dressed, with a headful of curly hair. It was a little early for ale, so they ordered tea. A few other people were in the tavern, but none at tables near them. Dalbin told Corsano what he had learned about the pressure on the district administration.

"Without knowing specifics, do we have enough to confront the administration?" Beldan asked Corsano.

"Probably. But you may not have to use that." He removed a sheaf of papers from his satchel. "I've been going over the contract. I remembered the innovative points, involving the new techne, but most of the contract is standard, so I looked near the end. Sure enough, it's in the fine print."

"What are you talking about?"

"Don't read your own contracts, eh? There's a clause calling for penalties if progress is delayed—penalties on your concern if it's your fault, but on the district if it's theirs. If you invoke that clause, it's enforceable in the magistrates' chambers."

"And if the district fights it there?"

"My professional opinion is you would prevail. The case is clear. Flammer has appointed a number of magistrates, but not enough—at least not yet—who simply approve any of his actions by twisting interpretations of the codes beyond recognition. The outcome is likely to be positive."

"So if we threaten to invoke that clause, they may give in."

"I can't predict what they'll do—but that would be sensible. Going to chambers will produce plenty of publicity, negative publicity for the district. The digests will be on it. Compactors may have a majority on the Council, but they'll have a hard time justifying clearly going against the codes. And the Flammer regime won't relish having their activities in the shadows exposed."

"Getting back to the question of pressure. If we can't find out exactly what it is, can we go to the magistrates' chambers nonetheless?"

He nodded. "We can file a motion for discovery. The district will be compelled to provide information."

"If we can find out what the pressure is, can we file against the Flammer regime in the magistrates' chambers?"

"Not only can you, it might be a good move on behalf of the entire alternate-techne sector. Force into public view the activities of Flammer and the mining concerns against the alternative concerns."

"I have an idea in that regard."

They got an appointment with Pemera Lingolo, the district administrator, the next morning. In her spacious inner office, a large desk stood out from several large windows, and the large upholstered chairs in front of it were now occupied by Beldan, Dalbin, Winnie, and Corsano. A middle-aged blonde woman sat behind the desk. Beldan introduced Winnie as a digest reporter.

"This conversation is off the record," Pemera told Winnie.

"I don't have a problem with that—unless it needs to be on the record."

Pemera frowned, but then turned to Beldan. "Look, I know you're here to ask about the delays. They're unavoidable, I'm afraid. The survey on suitability is necessary."

"We know about the pressure from the Flammer regime, Pemera," said Beldan. "We know it's against the codes."

"Who told you that?"

"We're not free to say," said Dalbin, "but it was a well-informed source."

She looked intently at Dalbin and then Beldan. "Political pressure is part of most public procedures," she said finally. "There's nothing unusual going on here."

"You can tell us what it is," said Beldan. "That's the easy way. If you won't, we'll have to do this the hard way."

"Hard way?"

Beldan nodded at Corsano. He pulled out the contract and told her about the penalty clause, and their intent to invoke it.

"You don't want to do that," she said.

"I don't want to," said Beldan, "but I will, if you don't drop the delays and proceed with installation."

"Financial penalties—that will really strap the district."

"There's an easy way to avoid that."

She stared at him for a moment. "Do you realize what a hard place this puts us in? Between two rocks, the threat from the Flammer regime and this threat from you."

"We might be able to help. We're going to file against the regime in the High Magistrates' Chamber. If we don't know what the pressure is, we'll file for discovery. It would be better to know going in."

"How does that help us?"

"If the district will file a supporting motion for our case," said Corsano, "it will strengthen the case and not only put a public spotlight on the regime's actions that violate the codes but also make it official that the district is an aggrieved party. It's a more sheltered position."

Pemera thought for a moment, then called to her young assistant in the outer office. "Tell Tomolo to come here."

A few minutes later, a sixtyish man walked in. She briefed him on the discussion and then asked what he thought. He considered for a moment, asked for the contract and looked it over, then said, "It's true that they can invoke the clause. As for filing in the High Magistrates' Chamber, my opinion is that they have a strong case. Supporting it would seem to give the district some cover."

Pemera was silent for a short while, then said, "All right, that seems the best option. We'll go ahead with installation. Tomolo, instruct the district advocate's staff to file the supporting motion. They can coordinate with Corsano."

"Wise choice," said Beldan. "Thank you."

"And the pressure from the regime?" said Corsano.

Pemera hesitated, then said, "Flammer's people have threatened to withhold the scheduled allocations to the district."

"The regular distributions, like all the districts get? The routine ones?"

"Yes. All of them."

Corsano looked at Beldan. "There's no doubt that's against the codes. Flagrantly."

"The digests will have a field day with that, when it comes out in the chambers," said Dalbin.

When they returned to the Placid Glade, Allie sat in a chair in the lobby, looking distraught. There was an ugly bruise above her elbow.

"What's wrong?" exclaimed Winnie. "What happened?"

Allie looked up at Beldan. "Your store manager came here very upset, looking for you. He said his son had been stopped by constables looking for a missing skimmer. His son had the registration for his skimmer, and answered them respectfully—Jandar said he'd taught his children to do so, as brown-eyes, to not provoke constables. But they said he was acting suspiciously, and they took him off toward the jail.

"I told Jandar you had an advocate here who might help, but meanwhile I went with him to try to intercede. We found them near the jail. Jandar pleaded with them, but they roughed him up. I yelled at them to quit, that we had an advocate, but one shoved me—hard." She examined her bruise. "He told me to shut up and said I was lucky they didn't arrest me, that I was a brown-eye trouble-maker."

"I'll contact Corsano right away," said Beldan grimly. "His firm has someone who will deal with this sort of thing—unfortunately, there's too much of it still going on. It sounds like the boy did nothing wrong—knowing Jandar, I'm sure that's correct."

"We should have a healer look at your injury," said Dalbin.

"It's nothing—I'll be fine."

9

— · —

THE SEARCH FOR THE MENTOR

Sam and Eddie each had a bench of the hauler to themselves, their duffels next to them. The damage became less visible and more sporadic, though they would occasionally pass a large boulder or a crack in a hillside. Gradually the ground flattened. At midday they stopped for lunch at a tavern in a small crossroads.

Katera had told them they'd have a long drive that day and stop for the night in an inn, then reach Buscara by late afternoon on the following day. So they were soon back in the hauler. As Katera started to turn back onto the road, a woman limped toward them from the direction from which they had come. Katera stopped and looked intently at her.

"I know her. She works for an organization helping Newcomers. Our organizations coordinate at times." She climbed out of the hauler and hailed the woman, who looked at her uncertainly before her face registered recognition. "Celera," said Katera. "What are you doing here? What happened to you?"

Celera glanced at Sam and Eddie. "How free are you to talk?" she asked Katera in a low voice.

"You can speak freely. These are friends."

"I'm shepherding a family of Newcomers to a sanctuary camp. There is an MNAA patrol behind us, not far, scanning for Newcomers. They must have had a tip that we've been operating in this area."

"Where are your Newcomers?"

"I left them hiding in the woods back there while I got food for them from the tavern."

"You're guiding them on foot?"

"Yes."

"You're not going to make it far at that rate, especially with your leg."

"I twisted my knee scrambling for cover when we were evading the patrol."

"How far are you going?"

"There's a side road about twelve miles ahead, and there's a spot a few miles down that road where we're to rendezvous with a hauler. It will take us to the camp."

"We can drive you to the rendezvous point."

"I can't ask you to do that. You'd be taking a big risk if you're caught."

"You're already taking a huge risk. It's the least I can do." She looked back at Sam and Eddie. "If we're stopped, we risk getting delayed by the MNAA—at the least. I'll tell them you're just travelers I was giving a lift. They might accept that and not detain you. But you should know the risk."

Sam hesitated. *We can't get caught, we just can't. And a delay might cost us the chance to find Perroso. But we can't just abandon these people.* "We're willing to take the risk. Right, Eddie?"

"Apparently you're in charge, Captain—it appears I don't get a say. But I don't mind a little adventure."

Katera turned back to Celera. "Best to skip the food and avoid the MNAA—let's go pick up your family. Hop in. Bad choice of words—get in."

Celera pulled herself into the hauler, wincing. Katera drove back up the road half a mile before Celera told her to stop. Celera limped through some tall grass for about ten yards before reaching the fringe of the woods. She thrust aside some bushes as she disappeared into the trees. Before long, she returned with a father and mother and three young children, the older two a boy and a girl, around eight and six, the youngest a girl, maybe three. They all had red hair and ruddy complexions. The parents looked relieved and thanked Katera profusely as they boarded the hauler. They had accents, but not ones Sam could place. He wondered again about how the linguistic parallelism worked.

As the hauler turned back toward Buscara. Celera glanced frequently behind them. They had driven for a short while when she inhaled sharply.

"What is it?" said Katera.

"The MNAA patrol hauler. It's behind us." Sam looked back and could make out a red hauler a quarter mile behind. Celera pointed ahead. "There's a sharp bend up there, and we have enough of a lead that we'll pass out of sight. I need to get my family out there and lead them through the woods. I can tell you where we can meet you again."

"You're in no shape to lead an escape," said Katera.

"I don't have any choice."

"I'll guide them," said Eddie. The two women stared at him.

"You don't know anything about this area," said Katera, as her attention turned back to the road.

"I'm experienced at making my way through woods and through unfamiliar terrain. Tell me where to meet and give me some general direction. I'll get them there."

"Eddie *is* good in an emergency," said Sam.

Celera glanced back at Katera, who nodded. "We're going east on this road," said Celera. "Head due south in the woods, and you'll come to a trail, going east-west. Follow it east and eventually you'll hit a road. If you follow it back to the north, you'll reach this main road again. The road we need to turn on isn't far up the main road from there."

"How far to the trail and to the road?" said Eddie.

"I would guess the trail is two or three miles, and the road perhaps another couple. I can't give you exact distances because I'm not sure in this part of the woods—I haven't been in it before. I'm sorry."

"We'll find our way."

"Thank you," said Katera.

"Be careful," said Sam. "The others will be pissed if I lose you."

Celera made sure the husband and wife understood what they were about to do. A couple of minutes later they reached the bend and started around it. When they lost sight of the MNAA vehicle, Katera jolted her hauler to a sudden stop. "Now!" she cried. Eddie jumped out and waved the family after him. They clambered out, the parents and Eddie helping the children down. Here the grass stretched for about thirty yards. They began hurrying through it toward the trees.

"You'd better go now," warned Celera. "That hauler will round the bend any second."

Katera drove away. The family had reached within ten yards of the trees when the three-year-old stumbled and fell. The others halted, then Eddie motioned the parents on and leaned down and picked up the child and carried her as he ran toward the woods. The MNAA hauler came around the bend just as Eddie and the child reached the outlying trees. It had a logo on the side, two white squares, one on top of the other, joined by a vertical white line.

"I hope they didn't see them," said Celera.

The MNAA hauler sped up and a man in the front gestured to Katera and yelled at her to pull over. As she did, so did the red hauler and the man emerged and strode to her door. He wore a black tunic and gray pants. Sam could see several other men in the hauler, all in the same uniform.

"Did you see anyone over there?" the agent said, pointing toward the woods.

"No," answered Katera.

The man looked over the passengers, then back at Katera. "You slowed down around this curve. We caught up to you quicker than we should have."

"I don't know this road. I wasn't sure what lay around the curve, and I didn't want to take it too fast."

He looked hard at them all again. "We're looking for Newcomers. We have information there are some traveling through this area. It looked like a couple of people disappeared into the woods there."

"We haven't seen any Newcomers. Like I said, we didn't see anyone around here."

"We'll check to be sure. There's an MNAA roadblock ahead. If you spot any Newcomers, or anyone acting suspiciously, inform the agents there."

"We'll be sure to."

The man went back to his hauler and spoke to the others inside. Three men got out and strode toward the woods.

"We have to go or they'll get suspicious," said Katera. "We just have to hope they don't find Eddie and the others." Her hauler pulled away again. "I wonder where the roadblock is."

"I wasn't aware of one around here," said Celera. "But they move them around—they don't keep them in one spot for too long."

It didn't take them long to find this one. After another couple of miles, traffic ahead was stopped, with five or six skimmers interspersed among three haulers waiting in a queue.

"Oh no," said Celera. "It's right at the intersection with the side road I mentioned! If the family comes back to the main road, they'll walk right up to the roadblock."

"We've got to head them off," said Katera. She looked at Sam. "I don't have any right to ask, but—"

"I'll go," said Sam. "We don't have any choice. Where the trail hits the road should be clearly visible?"

"It's screened by some bushes," said Celera, "but if you look carefully you'll see the trees aren't as thick where the path leads up to the bushes. There's a narrow gap, though you have to be looking to notice." She peered ahead at the roadblock. "They're questioning those skimmer drivers now. But they'll really focus on checking the haulers. If you slip out now, I think you can reach the trees unseen."

"If they do see you, we'll claim you're attending to nature," said Katera. Sam laughed.

"You'll have to lead the family on by the trail across the side road until you reach the next road," said Celera. "That's the one we're making for. We should be waiting for you by the time you arrive at the road. I just hope you find them." She looked back at Katera. "I'm sorry I got you all into this mess."

"We knew what we were getting into. Don't worry about it."

Sam walked nonchalantly toward the trees, resisting the urge to look toward the roadblock until he reached the edge of the trees. None of the MNAA agents appeared to be looking his way. He plunged forward into the trees, and after a few minutes turned and headed obliquely. He had seen enough of the sun warming Melenca to know it matched Earth's, and he felt confident he was moving southeast toward the side road. It was slow going as he dodged or swatted away branches and worked his way around trees. After half an hour, he pushed aside the outlying branches of a large bush and suddenly stepped out onto a strip of grass that bordered the road. Hastily he glanced back to the north. He couldn't see the intersection. There was no traffic.

As he walked along the side of the road he increased his pace, though not enough to appear to be fleeing anything, and made better time. It was good to walk briskly after sitting in the hauler for much of the day. Birds chirped, and a hawk soared elegantly not far overhead. Sam spotted a cardinal and a few wrens in trees, and then an unfamiliar pair of birds that somewhat resembled parrots but were considerably larger with a much wider wingspan flew over him. A few cumulous clouds drifted in a blue sky. It was warm. Nonetheless, he was tense. The journey from Pelora had been smooth so far. Now everything was uncertain. *Can I find Eddie and the Newcomers? Can I find Katera and the hauler? What happens if I lose them?* He was taking a big risk.

The road was mostly flat, but after fifteen minutes, it rose ahead to a hill, beyond which he couldn't see. Suddenly over the crest of the hill came a red hauler. He had no time to do anything except keep walking, hoping he was inconspicuous enough. The hauler stopped beside him. It had the logo with two white squares. A black tunic called to him out a window. "There are few travelers on this road."

"I haven't seen many," he agreed.

"Not many? Meaning you have seen some?"

"Well, not in a good while."

"Where are you traveling to?"

"Buscara. Why do you ask?" He hoped the question didn't make him seem impertinent. No point in courting trouble.

"Buscara is to the east. You're going south."

"I'm meeting a friend who's going to give me a ride. A friend coming from the south."

The man stared at him for a moment, then said something to the driver, and the hauler drove off. *Apparently I'm innocuous. I'll stick to the road.* He continued to make good time, not encountering anyone except a skimmer that flashed by. He told himself he needed to pay more attention to the woods to his right. They remained uniform, oaks and beeches interspersed with the tangled undergrowth through which he had fought to reach the road. The monotonous view combined with his regular pace to lull him into a rhythm, which reduced his awareness to scanning only the view to his right.

After another fifteen minutes he noticed some bushes beyond the strip of grass that appeared thinner than the undergrowth so far. When he spread them apart, he found a small opening. Down a narrow alley he saw no trees directly ahead. He pushed through into the opening. Sure enough, the ground, mostly clear of undergrowth, formed a trail into the woods as far ahead as he could see, wide enough for three or four people to walk abreast. He was sure Eddie could not have come this far yet—if he made it at all. He glanced around. A few feet ahead on the side of the trail was a large oak in a small clearing. Sam sat down with his back against its trunk. He couldn't be seen from the road or the trail, at least not until someone was right on him, and he felt sure he could hear anyone approaching on the trail. There was nothing to do but wait.

His mind drifted back to the seaplane, to jumbled thoughts of the bizarre environment he had landed in, to the strange events he and his companions had experienced. The whole sequence struck him now as dreamlike. *How do you process this, cope with it? The human mind has no experience with it.* He was absorbed in these thoughts when suddenly he heard low voices and a faint sound of movement on the trail. He jumped to his feet and drew himself against the tree. After a moment, he peered cautiously around the tree, hoping whoever was coming would not be looking to the side. It was Eddie, leading the Newcomer family.

"Why are you hiding behind a tree, Captain?" called Eddie. "Why are you here, period?"

"I was hoping you wouldn't spot me."

"That's not hard when you leave your face hanging out."

Sam told them what had happened since they'd left the hauler. "Did you hear any pursuit?"

"We heard some noise. It sounded like an elephant thrashing around—the MNAA must not be used to chasing people in the woods. I just drew us off into a clump of big bushes. After a while, the noise faded away."

Sam pointed in the direction of the road and said they needed to cross it and continue along the trail. He went first and looked in both directions. Seeing nothing, he called for them to follow. He noticed that the three-year-old stuck close to Eddie. "You seem to have a fan."

"Can you blame her? I think she feels safe around me after I carted her into the woods."

The trail was screened by bushes on the other side of the road as well, but since they knew where to look, they had no trouble finding it. Their going was slow walking at the children's pace, but eventually they spotted an empty space ahead: the other road. Sam had them wait while he walked out to the road. Sure enough, there was Katera's hauler, parked along the side, only a few yards away.

"Sam!" exclaimed Katera. "Did you find them—oh, there's Eddie! And the family. We were worried." Celera hugged the Newcomer parents. After hearing Sam's and Eddie's reports, Katera told them they had best be on their way. "An MNAA patrol hauler passed us not long ago. We can't chance being on the road long." They quickly resumed their drive, Katera glancing back over her shoulder. "We can't tell you how thankful we are for what you've done. This isn't your struggle, and we're truly grateful to you." Celera echoed her remarks.

"You needed help," said Sam, embarrassed. "It was the least we could do after all you and your family have done for us."

"Besides," said Eddie, "it let us stretch our legs after you've had us cooped up in this hauler. If it hadn't been the MNAA, we'd have had to find another excuse."

Katera laughed. Then Celera told the Newcomers they'd better slouch down as they rode. In five minutes the hauler reached an intersection, at one corner of which, set back from the road a hundred feet, was a building. It showed no signs of activity, no lights on inside, no vehicles parked outside. Weeds grew around the edges. "Pull in here," Celera told Katera.

"What is this place?" said Eddie.

"It was one of the research stations on crystal waste," said Celera. "Where they were looking at new ways to dispose of it safely. Maybe even find uses for it that wouldn't be harmful."

"But it's empty," said Sam.

"Flammer's regime closed it down," said Katera, "and the others as well. Unnecessary and a waste of money, they claimed."

Celera scanned the horizon anxiously in all directions. "The sanctuary hauler was supposed to meet us here. We're a little late, but they would have waited. Something must have happened."

"The MNAA?" said Katera.

"That's my guess. We didn't know they were active here—our teams have had pretty free passage." She sounded pensive. "That's really worrisome—if they're managing to track us where we're being active."

"Or being told."

"It's possible. It doesn't have to be someone in our organization alerting them, though; it could be Flammer supporters in the area spotting activity and reporting it." She looked at the Newcomer family, who had straightened up when they stopped. "In any case, you've brought us to the rendezvous site, and I'm very grateful. I can't expect any more. We'll leave you here, and I'll lead them on to the camp."

"How far is it from here?"

"It's in Cantorba—sixty-five or seventy miles from here."

"That would take you more than two days on foot, at least, assuming your leg injury doesn't get worse—and you're traveling with children. Do you really think you can dodge the MNAA on foot throughout that long a hike?" Katera turned to Sam. "We have a choice: leave them on their own and turn toward Buscara or take them to Cantorba. If we take them, we'll lose time—considerable time. But I promised to take you to try to find Mentor Perroso. I'll do what you say."

Sam tried to think through the options. If they took the family to Cantorba, they risked missing Perroso—worse than a risk, they likely would miss him. But if they dropped the family off here, the Newcomers' odds of reaching Cantorba safely seemed less than slim. "What do you think we should do, Katera?" he said finally.

"Since you asked, I hate to just leave them here. We stopped to help them, after all. The MNAA is a real danger." She paused. "But I told you and Eddie I would drive you to Cantorba. It's your decision, Sam, and I'll go with it."

Thanks for putting it on me. Sam looked at Eddie. "What do you think?"

"We'll probably miss Perroso. This little side trip will be a waste. But you're the one so fired up to find him right away, not me—like I said, I don't mind some adventure." He hooked his thumb back at the family. "And these kids won't mind spending extra time with me."

Sam looked at the Newcomer family, especially the children. The parents looked at him anxiously. "I don't see how we can just abandon them," he said finally. "Let's take them to Cantorba."

"Thank you, Sam," said Katera, smiling at him. "I won't forget this." She looked at Celera. "I know the general direction of Cantorba, but what's the best way to go now, with the MNAA swarming around here?"

Celera thought for a moment. "They won't expect anyone moving Newcomers to be heading south. If we stay on this south road, even if we do run into a patrol, they might not stop us. And we soon should be out of the area where they're likely concentrating."

"We can make our guests more inconspicuous, I think." When Celera and the Newcomers had joined their party, Eddie had moved up beside Sam and brought his duffel, and Celera joined them on their bench, while the family took the back bench. Katera now directed the Newcomers to lie on the floor, and she took papers from boxes behind that bench and spread them out over the family, then had Sam and Eddie stow their duffels on the back bench. "I'm sorry, I know it's uncomfortable," she told the family, "but it should just be for a short while." The parents complied without complaining. The two older children whined about being crammed onto the floor until their father shushed them.

After they traveled for about ten minutes on the south road, one of the red haulers approached. Sam's stomach tightened. *If they stop us and search the hauler, we'll be delayed more than a day. We might not get back to the others period.* The red hauler rushed toward them at high speed. As it passed them, it didn't slow down, and a couple of the black-tunic men glanced their way, but they were in the clear.

"They think the Newcomers are back in the woods," said Katera.

"I think we should be out of danger soon," said Celera. Still, they kept the family hidden for another half hour, during which they encountered little traffic and no more patrols. Eventually they stopped and the family climbed back onto the bench, with the duffel bags rejoining the men on the crowded front bench. An hour later, they approached the outskirts of a town. "We need to turn toward Cantorba now," said Celera. "I think we've gone far enough south. I haven't been this way in a while, but if I remember correctly, there's an intersection not far ahead where we can take a road going northeast." She asked the family to crouch down on the floor once again as they neared the town. She was right: in the town they reached an intersection with a major road, and Celera told Katera to turn. As they left the town behind, the family regained their bench.

As they reached the outskirts of Cantorba, a town of some size, deep twilight had fallen. "Where's the sanctuary camp?" said Eddie.

"A large set of fields in the town center that was used for sports has been converted," replied Celera. "Cantorba is a town dominated by Unifiers, and the local council here permitted the camp to be erected. The constables have refused to help the MNAA or allow its agents near the camp."

"That takes courage, I guess," said Sam.

"They've angered the Flammer regime, and the Compactors in the Grand Council have threatened to act against them, but so far the High Magistrates' Chamber has not supported such threats. It's a tense standoff."

They passed large buildings into the center of town, where off to one side of the road ahead stood tents in rows. Celera directed Katera to a narrow street at the edge of the camp, where they parked. Celera led them between two lines of tents, some larger than others, to a particularly large tent. People filed in and out of it. A man was seated behind a table studying some papers. He looked up and greeted Celera by name. Over to the side a Newcomer woman was sobbing, and a Newcomer man was comforting her.

"What's wrong?" Celera asked the man at the table, clearly a sanctuary official she knew.

"They managed to get away from the MNAA, but only after the agents had separated their children from them."

"Oh no." Celera looked at Katera. "That means they'll send them to the mines."

Katera turned to Sam and Eddie. "That's one of the MNAA practices—Flammer's regime started it. They send Newcomer children to work in the crystal mines."

"You don't know about the mines?" the official said suspiciously to Sam and Eddie.

"My friends are from the Lands Beyond," Katera told him quickly. She looked back at Sam and Eddie. "It's very hard labor, dangerous work. Most children sent there don't reach adulthood."

"Can you track down the children, do something to distract the MNAA?" said Eddie.

"They'll have already put them on a transport, most likely," said the official.

"There's nothing we can do now," said Celera. "This job often makes you sad."

Katera looked out the tent entrance, where twilight was deepening into night, then at Sam and Eddie. "Even with the light on the hauler, I'm not sure how far we'd get in this darkness. It's better, I think, to spend the night here, and then leave early in the morning."

Sam looked into the darkness. He wanted more than anything to reach Buscara in time to meet Perroso. *If we keep going, we'll only make a couple of hours before we'd have to stop—unless we drive all night. It'll be risky on unlit back roads. I can't ask Katera to take that risk.* Reluctantly, he agreed.

Katera turned back to Celera. "We've delivered you, safe and sound. I assume there's a decent inn nearby?"

"No."

"In Cantorba? *No* good inn?"

"I didn't mean that. We'll find you room in one of the tents." She talked with the official for a minute, then said a few words to her Newcomer family. The parents embraced her. The children hung back shyly—except for the three-year-old, who came up to Eddie and hugged him. He put his arms around her little shoulders, then looked sheepishly at Sam.

"Be careful, or you're going to ruin your macho image," said Sam.

Celera led them over a few rows to a tent roomy enough for the three of them. "Let's go eat," she said. They hadn't had time to think about food, and Sam was famished. Celera led them over past several more rows to an open space with another very large tent in the middle. People sat at tables around it eating, both Newcomers and sanctuary workers. Just inside the tent were a couple of long tables with platters and large, steaming bowls. People had formed lines and were serving themselves.

When they finished, Celera hugged each of them. They retrieved what they needed from the hauler, then returned to their assigned tent. A curtain divided the tent in half, with cots on each side—clearly a men's side and a women's side.

"Thanks for the entertainment on the journey," Eddie said to Katera. "I was afraid we'd be bored."

"Less entertaining the rest of the way, I hope," she said.

"Dalbin told us the MNAA hunted down Newcomers," said Sam, "but that was abstract. This is real."

"At its best, Melenca has been open to people moving in from outside, but it hasn't always been at its best. It isn't now. The Flammer regime has inflamed attitudes toward Newcomers. More division."

"After seeing the MNAA in action, I'm glad we helped." He couldn't erase the image of the crying parents in the tent from his mind.

"So am I—thanks. It was a difficult decision, I know. I respect you for it." Sam caught a hint of something else besides gratitude in her voice, then suddenly knew what it was:

affection. And as he looked into those deep blue eyes, he realized he felt it too.

After an awkward pause, he said, "Eddie's the one who really came through, leading our family through the woods."

She looked at Eddie. "Yes, thanks. You took a big risk."

"Just a day's work for me." Then Eddie brushed aside the curtain and entered the other side.

She hesitated, then said, "Well, goodnight, Sam. Sleep well."

"You too, Katera." He went into his and Eddie's side.

He slept soundly. It had been a long day. Katera woke them at dawn. After a quick breakfast in the mess tent, they set off again.

The countryside was sparsely populated, mostly woodlands. They stopped for lunch at a small, dingy tavern. The food was mediocre, the tea weak. Afterward, they drove until the sky was growing pink in the west. At last Katera said they would stop at the next decent inn. They passed a couple at crossroads that appeared a little short of the "decent" criterion. They were well into twilight when they reached a small town, in the center of which a larger inn loomed over one corner, the Soaring Cloud. Katera parked behind it. It looked respectable enough in the lobby. The common room wasn't overly busy. Sam and Eddie had tankards of ale in front of them and Katera a glass of wine and they had ordered food when a man entered and sat at a nearby table. His clothes were muddy and torn, his hair disheveled.

"Looks like you've had a rough time," said the landlord to the man.

"Out past Buscara. Ground's collapsed. From the subsoil eaten away by crystal waste they've buried for years. It's just what the technists have projected."

"Technists have predicted those kinds of things for years and nothing's happened. We don't put much stock in those predictions in these parts."

"And I'm telling you it's happened now beyond Buscara."

"Stay this side of Buscara, then. That's my advice." He took the man's order and left.

"Were you caught when the ground collapsed?" Katera asked the man.

"Barely got away from the big trench. Others weren't so lucky. Folks there were just like that landlord—didn't believe anything was going to happen, or it wasn't going to affect them."

"We're headed to Buscara. I need to check on conditions where you were."

"You can't get there. Ground is shifting near Buscara. And not only that—there's some sort of poison gas that's erupted from the sinkholes."

Katera glanced at Sam and Eddie. "We've run into that elsewhere. Is EmRes there? Are they evacuating people?"

"They did for a while, those who would leave. But they've had to pull back. The gas is spreading."

"Do you have anywhere to go?"

"Sister lives west of here. I'll go there."

The landlord delivered a tankard of ale to the man.

"Sounds like you're stuck with us, Katera," said Eddie.

"I'll assess when we get there," she said.

When they reached their rooms, Katera said, "We've made good time today. If we delay lunch, we should reach Buscara by early afternoon."

"Let's hold off on lunch tomorrow, then," said Sam. "And get an early start again."

"I'll knock on your door."

"I can hardly wait," said Eddie. He went on into the room he and Sam were sharing.

Katera gave Sam a searching look, as though she expected him to say something. After a moment, she said, "Could be a long day tomorrow. We should get some sleep."

Sam nodded, unsure what he should say. "See you in the morning," he said after a moment, feeling that was a weak goodnight.

Suddenly, she moved closer and embraced him. He held her tight for a moment, then let go. She left for her room.

In the room, Eddie said, "Out late again. Hitting on Katera again?"

"You're crazy."

"It's working—she likes you."

"She's glad we helped, that's all."

"I bet. And I bet you're happy she does—like you, that is."

"You've got a one-track mind."

"What will Allie say?"

"Allie?"

"Come off it. You've been hitting on her too."

"I haven't been hitting on her either." He paused. "I do like her."

"If you want to know how to balance more than one woman at the same time, you've come to the right man."

"You're the first one who comes to mind for advice about women."

Eddie laughed. "All you have to do is ask. Tell you what—you can have Katera and I'll take Allie."

"Go to sleep, Eddie."

Katera was right: they reached Buscara early the next afternoon. "If Mentor Perroso is still in Buscara, he's likely at Caldan's meeting house," she said as they drove through the outskirts. "We'd best head there first and see if he is."

10

— · —

REUNION

Soon they stopped in front of a building downtown. "Buscara Wayfarer Center" a sign above the double doors read. As Katera opened one of them they could hear singing.

"Sounds like a service is just starting," said Katera. "Let's go in and sit, and see if the mentor is here. If he is, I'm sure you can talk with him after the service."

"Like a church service?" said Eddie. "No thanks, I'll pass. Maybe I'll look around town."

Inside a large room off the vestibule, people sat in rows of chairs, facing a lectern where Caldan Garolo stood. As Katera and Sam took seats near the back, she said, "This should make my mother happy. I haven't been in a while." Sam's family had gone occasionally to a Methodist church when he was growing up, but the only time he went now was at Christmas with his family. He believed vaguely in God, but he didn't spend a lot of time on philosophical or religious contemplation.

After the song concluded, Caldan led congregants in reciting what seemed to be either a prayer or a confession of faith. Then he told them, "You heard Mentor Perroso speak here this morning on the beauty of our land and the threat to it from unstable crystal mines and toxic spent crystals, and on our duty to preserve the land."

So he was here!

"Does that relate to our beliefs? The Chronicles address that question." Caldan opened a thick book on the lectern to a page close to the front, and read: "After the Essence had created the fields and the streams and the mountains and the forests, indeed all of the lands and all there is, and then the animals, the Essence created Borel and Dremila. And they had three children, two sons and a daughter, and the Essence gave to each child a respective task in life. Jardal was to tend fields and flocks, Finraba was to harvest from the forests, and Langar was to work the caves." He closed the book. "Now tending fields means keeping them free of poison. To keep harvesting the forests, we have to keep them safe from destruction—the kind of poisons and destruction we are seeing in the north. And working the caves means managing what they contain for our benefit—and unleashing destruction in the course of using the mines is not to our benefit." The crowd murmured assent.

"Many Proclaimers confuse the surface details of the stories with their deeper meanings. In this case, they contend that we have a sacred obligation to keep mining, regardless of the consequences. But that is a misreading of the Chronicles. The deeper meaning is that the Essence has given us the means to sustain ourselves, but those means can take many forms, and those forms can change as conditions change. And sustaining ourselves does not mean poisoning the lands and the waters, and now the air as well, around us."

He paused for a moment and looked around the room at his listeners. "Now I'm going to read what the One had to say, as the Chronicles also tell us." He opened the book again and turned much further back: "And the One told them, 'I announce to you the coming of the Dominion of the Essence, in which the poor will have enough, the oppressed will receive justice, the farmers and herders will tend fields and forests that will yield bountiful harvests, and the rivers will teem with fish. Peace will descend upon all the lands, neighbor will look upon neighbor with goodwill, and strangers will be welcomed.'" He closed the book again.

"The One tells us we are all responsible for the fields and the forests and the rivers. We must care for them—or there will be no bountiful harvests. And we will not have peace and goodwill if our land is being ripped apart and Melencans attack Melencans." More murmurs of approval arose from his audience. "So Mentor Flourish's message resonates with the teachings in the Chronicles. We have a sacred obligation, all right, but it's to preserve our land, and to adjust to changing conditions with new methods. They're out there, and we need to embrace them."

Caldan led them in another song, and concluded with a prayer: "Oh mighty Essence, we beseech you to enlighten the minds of Proclaimers so that they see the errors of their ways and come to tend the land as the Chronicles so clearly direct all of us."

The congregants chanted in unison: "Let it be so."

As the crowd broke up, several people approached Katera and greeted her as an acquaintance.

"Do you come to Buscara often?" Sam asked her.

"Not often. I've been here a few times."

"You seem to know some of the members here."

"I've been to Wayfarer meetings that involved people from throughout Melenca. Mostly when I was in senior school and the Academy. I do run into a couple now and again through my work." She glanced at Caldan, who was talking with a couple of members. "I fear Mentor Perroso is no longer here. But let's ask Caldan. Shall we wait outside?"

As they walked out, Sam said, "You don't go to services—did you stop going to the services because you studied techne?"

"I didn't stop—just don't get to them that often." She paused. "It's true that Technians don't see worship of the Essence and techne as compatible. So they reject belief in the Essence. And many Proclaimers don't see techne as compatible with worship of the Essence. So they reject techne. But I don't see any discord between my beliefs as a Wayfarer and techne. And many technists who aren't Technians don't see any discord either—even those who don't necessarily believe in the Essence themselves."

"Obviously then you agree with Caldan that protecting the land and water fits your beliefs."

"Not just fits—it's a central part." She paused again, then said, "What about you, Sam? Do you believe in anything like the Essence?"

"A similar belief, yes. But like you, I haven't gone much to our services. I don't think that bothers my mother, though."

She laughed

The door opened, and Caldan came out. "Katera!" he said. "Nice to see you." He turned to Sam. "You look familiar. Have we met?"

"At Ravinn's. You told us Mentor Perroso was coming here. I wanted to speak with him."

"Ah, I remember now. I'm afraid you're too late. He left a few hours ago."

By now, Sam was prepared for this news. "He didn't happen to mention where he's going next, did he?"

"Sorry, I didn't think to ask. You should have heard him. He inspired us all."

I don't want inspiration, I want information.

"That reminds me," continued Caldan. "I had a message for Katera and her companions from Miraban." He told them of Allie and Winnie's journey to Kerela.

That news made Sam uneasy. *I hope they're not running toward violence. I hope they're OK.* Just then Eddie strolled around a corner.

"I need to find out more details of the devastation east of here," said Katera. "I don't know how close I can get, but I'll go as far as I can. You two may need to go back to Pelora if you can't wait another day or so."

"You can't go far past Buscara," said Caldan. "Not close enough to observe much. It's too dangerous."

"Even if it is, I have to find out more. It's why I came."

"Listen, my daughter is coming for dinner tonight. She lives out that way, and she's been helping with the relief efforts, refugees and so on. If you talk with her, she can give you a firsthand account."

"Is that an invitation to dinner, Caldan?"

"I suppose it is, now that you mention it."

"If I can find out enough to satisfy me, can you two wait until the morning to return to Pelora?"

"It's too late to set off now anyway," said Sam. He looked at Eddie.

"Don't ask me, Captain. I just do what I'm told."

Caldan lived in a two-story house in a modest but well-kept neighborhood. He led them into a comfortable study, where bookcases lined three of the walls, then served beer to Sam and Eddie and wine to Katera and himself. His wife had died two years before, Katera had told her companions. "Are you coping with living alone, Caldan?" she asked.

"Fair enough. I see my daughter and her family regularly—Urbela comes frequently, and she's a big help. And my faith gives me a purpose. My work keeps me busy."

Katera nodded. "It gives you a purpose. That's important."

"Yes. You're doing valuable work too, Katera."

They heard the front door open, and a thirty-something woman entered the room. Caldan told Urbela why Katera was there, then left to prepare dinner.

Katera told Urbela of the reports they'd heard at Ravinn's about the crevasses and sinkholes and poison gas. Urbela confirmed the reports and gave them details of what she'd seen, including casualties, both from the collapsing ground and the gas.

"It sounds like what we saw in the north," Katera said. "Were people who refused to leave screaming that their rights were being violated?"

"Rights? From what I heard, most people who didn't leave when the damage started didn't think it was going to be serious, thought they'd wait it out. Folks around here haven't paid attention to predictions of this sort of thing. Or the reports about damage from the mines in the north—didn't think that kind of thing was going to affect them."

"Will you have to evacuate?"

"The collapse appears to have stopped spreading west, at least for now. But it's expanding south. For now we're staying put."

"If it keeps spreading south, it may interfere with east-west travel," Katera said, looking at Sam and Eddie. "That would be a factor if you try to go to Remora."

"Cause detours, for sure," said Urbela.

"I hope we won't have to go there," said Sam. "I hope we can find Mentor Perroso soon."

"I hear he's become quite elusive. You may have a hard time."

"So we're finding."

Katera pressed Urbela on more specific details of what she had seen and finally told Sam and Eddie she had enough information for a report and would return to Pelora in the morning. Caldan insisted they spend the night there.

After a simple breakfast the next morning, they got an early start.

Allie was in a chair in the lobby, reading a digest. "Looks like Arban and Felbin worked something out," she said. "There's a story in both digests, citing 'some of our correspondents who are familiar with Proclaimer services,' that a large group of rightcakes is on the way to Penrala, believing Mentor Perroso will speak there and intending violence."

"That's enough to alert Perroso and his followers," said Dalbin.

"It should prevent the violence—for now," said Beldan. "At least in that place."

"If they found out that Perroso really was going there," said Winnie, "they can likely learn about his other destinations."

"We need to go back to Pelora, to see if there's word from Sam," said Allie. "If he hasn't made contact with Perroso, we've got to figure out how to find Perroso now."

"Agreed. But how?"

Allie turned to Dalbin. "First step—are you returning to Pelora soon? If not, Winnie and I will have to go back on our own."

"That depends on what Pop has in mind for me next."

"I'm headed for Calabra," said Beldan. "I need to consult with our chief advocate there about our case. I need you to stay here and make sure Pemera starts following through."

"That answers our question, then," said Allie. "We'll have to return to Pelora by ourselves."

"How are we going to travel?" asked Winnie. "We'll have to spend the night—how are we going to pay? And don't tell us you're going to, Beldan. We need to come up with a source of income to finance our search for Mentor Perroso. We can't just keep taking money from you."

"I have an idea," said Allie. "I need to ask Beldan something." She led him a short distance and they talked in low tones.

"You could rent skimmers," said Dalbin to Winnie, "but it might be easier since you haven't operated one since our lesson to take a transport—let someone else drive." He told her he could show them the transport station.

Allie and Beldan rejoined them, and Allie told Winnie she needed to go out. Beldan went to his room, then soon came back to the lobby and checked out of the inn to leave for Calabra.

An hour later, Allie entered the inn.

"You're being secretive," Winnie told her.

Allie pulled a drawstring cloth bag out of her purse and opened it. It was filled with golden coins.

"How in the world—" began Winnie.

Allie interrupted her. "I asked Beldan about a reputable jewelry store in town. You know how mesmerized people were with my carnelian necklace. So I also asked Beldan what sort of price he thought I might get for such a unique and precious gem." She laughed. "I bargained with the jeweler, who was eying it covetously, I can tell you. At one point I told him I'd try someplace else, and he upped his bid considerably."

"I didn't know you were such a shrewd trader."

"Neither did I. But now we can travel without worrying about how to pay for it."

"That's a good day's work—you've certainly shown some spunk."

Allie shrugged. "I didn't see how else we were going to make any money."

"There's always the choice house."

"Don't make me hit you with this bag."

After lunch Dalbin led them to the transport station. It was a large hall with benches for waiting passengers and a ticket counter. Several large vehicles were parked in a lot behind the building, much bigger and wider than haulers. After Allie purchased tickets, they hugged Dalbin and he left, and they waited a short while until their transport was announced. The transport they boarded had a double row of benches with a center aisle, like a bus at home. Winnie estimated the vehicle would hold at least forty people.

They had ridden for an hour when the transport began to travel next to a river. After a few minutes, Winnie noticed that the river had a yellow, foamy film swirling on its surface. "I wonder why the river is yellow," she said to Allie.

"Spent crystal waste," said an old woman across the aisle from them. "We've dumped that residue for decades, in rivers like this one, and in fields, too. It's toxic, we eventually realized—poisons people slowly, fish and animals more quickly."

"That's nonsense!" said a man in the seat in front of the old woman, turning to face them. "That's just more Unifier propaganda, trying to undercut our way of life."

"Nonsense, is it?" said the old woman. "Then why are fish floating belly-up by the score, dead, on the surface of stretches like this one?"

"It's an improved method of catching fish," he said. "And puts crystal waste to good use. It's more efficient than the old ways—and you can think Compactors for sponsoring it, and the Supreme Leader for making sure it keeps being implemented."

"Catching fish is right—poisoned fish. Technists have shown eating such fish slowly poisons people."

"Technists!" he sneered. "What do they know?"

"They've studied such things for years, in detail. Have you?"

"I don't need to. The Supreme Leader has made it clear—we don't need to listen to technists, only to him."

"That's enough arguing," snapped a woman in front of Allie. "The rest of us want to travel in peace."

Winnie and Allie spent the night in the Placid Repast in Buzakor and took a different transport the next morning. After several stops, they reached Pelora late the next afternoon, and took a taxi hauler to Ravinn's complex. Peter was taking a break from his interviews and greeted them warmly. He'd had no word from Sam or Eddie. Rafe was huddled with one of Ravinn's midlevel managers, pumping him for details on how Ravinn's concern operated. "That's how he's passed the time," said Peter. "Trying to decide what kind of concern he can start, and how. Maybe we should be doing more of that ourselves."

"I'm putting my energy into finding Perroso, and a way home," said Allie. "All my energy."

"Allie's right," said Winnie. "Finding Perroso should be our priority. If we can't find a way home, or if we find out for sure there isn't one, then we can worry about how to live here."

"Priority fine," said Peter, "but I think it would be prudent to start forming a backup plan."

They were just gathering outside the dining hall for dinner when Katera, Sam, and Eddie joined them. The two groups greeted each other with relief and then brought each other up to date on their separate doings. When they sat down at a table, Miraban and Jalno joined them, and soon Ravinn as well.

After welcoming the returning voyagers back and filling his mug with beer, Ravinn looked at Jalno. "You have news from Calabra?"

"As we feared. Compactors are introducing the act to prohibit harvesting silverbark. Word is, they're considering a further step—requiring use of crystals in all vehicle engines."

"Do they not understand what is going on around us?" said Katera. "Do they not care?"

"Care? Hah!" said Ravinn, slapping the table. "Certainly those buffoons care—about protecting the pockets of mine owners." Then he drained his tankard.

"We need you in Calabra, Ravinn," said Jalno.

"That's what I employ people like you for, Jalno. To wage the battle there."

"This is an emergency. You've got a high profile with the public. If you're there speaking out against this proposal, the digests will cover it. It will draw more attention to what's going on."

"Pop and other alternative power producers are gathering there," said Katera. "We all know what the stakes are."

"I've just learned, too, that the Council is going to summon Mentor Perroso to appear before it," said Jalno. "The Compactors want to grill him and try to discredit him. The Unifiers are eager to praise him and give him a prominent platform for his views."

"Will he go, though?" said Sam. "He's supposed to have been other places where he hasn't shown up. And if it's publicized, rightcakes will gather."

"He's courageous," said Miraban. "But he's also prudent."

"He won't disregard a summons from the Grand Council," said Ravinn. "He'll relish the opportunity—I know him. And if the Council summons him, it will have to provide security for him. Unifiers will see to that."

Sam looked at his companions. "I think I know where we're going now."

Ravinn refilled his tankard, glanced at Jalno and then Katera, and sighed. "I think people are forcing me to the same conclusion."

11

— · —

ACTION IN THE DOME ZONE

The voyagers rode with Katera after breakfast the next morning. She carried reports to deliver to Rally Round officials in the capital. The hauler reached outlying houses by late afternoon and in the distance they could see taller buildings. The traffic picked up, in both directions. Clearly this was a real city, larger than any of the towns they had been in so far. As the distant buildings grew closer, they noticed a large white dome.

"This is Calabra, I presume," said Winnie. "What's that big dome?"

"The Grand Council Chamber," said Katera. As they drove into the city, they passed large buildings of stone, some white, some gray—"the Dome Zone," she called it—administrative buildings housing secretariats and agencies. The domed building loomed larger, more impressive as they drew closer, and then they passed it.

"Where are we going?" said Sam.

"The guest house of the Association of Alternative Power Producers. Members stay here when they're visiting the capital. Pop's staying there—we will too."

They passed into a mostly residential area, though with some buildings scattered here and there that housed private organizations, Katera said. She finally turned into a drive at a large stone house with a wide veranda in front. Several haulers and skimmers were parked behind the house.

The lobby they entered was wide and high. Some portrait busts stood on pedestals or tables. Paintings hung on the walls, landscapes and geometric designs. Large, overstuffed armchairs surrounded a large central area. Against one wall was a short counter. Katera asked the white-haired woman behind it for Beldan. The woman smiled pleasantly and said he was in his room. Katera left to greet her father and bring him downstairs.

They gathered in the guest house's large dining hall. As they were sitting, Dalbin entered and joined them. Beldan asked, "Did Mentor Perroso show up in Buscara? Did you speak with him?" Katera filled him in on their experiences. He shook his head. "The

MNAA is expanding its reach, then. In the past they only operated near the Borderlands. It sounds like they're hunting down Newcomers in a wider area."

"They'll be casting their net wider for Outbounders as well," said Dalbin. "You can bet on it."

"It's not far-fetched to expect they'll set up roadblocks to question travelers," said Katera.

"On Melencan culture?" asked Sam.

"If any patrols are looking for Outbounders specifically."

"Then we may need to look for backroads. But we can worry about that after we talk with Mentor Perroso."

"He's due to address the Grand Council tomorrow morning," said Beldan.

"Can we hear him?"

"There's a gallery for spectators."

"Enough small talk," said Dalbin. "Let's eat."

The next morning, most of them left for the Grand Council Chamber. Katera headed to a meeting at Rally Round headquarters.

"I've had my fill of politicians at home," said Eddie. "I'll pass."

"Yeah," said Rafe. "I don't care anything about watching them argue."

Once they reached the Dome, they entered a huge vestibule. Staircases on both sides led to several upper floors, but the space immediately above the vestibule was empty, allowing an unimpeded view to the rotunda. Opposite the front entrance, two large doors opened onto a large room. A guard scrutinized them, then waved them in. In the large central chamber, a semicircle of seats faced a dais. On the sides above, seats rose up multiple levels—probably the gallery, Sam guessed. Men and women stood talking in small groups in the central space, while others sat. The gallery was filled with spectators.

Beldan led them up steps on one side of the gallery, past a number of rows, and into one row with a stretch of empty seats. They made their way past five or six people to the seats. As they settled in, a man on the dais rang a bell on the podium in front of him. The hubbub of conversation subsided. After a moment, he rang the bell again. The great room was soon reasonably quiet, though Sam could hear murmurs behind him. Beldan and Dalbin had interspersed themselves among the voyagers, Dalbin on Sam's left, so that they could explain the proceedings.

The officiant spoke, his voice carrying throughout the chamber: "First on the docket is testimony of Mentor Perroso, summoned to appear before this council."

A man in the chamber rose to his feet. "I rise in a point of privilege, Convener. Mentor Perroso is scheduled to address a large crowd outdoors tomorrow. I move we delay his testimony for two days."

"What's he up to?" said Dalbin. "He's a Compactor."

A murmuring swept through the seated delegates. A couple of Unifiers questioned why a delay, but Compactors provided no clear reason for it. In the end the motion carried with only a few no votes.

"Next on the docket is introduction of an act to ban harvesting silverbark in the Darkling Wood," said the convener. Loud, heated argument broke out as speakers from both sides took the floor.

"What happened to Compactors' vaunted belief in allowing concerns to carry out their trade free of interference by the governors?" said a Unifier.

"We're merely trying to protect a precious resource from exhaustion," said a Compactor.

"Sap from silverbarks is endlessly renewable. Unlike crystals. And you are well aware of the threat that crystals pose, but you deny it, because of the profits accruing to the mining concerns."

"Threat! These reports of threats are phony stories, as the Supreme—ah, the chief administrator—has demonstrated."

"You seem to be a little confused about vocabulary. The word you want is 'denied.' Flammer hasn't demonstrated anything, just denied the truth."

"Blatant falsehood! That there's nothing to these reports has been verified by digests—*credible* digests, that is." He turned and looked at a row in the gallery, staring at a woman writing on a notepad.

"The *Weasel* reporter who covers the Council," said Dalbin. "That's the row reserved for digest reporters."

"Did you catch that?" continued the Compactor, still staring at the woman. "Make sure you have the name right—Councilor Blathna." The reporter nodded.

"But they're not phony stories!" said Allie, forgetting to keep her voice low. "We've seen the results in the north."

A woman in front of her turned and glared at her. "Don't go spreading those falsehoods here in the very Council."

"They're not falsehoods. We've witnessed houses damaged and destroyed, cracks in the land."

"Try peddling that Unifier propaganda somewhere else." She squinted at Allie. "What a surprise, that it's a brown-eye talking such rot."

"There's no call for that kind of talk," interjected Dalbin. The woman stared hard at him for a few seconds, then motioned to an usher.

"This brown-eye is being disruptive," the woman said.

"All right, let's go," said the usher. "We don't tolerate unruly behavior in the gallery."

"She wasn't being disruptive!" exclaimed Sam.

"Stay out of this." He motioned for Allie to follow him. Slowly, she rose and walked to the aisle. Sam rose as well.

"I'll go with you."

"He's right," said Dalbin.

"If you abuse her, you'll answer to my advocate," said Beldan.

The usher started to reply, then stopped and, glaring at Beldan, grabbed Allie's arm and pulled her after him. Sam followed them. As they walked down the steps, a cacophony erupted on the floor below as opposing councilors shouted at each other.

When they reached the front entrance, the usher shoved Allie through one of the doors, then snapped, "Don't try to come back in, brown-eye."

"Leave her alone," said Sam as he pushed past the man. The usher stared hard at him for a moment, and Sam tensed, anticipating possible violence. Then the man slammed the door. "Are you all right?" Sam asked Allie.

"I'm OK. A slight bruise, the bastard."

A few minutes later, the doors opened and a few people walked through them, then more. Soon Beldan and the others joined them. Beldan asked Allie if she was hurt, then told them "the motion carried—Compactors all in favor, Unifiers opposing as a block." He shook his head. "Well, we'll just have to deal with it in magistrates' chambers. I'm due to meet our advocate in the tavern at the Domeside Hostel. Let's go there." He led them past a number of large granite buildings, similar to buildings on Earth in classical style. The area would certainly awe someone coming from one of the small towns they'd seen, Sam thought.

Winnie said, "This is very impressive. Looks like a governing district should."

"And now you see why Compactors are willing to put up with Flammer and his antics," said Dalbin. "The power you see symbolized in these buildings is a mighty temptation."

"Still, there are people standing up to him, it appears," said Peter.

"Yes," said Beldan, "but how long can they keep the forces, the impulses Flammer has unleashed, at bay?"

The Domeside Hostel was a large hotel. "Domeside" was not entirely accurate: while the dome of the Grand Council Chamber was visible, the hostel was nowhere near adjacent to it. Inside, the lobby made the spacious one in the association guest house seem cramped. A long counter ran along one wall, with several clerks standing behind it, checking guests in. People milled around in a long and wide central area with stuffed chairs and small tables. Ornate vases graced many of the tables, large paintings decorated the walls, elegant chandeliers suspended from the high ceiling. Beldan led them into a large, crowded bar, looked around, then gestured for them to follow him to where Miraban and Jalno sat, along with a heavyset sixtyish man. At a nearby table, Ravinn sat surrounded by Ralbo Jasko, Devis Belbar, and a couple of other men and a woman—also reporters, Sam guessed.

"Gondal," said Beldan to the heavyset man. "I didn't expect to find you with Ravinn's contingent."

"If you're going to bring a case to the High Magistrates' Chamber you want to be in the best hands. Ravinn knows that, so naturally he's hired me. Surely you didn't think you were my only client, Beldan."

"I'm just surprised Ravinn is already moving on the silverbark act. I shouldn't be, I suppose." He turned toward his companions. "Gondal Barumba—as you've no doubt figured out, he's our advocate for the Kerela lighting case." If Beldan and his family dressed in brighter colors than less affluent Melencans in their drab outfits, they dulled compared to Gondal, who wore a lime green tunic, bright yellow pants, and white shoes. He would stand out in any crowd. "And speaking of our case, what progress?" said Beldan.

"You'll be pleased to learn that the High Magistrates' Chamber has agreed to consider our motion—and set initial proceedings for tomorrow. If the administration's advocate has any sense, she'll agree to our terms and we'll settle. If not, she'll learn a lesson in advocacy, one that will chasten her."

"You seem highly confident, Gondal," said Dalbin.

"Experience, my boy. I have a keen sense of how cases are likely to unfold—and how to lead them toward the disposition I favor."

"And Ravinn's case?" said Miraban. "I know it's early on."

"I'm optimistic. Aside from Ravinn's wise choice of advocate, this kind of meddling by the Grand Council that blatantly violates the Compact is not likely to receive a warm reception in the High Magistrates' Chamber, in my view. We'll ask for a stay at the least to begin with, so production can continue."

"So Ravinn has been addressing reporters?" said Winnie.

"Ravinn doesn't take half measures," said Miraban. "He's accused Compactors in the council of not only failing to act in the face of the spreading damage but of accelerating it. And he's accused Margan by name of backing these efforts, and profiting from them."

"Margan will step up a response accordingly," said Beldan.

"So what? He's been ramping up, and would continue to do so regardless. Ravinn may be volatile, but he's also shrewd."

"We're wondering why the Compactors postponed Mentor Perroso's testimony," said Dalbin.

"I wonder too," said Jalno. "The councilor who introduced the motion is a pawn of Margan. What purpose does the delay serve? Certainly not for solicitude over a scheduled address by the mentor. They're up to something."

"Could they intend to abduct him—or worse—Margan and the other mine owners, I mean, or the Proclaimers who are hunting Perroso?"

"Possibly. But the Council is to provide constables from the Dome Force. Still, it is worrisome."

At breakfast the next morning, Sam told his companions he was going to Mentor Perroso's address and would try to meet with him afterward. "I'll go too," said Allie. "I want to hear what he says."

"In case there's trouble, obviously you'll need me," said Eddie.

"And me," said Dalbin.

None of the other voyagers volunteered, and Beldan and Katera both had meetings scheduled. Beldan held up a digest. "They're already at it," he said. "The *Weasel* reports the latest posting from Flammer. I'll read, emphasizing his capitals: 'These enemies of our way of life NEED TO BE TAUGHT a lesson! Prepare for action! Prepare to TAKE ON those who would TAKE AWAY our property and those who would SABOTAGE our wonderful economy!'" He put down the digest. "Immediately after this the *Weasel* has a passage about Mentor Perroso's address, saying he intends to bring the economy to its knees, and spelling out where and when he's to speak. It's not hard to connect the dots there."

"Will there be enough constables there?" said Allie.

"Let's hope so," said Dalbin. "Enough to handle a large contingent of rightcakes—let's hope so."

By the time the address was scheduled to start, the three voyagers and Dalbin stood among a large crowd in a wide, deep greensward within a park on the outskirts of the Dome Zone. They had pushed in as far as they could, about a hundred feet, but could go no farther through the mass of people. Many of those around them were young, but not all. Sam wondered if Mentor Perroso was to speak from a large open space in the center, and if so, how he would ever approach him. *I'll have to wait until he finishes and the crowd starts to disperse.* Then he thought, *What if he walks toward the far side after he finishes and I can't catch up to him before he's gone?* The edge of the greensward bordered a row of trees, and there weren't many people close to the trees. He'd have to reach the edge and hurry, unless the mentor walked in their direction.

After ten minutes, a small group emerged from the trees on the far side of the greensward and strolled purposefully to the center. A young man with a megaphone called for silence and announced without preamble that Mentor Perroso would speak on the most pressing crisis Melenca faced. He handed the megaphone to a tall, erect old man with a head full of silver hair.

"My friends," he began, "we face a choice. Melenca's path diverges just ahead of us. We can. . . ."

His words were drowned out by a loud cry emanating from various directions in the crowd: "Now! Grab him!" Around Sam and the others a number of spectators, mostly older, surged forward, shoving aside the mostly younger ones in their path and when some of those finally reacted by shoving back, fighting broke out. Shouting and cries of pain filled the air. The struggling mass surged toward the group surrounding Mentor Perroso.

"Where are the constables?" someone shouted.

"They must not have considered rightcakes would infiltrate the crowd," yelled Dalbin to his companions. "I'll go back and find them. They've got to get through to the middle."

Sam stumbled as someone pushed him, then regained his balance and shouted over his shoulder, "I'm going to reach him," as he forced his way through, his plan to head for the edge forgotten as he reacted. Having played football in high school, he wasn't afraid of rough contact.

"Don't be crazy!" yelled Allie. "You'll just get hurt. You can't accomplish anything."

Eddie reached him and swung him around. "Save the heroics for another day, Captain. Allie's right. Let's get out of this scrum."

Allie grabbed his hand and pulled him back in the direction they had come from. They struggled through the crowd, suffering a few bruises, but finally regained the entry to the greensward. Sam spotted Dalbin. When they reached him, he shook his head. "No sign of the constables. I think they didn't show. The handiwork of Compactors in the Grand Council."

"What do we do?" said Allie.

"Head for the edge of the greensward and then along it through the trees to the far side," said Sam. "It's probably hopeless, but maybe we can at least spot where they're taking him."

Dalbin nodded and they raced along the back of the crowd, where the melee was still raging, until they reached oaks and elms and circular clusters of gladiolas and unfamiliar red and yellow flowers and could turn and follow that line toward the far end of the greensward. Several younger people saw them, grasped what they were trying to do, and followed them along the tree line. At last they reached the opposite side of the greensward from where they had stood. Fighting continued among the crowd that had surged to the trees at the back of the greensward, and the din was deafening.

They turned along that tree line, and when they came to a point parallel to the center of the greensward, they were alone except for the handful who had followed them. "This way," Dalbin called from a faint path away from the greensward. They followed it for a few hundred feet without spotting anybody, then saw a young man sitting with his back against a tree. Blood oozed from a cut on his forehead. A young woman knelt next to him. Tears ran down her cheeks.

"They've taken the mentor," she said, her voice breaking. "They've taken him away."

Sam and Allie were sitting in chairs in the lobby of the guest house. "Some leader I've been," he said. "I thought I could keep us together and find Mentor Perroso, and then we'd find out how to go home, just like that. Well, I can't."

"It's not your fault, Sam," she said. "We couldn't control what a horde of rightcakes did, or Compactor leaders in the Grand Council."

"I don't have any more ideas. I'm at a dead end."

"You'll think of something—or I will. There has to be something."

"Perroso was our only hope. Now he's gone."

"Maybe he wasn't our only hope. There have been other Outbounders. Maybe there's someone besides Perroso who knows about the portal."

"How would we ever find such a person?"

"Start by asking Wooden, and Beldan, and Ravinn. They seem likely sources of information. Beldan told us he'd known other Outbounders, and I'll bet Ravinn has too." She put both hands on his shoulders and leaned in, then she kissed him.

"I'm not giving up. You can't either." She walked away.

In spite of his depressed spirits, he felt an exhilaration at her touch. But then he thought, *I couldn't handle this, just like I feared. The same way I've felt about running the company. I told my mother that, but she wouldn't believe me. She would if she could see me now.*

He thought now about the future. Should he figure out how to adapt to life in Melenca, as Wooden advised them? Were they stranded here forever? *That's crazy. Allie's right. We can't just give up. I'll have to look for something. Think.*

"We've lost an important voice," said Miraban. They were sitting in the tavern at the Domeside Hostel, plotting strategy.

"Compactors in the Grand Council are denying any knowledge of Mentor Perroso's whereabouts," said Jalno.

"What happened to the constables?" asked Dalbin.

"An outbreak of rioting at the same time in another part of Calabra, they claim. There was a tussle between two small groups—but the *Current* and the *Vantage* reported that some prominent rightcakes were on both sides, and they were spotted laughing together shortly afterward at a tavern."

"What a surprise." Dalbin took a sip of ale. "But I can tell you his followers, like my brother, aren't just going to give up."

"They're not alone," said Ravinn. "I have ways of finding out things. I'll use them to learn what they've done with the mentor."

Should I say anything? thought Sam. "You might ask Arban Melroc," he heard himself say.

"Why is that, young Earthling? Are you suggesting a digest reporter has more insight into the shenanigans of a plunderer like Margan than I have?"

"I can't say any more. Just ask Arban—he may be able to find out something."

Ravinn gulped from his tankard. "Perhaps I will. Now, if you're finished telling me how to run my affairs, young man, we'll turn to something else urgent. Miraban?"

"Have you seen today's *Weasel*?" No one had.

Jalno held up a digest. "It's on the front page, an article on how the DynaStream facility at Mencara is gearing up to put into production vehicles using alternate sources. Then it quotes Flammer's latest posting: "THIS ASSAULT on crystals and our way of life MUST BE STOPPED! March there and give them a SHOW OF FORCE!'"

"It doesn't take much thinking to draw out the implications," said Miraban. "And rightcakes will draw them out."

At that moment, several people entered the tavern, including Katera. When she saw them, she spoke to her friends and then joined them. She sat down in an empty chair next to Sam.

Beldan filled in Katera on the posting. Then he said, "I should explain for the Earthlings. My concern is supplying engine parts to DynaStream for their prototype alternative vehicle—the engines Ravinn's concern designed. They've started testing that vehicle now, and then DynaStream will produce thousands of those skimmers and haulers. It's a major step."

"Not if a horde of violent rightcakes wreak havoc," said Katera.

"Can DynaStream provide enough guards around the facility?" asked Miraban. "It *is* a major concern."

"They're not in the habit of fending off major attacks," said Dalbin.

"Bah! Do you think they'll take this seriously?" snorted Ravinn. "Like any other major concern—excepting mine, of course—they have a bureaucracy. It will take them forever to decide anything."

"And I'm not sure how much credit they'll give to rumors about rightcakes and the rantings of Flammer," said Miraban.

"If trouble arises, the Mencara constabulary will deploy in force," said Dalbin.

"If they have enough warning," said Beldan. "That's a big question."

Jalno waved the digest. "The *Weasel* also has a separate piece quoting Flammer. He starts by insulting Mencara and its inhabitants."

"Not surprising," said Dalbin. "It's a Unifier stronghold."

"Not just Unifier," said Katera. "Many Mencarans go well beyond Unifier positions, especially in the Academy."

"What's new is that he threatens to increase the levies on Mencarans," said Jalno.

"He tries to cut the allocations to Kerela, then tries to boost levies on Mencara," said Dalbin. "Just so happen to both be places where we're involved."

"Sheer bluster!" said Ravinn. "The Illusionist has no authority to increase levies on his own. That's Grand Council business—it's in the Compact." He gulped from his tankard.

"That doesn't mean the Compactors in Council won't back him," said Miraban.

"The magistrates' chambers won't allow that to stand," said Katera, "not the district chamber and not the High Chamber."

"I'm sure you're right," said Jalno. "So far, the chambers have blocked anything that strays from the Compact so egregiously."

"Many of the Compactors' actions, for instance?" said Dalbin.

"If we can get back to what affects us urgently," said Beldan, "I need to go to Mencara. Dalbin, you've dealt with the local DynaStream people more than I have—I need you there."

"Certainly. I don't want to miss out on the action."

"We can stay with Lirea." He took a swallow of ale. "Ravinn, what about you? You've got a major stake in DynaStream's facility, obviously."

"I'll send some men there, stout men." He looked down at his stomach and laughed. "Not stout like me, I mean in the other sense. They can help when rightcakes try to storm the place. But I don't have many to send against a horde of rightcakes."

"We'll have to count on the constabulary, then, and try to give them more than a moment's notice." Beldan snapped his fingers. "I'd almost forgotten. I received a message from Silenda. She's going to Mencara for a big art exhibit. In light of this news, perhaps I should discourage her."

"She won't listen," said Katera. "A threat to DynaStream from rightcakes won't keep her away."

Suddenly a thought flashed into Sam's consciousness. "Do you know if Wooden is going to the art exhibit?" he asked.

"I expect so," said Beldan. "He's part of that world."

Sam looked at the other voyagers. "I just thought of something. We need to head for Mencara."

12

THE HOUSE OF LIREA

The voyagers were seated in the lobby of the guest house after lunch, the first time they'd been by themselves in a while. "Was that wise, telling them about Arban?" Winnie asked Sam. "He told us that in confidence."

"What I said was vague, and general," Sam replied. "I was trying to get Ravinn to ask for help. I don't think that's too bad a breach. Even if it is, if his source can find out where they're keeping Perroso, it will be worth it."

"Why should we go to Mencara?" said Allie.

"I'm tired of chasing rumors," said Rafe. "We don't have any reason to go there—this isn't any of our business."

"It does sound like a situation that could get out of hand," added Peter, "really violent."

"Tell me, Professor," said Eddie, "is there anything you don't worry about?"

"My name is Peter, damnit. And I'm not afraid! I'm just counseling prudence. Asking for trouble doesn't strike me as intelligent. I question whether having an idea is worth placing ourselves in danger."

"Obviously, that depends on what the idea is," said Winnie. "So why don't we find out? Sam?"

"Allie set me on the right track. We've been thinking all along that Mentor Perroso is our only hope. What if he's not?"

"You know something Wooden didn't tell us?"

"If you remember what he did tell us, we're not the first ones seeking Mentor Perroso."

"Yes, two other Outbounders went searching for him," said Allie.

"And one of them couldn't find any portal," said Rafe, "and the other most likely got killed looking for it."

"We don't know any such thing. We only know he never showed up again. If he found a portal, he wouldn't have."

"What does that have to do with Mencara, Sam?" asked Peter.

"We ask Wooden those two Outbounders' names, where they lived, anything else relevant he can recall. Then we track them down. And talk with—well, with the one who's left."

"He's the only one we need to find," said Winnie.

"On the contrary, there may be people the other talked with, people may remember something he said. Maybe he just moved somewhere else in Melenca."

"Even if we manage to track down the one who couldn't find the portal," said Peter, "how is that helpful?"

"He must have talked to Perroso. At the least, he found out something about the general vicinity of the portal. That's more than we know now. And maybe he found out more than that."

"Still, he didn't find the portal," said Winnie.

"Maybe he just did something wrong at the end. It's worth a shot to follow up—better than sitting here helplessly."

"If we can't find Perroso, we have to try something else," said Allie. "Going to Mencara is doing that. Sam's right—let's go to Mencara."

After a moment's silence, Winnie nodded. "Yes, that makes sense as the next step. I say we go."

Eddie shrugged. "Probably useless, but we'll see more of Melenca. OK."

Peter looked troubled. "We can't just flail about, following one longshot after another." He sighed. "But if you're all set on going, I guess I will too."

When Winnie asked Rafe, he shook his head and refused to say anything, though they pressed him.

At dinner, Sam told Beldan and the others of the voyagers' decision to go to Mencara—at least all except Rafe. Sam didn't know what he would do—go off on his own?

"You're welcome to stay in Mencara with Lirea as well, then," said Beldan.

"You mentioned Lirea earlier," said Winnie. "Who is that?"

"She's my cousin. She and her husband own a wine concern."

"You're just going to drop six of us on her without warning?" said Allie. "Plus the rest of you?"

"She has plenty of room, and she's hospitable. Besides, Katera's leaving for Rally

Round again."

"Toward the mines again?" said Sam.

"North again, but farther east, almost due north of Mencara," said Katera.

"The damage is spreading fast," said Dalbin.

"Until now, our move into alternate power has been theoretical, responding to technists' projections," said Beldan. "It's not theoretical anymore. It's urgent. So is warding off an attack on DynaStream."

The digests the next morning were full of reports of disaster at Kondora, a large town in the north. Quakes had rumbled through the town, creating crevasses and sinkholes. Kondora was heavily damaged, some parts destroyed, as buildings collapsed or vanished. Casualties were high. The reports in the *Current* and the *Vantage* were consistent. Only the *Weasel* had a different slant. It referred to "rumors circulating of mild tremors around Kondora" and then quoted a leading Compactor councilor who said that there was only slight damage in a few neighborhoods, and that the tremor was unrelated to the "rumored turmoil in the land near the mines." He went on to accuse Unifiers of fabricating threats of damage in order to cripple the mining concerns.

"There's another Flammer post that should alarm you," said Beldan as they ate breakfast. "It alarms me." He picked up the *Weasel* and read: "Horrible creatures have infiltrated Melenca! These Outbounders aim to sabotage our economy by DESTROYING the mining concerns and SHUTTING DOWN the mines. They are behind this movement to build so-called ALTERNATIVE SOURCES, which will DEVASTATE our beloved society!"

"What's he say to do about these terrible Outbounders?" said Dalbin.

Beldan continued reading. "The Supreme Leader has directed the MNAA to hunt down these creatures. Patriotic Melencans are urged to be on the lookout for them, for anyone acting strangely."

"That explains this item in the *Current*," said Dalbin. "Compactors intend to introduce an act forbidding Outbounders from entering Melenca and authorizing the MNAA to lock up any they find and hold them indefinitely."

"An old trick," said Katera. "Invent an enemy to divert attention from the devastation—which they'll have a hard time to keep denying when it's happening in more places."

"Watching rightcakes try to figure out what Outbounders look like should be amusing."

"It's no laughing matter," said Beldan, glancing at Sam. "You need to be very careful—keep to yourselves as much as you can. If you appear unfamiliar with our ways, you could be in great danger. There's no telling what some of these rightcakes might do."

They left soon after breakfast, passing through countryside and small towns until late afternoon, when they drove into a more developed area, with tall buildings visible in the distance, clearly the outskirts of a city perhaps on the scale of Calabra. Soon, however, they took a side road and followed it through a residential area of substantial houses, and turned into a long drive leading to an impressive two-story house of white stone, with wide grounds around it. Several skimmers and haulers were parked behind the house. A wide veranda wrapped across the front and around both sides. As they approached the veranda, two dogs trotted up to them wagging their tails. One looked like a German shepherd. The other was like no dog Sam had ever seen, as big as a greyhound but stocky and red and brown in color, with white spots on the brown parts. When Beldan knocked on the front door, a young, dark-haired man opened it, smiled, greeted Beldan and Dalbin, and then looked curiously at the others. Beldan clapped him on the shoulder as he walked in.

"Lirea's son, Kandar," he said over his shoulder.

They followed Kandar through the large foyer and down a corridor to a huge room halfway down. Along one wall ran a bookcase, and on the opposite wall a long case held flagons of wine and award certificates. Landscapes hung on the walls. A tabby cat rested on a window sill. Two women in chairs in the middle of the room were talking and looked up. One was Silenda. The other, presumably Lirea, appeared to be a few years older, plump, of average height, with blonde hair beginning to gray. She stood up, as did Silenda, and Lirea approached Beldan and hugged him.

"Greetings, cousin," she said. Though the words were formal, her tone was warm and casual. Beldan and Silenda embraced.

"I've come to impose on you, Lirea," he said. "I told my friends you could put them up."

"If they're your friends, they're welcome here. Who are they, by the way?"

"Outbounders. You'll be harboring fugitives."

She laughed. "If it's a chance to defy Flimsel Flammer, we'll take the risk, and relish it. But why are you escorting them, Beldan? Transporting them across district lines, I should think. That should interest the MNAA."

Now he laughed. "They're trying to find Mentor Perroso, and our paths have converged."

Lirea shook her head. "A sad day when rightcakes can just abduct someone as peaceful as the mentor, in plain daylight in the middle of Calabra." She looked toward the voyagers. "But why Perroso?"

"We believe he has knowledge that will help us find a way to return to our land," said Sam.

"Remember? Perroso is an Outbounder," said Beldan.

"Of course," said Lirea. "I'd forgotten."

"Most people have forgotten, those who knew in the first place."

"Do you suspect they're holding him in this area? It seems unlikely."

"We're looking for Wooden now," said Sam. "Will we find him at the exhibit, Silenda?"

"He's an Outbounder too—is that it? He said he would come."

"We'll attend the exhibit, then."

"You must be famished after your journey," said Lirea. "I'll have cook bring some food and drink in to hold you until dinner."

As they waited, amid snatches of conversation, Sam looked around the room more attentively. The wine flagons had labels with an image of a vineyard and "Dorwin Wines" printed on them. The landscapes showed various settings: broad vineyards, a stream tumbling down from hills over a rocky course, a meadow surrounded by trees leafed out in the bright green of spring, houses clustered along a road with fields stretching out to woods.

Allie gestured at a painting. "Did you paint these scenes, Silenda? Lirea's vineyard, perhaps?"

Silenda smiled. "It's not hard to find inspiration in the area where Lirea and Stefar's concern has its vineyards."

Lirea came back into the room, followed by a stout woman pushing a cart bearing various bite-sized foods, several flagons of wine, and a pitcher of beer.

"This is Percela," said Lirea. "She is responsible for the delightful spread you see before you—not the wines, though. I claim those!" Percela beamed and bowed, then left the room. "You see, we're broad-minded," said Lirea, "offering in addition to samples of our wines ale for anyone inexplicably preferring it to the wine." She laughed.

To be polite, Sam poured some wine into a goblet. He usually drank beer, but he did drink wine on weekend dates from time to time. Winnie must have been thinking the same—she poured a goblet of wine. So did Peter and Allie as usual. Eddie and Rafe stuck with the beer. Sam didn't understand terms used to describe wines, but he recognized quality when he tasted it, and this white wine was exceptional, rich but dry. The food was as good as that at the Domeside Hostel or Ravinn's house.

After a silent moment, Allie said, "Lirea, I noticed that Percela is a brown-eye."

"I didn't know whether Outbounders included brown-eyes or not, but now that I've met you, I see that they do. I don't know much about Outbounders—I may have met one or two over the years, but I don't remember much about them if I did."

"Are most cooks in Melenca brown-eyes?"

Sam hadn't noticed that Percela was a brown-eye. He realized now that having been abused because of her eye color made Allie attuned to this small characteristic—and its implications.

"In houses," said Lirea. "They've always been easy to hire, because many jobs were not open to them in the past, so they were not well paid, I'm sorry to say. If you're wondering, Percela is well paid. She has had offers at some of the fancy taverns in Mencora, but she prefers to remain with us."

"I didn't doubt it," said Allie.

There was a moment of uncomfortable silence, then Beldan said, "Now then, shall we tell you about our adventures?"

An hour later they were gathered in Lirea's large dining room around the long table for dinner, with different wines from those earlier and another flagon of ale. Stefar Dorwin sat at one end of the table, Lirea at the other. Stefar had arrived just before dinner. He was tall, trim, dark-haired, around Lirea's age. Kandar was not there, having returned to his own nearby house, where his wife and two-year-old son awaited him, but Lirea's daughter, Renala, had joined them. She resembled Kandar but looked younger, in her late twenties. Also present was Stefar's mother, Alcinda, a women in her eighties, who lived in the house.

"I see it's not just Outbounders who are Flammer's targets," said Stefar. "So are you, Beldan. And Ravinn and the others."

"Did you see the *Weasel* unmasks you as a plandist, Beldan?" said Renela.

"*What?!*"

"Behind the 'assault on crystals' are Unifier leaders, who are anti-Melencan and plandists, it says. And heads of concerns developing alternative vehicles—also plandists."

Stefar laughed. "That's preposterous. No Unifier leaders are plandists. Some in the Academy, true, unfortunately, both scholars and students. But leaders of concerns out to turn a profit? Can you see Ravinn wanting the governors—or anyone—to tell him how to run his concern? The idea is so laughable it's hard to see how anyone could swallow it."

"Have you met any rightcakes, Stefar?" said Dalbin.

"Anyone who claims Unifiers in the Grand Council are plandists doesn't know what they're talking about—they don't understand what plandistism is."

"Neither do I," said Winnie. "What is plandistism?"

"It's short for 'planned distribution,' the idea that the governors would own the production of goods, specify how that production should proceed, then plan and oversee how the goods are distributed."

"I get it. We have a similar concept."

"If they're trying to paint Unifiers as opposed to concerns making money," said Beldan, "Compactors are getting desperate."

"It's the trendy new insult,'" said Dalbin. "Rightcakes have been calling anyone who disagrees with them anti-Melencan for years. And anyone who criticizes anything that goes on in Melenca. Now they're suddenly plandists as well."

"So as merchants you oppose plandistism," said Peter.

"Plandists are a threat to open venturing," said Stefar, "and open venturing is one of the values Melenca has always stood for."

"Open venturing?" said Winnie.

"The right of anyone to open their own small concern, and if they work hard and are smart, making a success."

"You're exactly right," said Rafe. "We call it entrepreneurship."

"So you have that concept too beyond the Boundless Sea? It may sound abstract, but it's personal to me and my family. My great-grandparents immigrated to Melenca from Kasemu, from poverty. In that static society they had no chance for advancement. They came with very little, but opened a grocery shop and built it into a thriving, highly successful one."

"A lot of Melencans had ancestors who did the same," said Renala, "fled poverty, no opportunity, persecution, and succeeded here.”

"Your ancestors turned a small grocery into a big wine concern?” said Allie.

"Wine was a large part of their culture in Rasemu, and they featured it prominently in their store. My grandfather then started Dorwin Wines, and my father expanded it. Now we focus on maintaining quality and reputation.”

"The reputation is deserved,” said Allie. “This wine is excellent.”

"I’m one of those yahoos who prefer ale, Lirea,” said Winnie, raising her wine glass, “but damn, this is good—keep it flowing.”

"Always happy to refill wine glasses,” said Lirea.

"Changing the subject,” said Silenda, “do you all wish to go to the exhibition?”

Eddie said he would instead look around town if he could borrow a skimmer, which Lirea told him they would provide.

"I’d like to see how your wine concern operates, Stefar,” said Rafe. “I’ve started some small concerns myself.”

"We’ll be glad to show you this end of the operation. The vineyards, of course, are not here.” He looked at Eddie, then back at Rafe. “For all of you, a word of caution: be careful what you say when you’re in Mencara.”

"Say about what?” said Eddie. “Why careful?

"Nothing that might be construed as disparaging brown-eyes or Newcomers, for instance.”

"Don’t worry—we wouldn’t say anything like that.”

"I’m sure not. But note I said ‘construed.’”

"There are some in Mencara who become offended at what seem innocuous remarks,” said Lirea.

"And brown-eyes and Newcomers are just the most obvious examples,” said Stefar. “There are others, which perhaps might not occur to you as controversial.”

"Like what?” said Rafe.

Stefar shrugged. “There can be many triggers. Just choose your words with care, and perhaps concentrate on listening rather than speaking, at least until you have a sense of how your words are perceived here.”

"Let’s talk about lighter things, shall we?” said Lirea. Stimulating conversation followed until people began yawning, and the evening wound down.

13

— • —

PREPARING FOR THE ASSAULT

First thing after breakfast, Beldan and Dalbin prepared to go to the DynaStream facility. Dalbin had asked Winnie and Sam to accompany him to talk to DynaStream officials, reporting the conversations they had overheard.

The DynaStream facility was a huge building outside Mencara, with a two-story office wing, a long one-story center for prototypes and testing, and a large, square one-story wing for production, which would ramp up rapidly once the prototype testing stage was finished. After they parked beside many skimmers and haulers, Beldan headed for the prototype section, while Dalbin led Winnie and Sam to the office wing.

They entered through a reception hall. Dalbin nodded at the woman behind the desk, and they continued down a corridor to a large office. Another woman behind another desk inside greeted Dalbin by name. She rose and walked into an inner office and announced their arrival, then ushered them in.

A stout middle-aged man sat behind a desk. Facing him sat two other middle-aged men, one tall and slender with dark hair, the other short and stocky and graying. The short man moved three chairs from one wall over for the visitors. Dalbin introduced Sam and Winnie as associates.

The man behind the desk, Rofar Conto, said, "You mentioned urgent business to discuss with us—too complicated to include in a message, was it?"

"Not complicated, confidential."

"You have piqued our curiosity—please elaborate."

"I'll let my associates tell you what they have heard, and then I'll need to supplement their accounts." First Sam and then Winnie described the context and then the content of the conversations they'd overheard. When they finished, Dalbin mentioned the bulletin board posting from Flammer. "If you connect the dots, you see where this is leading—a great threat to this facility."

Conto looked at the other two men, then said, "That seems far-fetched. Idle talk from rightcakes is nothing new. It seldom leads to much real trouble—though, granted, it's annoying."

"Surely all of Melenca is used by now to the blustering of Flammer," chimed in the tall man, Torban Pelgor.

"You shouldn't underestimate the devotion of the True Believers in Flammer's cult," said Dalbin. "They believe anything he tells them, and they're being increasingly fed a stream of lies to convince them their way of life is threatened. They've already become violent—witness their assault on Mentor Perroso, and his abduction."

"Even if you were right," said Conto, "which I'm by no means conceding, what do you think we could do about it?"

"You can increase the security guards around the facility, by a lot. Just in case."

The stocky man, Dancar Keldo, said, "That would be expensive, just on a chance, a slim chance, that events might unfold as you fear. We're on a tight budget on this project as it is."

"If a rightcake mob damages the facility, it will be a lot more expensive."

"We have to weigh risks and costs in managing this project. We may have to take some chances, as you see it." He glanced at the other two. "I think we're comfortable with that."

"Besides, if a mob did materialize, we would notify the constabulary in Mencara right away," said Pelgor. "I have no doubt they'd respond in force quickly. We have good relations with them."

"It would take them some time to get here," said Dalbin. "Time during which a large mob can do a lot of damage. These True Believers are being whipped into a frenzy, and not just by Flammer. Margan Anthrite, for instance. He's riling them through the *Weasel*—to boost his profits."

Conto looked at Keldo, then Pelgor. "I think you're exaggerating the risk," he said. "But what we can do is project the costs of bringing in more guards against the potential costs of damage from a mob, as you seem to fear. We'll give this careful consideration."

"All right. Don't take long. The danger is imminent."

"Is that what you expected?" Winnie asked Dalbin as they left the office.

"I didn't know what to expect for sure, but it doesn't surprise me. Ravinn was right—it's a bureaucracy. Those in it are reluctant to take risks. To reach a decision and approve something often takes time—which we don't have."

"What will happen, then?" asked Sam. In his small company, he didn't have to deal with a bureaucracy, and when he'd been a middle manager, he certainly hadn't dealt with an issue like this.

"They'll study it all right, but then they won't do anything—or they'll delay a decision as long as they can. And it will be too late."

At Lirea's house, Silenda and Kandar were preparing to leave, along with Allie and Peter. Beldan sent Dalbin to persuade a city official he knew to alert the Mencaran constabulary to the attack they expected. Renala was running an errand but would meet them later at the exhibit. Sam and Winnie joined Silenda's group. Just past downtown was the Academy, which looked institutional, with large buildings and open spaces between them. Silenda identified dormitories and classroom buildings as they passed, then parked off the main street, across from the campus. The gallery was adjacent to the campus but not part of it.

They had just passed a building and come to the edge of a large open space to their left when they heard a commotion and saw a crowd gathered. Opposite them across the space were two pedestals, each containing several vaguely human figures. Sam couldn't tell what they were meant to represent, if anything, since they didn't have distinctive enough features to be recognizable historic individuals. People stopped as they entered the space, dropped to their knees, bowed before the statues, then rose and moved into the throng beyond.

"What's going on?" said Winnie. "What are those statues?"

"The one on the left is called 'Diversity' and the other is called 'Tolerance,'" said Kandar.

"But why are people bowing down? Is this a religion, like Proclaimers and Wayfarers?"

"Not exactly," replied Silenda, "at least not officially. But they are sort of like idols."

"It's good to celebrate tolerance and diversity, no?" said Allie. "Why do you call them idols?"

"Celebrate as values, certainly."

"When they're practiced," added Kandar.

Over the hubbub a man's voice was audible, and the crowd noise subsided. A fiftyish man, stocky with a paunch and a receding hairline stood on a raised platform. "Melenca, the land of promise!" he called out. "So proclaim both Compactors and Unifiers, and they talk reverently about the Compact. But the Compact just cements exploitation of the laborers, to keep not only the great merchants but also burghers at the top, in positions of privilege." The crowd, most of them young, erupted in shouts of approval. "Our governors for centuries have subjugated and abused brown-eyes and Newcomers especially. Melenca the land of promise? No, Melenca is just a typical example of the concern structure, of exploitation and subjugation, as in the Lands Beyond."

"Good thing Stefar is not here to hear this," said Silenda.

"Good thing Renala is not here," said Kandar. "She can be hotheaded. We wouldn't want her arguing back in this crowd."

"Not a land of promise?" yelled a man in the crowd. "Many Melencans' ancestors came here to escape poverty and oppression in other lands so they could better themselves, and they did!" Angry jeers from the crowd interrupted him.

"Our friend here is blind to his privileged background as a burgher in the concern structure," called the speaker.

"Many burghers worked their way up from modest beginnings—I did," the man shouted. "And many operate small concerns that struggle—not everyone is a great merchant."

"He's certainly brave," said Silenda.

"Or foolish," said Kandar. "He's taking a risk. He must be from outside Mencara."

"Do we have to listen to this abuse?" yelled a student.

"Why is he allowed to spread these vile ideas?" shouted another.

Before the speaker could respond, there was a stir in the crowd, and several men in red tunics forced a path through the crowd until they converged on the man. Two of them grabbed his arms and led him away.

"Who are they?" asked Winnie.

"The Correctness Patrol," said Silenda.

"Where are they taking him?" said Peter.

"If he's lucky, they'll just expel him from the campus," said Kandar. "If he's unlucky, they'll detain him and he'll have to appear before the Commissars of Correctness."

"The what?" said Winnie.

Silenda started to answer, then paused as the Correctness Patrol emerged from the grounds not far from them. Each patrol member had an armband on each arm, with "Tolerance" on one and "Diversity" on the other. "The commissars assess allegations of improper statements," said Silenda. She sighed. "I'll explain more later—let's go on to the exhibit."

A few minutes' walk later, they came to a two-story building that stretched farther along the street than the typical storefront. They entered a wide and deep room where people in small groups milled around various objects standing on pedestals or mounted on the walls. Silenda looked around for a friend she'd met through art shows, then spotted a woman standing by one of the pedestals, who saw them and advanced to meet them. Lenara Holpar was around Allie's age, wearing an orange tunic and purple skirt.

"I'm so glad you've all come to see the exhibition!" she said. "It's good for the artists to gain broader exposure than just in the Academy—you aren't in the Academy are you, any of you?" Before anyone could respond, she said, "Come look around! There's so much to see. I'll guide you if you like." She led them to a painting on the wall, on which streaks and smudges of black paint stood out against a white background. "Clearly here you see the artist's cry of despair at the futility of modern life," said Lenara. As she explained the artist's protest against the unfairness of the universe (the one they were in now, Sam guessed), they heard a voice that sounded vaguely familiar. Tim Wooden stood talking to a couple of people at a pedestal ten feet away.

Silenda called out, "Wooden! I told them you'd be here."

He looked and recognition registered in his eyes. He excused himself and joined them. "Silenda," he said, "I'd think a lot of the work here isn't your style."

"It's not. But I like to keep up with trends." She introduced Lenara to Wooden. Lenara could hardly contain her enthusiasm.

"It's such an honor to meet you, such a distinguished artist. I have followed your works for years."

"You're very kind," said Wooden. He looked at the voyagers. "It's good to see you again. How have you fared? You were going to seek Mentor Perroso. Did you find him before. . .?"

Sam shook his head. "That's what we want to talk to you about."

Before Wooden could respond, a woman's voice rose above the din: "Can I have your attention?" A middle-aged woman stood on a small platform. As the clamor died down some, she said, "We're honored to have the great scholar Pondol Garolo here this morning to comment on the exhibition." The crowd murmured.

"Oh we are fortunate!" said Lenara. "You're familiar with his work, I assume?" When several of them shook their heads—including Silenda and Kandar—she went on, "You know of him, of course."

"Sorry, no," said Silenda. Kandar also shook his head again.

"Well, he's very influential in the Academy." She looked puzzled. "I thought his fame had spread to the general culture. Oh well, we're in for a treat."

The woman on the platform spoke about Garolo's influence on cutting-edge thought in the Academy, through his observations on Melencan society and its institutions.

"Sounds right up your alley, Peter," said Allie.

"I'm listening."

The woman stepped down from the platform and a man stepped onto it. They immediately recognized him as the speaker they had observed in the open space on campus that morning. But if Peter hoped Garolo would talk about aspects of Melencan society he would find interesting, he was to be disappointed. "How inspiring this exhibit is in capturing the cry of the oppressed for liberation, the defiance of privilege," said Garolo.

"Says the man who holds a cush position in the Academy, for which he's well paid," said Kandar in a low voice. Lenara frowned.

"These works in general reflect the voice of the hitherto powerless in asserting their identities in the face of the ruling class, an assertion that's refreshingly replacing such hegemonic concepts as beauty and symmetry." He pointed to a pedestal not far from where he stood, and his introducer held up the object on it, a wood carving. "Look, for example, at this work by the noted artist Wooden."

Sam peered at the carving. It looked familiar. Allie said, "Is that a Corvette, Tim?"

Wooden grinned. "I dreamed about having one as a teenager. Obviously we couldn't afford one."

"It's actually rather convincing," said Peter.

"Here we have a sculpture that in its shape represents the imprisoning confines of the laborer's lot," said Garolo. "The ominous curves enclose the poor laborer, leaving no escape, stuck inside this limited space. And in so doing, the sculpture cries in protest against the oppressors."

"Way to go, Tim!" said Winnie. "Stick it to the man."

Garolo pointed to another pedestal, and the host held up the piece on it. It was a cup such as they'd been served tea in—a real cup, not a sculpture—sitting on top of a wooden box, also real. "These common objects express the artist's rejection of the concern structure, and her endorsement of solidarity among laborers."

"He gets that out of a teacup and a box?" said Kandar with a smirk. "Impressive!"

Garolo continued for a few more minutes in the same vein, singling out other objects. As he was winding up, Renala joined them. "When we're through here," said Wooden, "let's get lunch, and discuss your search for Perroso." They wandered around the exhibit for a while, guided by Lenara, with Silenda and Wooden occasionally commenting on objects they admired. When they finished touring, at Silenda's suggestion they headed for a café a few blocks away, all except Lenara, who still had work to do at the exhibit.

The café was on a corner of the same street. Like the gallery, it was adjacent to the campus but not part of it. Many of the tables were filled with students and some older adults, presumably faculty. The café was noted for its varieties of tea, Silenda told them, and they tried some, along with sandwiches.

Talking to Wooden about their quest in front of the Melencans was delicate, Sam thought. Wooden seemed to be waiting for them to open the conversation. "We're not going to be able to talk to Mentor Perroso anytime soon," said Sam.

"Not likely," said Wooden. "You want advice on adjusting to life in Melenca, then, as I recommended?"

"You mentioned two Outbounders who found him."

"What about them?"

"Can you tell us their names and where they lived?"

"One didn't find . . . what he was seeking. The other has never shown up again. I don't see how that helps you."

"It's our best hope now. Maybe we can get some helpful information from the one, general location maybe. Maybe the other said something to an acquaintance. It's worth a shot."

"You're making a mistake, I have to say. Wasting time when you could be starting out here."

"We have to try," said Allie. "Don't you have that information?"

"I don't see how it can do any good." He sighed. "But if you're determined, I can provide names and locations—towns, not addresses." Suddenly there was a commotion several tables away, where two red-clad Correctness Patrol members stood flanking a middle-aged man at a table with a couple of other older adults. A student stood with the patrol officers.

"Scholar Jogonda?" said one. When the man nodded, the officer continued, "You're charged with violating the principles of tolerance and diversity by promoting study of a book on the proscribed list." He cited the title of the work.

"But it's a classic of our literature!" Jogonda protested.

"It is flagged for offensive remarks about brown-eyes," said the second officer.

"It contains stereotypical images!" said the student.

"It was written a hundred years ago," said Jogonda. "It reflects cultural attitudes of the time. Is that a reason to prohibit the teaching of literature? It records our history, and it touches on some of the great themes of life, of being human."

"I am offended by the promulgation of such bigotry! It has no place in our culture, and we students should not have to endure this assault on our sensibility."

"The stereotypical images you mention are incidental, and in fact they are few. Besides, do you think you can avoid being confronted in life with things that offend you?"

"Save your speech for the Commissars of Correctness," said the first officer. "On your feet! Let's go!" Jagonda stood up and they led him off as his colleagues watched helplessly.

"Poor man," said Silenda.

"What will happen to him?" asked Allie.

"If he's found guilty by the commissars, he may well lose his position at the Academy," said Kandar.

"Isn't there anything anyone can do?"

Silenda shook her head. Kandar shrugged. "If you ask me," said Renala, "there aren't enough people with spines to stand up to the commissars."

"A sad state of affairs Melenca has reached, on both sides," said Wooden. "Ah well, you wanted information." He told them the names and the last known towns of the two Outbounders. When they finished lunch, he returned to the exhibit, and they left for Lirea's house. Eddie and Rafe were still out, as was Dalbin, but Beldan had returned. They were in the large living room when Dalbin burst in through the doorway.

"I've just learned a large mob of rightcakes has been spotted approaching Mencara," he said, breathing hard. "They're not far from the DynaStream facility."

"How do we know they're rightcakes?" said Beldan. "They probably are, I agree, if there's a mob headed this way, but still, we need to be sure. I need a solid reason before I panic."

"I was told that several in the front rank were carrying a large banner with 'Flammer!' and 'Save Melenca for the Supreme Leader' written on it, and another banner farther back said 'Melenca for Real Melencans.'"

Beldan frowned. "Yes, that's them."

"You can panic now."

Beldan didn't panic, though; instead, he looked thoughtful. "We need to inform the constabulary right away. Meanwhile, we need all the able-bodied men we can muster.

Dalbin, I need you to go with me. Kandar, are you willing?" Kandar nodded.

"I'll go too," said Sam.

"You're not obligated to," said Beldan. "This isn't your fight."

"After all you've done for us, I do feel obligated."

"I'm not much for fisticuffs," said Peter, "but I'll go and help however I can."

"Eddie would be good to have around in a crisis like this," said Sam. He looked at Allie and Winnie. "Send him on when he comes, will you? And see if Rafe will come too."

"Then you'll need someone to fetch the constables," said Renala. "I'll do that."

At Beldan's direction, Lirea brought some garden tools—shovels, spades—as makeshift weapons. They were passing these out in the foyer when the front door opened and Eddie hurried in.

He paused for breath, then said, "Rafe's been arrested!"

14

— · —

THE ATTACK ON DYNASTREAM

For a moment they were speechless. Then Winnie said, "Arrested? For what?"

"By constables?" said Lirea.

"They didn't look like constables—at least the ones I've seen so far," replied Eddie. "There were a couple of guys wearing red tunics and with armbands on. They carried him off."

"That's the Correctness Patrol," said Renala.

"He hasn't been arrested for legal offenses, then," said Lirea. "But he has been detained, nonetheless. He'll have to appear before the Commissars of Correctness."

"What's the difference?" said Winnie. "From what we saw today, I thought there were serious consequences for the people we saw carted off by the Correctness Patrol."

"Oh there are—but they're not legal ones, strictly speaking. There haven't been acts passed for these so-called offenses, and the commissars don't have legal authority."

"Why the hell do people put up with such bullshit, then?"

"Social pressure. Everyone is afraid to run counter to the commissars, and risk ostracism. That includes concerns, even the big ones, so people can lose their jobs if they're sentenced by the commissars."

"What did Rafe do?" asked Sam.

"We split up soon after we went out," said Eddie, "but I came across him later listening to some guy making an announcement to a small crowd. He said he was introducing a new list of 'proscribed words from the commissars'—I didn't know who he was talking about—and then he read from the list. It was crazy."

"How so?" said Beldan.

"He said 'sick' could no longer be used to refer to people because it would make them feel inferior to well people, so from now on people would have to say 'temporarily inconvenienced.' Some smart guy in the crowd said, 'What if it's not temporary?' and someone told him he was insensitive and to be quiet."

"He was daring," said Lirea.

"The announcer stared at the guy for a moment, then moved on—he said 'fat' could no longer be used, because it would hurt the feelings of someone who was called that, so the new term is 'geometrically distributed.' Someone else called out, 'Does that mean wide-angled?' and people told her to quit criticizing sensitive people, and to be quiet."

"I'm surprised," said Kandar. "Those speaking up must be unfamiliar with things in Mencara."

"Maybe they're just fed up," said Renala.

Eddie continued, "The next word was 'dead,' the announcer said—it was taboo because it would arouse grief in family members, so from now on people should say 'alternatively positioned.' Another guy said, 'Why not horizontally positioned?' and the crowd really became agitated."

"But Rafe hadn't said anything?" said Allie.

"Not yet. But then the announcer said 'laborer' couldn't be used anymore because it carried 'pejorative connotations reflecting a history of exploitation by merchants and burghers,' so the new word would be 'builders of society.' And that set Rafe off. He said that burghers are builders of society, too, and someone else said, 'Everyone knows burghers just live off the work of laborers.'"

Lirea sighed. "Stefar did warn him to be careful with his speech."

"He did, yes," Eddie agreed. "So Rafe argued back that a lot of burghers have started concerns and contribute money and jobs to the economy."

"Rafe does like to harp on entrepreneurs," said Winnie.

"He couldn't help himself, the dumb-ass," said Eddie. "So someone else said burghers keep laborers—'I mean builders of society,' the guy said—locked into their lower place on the social scale. And Rafe said that laborers could advance if they founded small concerns."

"Not all who start out without much can afford to do so, or advance to that degree no matter how hard they work," said Silenda.

"Still, some can," said Renala. "Like my ancestors—the opportunity exists."

"The point here is that Rafe couldn't read the crowd," said Allie.

"That's not his strong suit," said Winnie.

Eddie nodded. "That was the last straw for the announcer, so he signaled to these

Correctness Patrol dudes who were walking past and pointed to Rafe, and they went up and dragged him off."

"So he'll have to appear before these commissars," said Winnie. "Do we know when?"

"I'll try to find out," said Lirea. "We can at least go and see what happens to him, and try to speak on his behalf if the commissars will allow it."

"Can't we hire an advocate for him?" said Allie.

Lirea shook her head. "It won't do any good. As I said, it's not a legal matter."

"I don't mean to downplay the seriousness," said Beldan, "but we have a more pressing need." He told Eddie about the mob approaching the facility and that Beldan and the others were heading there. Eddie immediately volunteered to go as well.

"What if Rafe has to appear before the commissars while you're gone?" asked Allie.

"I'll take you there," said Renala.

"I'll go too," said Winnie. "We can handle this. You three go on with Beldan—and watch your asses." They promised to, and then they followed Beldan and the others, with Renala trailing behind.

As they approached the DynaStream facility, there was no sign of the mob yet. But outside the building they found a handful of waiting men, who carried long staffs, thick enough to seriously damage anyone they made contact with.

"Ravinn followed through," said Beldan. "Those are his men. That's Ralkar Bodeno." Beldan walked up to a tall, well-muscled man, with close-cut, graying hair.

As the others followed, Dalbin said, "He served in the regiments. He's a good one to have here."

"I'm glad to see you and your men, Ralkar," said Beldan. "Not many, as Ravinn said, but these look like good men to have in a pinch."

"They are," said Ralkar. "Those of us deemed useful were scattered, so it took some time to gather us. But we're here."

"How many?"

"Fifteen. It's all Ravinn could assemble."

"We're few against a mob."

Ralkar nodded. "The best we can hope to do is hold them off as long as we can, to gain some time for the constables to arrive in force."

"What if they have firetubes?" asked Dalbin.

Ralkar glanced back at two of his men closest to the building. "We have a couple, if necessary—but I hope they won't become necessary. That would lead to a bloodbath—civil war."

As he looked around the group of defenders, Sam noticed Rofar Conto and Torban Pelgor, two of the DynaStream officials he and Winnie had visited with Dalbin, standing near the front door, looking around uncertainly.

"I see the DynaStream bureaucrats are ready for action," said Dalbin.

Ralkar snorted. "I wouldn't count on much help from them."

"We need to sort out what we'll do if the mob gets inside," said Beldan.

"They'll try to damage things," said Dalbin, "but I'm not sure they know what exactly is valuable to us."

"My guess is they'll just break random things," replied Beldan.

"You have a pretty good idea of what is hardest to replace," said Ralkar. "The six of you can contribute more by preparing inside for when they do break in. Lock up anything you can, hide things."

"I hate to leave you and your men by yourselves out here, but no doubt you're right." Beldan turned back to Dalbin and the others. "Let's go into the prototype and testing areas." He led them to the main door of that part of the complex. They entered a narrow foyer, with a corridor on the left leading to the offices and one on the right leading into the testing area.

"Beldan, you and Dalbin know the ins and outs here," said Sam. "The rest of us don't. Should we stay here and try to delay the mob as long as we can?"

Beldan shook his head. "When the rioters get in—and they will—Ravinn's men will have to retreat inside. Four of you won't make any difference against that mob. But we can try to misdirect them once they're looking for things to damage." They followed him down the right-hand corridor past a number of rooms. Some doors were open, others closed. They saw no one in the first open rooms they passed. Then Beldan paused beside the door to a large room with several pools. "Here's where they combine the resin and the powder and heat them, fine-tuning various ratios. The pools are for testing the amounts needed for skimmers, haulers, and transports. The vehicles should soon go into production." A man stood next to one pool, fiddling with some sort of control on a stand next to a chute. Liquid splashed out of a large, long container attached to the chute and down into a rectangular metal box in the water attached by a pipe to the stand, and across from that first chute a powder slid down another chute into the box. The man looked up, then turned another control. Then he stepped over to another pool, with a similar arrangement, where suddenly the water in front of the box began churning, then sent out waves that propelled a small floating square. Beldan said to his companions, "If we can lure a number in here, making them think it's something they can sabotage, we can lock this door." It was thick and metallic. "They won't be able to break out. Any damage here will be more easily repaired than in some of the key rooms." He turned toward the employee and warned him what was about to happen.

"So I heard," the man said. "Most people in this area have already been evacuated. I'm waiting to get this last batch mixed for now."

"Evacuated? To where?"

"To the large back hall in the office wing, where group meetings happen."

"Why didn't they stay to help defend this area?" said Kandar.

"Maybe it's better they didn't," said Beldan. "We don't need mass casualties against this mob." He looked back at the employee. "You need to clear out as soon as you can. They'll be here soon, and Ravinn's men outside won't be able to hold them off for long."

The man nodded. "Don't worry. I'm not a martyr—DynaStream doesn't pay me enough."

"Where's the key to the door?"

The man gestured over to a counter against one wall. "In the third drawer."

"At the first sign of trouble, some of us need to get back here and retrieve the key, and get ready to use it," Beldan told his companions. A couple of doors farther down was a room in which several large machines stood. No one was in the room. "These devices test the boxes for the various kinds of vehicles, and they calibrate the regulators," said Beldan. "There's an optimal size for producing the proper force, without it becoming too great." He went to a counter behind the machines. He leafed through some paperwork in two piles on the countertop, then put each pile into a separate pocket of his pants. "These are charts from the testing, noting the right adjustments. It's important these be kept safe." He glanced back at the devices. "They're too big and stationary to hide, I'm afraid. If there's any way to keep the rioters out of this room, we need to do so."

He led them past a few more rooms, to where the corridor ended in a door. They pushed through it. A few doors down, a branch hallway led into the heart of the facility, and a stream of employees hurried toward them and turned into the branch. Dancar Keldo, the third member of the DynaStream triumvirate, stood in the main corridor amid the onrushing people, directing them. Beldan and the others pushed past the approaching throng and reached Keldo.

"You're making yourself useful in this emergency," said Dalbin. "Rofar and Torban don't have a clue."

"We heard a mob had been sighted. We continue to think the risk is exaggerated, but there's no point taking chances."

"Fine time to figure that out."

"Have you been to the engines room yet?" asked Beldan.

"I haven't made it that far. I'm trying to keep this, uh, evacuation orderly."

"We're headed there. We'll warn them." They rushed past more rooms, struggling to avoid more people going the other way. In a moment, however, the crowd thinned out. Beldan halted next to another open door. "This is where they're putting everything for the engines together, testing to make sure they're working correctly, and fine-tuning them as necessary." Inside the large room, several people were at work at long tables. Metal shells of various sizes—apparently the exoskeletons of future vehicles—stood locked into narrow ruts on each table. The workers looked up as Beldan and the others entered. Beldan explained the approaching danger to them. They looked surprised. "We have people outside who will try to stop them, and we've sent word to the constabulary to send reinforcements, so we hope they won't be able to stay inside long," he said. "But you need to know what's likely to come. Anyone who wants to leave can gather in the large meeting hall in the office wing."

"What about the engines?" said one man. "We've put too much work into them to just let someone trash them."

"Some of us are going to resist them—we'll try to misdirect them if we can. If any of you want to help, you'd be welcome."

"What if you angled these tables toward the door so the engines pointed toward the mob," said Dalbin, "and then removed the containment boxes at the end, wouldn't they propel the gas out in a forceful stream?"

"I see what you mean," said another man. "It might be effective. Though I'm not sure how long it would delay a mob."

"And what if you then turn off the regulators so everything feeds at once? Wouldn't that produce a more powerful burst?"

"We couldn't control it," said a woman. "Sprays of gas would go all over the place."

"It's a chance worth taking—this is an emergency—not normal use to power a skimmer."

"He's right," said the second man enthusiastically. "The burst of pressurized gas would knock back anyone trying to force their way in here. We can rig the engines up in a few minutes." He looked around the room. "And we can concentrate on the transport engines—they'd give the biggest blast." Several other employees made supportive comments.

"Go ahead—I doubt the mob is far off now," said Dalbin. "We'll try to give you a little advance notice, but stay on your toes. Once the rioters are in, things will be chaotic." He looked at Beldan. "Well, Pop, where to next?" Beldan glanced around the room. At the back wall were some cabinets. He opened one, sorted through some objects—metal parts, cloths, bottles—stored in it, then stashed the charts behind the objects.

"If your defensive measures work, these will be safer in here than on me," he told the employees. Back in the corridor, Beldan glanced farther down to its end in another door, presumably leading into the production area. "There's not much we can do down there. Let's go back and see if anything's happening outside."

They had just pushed through the door into the first prototype area when Dalbin said, "Uh oh," and pointed out a window. A disorderly throng swarmed around the facility, mostly men but some women. Several men in the front ranks carried a large banner that read "Follow Flammer's Commands!" in large print and underneath it in slightly smaller print "Save Our Mines!" Dalbin and the others stood watching. As the ragged first row of rioters surged near the entrance, Ralkar held up his hand and spoke to them. Whatever he said had no effect. They drew even with Ravinn's contingent, who raised their staffs in an unmistakable posture, ready to strike. The leading edge of the mob began grappling with the defenders, who began to swing their staffs. Rioters went down right and left. For a few minutes the defenders managed to keep them at bay. But the rightcakes behind the front ranks kept pressing forward, and the surge of humanity was too strong. A couple of Ravinn's men went down, overwhelmed. Eventually the rest retreated through the main door.

While a mass of rioters banged against the door, others spread out along the facility. "They'll get in other doors," said Beldan, "Let's go back the way we just came, so we can try to misdirect them." He looked back down the corridor. "The main door won't hold that mass of people for long. We ought to send someone to alert that man in the pools room."

"I'll go warn him," said Eddie. "I'll get the key too."

"I'll go with you," said Sam. "If they reach that room, we'll be better off with more than one."

They hurried away. The others pivoted back through the doorway. Sam and Eddie hadn't gone far when a window broke with a loud crash perhaps fifteen feet ahead of them. A metal rod poked in and shattered more of the remaining glass, and two men climbed through the window. Both had hats on, one reading "Restore Melenca to Glory" and the other just reading "Flammer." They spotted Sam and Eddie and ran toward them, one carrying the rod, which he swung as they closed on them. Eddie dodged the blow, grabbing the rod and pulling it in the same direction, the momentum carrying the man with it. He stumbled and fell, and as he scrambled to his feet, Eddie punched him hard in the stomach. The other man had charged Sam. Sam wasn't used to fighting, but he reacted instinctively, his muscle memory from football kicking in, as a thought flashed through his mind: *hit him like he's a wide receiver*, and he crashed into the man and slammed his body into the wall. The man cried out in pain and went down. Eddie brought the rod down hard on the first man's shoulder, then onto the second man's back. Both screamed and writhed on the floor.

Eddie grabbed the hat that read "Restore Melenca to Glory" and put it on, then flipped the other to Sam. "Maybe that will fool some of them for a few minutes," said Eddie. They raced to the pools room and told the worker it was time to flee. True to his word, he didn't hesitate but ran to the door and then toward the testing wing. Now they could hear a commotion toward the center. "I'll get the key, then we'll go see what we can do," said Eddie. He found the key in the drawer, as the man had said. They hadn't gone far in the corridor when in the distance they could see a couple of men swinging staffs against a number of rioters, backpedaling as they did. Abruptly they plunged into one of the rooms and closed the door.

As several rioters banged away at the door, another yelled, "Forget them! We need to find where the main work's going on and destroy things." And the mob pressed on toward Sam and Eddie.

Eddie waved his hat. "This way! I found where they're making their fuel." The crowd surged toward him. He signaled with his arm, pointing to the pools room, where the door was still open. "In here!" As the first few rioters reached him, he grabbed one's arm and shoved him on in. Sam grabbed another and gave him a push.

"The fuel's in there!" cried Sam.

"Hey!" someone yelled and they heard a splash.

"Hey, watch it!" yelled someone else and they heard another splash, then another.

But the momentum of the crowd behind them, aided by Eddie and Sam offering helping hands and encouraging words, was strong, and to aid it, Eddie moved back a few steps and yelled toward those in the rear of the crowd, "They're meeting resistance! We need you in there, quickly!" That sped the rioters up as they shoved those in front of them and they piled in, even as the sounds of people splashing into water and yelling carried. There were maybe fifteen or twenty in this group, and when the last batch were pushing at the doorway, Eddie and Sam shoved them in and Eddie slammed the door shut and turned the key in the lock. "Hope they like swimming," he said with a grin.

"We better get out of here," said Sam. "There'll be more of them before long." They raced back toward the end of the corridor. As they pushed through the door, they could see far down the hall people sitting on the floor, some with backs against the wall on both sides of the corridor, others in the middle, cross-legged.

"What the hell?" muttered Eddie. "Has this turned into a sit-in?" He and Sam stopped for a moment to take stock.

"Let's see what's going on," said Sam. "Just be ready to react, or run if need be." Eddie nodded and they headed cautiously toward the seated group. As the two drew closer, a couple of those seated shifted position, and Sam saw Dalbin walking toward them from beyond the sitters. Dalbin picked his way among them and stopped outside the doorway from which people radiated out in both directions. Clearly, these were rioters. A number had hats on with the Flammer slogans on them, and a banner was laid up against the wall. As they reached the lead sitters, Sam said to one, "What's going on here?"

The man smiled beatifically and said, "Hello, friend. We're just taking a break."

"Yes," said the woman seated next to him. "Take time to enjoy the beauty of this day."

"Yeah, we'll be sure to do that," said Eddie. They reached Dalbin, who was smiling broadly.

"We had a couple of tussles with rioters," said Sam, "but I have to say, things look pretty peaceful here."

"The heated gas from the silverbark compound produces a mellowing effect," said Dalbin. "The blasts from the engines worked perfectly. As you can see."

"How long will this effect last?"

"It should be long enough for the constables to get in here and process this group. I don't imagine they'll object." His smile disappeared. "We've had some encounters ourselves. Pop is down there with Kandar and Peter. Some of Ravinn's men have joined them, and they managed to hold at bay several groups. We better go see if they need help." They maneuvered their way through the sedate rioters and then hurried down the corridor. Several people were stretched motionless on the floor in the distance, and as they drew closer they could see a corner to the left where a side hall branched off before the far door. As they reached the corner, they saw seven or eight people standing a few feet down the hall. Two men with staffs hoisted them menacingly at Sam and Eddie. "No!" cried Dalbin. "They're with us." He looked back at the two. "You might want to take off those hats." Sheepishly, they did.

A few injured people sat among the standing men, one with his arm hanging in a makeshift sling from a tunic, another with his leg stretched out in front of him, groaning. Peter sat next to them, looking dazed, a nasty gash on the side of his head.

Beldan gestured toward Peter. "We managed to stop the bleeding, but we need to get him to a house of healing. He took a bad blow."

"They're here!" a man called out. One of Ravinn's men was looking out a window of the main corridor. "The constables are arriving in force. They're wading into the mob still outside."

"It shouldn't be long before they can force their way in here," said Beldan. Those in their group who could move congregated around a few windows. Sam could see a melee outside: blue-clad constables carrying shields and wielding truncheons clashed with the rioters. Many rightcakes broke and ran. Some ran into other constables and were apprehended, while others evaded the ranks of constables and fled the grounds. The figures in blue outside methodically turned the rioters away from the building and began to enter. Beldan looked down the corridor toward the door to the production wing. "I doubt more of the rioters will break in down that way," he said. "They have their hands full now with the constables. We should head back this way to cut off any trying to escape."

After they passed the erstwhile rioters still peacefully seated outside the engines room, they hurried down the corridor and soon saw a struggle ahead, as a band of rioters desperately fought with constables. As Beldan and the others reached the rightcakes from behind and laid into them with their staffs and the makeshift weapons from Lirea's house, the rioters soon gave up.

Dalbin directed some of the constables to the engines room. "You'll meet a group who won't be any trouble—they'll do whatever you say and go wherever you tell them, like the magistrates' chambers, say, or the jail."

It took a while, but gradually the constables both outside and inside gained control and broke the resistance of the mob. The blue tunics began loading the hat wearers into transports.

Beldan, Dalbin, and Kandar, followed by Sam and Eddie, who were supporting Peter, eventually went back outside and found Ralkar conferring with a couple of high-ranking constables. When Beldan had a chance to speak with him, they compared notes. Many of Ravinn's men had been injured, a few seriously, and needed to go to the nearest house of healing. Beldan told Dalbin to drop him, Sam, and Eddie off with Peter at the house of healing, and they returned to their hauler.

15

— • —

BEFORE THE COMMISSARS

Winnie sat with Allie, Lirea, and Renala in the building where the commissars met. Renala had led them there, and Lirea had gone with them, to make sure Renala didn't become so irritated she became disruptive.

"We don't need two of our group in front of the commissars," Lirea told her. Renala said nothing but after a moment nodded slightly. They sat now in pew-like benches in a large hall, inside an imposing stone building, with a handful of other people scattered among the benches. Over the entrance were carved the words "Hall of Judgment." In front of the rows of benches were a dais with a long table and behind it a row of chairs. Flanking the table were two statues of idealized human figures, one male, the other female, about eight or nine feet tall. At the base of the female was carved "Tolerance," at the base of the other, "Diversity."

After a few minutes, a line of figures filed in from a door to the side of the dais. They wore black robes and hoods with slits for their eyes, noses, and mouths. One by one they knelt and kissed the statue of Tolerance and then Diversity. As they took seats behind the table, a man came out of the same door and strode to the center of the table, in front of the dais. The only apparent indication of any sort of official status was a red armband he wore with "CoC" in white letters.

He now read from a sheet of paper: "The case of Baldor Katerbo." He turned and went over to the door.

"Oh my," whispered Lirea, who was sitting next to Winnie. "He's one of the founders of the Unified Districts and one of the authors of the Compact."

"Wasn't that a long time ago?" said Winnie in a low voice.

"A couple of centuries. He's been dead for a long time."

The commissar in the middle spoke. "The defendant is charged in absentia with exploiting brown-eye indentured servants and illegitimately extending their terms. He is also charged with deviant writings that violate the core principle of tolerance."

"They reflect his times," muttered Renala, who sat on Winnie's other side. "He was one of the heroes of the system we have today."

"He had real flaws, true," said Lirea, "but the same can be said for many people today. He also contributed much."

The commissars consulted among themselves for a minute or so, though Winnie heard only a low hum of voices. Then the one in the middle spoke again.

"We find the defendant guilty, in absentia. He is sentenced to be purged from the history texts that our students study, except to be described as an example of intolerance. Governors throughout Melenca should be encouraged to change the name of any streets called by his name." Renala snorted, and her cheeks reddened. "Next case," said the commissar in the middle, who apparently presided over the panel.

The armbanded man came back and read again: "The case of Fordel Lingabar." He went back to the door and this time opened it, and a sixtyish man was escorted into the room by two red-clad Correctness Patrol members, one on either side guiding him by the arm. They led him to the center of the table, beneath the dais, facing the commissars.

"You are charged with using offensive language and practicing social intimidation," said the commissar.

"What did I say?" said the man, sounding puzzled.

"Bring forth the witness."

The CoC man came back and gestured to the group of spectators. "Pardela Mandar, please come forward." An older woman got up from the bench a few rows behind Winnie and her companions and to their right and slowly, unsteadily made her way to the front of the dais.

"Proceed with your testimony," said the commissar.

"What was it? Oh, I remember. He told a joke about brown-eyes. Yes, I think that's what it was." She paused.

"What did he say?"

"Let me think." She concentrated for a moment. "Was it about the brown-eye who had been promoted to one of the lead managers in a concern that built canals? I think maybe it was. That article was in the digests."

"What about the manager?"

"I think he said he ought to be good at digging ditches. Wait a minute, no, I'm not sure that was it. Maybe it was about the brown-eye who'd been named lead cook in a fancy tavern—that the patrons there would be getting a lot of roasted galupa."

"Well, which one was it that he told?"

"I'm not sure," she said, sounding flustered. "It *was* forty years ago."

"Try to remember."

She concentrated again. "You know, it could have been the one about which side of the sod to lay down. I'm sorry, I'm not sure."

The commissars conferred among themselves. Then the presider said, "It's clear from the trend of the witness's testimony that the defendant did indeed use offensive language in an effort to create an intimidating and intolerant atmosphere in which diversity was assaulted." He looked at Pardela Mandar. "You may return to your place." She stepped away, and the commissar addressed Fordel Lingabar. "Do you have anything to say on your own behalf?"

"I don't know what she's referring to, but if I did say anything along those lines forty years ago, well, attitudes at the time were different. And I was very young. My thinking has changed since then. I've matured. I wouldn't say anything like that today—whatever 'that' was."

The presiding commissar glanced at the CoC man. "Add unrepentant attitude to the charges." He looked back at Lingabar. "You are found guilty of the charges. You are sentenced to dismissal from your job. We shall coordinate with your employer."

"But—but my wife doesn't make much. One of my grown children needs special support—I pay for that from my income."

"You should have thought of that when you used the offensive language." He looked at the Correctness Patrol members. "Remove the defendant from the building and release him. Next case."

As the patrol members led Lingabar, who continued to protest desperately, out of the building, the CoC man returned to the table and read again. "The case of Rafe Thomas." From the side door, two more patrol members emerged holding Rafe, looking disheveled, between them.

"You are charged with creating an oppressive atmosphere and expressing deviant thought."

"I'm not a deviant!" exclaimed Rafe.

"Silence. Is there a witness?"

"None could appear at this time, so we took down testimony," said the CoC man.

"Read it."

The CoC man looked at a separate set of sheets and began to read. "'He said laborers'—the witness meant builders of society—'were not kept in their place by burghers but could climb out of it if they just acted like burghers and exploited their fellows.'"

"Shameful," said one of the other commissars, the first time one had spoken other than the presiding commissar.

"I didn't say they could exploit their fellows," said Rafe. "I said some could advance if they struck out on their own."

"You have been warned about interrupting the testimony," said the presiding commissar. "Keep quiet or we will add new charges of disrespect for the process of ensuring diversity and tolerance." He looked back at the CoC man. "Proceed." The man went on to read several similar statements. Rafe looked frustrated but managed to keep silent. At the conclusion of the statements, the commissars spoke among themselves again, and then the presider said, "You are found guilty of using abusive language and promulgating harmful thinking. We will not tolerate such divisive speech and thought."

"Don't I get to say anything?" said Rafe.

"You have interrupted the testimony and your thinking is quite clear. You are sentenced to dismissal from your job."

"Uh, your eminence, there's a problem," the CoC man said. "We can discover no place of employment for the defendant."

"Where do you work?"

"I work for myself," said Rafe. "I own my small concern."

The commissars spoke among themselves for a moment, then the presider looked back at Rafe. "You are sentenced, then, to undergo a six-day session of enlightenment training, where you will have your attitudes and thinking adjusted so that you appreciate diversity and tolerance, in one week's time. Until then, you are remanded to the detention rooms, to await your session."

"You can't keep me imprisoned!" said Rafe. "I haven't done anything wrong."

"Remove the defendant from the building," the commissar told the Correctness Patrol members. The two patrol members grabbed Rafe's arms and dragged him from the room as he shouted defiance.

The CoC man addressed the audience: "Judgment Panel is adjourned for the remainder of the day."

At Lirea's house, everyone was gathered in the living room—everyone except Peter, who had drifted in and out of consciousness and was being kept at the house of healing for treatment and observation. It was the normal late-afternoon time for drinks, and after the events of the day, drinks were badly needed.

"What would happen if Rafe just left?" Allie asked Lirea. "If he could."

"People don't—they're afraid of the commissars."

"But what if he did?" said Winnie.

"I assume the Correctness Patrol would hunt him down and return him, probably to face more severe penalties."

"A stay in detention might not be such a bad idea for Rafe," said Eddie.

"We can't just leave him locked up," said Allie. "We've got to look for the other Earthlings Wooden knew. Suppose we find out something and have to leave. We can't just abandon Rafe."

"We can't delay searching for the others because of him, either," said Sam.

"We won't leave him behind," said Winnie. "We'll come up with something."

Dalbin had gone from the house of healing to the DynaStream facility to check on the damage there and had just returned to Lirea's house, and he changed the subject to report that the pools equipment had not been badly damaged nor the engines harmed. Unfortunately, though, the calibration devices had been damaged considerably. Dalbin, however, had retrieved the charts from where Beldan had hidden them.

"What does this mean for the alternate vehicles?" said Lirea.

"This will set us back, no doubt," said Beldan grimly. "There will be a delay in getting them into production, haulers and transports particularly—skimmers will be easier. But we can repair or reconstruct the devices, and having the charts will save us from considerably longer delay."

"Still, this transition is long-term," said Stefar. "The geological damage is here now, spreading to the east, close to our vineyards. It's a threat we face immediately."

There was a momentary silence, then Lirea said, "Are they sure it will continue to spread?"

"Where we were, the land just kept splitting wider and wider," said Dalbin.

"The crumbling will happen in those mines that are unaffected so far," said Beldan. "The same conditions prevail there. So it's going to come from new directions. Then there's the damage in the lowlands as a result of the crystal residue—it's spreading there too."

"Also," said Dalbin, "the Flammer regime has started opening new mines in areas in the Hazy Mountains where there haven't been any before, ignoring the risks."

"What kind of damage near the vineyards, Father?" said Renala.

"Cracks in the surface, widening sinkholes. I didn't hear about toxic gas, but that's a big concern too. Aside from the danger to people in the vicinity, will its residue on grapes linger in the wine? Poison it?"

"What are we going to do?" asked Lirea.

"We'll have to move equipment. We may have to transplant vines—we'll have to at least get cuttings to replant farther south. I'll need you, Kandar and Renala. It will be a big job."

"I wish we could help too," said Beldan, "but Dalbin and I are needed for repairing the DynaStream facility."

"Not needed, Beldan. We have a number of good employees in Barella. I mostly need these two to help organize and to communicate there and to the office here."

"Stefar and Lirea, I need to impose on you again and ask if I can borrow a skimmer," said Sam.

"You learned something helpful from Wooden, then?" asked Silenda.

"I need to try to track down a man he told us about."

"An Outbounder, I presume—excuse me, Earthling," said Beldan.

"We can spare a skimmer," said Stefar. "Where is this Outboun—uh, Earthling?"

"In a place called Carcella," said Sam. "I'm not sure where that is. I'll need directions."

"I can tell you where it is. It's not far from Barella, to the northeast. We can give you a ride as far as Barella. Then you'll be on your own."

"Directions aren't all you need," said Allie. "You can't go alone. I really want to go, but I feel strongly I should stay and look in on Peter. I hate to think of him in that house of healing all by himself. If he—when he—fully awakens, it would be scary to find himself somewhere unfamiliar, with none of us around."

"Allie and I talked," said Winnie. "We agreed she's better suited for nursing than I am. More patient and understanding. I'm from the suck-it-up-and-get-on-with-it school."

"It's obvious who else should go with Sam," said Eddie. "You people rely on me—with good reason."

16

— • —

THE WINE COUNTRY

Stefar's group left after breakfast the next morning, while Allie set off for the house of healing on a skimmer, confident she could find her way there with Lirea's directions, and Silenda returned to Secora to manage their concern's business.

Before long, the hauler reached wooded hills north of Mencara, steeper than those they'd encountered after leaving Pelora, interspersed with valleys. They passed fewer towns and farms than on their previous journeys. They had driven through this country for two more hours when Eddie called out, "Look! At the bottom of that hill over there." Sam glanced in the direction Eddie pointed and saw a group of large rocks clumped together."

A moment later, Sam said, "There's a crack in the hillside over there," pointing to the opposite side of the road.

"Where there's one, there're likely to be more," said Eddie. Sure enough, within a few minutes, they spotted several more cracks and scattered rocks. Suddenly, Eddie cried out. "Stop! There's a hole in the road!" Stefar braked and the hauler shuddered as it slowed, stopping within six or seven seconds, a few feet from the edge of a chasm that spanned the road. It extended on both sides past the road.

"We're not going to cross here," said Stefar.

Kandar scanned the countryside. "Can we take the hauler through the woods?"

"That would be really hard on it," said Renala.

"We might hit similar obstacles ahead even if we could," said Stefar. "We need to go back to the last crossroad and detour." He maneuvered the hauler around and they headed back. They drove for ten minutes before they reached a crossroad. After twenty minutes on it, Stefar turned onto another road heading north and followed it for an hour until they reached the outskirts of a town, Karament. Soon there were more houses grouped closer together and more side streets branching off the main road.

Suddenly traffic in front of them slowed. Several vehicles ahead waited to turn right onto a cross street. As they got closer, they saw skimmers and the occasional hauler parked on both sides of that street. They heard a rumble of voices. When they reached the street, Stefar turned left instead and parked ahead of several skimmers. In the distance across the road a crowd gathered around a house. Closer to Stefar's group, several people stood or sat on the ground near another house. A man and a woman among them wore EmRes armbands. They looked exhausted. Stefar asked them what was happening down the street.

"A large crevasse," the man replied. "It's already taken a couple of houses, and it's widening."

"But what's this crowd?" said Kandar.

"Not all rescue personnel, I wager," said Renala.

"It's a bunch of rightcakes, yelling that we're violating their rights," said the EmRes woman. "And they're interfering with our efforts to rescue people—some of them don't want to be rescued and are screaming the same gibberish."

Another man standing nearby was writing in a notebook. "Are you a reporter?" Sam asked him.

"There are some up there, from the *Vantage* and the *Current*. I'm with Rally Round. We're documenting what's going on."

"Rally Round? Is Katera Falembo here?"

"She's up there. You know her?"

"She's our cousin," said Renala, gesturing toward Kandar.

"Let's go see," said Sam.

"Watch out," said the EmRes man. "Between the crack and the crackpots, it's not the safest place to be. The constables already have their hands full."

After five or six more undamaged houses, a woman in front of a house faced a throng. A man and a woman stood on the stoop. Several in the crowd were yelling angrily at the woman facing them.

"Please listen to me!" she called out over the crowd noise. "We're trying to save lives!"

"Don't lie to us!" shouted a man. "You're trying to take our property and give it to Outbounders and force us into a shantytown. You'll separate us from our kids and give them to Outbounders, so they can brainwash them with deviant Unifier notions."

"We know all about their plot!" yelled a woman. "The Supreme Leader has warned us."

Sam noticed several people standing to the side of the crowd, holding notepads, and recognized Ralbo Jasko. He went up to him and reintroduced himself. Ralbo looked at him, then the others. "I remember—you were with Katera, at least a couple of you."

"Who's the woman in front?" asked Sam.

"A local administrator. She's been warning residents on the street of the danger and telling them they need to evacuate—especially the children. There are kids in several of these houses, and the parents won't let them leave. This lot showed up to interfere. Several have threatened the administrator."

"Where are the constables?" said Stefar.

"They're up ahead, trying to evacuate people—not easy when they're also trying to hold off these loonies. They've called for reinforcements from the next town, but they'll take a while."

Suddenly they heard a loud crack, and the house swayed up and down. "I want to get away!" wailed the woman on the stoop.

"No, we're staying here!" yelled the man with her. "They're not going to confiscate our house."

"I don't want to die!" She started to move, and the man grabbed her arm and held her. Eddie bolted from the group and raced to the stoop. He pulled the woman away, and escorted her quickly toward the others. His action seemed to freeze the crowd momentarily, but then one moved into his path and raised his arm, his hand clenched in a fist. Before he could swing, Eddie punched him in the stomach, and he staggered back.

As Eddie reached the others he said, "Where should we take her?"

"Maybe back with EmRes," said Sam.

Ralbo nodded. "They'll take care of her." Eddie left with the woman, who was crying softly and letting Eddie steer her. Several rightcakes had moved a few steps toward them, but then others began yelling at the administrator again, and they turned back toward her.

"We heard Katera is here," said Sam.

"Several houses down," said Ralbo.

Sam turned to Stefar. "Maybe you and Kandar better wait here for Eddie—that poor woman in front may need rescuing herself."

"I'll go with you," Renala told him. More protestors spread in front of three other houses they passed, which were also shifting some, though no residents or rescue workers were visible. At the fourth house, however, several people stood a few yards out from a wide porch in front of the house, apparently trying to coax a man on the porch away from the house. Part of the house had collapsed, and beyond it was a chasm. On the other side of it, the rubble of houses was scattered across the ground. The man on the porch shouted back angrily and refused to move. Two of the people talking to him were EmRes personnel. Sam guessed the others were likely local officials. Behind them a line of constables was standing their ground against protestors who surged forward.

"You can't take away our rights—or our kids!" yelled someone. Those in the vanguard of the crowd pushed at the constables, who shoved them back. Sam scanned the area, then spotted Katera, standing at one end of the porch, apart from the crowd, writing on a notepad.

"Wait here," he told Renala. He kept behind the mass of people as much as he could but still had to force his way toward Katera. He glanced over to the front of the house at one point and saw several people assault an EmRes worker and then a constable lay into them with a nightstick. Before Sam could reach Katera, the tussling mass engulfed her, and he saw her drop. She groped on her hands and knees for her notepad among trampling feet. When Sam was a few feet from her, suddenly a loud cracking rent the air, debris tumbled to the ground, the corner of the roof at their end broke off, and a large beam fell toward Katera just as Sam reached her. He pulled her up and yanked her to the side as the beam crashed into the spot where she'd been crawling.

"Thank you—" she started to say, breathing hard as she turned to face her rescuer, then she broke off. "Sam! How did you get here?" And then she hugged him tightly. He hugged back. They held each other for a long moment, and then she kissed him on the cheek.

"Let's get out of here before that house goes," he said.

"Wait!" she said, and she stumbled a few paces and picked up her scuffed-up notepad. As Sam led her away, more of the roof broke off, and then the whole structure collapsed with a loud roar. Constables and rightcakes scrambled back toward the street as the building fell apart, though small groups of rightcakes and constables continued their altercation. There was no sign of the man on the porch amid the rubble. Sam and Katera hadn't progressed far in the sea of humanity when they ran into Renala.

After the two cousins greeted each other, Renala said to Sam, "I saw you pull her up."

"He saved me from serious injury, or worse," Katera said.

Many of the constables and officials and even rightcakes had retreated to the next house down the street. As the three of them walked past, it began creaking, then cracking, and then parts of boards and pieces of stone tumbled to the ground. A cheer rose from the crowd.

"Try to steal that house now!" someone yelled at the officials.

"You won't steal our freedom!" someone else shouted.

"We'll defend our property and our children from Unifiers and Outbounders!" yelled another. "We know our rights!"

"They do cherish their right to die," said Katera.

"And to take others with them," said Renala. "Including their own children."

When they reached the others, Katera told them she and other Rally Round observers had been working in areas due north, but the damage was so widespread there, they'd had to withdraw.

"I need to ask you about what you've seen, Katera," said Stefar. "We haven't had lunch. Join us?" He glanced back toward the main street, still undamaged. "There must be a tavern around here, away from the damage."

Katera shook her head. "It's spreading too fast. This whole area is unstable. We'll have to go south to be sure we're safe."

"It's that bad?"

"I'm afraid so. It's getting worse."

Back across the main road, a man with a notepad stood talking with a man on the stoop of a house. The man with the notepad looked vaguely familiar to Sam.

"Who's that guy?" asked Eddie, pointing. "I think I've seen him before."

"Axo Saltar," said Katera.

"The *Weasel* reporter?" said Kandar.

"Getting close to the action, I see," said Renala.

Katera laughed. "And he'll file a report from the heart of the action, according to him."

After fifteen minutes in the hauler returning the way they had come, they came to a crossroads with a few buildings, including a dingy tavern. For a hole in the wall, the food was surprisingly tasty, as was the ale.

Stefar questioned Katera about where she'd been exactly and how fast the damage was spreading. Then he said, "I didn't see any sinkholes. I'm concerned about the toxic gas we've heard about. Maybe it hasn't spread far?"

"I'm sorry, Stefar," said Katera. "There was a major eruption not far north of here. It spread rapidly, caught a number of towns unawares. EmRes got many people out, but the death toll is high. The number of people in houses of healing is even higher. Many of those are very sick."

"Does it just keep spreading, or does it dissipate eventually?" asked Renala.

"It thins out. But it can spread quite a distance from its initial point. That cloud won't reach this far, I don't think. But who knows what combination of factors causes the gas? Where it just erupted was a long way from the mines. And sinkholes have been spotted this far south."

"Does anyone know what this gas does to crops?" said Stefar.

"Our technists who've managed to visit stricken areas after several days report withered foliage. And grapes. . . ."

"Would wither too," said Stefar grimly. He looked at Kandar and Renala. "We'll have to transplant the vines and hope the grapes can withstand it. We don't have much time. And we're facing disaster."

When they dropped Katera off in Karament, the crowds had moved across the main road to the other side of the street, where Stefar had originally parked. The action was now down this street. Where several houses had stood near the main road, there was a large gap. The house where Axo Saltar had conducted his interview was gone. Damage had reached the middle of town, and as they drove east they passed more scree at the bottom of hills and cracks in hillsides, but the road remained passable. Eventually they turned south on another road. Finally, they passed into country where the damage was no longer visible. The hills became higher and the slopes steeper, separated by valleys often with rivers or streams flowing at the bottom, with towns scattered along the valleys. Sometimes buildings sprawled on hillsides or ran along hilltops. The slopes were wooded between towns, firs and spruces.

In early evening, they reached the outskirts of Barella. The architecture was different from any they'd seen in Melenca. The roofs were steeply pitched, like those of chalets Sam had seen in the Alps. A river ran swiftly through the town center, which rose from the valley floor on both sides of the river. Stefar and Lirea had a house perched on the hilltop with a good view of the river and the lower town, a two-story stone A-frame house. As they tried to relax over drinks and hors d'oeuvres in the large living room, tall windows gave them a fine view of the slopes, the valley, and the river as the sun set over the hills. Lights twinkled in the gathering gloom in houses down the hillside and in the town below.

There was no Percela here, but Kandar enjoyed doing much of the cooking in his own household, and he busied himself in the kitchen. He proved to be an adept chef. One wall of the dining room was mostly glass and gave them another lovely view of the hillside down to the river and the hillside across the river, with lights glimmering in houses on the opposite side.

The next morning over breakfast, Stefar perused a digest. "Listen to this from the *Current*. Flammer's latest bulletin-board posting praises 'the BRAVE and LOYAL ordinary Melencan citizens who took the initiative to DEFEND our way of life from those at the DynaStream facility who are LEADING THE ASSAULT on crystals.'"

"Those brave and loyal Melencans may not be so happy they took the initiative today when they're being charged in the magistrates' chamber," said Renala.

"He's going to get rightcakes even more riled up," said Kandar.

"That's his idea of governing," said Stefar. "Divide everyone. Create enmity. But if he thinks he's going to stop Ravinn and the others in this way, he's going to be disabused of that notion."

"Have you read the *Vantage* yet?" said Renala. "Compactors have introduced an act in the Grand Council to prohibit manufacture of several components of the alternative engines."

"Ravinn's advocates—and Beldan's—will fight it in the magistrates' chambers. They'll likely prevail. But what else will they do to stop the alternative vehicles? Melenca doesn't have the time for this."

On their way to the Dorwin vineyard, where Sam and Eddie would set off on skimmers, the hauler stopped at a local administrative office. A tall, thin man stood behind a large desk near the wall opposite the door, talking with a short, stout, balding man in front of the desk, holding a digest. They paused and looked at the group.

"I'll be with you in just a minute, Stefar," said the thin man,

"Fine, Jerdel," said Stefar. He nodded at the stout man. "Councilor Polgo."

"Barella's representative in the Grand Council," said Kandar in a low voice.

Jerdel and Polgo resumed their conversation. They spoke for another two or three minutes, and then Jerdel looked at Stefar expectantly. Polgo looked at him too, but showed no inclination to leave.

Stefar asked if the town was coordinating a disaster response.

"Like what's supposedly happening up near the mines, you mean?"

Before Stefar could reply, Polgo said, "There's nothing to worry about. These rumors about damage are just wild exaggerations."

"We've seen the damage ourselves," said Stefar. "We've just come from Karament—the damage has spread there now, a long way from the mines—and it's headed here."

"Whatever you saw was local—nothing of the sort is happening to the mines. We've had reports in the Council—these are just rumors spread by Unifiers for political advantage."

Stefar kept his cool, Sam thought, though Renala's face turned red. "With all due respect, Councilor," said Stefar, "what has happened in Karament is major damage—quakes, rockslides, sinkholes. We saw it."

Polgo waved the digest in his hand. "Here's an article in today's *Weasel* investigating the tales of damage in Karament. It's by Axo Saltar, a renowned reporter. He says there was no visible damage, and he quotes a homeowner who says the local administrators are trying to seize his property—that's another Unifier motivation behind propagating these rumors."

"We saw Saltar. The damage was up the street across from where he stood—though it reached the part of the street he was after he left."

"As I said, it was very localized—likely damage to one street."

Stefar started to respond, then stopped and looked at Jerdel. "I don't want to argue with you, Councilor. I'm just telling you what we saw."

"And I'm telling you, nothing to worry about."

Stefar didn't say anything more, and there was an awkward silence for a moment, then Jerdel thanked Polgo and said he would get back to him. Polgo nodded and ambled to the door, *Weasel* still in hand.

"The pompous ass," said Renala, "lecturing us about what we had or hadn't seen."

"Renala!" said Stefar sharply.

"He's a Compactor, I take it," said Sam.

"How could you tell?" said Renala.

"Regardless of what he believes," said Stefar, "the threat is real, headed this way. You need to act, and warn concern owners. Their livelihoods are threatened."

"People here haven't worried about it, whatever's been happening. It's been far away," said Jerdel. "But I guess if you've seen something, and it's as bad as you say . . . well, I'll speak to some—discreetly."

Beyond the town, vines full of grapes spread down the hillsides toward the river and along the hilltops in every direction—Dorwin wasn't the only concern with vineyards in the area. The Dorwin complex consisted of several large buildings grouped around a central courtyard. Sam and Eddie soon rolled out the skimmers and set off. It was a sunny day under a cloudless blue sky, pleasantly warm. After a few minutes' leisurely drive on the winding road along the hillside, they rounded a bend and the whole valley spread out below them, a spectacular view. Sam stopped on the roadside, as did Eddie.

"I'd love to see all of this from my plane," said Eddie. "What a view just from ground level." He looked around for a moment. "But when the sinkholes and all that reach here. . . ."

"Stefar can build new facilities somewhere else, but it will take time to transplant all his vines. And that seems chancy."

Eddie nodded. "They can't outrun the damage forever."

"Neither can we. I don't think we have a lot of time."

"Oh, I bet you wouldn't mind spending more time here. Renala told us about the reunion between you and Katera yesterday."

"I saved her from a falling beam, Eddie. She was grateful—as anyone would be."

"You were pretty grateful back, I heard."

"There's nothing between us."

"Just trying to be helpful, Captain. I don't know what sort of measures they use in Melenca to ward off surprises, but you don't want to leave any little half-Earthlings running around here. I don't even want to think about trying to coordinate child support across dimensions."

"Very funny." Eddie seemed to think so, and laughed. Sam didn't want to talk about his feelings for Katera. He didn't want to think about them either. Or how they complicated his feelings for Allie. "Let's go. We need to find Guy Robinson."

They drove on and reached Carcella in forty minutes. "OK, we're here," said Eddie. "What do we now, Captain? All we have is a name."

"The local administration. Maybe they have a directory of residents."

"And they'll just lay out the welcome mat for strangers asking questions?"

"All right, what do you suggest?"

"I'm just following along, Captain. This is your mission."

In the administration building they asked in several offices with uninterested workers before they were directed to a room with a sign reading "Levies." The lone man inside grunted and said nothing when they told him what they needed, but he pulled out a large, thick book and skimmed through it, moving his finger down the pages. Finally he looked up.

"Nothing here. If he lives here, he's not being assessed the levy."

"Is there another way to find someone here?" asked Sam.

The man thought for a moment, then told them to wait. He disappeared down the hall. A few minutes later he returned with an older man.

"Guy Robinson, eh?" said the older man. "I remember him. Prickly chap, could be. He lives out on the Longwood Crescent—or used to. I hadn't heard that he'd died or moved. But if he's not on the levy roll. . . ."

"Do you remember an address?" said Sam.

"Sorry. It was near the big grain storage bin, as I recall. You might ask around there."

They followed his directions to the Longwood Crescent and soon spotted a large cube looming in the distance. Set back from the road, it was the only commercial-looking building, flanked by houses on either side. They halted just past it. As they pondered their next step, a woman came out of a nearby house. Sam called out to her about Guy Robinson.

She pointed to one of the houses. "He did live over there."

"What happened to him?" asked Sam.

"He got old. Even more cantankerous. And not all there. Eventually he had to move into the Elder House."

"Where's that?"

She gave them directions.

Ten minutes later they stood in the lobby of a two-story building. A middle-aged woman behind it affirmed that Guy Robinson was a resident.

"Are you relatives?"

"Friends, sort of," said Sam. Eddie smirked.

She told them his room number. "He's lucid occasionally, for short spells. Usually he's not."

The old man's room was small, with a bed, a dresser, and a small armchair. He was sitting in it, staring out the window. He looked up at them blankly.

"Mr. Robinson," said Sam, "we're Outbounders, like you."

"Outbounders?"

"From Earth. Americans." A faint glint of recognition appeared in his eyes. "Tim Wooden sent us. He said you found out from Mentor Perroso about a portal to return to Earth—where it is, and when it appears."

"Portal?" he said dully.

"The whirlwind? To go back to Earth."

"Whirlwind?"

"You must remember!" Sam realized he had raised his voice. He tried to calm down. "Were you in the Bermuda Triangle? Was there a whirlwind that swept you up? Landed you in Melenca?"

Suddenly Robinson's eyes grew bright. "I wanted to go home. I talked to Perroso—followed his directions, found the place, and it wasn't there!"

"Where? The place, where is it?"

"In the Hazy Mountains."

"Where in the mountains? Near Remora?"

"North of there."

"How far?"

Just as suddenly the light in the old man's eyes went out. "Where is my lunch? Are you to bring it?"

"Where is the place where the portal appears, Mr. Robinson? How far from Remora?"

"Portal?" He looked out the window, then around the room. "Are there games this afternoon?"

"Please, it's important—try to remember. You came to Melenca in the whirlwind. You talked to Perroso and tried to find the portal. Where is it?"

The old man looked around the room again. "Are you here about the levy? I paid my share. I don't owe anything."

"Does it take you back to Earth? Did Perroso tell you?"

Robinson stared uncomprehendingly.

"Is there a portal?" asked Sam, growing desperate. "How often does the whirlwind appear?"

Robinson remained mute, staring at him.

Sam tried a few more questions but the light never came back on in Robinson's eyes.

Finally, dejected, Sam gave up, and he and Eddie left.

"Well, that was a howling success," said Eddie. "What now?"

Sam took a moment to answer. "Go to the other Outbounder's town. Then leave for Remora."

17

— • —

AN UNEXPECTED DETOUR

She should at least look in on Peter, Winnie thought. Lirea said she had an errand to run not far from the house of healing and would lead her there. She asked Winnie if she could drive a skimmer.

"Sort of," said Winnie, looking doubtfully at the vehicle she was being asked to mount.

"I'm sure you'll get the hang of it. Just follow me—I'll go slowly at first."

Winnie didn't like the sound of "at first," but she got onto the skimmer and unsteadily started off after Lirea, swaying back and forth. She was determined not to repeat her earlier performance, and she concentrated as hard as she could on steering it straight. After a few minutes, the driving did become easier. Downtown, Lirea stopped next to a large four-story building with many windows close together, more than the typical Melencan building. Inside the large lobby, a counter ran along a side wall and a broad staircase in a corner led up. A few chairs were scattered about. Lirea gave Peter's name to the woman behind the counter. His room was on the third floor.

The door was open. Bright sunshine flooded the room through three large windows. In a bed in the middle, its headboard against one wall, Peter sat with a pillow propped up behind him. He had a bandage across his forehead that wrapped around the back of his head. In a chair next to the bed sat Allie. She looked up and smiled.

"You don't look too bad off, Peter," said Winnie. "Why the hell are you still lounging around here?"

He laughed. "In fact, they are going to let me go today. I do feel better. I was apparently quite groggy when they brought me in." He pointed with his elbow toward Allie. "My nurse here has been conscientious about coming to see me."

"I wouldn't want to wake up in a strange place without anyone I knew there, or any clue about where I was," she said.

"It is true that I don't remember much after I got hit in that riot."

"It sounded pretty rough there, from what we heard from the others," said Winnie. They were interrupted by an early-middle-aged woman in a white robe who entered the room.

"Here's my doctor!" said Peter.

Lirea asked the healer when Peter was likely to be released, and she replied that it should be within a couple of hours. Lirea told Peter they'd return in a hauler, and she and Winnie left.

They had just reached the lobby when a loud voice boomed, "Friend? I'm not their friend, I'm their employer. Not that it's any business of yours." Ravinn stood at the counter, staring haughtily at the woman there. Winnie went to the counter, Lirea following.

"Ravinn! I didn't expect to see you here," said Winnie.

"Comforting my men stricken in the fray, my dear Earthling. And you?"

"Peter, also injured in the assault."

"Come over here with me." He steered them to a set of chairs near the back wall. "I have some information for you, if you can call it that. I followed your young friend's advice and talked to Arban Melroc. He was reluctant, but I wheedled out of him that the Illusionist's circle doesn't know where Margan has squirreled away the mentor—if he has."

"*If?*"

"Margan, it appears, is being coy. No surprise—he has only disdain for Flammer, he just uses him. He's not saying whether he knows where Perroso is. In other words, not revealing if he orchestrated the abduction or if rightcakes did it on their own."

"If rightcakes did take him," said Lirea, "wouldn't they boast about it and what they've done to him?"

"They don't have the sense to remain circumspect. So presumably you are correct, dear lady—Lirea, is it not? But it's not certain."

"So the upshot is we don't know any more than we did," said Winnie.

"Not appreciably. But my money's on Margan having him hidden somewhere. I'll continue to press for where. Such things do not always remain secret."

When they left the building, Lirea and Winnie drove down a side street to a building where Lirea conducted her business. Then they continued on that street and had slowed around a curve past a small park when Winnie noticed a group of people in the center of the park. They stood around a statue.

"What's going on?" she called to Lirea.

"Technians holding their service."

"I've heard about them. What exactly are they doing?"

Lirea stopped and pointed to the statue. "Do you see what that is?"

Winnie looked at the statue intently. It was of a man, who held some sort of rock in one hand and a magnifying glass in the other. "I just see a man with a rock. And a magnifying glass."

"The rock is a crystal, and the man is a technist studying the crystal to read its secrets. It's an idol, representing Great Techne. We can go closer if you want to hear what they're saying."

"It's OK for us to listen?"

"They'll be immersed in their service. They won't notice us." They moved almost to the edge of the crowd. As more people filed in, they bowed to the statue before joining the others in a semicircle around it. Then a man left the crowd and faced them from in front of the statue. He held up his hand and the hubbub of conversation diminished.

"There is no Essence," he called out. "There is only man and nature, and Great Techne is the master of nature."

"Praise to Great Techne!" responded the crowd.

"Great Techne enables us to unravel the secrets of nature and master the land around us."

"Praise to Great Techne!"

"Great Techne will lead us to greater and greater advances, to a more idyllic future."

"Praise to Great Techne!"

"There is no Essence. Afterward there is only the void."

"Hail to the void!"

Lirea shook her head. "They think themselves courageous because they believe there is nothing after this physical existence. That seems to me a way to be miserable, ultimately. And they think that is fact. They don't recognize that it's a belief."

"You're a Wayfarer, I would guess," said Winnie. Lirea nodded. Winnie was agnostic. She didn't spend much time thinking about philosophic or religious matters except insofar as they impinged on politics, which she had frequently covered. Now the crowd began chanting words that Winnie couldn't make out. "What are they saying?"

"Those are technical terms. They're part of the formulas they use, to understand how crystals work together and such processes."

"Do you understand what they're saying?"

"I didn't study techne much. Most ordinary people who haven't made intensive study of it don't really understand the formulas. In my view, Technians like it that way—they like for people to hold them in awe."

After listening for another minute, Winnie said, "That's enough—I get the flavor of it."

By lunchtime, they had retrieved Peter and Allie from the house of healing and were back at Lirea's. As they finished lunch, an idea was forming in Winnie's mind. She asked Lirea where Rafe was being held, and told them she was going to visit him. Winnie set off again on the skimmer and found the detention building without any trouble. A guard in the anteroom looked up in surprise; apparently, visitors to those being held awaiting a hearing were few.

"I'm here to visit Rafe Thomas," Winnie told him. "I'm his mother."

The guard fished a set of keys off a hook on the wall and led her to a room. Winnie took note of which key he used to unlock the door. He opened it and announced, "You have a visitor—your mother."

"My mother?" exclaimed Rafe. "She's not—"

"Rafey!" said Winnie loudly. "Are they treating you badly?"

"We don't mistreat people," said the guard huffily. "Call me when you're finished." And he walked back toward the anteroom.

"What the hell are you doing?" said Rafe.

"What does it look like I'm doing, dumb-ass? Working on getting you out of this joint. Now shut up and listen." She told him her plan. He was dubious. "If you want to get out of here, just do as I say. Or would you rather we leave Mencara without you? Then you can seek out ideas for your Melencan startup to your heart's content—you'll have plenty of time."

"All right, but I doubt it will work."

Winnie called for the guard. When he unlocked the door, she said, "I'll see you again soon, son."

Back at Lirea's, Winnie explained her plan to Allie, and Allie's role in it, which Allie agreed to. Then she asked Lirea to show her how to disconnect the main crystal box on a skimmer, telling her only that it was important. Lirea hesitated, clearly suspicious, but finally showed her what to do. Winnie borrowed the tool Lirea had used. Allie and Winnie went next to a clothing store, where Allie bought a blouse that was tighter on her than the ones Dalbin had purchased and a skirt that was shorter than her other skirts.

"Are you sure this is going to work?" said Allie. "What if he doesn't find a brown-eye attractive?"

"They're tolerant in Mencara, remember? It'll work."

They rode to the detention building. Winnie parked her skimmer around the nearest corner, out of sight of the building. Allie parked hers across the street and down several buildings from the detention building. Winnie disconnected the box. She took a deep breath. "All right, let's go."

She entered the anteroom and told the guard she was there to visit her son again. At that moment, Allie came in. The guard looked her over appraisingly.

"Could you possibly help me, sir?" said Allie. "My skimmer stalled out right in front and I can't get it to start again. I'm sorry to put you to trouble."

"Certainly, miss, I'll take a look, glad to help." He glanced at Winnie. "Wait here. I'll let you in to your son's room when I return." He and Allie left.

Quickly Winnie retrieved the keys and hurried to Rafe's room. He looked up in surprise when she appeared in the doorway. "Let's go," she said in a low voice. Rafe didn't hesitate. Once Winnie replaced the keys, she cracked the main door open and glanced out. The guard was bent over the back of Allie's skimmer. Winnie and Rafe ducked low along the side of the building and raced to the corner. Turning, they scrambled to Winnie's skimmer and mounted, Rafe holding onto Winnie's waist. In ten minutes they were back at Lirea's house.

Lirea stared at Rafe in surprise, then sighed. "So that's what all this intrigue was about. What happened to Allie?"

Winnie told her she should be back soon—she hoped. Indeed, Allie showed up ten minutes later, laughing.

"You were right," she told Winnie. "It worked like a charm."

"I knew it would with you as Delilah."

"That guard saw what the problem was, went to get a tool, and reconnected it. I hurried off before he could find out about his missing inmate."

"I hope we don't get you in trouble," said Winnie to Lirea.

Lirea thought for a moment. "No one knows where Rafe was staying, or you two. If anyone should come here looking, we'll deal with it somehow. But the three of you need to stay in here for now."

When Sam and Eddie arrived in Barella, Stefar and the others had just returned to the house from the vineyard. As they ate a hasty lunch, Stefar looked through the *Current*. After a moment, he frowned. "How predictable. The Unifiers in the Grand Council introduced a motion to censure Flammer for motivating the rightcakes to assault the DynaStream facility. The Compactors in the Council voted it down. They said he was just speaking in general terms about the importance of preserving traditions, not encouraging anyone to attack a specific facility violently."

"That's ridiculous," said Renala. "That's not what he said in his posting—he specifically told his followers to show up in force."

"What someone has actually said or done has not been much of a concern to Compactors lately. It's what they can make people believe."

"And as we've seen, rightcakes will swallow just about anything," said Kandar.

Sam told them he and Eddie had learned very little and needed to return to Mencara. Stefar said Renala was going there in the morning and if they could wait they could ride with her, which suited them.

After breakfast, Sam, Eddie, and Renala headed for Mencara. They had to detour for a short while in one place, but otherwise encountered no problems. They reached Lirea's house in late afternoon. In the living room, Sam was surprised, and relieved, to see Peter sitting up in a chair. Beldan and Dalbin sat nearby. Then he saw Allie, and he felt a jolt of affection and attraction. Her face lit up. *Does she feel the same?* he thought. *I'd say so.*

"Any luck?" said Winnie.

"Not much," said Sam. "A little."

"What the hell does that mean? Did you find Guy Robinson or not?"

He told them the little they had gleaned from Robinson in his brief lucid spell and that they could not get any more information from him. Since Perroso had told Robinson where to find the portal, Sam suggested they talk to Perroso's associates in Remora, and see if any knew of a place north of Remora Perroso went to, probably by himself, or spoke of. Sam added that it was likely remote.

"You're saying we just give up on tracking down the other Outbounder?" said Winnie.

"I didn't say that. A couple of people can look for him—or his traces. The rest can head toward Remora. We can rendezvous somewhere."

"I'll look for someone who knew Dan Caruso," said Allie.

"So will I. It was my idea, after all."

"So it's just you two?" said Eddie. "That's a nice setup."

"You've had all the fun so far, Eddie," replied Allie. "Time to let someone else have a turn."

"Not to mention," said Winnie, "if you want something done right, send a woman."

Dinner was another of Percela's culinary triumphs. Afterward, they gathered in the living room. Lirea spread out a large, detailed map on a table and pointed to a line. "Take the East Highway to Remora," she said. "Once in the mountains, you'll strike the Mountain Trail at Lingora. Take that back to the north, and it will lead you to Remora." She looked at Sam, then Allie. "You two can branch off here to go south to Bancara." She pointed to a spot. Sam studied the map.

"This place," he said, pointing to a dot. "The rest of you can wait here in Kedera for Allie and me—not long, I hope."

"No hurry," said Winnie. "I've always wanted to spend time in Kedera."

Lirea laughed. "You may change your tune when you see it."

Beldan said he and Dalbin were needed at DynaStream, so the voyagers would be on their own. "Try not to call attention to yourselves. Rightcakes, the MNAA—they're actively hunting Outbounders."

Lirea told them she and Stefar could "lend" them skimmers, though she made it clear if they succeeded in their quest, she knew they might not return them.

"The quakes and so on—they haven't reached the mountains yet?" said Winnie.

"Not that we know of," replied Beldan. "But you could run into blasting from the new mines."

"Dalbin mentioned that."

"No one's ever found crystals in the Hazy Mountains before, but some technists have speculated that there are crystals there under layers of rocks, deeper than in the mines in the Cleft. The concern excavating the new mines is blasting rock out. They've reported no problems so far, but. . . ."

"The blasts could trigger rockslides," said Dalbin. "Just be aware of that."

Over breakfast, Beldan held up a copy of the *Current*. "The move to censure Flimsel Flammer may not have worked, but it had an effect. He's gone from praising the rioters to blaming the imaginary enemies he invented."

"Meaning Outbounders?" said Dalbin.

"In his latest bulletin-board posting, he says the rioters weren't his followers. It was the Outbounders."

"I wonder how many Melencans have ever even seen an Outbounder," said Lirea.

"That's what makes them such a handy villain," said Beldan.

"Still, you don't look any different from ordinary Melencans," she said to them. "You have one brown-eye among you, but everyone's used to seeing brown-eyes. No one can jump to the conclusion that you're Outbounders just from your appearance."

"As I urged you before, don't get into lengthy discussions with Melencans," said Beldan. "Many people won't care that you're Outbounders. But people are jumpy these days. Others are all too willing to blame outsiders for any trouble—Newcomers, say—so blaming a new group finds receptive ground."

"What if someone asks us point-blank if we're Outbounders?" said Allie.

"You must follow your instinct—whether to admit that you are or just lie. It depends on the context. Many Melencans aren't susceptible to this kind of fear-mongering."

"And hate-mongering," said Lirea.

After breakfast they gathered with their duffels in the front foyer. Eddie carried the map Beldan had given them. Lirea gave Allie a smaller copy of the big map she'd shown them. She supplied each with a packed lunch. Knowing Eddie had seen how skimmer engines worked at Ravinn's, Dalbin suggested he be given a small bag of tools in case they needed repairs at some point, which Renala fetched for him.

Their farewells were emotional, particularly with Beldan and with Dalbin, who had escorted them around Melenca since they'd arrived, but also with Lirea and Renala. Then they mounted the skimmers.

As they drove off, Winnie said, "Not exactly Hell's Angels, but maybe we can intimidate some rightcakes." They followed the main road south out of Mencara, through woodlands and farm fields and occasionally a town. Once they reached the East Highway, they saw the Rushing River glinting not far off to the south. The current flowed notice-ably, though it wasn't what Sam would call rushing here. They stopped for lunch at the crest of a hill, where a scenic vista spread out below them, the river flowing amid green hills and woodlands and the hillocks tumbling down to farmland. Beyond the fields, the houses of a village appeared in the distance.

There was nowhere to sit but on the grass, but it was dry and not too high and the sun was warm as they ate. They lingered afterward, stretched on the soft turf, basking in the sun, conversing lazily. Sam felt himself falling into a semi-trance-like state halfway between sleep and wakefulness.

Suddenly he jolted himself out of his torpor. *We need to be on our way. Just because we haven't hit any obstacles so far doesn't mean we won't—including human ones.* He picked himself up and brushed the grass off. Reluctantly, the others rose as well, and they set off again.

When they reached the crossroads Lirea had pointed out, they stopped in front of a store.

"Well, this is good-bye—for now," said Sam.

"Yes, we'll see you in Kedera," said Winnie. "Make sure you're there—be careful."

"You don't have me to bail you out of trouble this time, Captain," added Eddie.

"He has me," said Allie.

"No offense, Eddie, but that's better," said Sam. He glanced at Allie. She looked back steadily. *What does that look mean?* He wasn't sure. Then the rest of them proceeded down the same road. Sam and Allie took the road south. By his calculation from the map, they should reach Bancara before dark. As long as no traffic was coming, they rode side by side.

They had driven for a while without encountering much traffic when an engine throbbed behind them. Sam glanced back. A red hauler caught up with them and passed. As it did, a man peered at them. The hauler had the MNAA logo on the side. It kept going and was soon out of sight.

"MNAA?" said Allie. He nodded. "Patrolling?"

"Most likely," he said. "Maybe we don't look too suspicious, but still, it makes me uneasy."

Not long afterward, at an intersection in a village, the road was blocked by a wooden barricade. They halted next to a storefront where a young woman and a middle-aged man stood.

"What's going on?" said Sam.

"The land's split beyond—there's a chasm," said the woman. "We've been warning people around here about what the technists have been saying, and they wouldn't listen—especially the older people. Even when it's been happening elsewhere."

"Yeah, they still just thought nothing would happen here," said the man. "Well, it has."

"How do we get to Bancara, then?" asked Sam.

The man pointed down the side street to the right and gave directions for a detour.

A mile outside the village the street merged into a wider road. They hadn't driven on the road long when suddenly Allie yelled as her skimmer jerked sideways, bounced, and skidded, throwing Allie into the grass beside the road.

"Allie!" shouted Sam as he dismounted. "Are you OK?" He reached her as she got to her feet.

"A little bruised," she said in a shaky voice. "I hit a crack in the road." He looked back. Some feet behind them, a split extended from halfway on their side of the road back across into the grass on the other side, widening away from them. He hadn't seen it but his skimmer had avoided it. He picked up her skimmer. The rear wheels were bent inward. The axle was bent as well.

"You're not going any farther on this skimmer," he said. "You'll have to ride with me."

She looked at his machine. "Can we both fit?"

"It'll be tight. We don't have any choice. Pile your duffel on, then hang on."

Her duffel looked secure enough on top of his. She put her hands around his waist. At her touch, a tingle coursed through him. They set off again. In half an hour they reached the town where they regained the Bancara Road.

"With the detour, we're not going to make Bancara by nightfall," said Sam as the sun set. "We'll have to stop somewhere."

"Look for an inn next town we come to."

Twenty minutes later they reached the outskirts of a town. They reached its center without spotting an inn. Soon it would be too dark to drive in unfamiliar country where the road might crack, even with the light on the skimmer.

As they approached an intersection, Allie said, "There's a tavern. We can ask about an inn in this area. Besides, I'm hungry."

Inside the tavern, people sat at tables, some eating, some just drinking ale, but there were empty tables as well, and Sam and Allie chose the one most distant from other customers. A waiter soon came over, a portly, balding man. Allie asked for a Dorwin white wine.

The waiter laughed. "Nothing that fancy here. But we have decent wine. Would a glass of the house white suit the lady?"

"Anything wet will at this point. We've been traveling."

"Speaking of traveling," said Sam, "is there a decent inn nearby?"

"Not just an inn, but a decent one—you're adding qualifiers. That makes it harder." He winked. "But you're in luck. The Floating Leaf is a fine establishment. It's on the edge of town, on the Bancara Road. Shouldn't take you more than ten minutes."

When he returned with the drinks, he recited the menu offerings—only a handful of dishes.

"What do you recommend?" asked Allie.

"Everything on the menu—they're all good."

"You seem proud of the establishment's fares."

"I should be—I run the place." He winked again. "So you know it's first class."

Over dinner, they talked at first about how they would go about looking for Dan Caruso once they reached Bancara. After his experience looking for Guy Robinson, Sam suggested they go to the town administration once again.

Then, as the conversation hit a lull, Sam thought, *I need to get this out in the open.* "These are strange circumstances we're in, Allie—not just strange, bizarre. I can't exactly ask you to go out to dinner like I could if we were on Earth."

"We're at dinner."

"Well, true. For an unusual reason. But in any case, I enjoy being with you. What I'm trying to say, Allie, is that I really like you, a lot. In spite of everything, being stranded in a place we can hardly believe, the anxiety, the uncertainty, meeting you was one really good thing to come out of it."

"I'm glad there was something good to come out of this mess." She paused, as if to gather her thoughts.

That's noncommittal.

Then she said, "I really like you too, Sam." She took a sip of wine. "Let's enjoy this while we can, in the midst of all this turmoil. Then, later . . . we'll see how things develop."

That's promising, anyway. There was an awkward silence. After a moment, he said, "So let's find this inn, then leave early tomorrow and search for Caruso. Let's hope we can find something out, one way or the other, in a day, then head for Kedera."

When they were back on the skimmer, within a few minutes an inn loomed ahead on the right, with a large sign reading "The Floating Leaf." From the outside, the inn looked well maintained, and so did the wood-paneled, well-lit lobby. The man behind the reception counter looked up as they approached.

"Good evening," said Sam. "Do you have any rooms available?"

"Certainly. One room? Or two?"

Sam hesitated. Allie said, "Just one room, please."

18

— • —

MISSING IN ACTION

At first, Winnie and the others encountered nothing out of the ordinary. The scenery was pleasant, the ride bracing. Then, ahead in the distance, a wooden barricade blocked the road just after the intersection with a cross road. People stacked wooden beams along the cross road in both directions. Several men stood at the barricade. When the voyagers approached the barricade, one man held up his hand.

"The road is closed ahead," he said. That seemed unnecessary advice.

"Why?" asked Eddie.

"The river has flooded."

The road beyond the barricade ran on as before. Other people laid beams alongside the river on both sides. Winnie squinted, looking into the distance ahead, and discerned a faint shimmering, stretching out from both sides of the river.

"Quakes, like in the north?" she asked.

"It's not quakes," said the man. "It's the new mines they're digging in the Hazy Mountains. They're piling the debris into barges on the Rushing River and sending them down this way, then dumping the debris in the river. We've warned them about the risk in doing so—both the authorities in towns around here and local merchants—but they've ignored us."

"The concern excavating the mines is owned by Flimsel Flammer," said another man. "They got the contract for the mines—what a surprise. And one of Flammer's sons is managing the whole enterprise. So incompetence is no big shock."

"All right, let's worry about the flooding, not politics right now," said the first man to the second. He turned back to Winnie and the others. "Anyway, a sandbar runs across most of the river up ahead a ways, and the debris has caught on it and finally collected enough to dam the river. This is the last crossroad before the flooding. You'll have to detour."

Eddie asked if they could reach the East Highway again above the flooding, and the man said that he'd heard that the road was passable as it neared the Hazy Mountains. Winnie asked about Kedera, and the man replied that reports they'd received indicated it was right on the edge of the flooding, so they might reach it—but he couldn't promise.

The voyagers pulled their skimmers over to the side of the crossroad headed south. A sign said "Delfera Road." Eddie pulled out the map and glanced at it.

"This road goes south, then it veers some to the east," he said. "When we reach Delfera, we'll be due west of Kedera. At Delfera, we should run into a road headed east to Kedera."

"What if he's wrong and Kedera isn't accessible?" said Peter.

"Then we keep going south at that point until we know for sure we can head east again. Unless you've got a better idea, Professor." No one did. They set off on the Delfera Road and within a few minutes reached the river. The bridge spanning it seemed sturdy enough, and they crossed it.

Eventually they came to Delfera. As they looked for the intersection with the Kedera road, they passed a red hauler parked outside a building on the left with a large sign above its front double-door entrance reading "Constabulary." On the side of the hauler was a logo: two squares connected by a line. Eddie glanced at the hauler. A few blocks later he turned right onto a side street and halted. The others coasted to a stop behind him.

"Why stop here?" asked Winnie.

"Did you see that hauler?" said Eddie.

"So?"

"It's the MNAA. I'm just wondering why they're around here."

"Do you think they're looking for Outbounders?" said Peter.

"I'd have said Newcomers, but with Flammer's comments targeting us, I'm not so sure. I'd like to know what they're doing in the area."

"From what I understand, this is not where you'd expect to find Newcomers sneaking in," said Winnie.

"There's a tavern over across the street," said Peter. "That's a good place to pick up gossip."

"It's also a good place to get picked up, if there are MNAA agents inside," said Eddie.

"Or zealous rightcakes who fancy themselves self-deputized," said Winnie. "We might overhear something, then again we might not." She pointed to an opposite corner. "There's a newsstand. If I go over there to buy a digest and mention something in the news, I should be able to refer to the hauler without raising suspicion."

"That's risky," said Eddie. "You might reveal how much you don't know."

"I'll stick to innocuous topics in the news—maybe things we've seen."

"Not too general, though," said Rafe. "We have to find out if Outbounders are on their radar."

"Believe it or not, Rafe, I know what I'm doing. I'll wing it, depending on what direction the conversation takes." She started off.

"I'm going to see what happens," said Rafe, following her.

"I'd better keep an eye on him," Eddie told Peter. "And a lookout for MNAA agents, as well."

At the stand, Winnie perused the front pages of several digests. The proprietor stood across from her behind the counter, talking to another customer to her side. Rafe came up and stood on her other side, glancing at some of the digests. Soon Winnie picked up one of the digests and then struck up a conversation with the proprietor about some of the events in the news. The other customer listened. So did Rafe. Eddie walked past the stand to the shop next to it and looked into the window.

After a moment, Winnie said, "I see there's an MNAA hauler down the street. Aren't they a little far afield? I wouldn't expect to find Newcomers around here."

"You'd be surprised," said the proprietor. "Some take a roundabout route through the mountains—trying to avoid the MNAA patrols. So they do patrol around here."

"Let's hope they're not looking for Outbounders," chimed in Rafe.

The proprietor and the other customer stared at Rafe. "Why do you think they'd be looking for them around here?" said the proprietor.

Rafe hesitated. "No reason in particular."

"Do you know they've been active around here?"

"No, no—there's just been a lot of talk about them, that's all."

Winnie looked for a chance to jump in and turn the conversation, but before she could say anything, the proprietor said to Rafe, "You're not from around here."

"No, I'm not."

"Where are you from?"

"The other side of Melenca—the far west."

"Which part? What district?"

"It's not a crime to come from another part of Melenca," said Rafe, and he turned and walked off. The proprietor and the other man looked at each other. Winnie paid for the digest and left. Eddie waited a moment, then turned and continued down the street. A few stores down he crossed the street and walked back to the skimmers. Across the street, the other customer at the newsstand strode down the street toward where the hauler was parked.

When Winnie reached the skimmers, she snapped at Rafe, "What the fuck were you thinking, Rafe? Why the hell did you want to arouse their suspicions?"

"I was just trying to get them to say whether they're searching for Outbounders around here—we need to know."

"There are more subtle ways, dumb-ass."

"If they weren't looking for Outbounders before, they most likely are now," said Eddie. He told them about the other customer's departure. "I don't know if he's making for the hauler, but we can't take any chances—let's get the hell out of here."

"We have to find the turnoff quickly," said Peter.

"Once we do, we need to pair off, and keep some distance between the pairs. Less conspicuous. If the hauler does follow us and spots us, split off by pairs down side roads as soon as we see any—take different roads, so they'll have to choose who to follow. But if we do see the hauler, stay in sight of each other so they can't just decide to follow the first pair—they need to see more of us. Rafe and I will keep going straight. If you two turn off, we'll slow down and try to draw them after us—maybe they'll think they can double back for you after that."

"You're just going to fall into their hands, Eddie?" said Peter.

"Don't worry about me, Professor. If they follow us, we'll do something to lose them." He grinned. "I've got a lot of experience maneuvering out of trouble."

"You know, I don't find that at all hard to believe," said Winnie, and she mounted the skimmer. "Let's go."

They turned back onto the main street and continued. They hadn't gone more than six or seven blocks before they came to an intersection with a sign for Kedera pointing to the left. As they turned, Winnie looked back and saw in the distance the hauler pull away from the side of the street, make a U-turn, and drive in their direction. *I hope those pricks in the hauler didn't spot us turning,* she thought. They soon passed into countryside again, putting some distance between the pairs. Before long, the land became hillier, slowing their progress as they ascended. Winnie kept glancing over her shoulder.

For some time she didn't spot any vehicles behind them, but then as they reached the crest of a hill, she saw in the distance a red hauler. As they coasted down the other side, then reached another hill, she saw that the hauler was gaining on them. "I'm going up to warn Eddie," she yelled to Peter. "I'll be right back." He nodded. She accelerated. Eddie and Rafe were at the crest of another hill. As she reached that crest, the two ahead were on a level stretch at the foot, and she sped toward them, passing a side road to the left before she caught up with them. She shouted her warning. Eddie nodded and pointed for her to turn off.

Winnie U-turned and met Peter as he approached the side road. She pointed and shouted for him to turn and she turned onto it just ahead of him and they accelerated. She looked back. The MNAA hauler was closer. The agents in it must have seen them turn off, but the hauler continued past the intersection. *Guess they think the ringleader is at the front of the column. Or maybe they think there are more than two ahead.* After a few minutes Winnie slowed down and pulled over. "We're going toward the river," she said as Peter stopped. "That's not how we want to go."

"So what do we do?"

"The hauler passed us. We could turn back and then go toward Kedera—we'd have to be very cautious. But that way, we might catch up to Eddie and Rafe—if they escaped."

"What if that patrol turns back? We'd risk running into them, and we might not have enough warning to avoid them."

"That's true." She paused for a moment, then said, "Let's retrace our route to the Kedera Road and take the last road to the right we passed. Eventually head to the east again." He nodded, and they returned to the main road and drove to the previous intersection. Peter turned to the south and Winnie followed. After ten minutes, they came to a narrow road leading to the east. Peter stopped.

"This looks pretty small," he said. "Are we sure it leads somewhere?"

"Hell no we're not sure. But we need to try it—it's heading east."

They followed the road for a good while, passing only an occasional farmhouse, and Winnie was wondering if they had made a mistake when they came to a village.

"We need to stop and ask directions," Winnie called out, "see if this road goes straight to Kedera." She pointed to a store ahead, and Peter waited with the skimmers while Winnie went inside.

When she asked the woman behind the counter if they were on the right road, the woman said, "Kedera's been cut off. Flooding. You can't get close to it."

Winnie thought for a moment. If they couldn't reach Kedera, neither could Sam and Allie. They hadn't formed a backup plan. *Should we head to Remora? Maybe we can reach Bancara before Sam and Allie leave it.* She asked the woman if Bancara was accessible.

The woman thought it was, and said it should take five or six hours on skimmers. She gave Winnie directions.

When Winnie told Peter her intention, he said, "What about Eddie and Rafe?"

"Shit. I hope like hell the MNAA didn't grab them. If they didn't, maybe Eddie will think of Bancara too. That or Remora. If they did get caught, . . . I don't know what the fuck we do."

"We can't just leave them behind if we find a way back to Earth."

"You think I want to? Don't fucking jump to conclusions. Maybe they got away. For now, I say we go to Bancara—if we can get there."

He looked uncertain, but nodded. "OK."

They drove for around two hours, stopping once at a store to replenish crystals. As the light faded into gloom and Winnie wasn't sure they could see well enough to drive much longer, they came to a town where they spotted a good-sized inn, the Goldenrod. Inside it was clean and, though simply furnished, seemed suitable enough for a night. After stowing their duffels in their rooms, they went to the common room for dinner.

19

— • —

A Discovery in Bancara

Sam and Allie sat next to each other in the common room of the Floating Leaf. A few others were breakfasting there. Despite being marooned, their chances of returning to Earth looking slim, their stay in Melenca on shaky ground—literally—Sam felt exhilarated after their night together. He had never felt like this before, even with Sylvia. He wanted urgently to press forward.

"Where do we go from here, Allie?" he asked her.

"To Bancara."

"I mean us, you and me, when we get home."

She hesitated. "Time enough for that when we do."

"I don't want to break it off like it was just some casual fling."

"I don't mean that, Sam—you know I really like you. Still, we've only known each other a couple of weeks. We need to give it some time to see how things develop."

"I don't need time. I've dated off and on for years and never felt this strongly."

"You never had a serious relationship?"

Now he hesitated. "Once. For a few years. We lived together. In the end it didn't work out."

"Why not? If you don't mind my asking."

He thought for a moment. "We'd grown comfortable, so I suggested we move in together, see how that went. We found out soon enough that being comfortable isn't the same as being committed. Really being in love. We'd been together for several years. But after six months living together, she broke it off."

"Sorry."

"I was really hurt. But looking back, I realize it was for the best. There wasn't a future."

"That's what I want to be sure of—that there's a future."

"Have you had a serious relationship?" She told him about her marriage and how it had ended. "Are you afraid to commit after that?" he said.

"Not afraid. I just need to be sure, not to make another mistake."

"I'm not a cheater, Allie."

"I believe you. I've got to make sure it's the right match, that's all." She took a sip of tea. "I want a family, Sam. But I'm not going to commit to someone just to have a family if I'm unsure about how the relationship will work out in the long run."

"And you don't feel a match with me?"

"I do, Sam. But let's give it time—give us both time, to be sure."

"Does time in Melenca count?"

She laughed. "It looks like we'll have a lot of time here to see how things develop."

"Let's see if we can shorten it. Let's go to Bancara."

As they reached the outskirts of Bancara, there was no uncertainty: Sam headed downtown, looking for the administration building. The journey had taken several hours but was uneventful: no opening sinkholes or crumbling hillsides, no MNAA patrols or crowds of rightcakes. The administration building was on a large square.

"We're trying to find out the address of someone who used to live here," Sam said to the receptionist in the lobby. "Is there someone we can talk to?"

"Why?"

"We want to talk to someone who knew him, to see if he told them something?"

"Like what?"

"Something that relates to a purpose of ours."

"What sort of purpose?"

"It's, uh—"

"It concerns a legacy," said Allie.

"Are you advocates?"

"Just interested parties."

She looked them over for a moment, then said, "Room 318."

As they climbed the stairs to the third floor, Sam said, "That was inspired."

"It just popped into my head."

In room 318, a trim man wearing a bright blue tunic and a red scarf around his neck sat behind a desk—not Sam's stereotype of a bureaucrat. When Sam told him what they wanted, the man leaned back in his chair. He didn't ask why they were looking for Caruso.

"Dan Caruso, eh? I knew him. He left several years ago. No one seems to know where he went. Anyway, he never came back—just disappeared."

"Can you tell us where he lived? Also, if you knew him, did he have any good friends who are still here we might talk to?"

"Hmmm. Good friends . . . I think Pello Fernlap was one—lived a couple of doors down from him."

"Where was that exactly?"

The man thought for a few seconds, then said, "The Candola Road, that was it. Let me think. Caruso was at 212. Pello was at 216."

"You've got a good memory," said Allie.

"One of my best talents." He waved off their thanks. "All in a day's work for a public servant." He gave them directions to the Candola Road.

Soon they were in the two-hundred block. Number 212 had a deserted look. Paint peeled off in patches. A few shutters hung askew. They knocked on the front door of 216. A balding, slightly stooped man answered.

"Pello Fernlap?" said Sam. "We understand you were a friend of Dan Caruso."

"So? What's that to you?"

"We believe he may have had information that's important to a project of ours. We're trying to talk to friends to see if he may have mentioned it."

Pello's face relaxed. "I don't know what sort of information Caruso would have had that would be useful to anyone. But come in."

"We're trying to go somewhere that's not easy to find, and we think he might have discovered how to get there," said Allie as they entered.

"That's vague." He studied them for a moment. "He was trying to find a way back to the land beyond the Boundless Sea, where he was from. He was an Outbounder—I don't know if you knew that."

"We did know that," said Sam. "That's why we're interested."

"Are you Outbounders?" he said.

They hesitated. Then Allie said, "We're from that same land. We're looking for that way as well."

"I don't know if I can help much. But I will if I can. I don't have anything against Outbounders. Caruso was my friend."

"Did he ever mention anything about finding out how to return to our land?" said Sam.

"You know, the day he left, he did tell me he had discovered something. He had gone off before, you see, and come back disappointed—didn't say what he was looking for. Months later, he said he had an idea and went again. He seemed satisfied when he came home, but he said the timing wasn't right."

"Timing?" said Allie. "Did he elaborate?"

"That's all he said. That last time, though, he told me good-bye—said he didn't think he'd come back. And he hasn't."

"Did he say what he discovered?" asked Sam.

"He didn't give—oh! I'd forgotten all about it."

"What?"

"Right before he left he gave me some pages from a journal he kept, and a letter. He told me to send them to Mentor Perroso—he didn't say why. He had to catch a transport and didn't have time."

"And you don't remember what was in them?" said Allie. He shook his head. "That leads us back to Mentor Perroso again," she said. "And obviously he's not available. So whatever was in those pages will stay unknown, unless—"

"No!" said Pello. "It won't. Wait a minute." He went into another room. After a few minutes, he came back in clutching some papers. "I delayed sending them. What if Mentor Perroso showed up and questioned me? With his followers? I didn't want to get mixed up in whatever this was about. I kept debating whether to send them, and eventually forgot about it." He handed the papers to Sam.

"Do you mind if we stay for a few minutes and read through them?" said Sam.

"You can take them with you. I don't have any need for them."

Sam glanced at the pages. There was a scrawled note to Mentor Perroso, then several pages torn from a notebook. Two journal pages appeared connected. A third started in the middle of a sentence, unrelated to the ending sentence on the previous page, and ended in a sentence that was clearly incomplete. "This last page breaks off at the bottom," said Sam. "It must continue to another page. Do you have it?"

Pello shook his head. "He took the journal with him. This is everything he left with me."

Sam and Allie sat next to each other in a tavern back in the commercial district having a late lunch, the pages spread between them on the table. The note to Perroso was brief, looking dashed off.

"I followed your directions to the valley," it read, "but was stymied. Later I figured out why. Things have changed. I have to leave now, so I'm enclosing a few pages from my journals to explain, since I think you'd want to know." The first two pages described how on his first search attempt he found a valley Perroso had described but didn't encounter the whirlwind, or other features Perroso had mentioned. The third page, referring back to an apparent earlier entry on his second attempt that wasn't among the torn-out pages, said that second attempt was successful. The page ended "I was right when I went back. Only one" and that was all. Clearly it continued on at least one more page. Had he neglected to tear that one off in his haste? Or had Pello lost it? Either way, they didn't have it.

"'Only one,'" said Sam. "Only one what? That could mean anything."

"He was stymied," said Allie. "Things have changed. You know what that means?"

"Something about the whirlwind's appearance isn't right?"

"Something about the directions Perroso gave him is wrong. So even if we found Mentor Perroso, we'd be in the same boat as Caruso."

"He never got the letter. Even if he had, unless Pello had the missing page originally and enclosed it right away, he wouldn't know what Caruso was talking about. Or at least I assume so."

"What now?" she said. "All we've thought about is finding Mentor Perroso, or failing that, finding out something from one of the Outbounders. What we've learned isn't good."

"First we go to Kedera. Meet up with the others. From there, head for Remora, like we'd planned."

"But even if some of Perroso's associates know something about where this valley is, there's something wrong, and they're not going to know that."

"Caruso figured something out. If he could, maybe we can too. It's better than just giving up. Do you want to stay here with Rafe?"

"You're right. Let's go to Kedera."

Winnie and Peter did not linger over their simple breakfast but got back on the road as quickly as they could. They were now on the edge of the hills, on more level ground. The area was mostly wooded. After around four hours, they came to Bancara, the largest town they'd seen since Mencara. In the commercial district, a park sat squarely in the middle of the broad street, which wrapped around the park on both sides before merging back into one road. People strolled through the park on gravel walkways or on the well-tended lawns amid beds of poppies and clusters of tall and slender silver birches and tall oaks with thick trunks. As if on cue, Peter and Winnie both slowed to a halt across from the park.

"We didn't think about how big Bancara might be and *where* exactly in Bancara we could find Sam and Allie," said Winnie.

"Any ideas?"

Winnie pointed at a bench about ten feet into the park directly across the street from them. "Let's take a break and figure out how to look."

On the bench, Peter said, "What would they do to try to find someone who knew Caruso?"

"Didn't Sam say he and Eddie went to the town administration in Carcella when they were looking for Guy Robinson?"

"So we find the equivalent place here?"

"We should be able to spot the building around here, and—"

"There they go!" cried Peter. "Sam! Allie!"

Winnie saw the passing skimmer with a man and woman on it slow, and she yelled and waved. The skimmer halted and the couple pushed it up onto the lawn and to the bench.

"What are you doing here?" said Sam. "I thought you were going to Kedera."

"Can't," said Winnie. "There's flooding upriver that's reached Kedera. And why the hell are you two on one skimmer?"

He told them, then asked where Eddie and Rafe were. Winnie told them of their encounter with the MNAA, and that she feared they'd been captured. Allie asked what Eddie and Rafe would do if they had managed to evade the patrol.

"Come here, maybe, or go on to Remora?" replied Winnie. "The same things Peter and I thought of."

"What if the MNAA caught them?" said Allie. "We can't just abandon them."

"There's nothing we can do," said Sam. "We'd have to see if Beldan has any suggestions. Or Ravinn. They know Melenca, and they have resources."

"Let's say they did escape," said Peter. "Do we wait here in case they come, or go to Remora?"

"Waiting here is a long shot, either way," said Sam. "We should leave for Remora. See if we learn anything there. If not, look for Beldan."

"It's been a long time since Winnie and I had breakfast. There's a tavern across the street. We can see oncoming traffic from there."

The tavern was spacious but crowded. They found a table one row over from the windows, from which they could see the street clearly. Winnie and Peter were finishing lunch when Winnie suddenly held up a finger and shushed them, then nodded toward a table behind her. Three men and two women sat around it eating. They were talking loudly.

"They say they eat their own babies!" one woman said.

"Then how do they continue to exist?" said a man.

"No, no, it's Melencan children they're kidnapping and indoctrinating, so they can turn them into unthinking servants—that's what I've heard," said another man. "And they're spreading throughout Melenca, infiltrating our institutions."

"Not just our institutions, Geldo," said the third man. "They secretly control the governors. That's what the Supreme Leader is fighting against—he's trying to overthrow them before they take over all of Melenca."

"How do you know all this?" said the other woman in a skeptical tone. "No one's ever said anything about Outbounders until the last few weeks."

"The Supreme Leader has made this known to his inner circle, and the word has gotten out, Recara," said Geldo. "He didn't want to alarm us, but now the threat is serious, so we have to act."

"And the technists are in cahoots with the Outbounders," said the first woman. "They've been co-opted. So when they make up these stories about so-called disasters caused by crystal mining and tell us we have to leave our homes, they're just trying to pave the way for these creatures to take over our homes and towns. We have to resist."

"And just how are we supposed to do that, Dandela?" said Recara. "How exactly are we supposed to recognize these Outbounders?"

"That's the thing," said Geldo. "They look just like regular Melencans."

"Not brown-eyes or Newcomers, you mean," said the first man. Geldo nodded.

"How are we supposed to stop them then, if we can't tell who they are?" said Recara.

The others were silent for a moment, then the third man said, "Look at their actions. Look out for suspicious activity. If you see any, turn them in to the constables, or the MNAA."

"Or act on our own," said Geldo. "The Supreme Leader has deputized private citizens to arrest Outbounders—and use force if they resist."

"Suspicious activity?" said Recara. "Like what?"

"Anything . . . you know, suspicious."

"Like pulling Melencan children off the street," said Dandela. "Or sabotaging crystal stores."

"Maybe all of them opposing the Anointed One or working to close down the mines are Outbounders," said Geldo.

"That's a lot of Outbounders," said Recara.

"Well, maybe not all of them," conceded the third man.

"Some are Melencans who've been turned and are doing the bidding of the Outbounders," said Dandela, "helping them take over."

"Be vigilant," said Geldo. "That's the key."

The server interrupted their conversation with a new round of drinks, and their conversation became more mundane.

Winnie shook her head. "Are we ready to go now?" As they moved their skimmers to the street, Sam glanced to his left, and saw a red hauler approaching rapidly.

"Oh no!" cried Allie.

"What do we do?" said Peter.

"That patrol earlier just got glimpses of us riding," said Winnie. "Maybe they won't recognize us."

They tried to act nonchalant as they waited for traffic to clear. The hauler slowed as it drew parallel to them, then accelerated. It turned at the far side of the park.

"Act like nothing's wrong," said Sam. "Winnie's probably right—they likely didn't recognize us."

"Just don't pull any Melencan children into the park," said Winnie.

But the red hauler drove around the park and pulled up next to them. Sam felt his stomach tighten. *What do we do—run for it? They may have firetubes.* The door at the front of the hauler opened. Out stepped a man. But he wasn't wearing a black tunic, and Sam realized with a jolt that it was Eddie. Then out came a second man—Rafe.

After a speechless moment, Winnie said, "What the fuck are you two doing?"

Eddie grinned. "Like our ride?"

"Impressive. How the hell did you—"

"Let's get out of here first," said Sam. "An MNAA hauler is likely to attract attention. And if it's not an MNAA patrol with it, that's damned suspicious behavior."

"Stow your skimmers in back," said Eddie, "and we'll get the hell out of here." They stashed their skimmers beside two other skimmers already there and got in, and Eddie drove on the main street out of town. "I'll look at the map when we're out of town," he said. "By the way, where are we going?"

"Remora, James," said Winnie.

As they drove, passersby glanced at them, but none seemed excited or agitated at the sight of the hauler. In the countryside, Eddie steered into a recessed area off the road where trees screened them from it. He studied the map for a moment.

"There's a road to the north not far ahead," he said. "It meanders, but it intersects with another road that will take us back to the East Highway. From there, it's not far to the foothills of the Hazy Mountains." They discussed what to do if the river was flooded at that point but decided they would have to figure out an alternate course if it was.

"Before we go any farther," said Peter, "you need to tell us how in the world you ended up driving this MNAA hauler. Where's the patrol?"

"Not digesting their lunch very easily, I can tell you," said Eddie.

"So they caught you?" said Winnie.

"After you turned off, we couldn't lose them. They forced us to the side of the road."

"They made us get into the hauler—didn't read us our rights or anything," said Rafe.

"They questioned us. We denied knowing anything about the people who turned off, but they didn't believe us—they'd spotted us in Delfera, they said. They were going to take us to an MNAA base for interrogation."

"Probably torture."

"Anyway, they stopped at a tavern for lunch—I guess chasing Outbounders is tiring work. They removed the power box that combines the different kinds of pulverized crystals from the other boxes—I learned at Ravinn's workshop that there are two other boxes that pulverize different crystals, then—"

"Skip the technical lecture," said Winnie. "Just tell us how you got away."

"The hauler won't run without that box they removed. They didn't bother locking us in—said they'd be watching us through a window in the tavern, and if we made a run for it—well, they had firetubes."

"If the hauler won't run without that box, how did you manage to drive it here?" said Sam.

"Because I'm a mechanical genius. I realized I might be able to hook the smaller boxes from our skimmers together to take the place of their box. That hadn't occurred to them."

"Wait a minute," said Peter. "How could you do all this taking apart and reassembling skimmer components?"

"I had the tools Lirea gave me in my duffel. So I managed to connect the skimmer boxes—and it worked. It's less powerful, won't generate as much speed, but it ran. So did the MNAA agents out of the tavern when we pulled away, but we must have gotten out of firetube range pretty quickly. So here we are."

"But they know you've got their hauler," said Sam. "They'll be searching for it. We'll be better off on skimmers."

"But I like my new wheels!"

"I'll buy you a cargo van when we're home," said Winnie. "You can paint the MNAA logo on it."

"Not only do they know you have their hauler," said Allie, "they have good descriptions of you two, and probably a general impression of Winnie and Peter as well. We need to avoid the East Highway, and any major roads—stick to back roads."

They pulled their skimmers out of the hauler. As Eddie started to disconnect the skimmer boxes in the hauler, Sam glanced at it, and looked around them. There was an opening between two large trees and no underbrush behind it for several feet. He suggested they move the hauler into the opening. Eddie nudged it through the opening and on a few feet. Then he broke off some large branches from nearby underbrush and piled them on the ground at the back of the vehicle until a heap concealed it. Then Eddie finished disconnecting the skimmer boxes and reconnected them to his and Rafe's skimmers. As Sam and Allie put their duffels on Sam's skimmer, Eddie looked at them with raised eyebrows.

"What's going on here?" said Rafe.

Sam explained what had happened. "Right, Captain," said Eddie with a smirk, "just happened to hit a rough patch."

I don't care what Eddie thinks, Sam thought. Allie rolled her eyes.

Just as they were about to take their skimmers out of the sheltered area, a red hauler went by, slowly. "They're looking for something," said Eddie.

"They're looking for us," said Allie. "They'll be all over this area. We can't afford to take the East Highway—they'll have it covered for sure."

"Allie's right," said Sam. "We need to take back roads. They'll likely expect us to take the easiest routes."

Before they drove away, Eddie looked at the map again and plotted an alternate course that would avoid the East Highway. They ventured cautiously onto the road and before long Eddie turned onto a narrower road. The area was sparsely populated. They had put some distance between themselves and the Bancara highway when Sam glanced back and saw a red hauler cruising on the highway, on past the side road. He could only hope the agents hadn't spotted them.

In the next hour they turned onto two other small roads. On the second of those, they hadn't gone far when Rafe called out, "Look!" In the distance, mountain peaks were faintly visible. The land grew steadily hillier, and by the time they came to a town two hours later, the mountains loomed larger, reaching high into the sky with white around the peaks. The town, Candola, was not on the river—or the East Highway.

20

On the Mountain Trail

Beyond Candola, the road rose sharply. It was early evening, and when they reached an inn as they entered Candola, the River Perch, Eddie stopped and said they should ascend the mountains in daylight. So they entered the inn behind two men.

"Welcome, gents," said the husky blonde woman behind the reception counter to those two. "If you're looking for lodging, you've come to the right place—best in the foothills. I'm Selva, and I make damn sure it's run well. Planning on going sightseeing in the mountains?"

"We're not here for pleasure," said one of them. "We're traveling for our concern."

"Where from?" said Selva.

Sam tensed up. *Is she going to question us and figure us for Outbounders if we're vague or evasive? Should we just turn and leave? No, that would just create more suspicion.*

"I'm from Cantorba," replied the man. "My colleague is from Kascara."

"Kascara—isn't that up near the mines, where there's been flooding and such?"

"I lost my house," said the second man. "We're in an inn now—my wife took off from work to find housing."

"That's not all he lost," said his companion. "He bought one of those plans that Flammer Enterprises put out when the flooding and rockslides started up north. Supposedly that plan would reimburse him if he suffered damage to his house—but he didn't read the fine print: the plan was void in the event of natural disaster, and of course they interpret the flooding as natural disaster."

"So I'm not getting reimbursed for my house, and I lost the money I spent on the plan. They've cheated me!"

"You should have known better," said Selva. "If Flimsel Flammer was sponsoring something, you should have known there was a catch."

"Oh no. I'm sure the Anointed One had nothing to do with this. I'm sure he didn't know anything about it. It's the people around him in his concern—they're the ones."

"Sure, you go ahead and believe that if it helps you sleep better. Speaking of which, you're bound to sleep better in the comfortable rooms here!" She finished checking the men in, and Winnie stepped forward, followed by the others.

Here we go, thought Sam.

"Been traveling long today?"

If she asks where from, do we say Mencara or Bancara? Which would be less likely to rouse her interest?

"All day," said Winnie. "A long day." She glanced around. "We'll need three rooms."

"Four rooms," said Allie. "Sorry, Winnie—I'm going to stay with Sam."

Winnie looked at her for a moment, then said, "Why am I not surprised."

"Neither am I," said Eddie. Peter did look surprised. Rafe looked sullen.

"Four rooms it is," said Selva. She entered something in the register on the counter and took four keys from beneath the counter. As she handed out the keys, she said, "You heard those gents before you? Poor sap doesn't want to believe he was swindled by Flammer, but that's standard procedure for him. He's swindled people for years."

"You know, we had that impression too," said Winnie. "Can't imagine why." Selva laughed. "I have to say," added Winnie, "you don't mind getting into a political discussion."

"I say what I think—whatever I want to say. People can think what they want. Though I think this isn't so much politics as, shall we say, personal finance. I guess that's what you'd call it when you get gulled by a swindler."

"Maybe so." Winnie turned to her companions. "Let's stow our stuff and get some chow." She looked back at Selva. "I'll bet your tavern has great food, as well."

"Best in a hundred-mile radius. You'll enjoy it!"

They did.

The next morning at breakfast, Winnie picked up a digest that had been left on the table. "Listen to this, from the *Current*," she said. "It has to do with the damage from the mines: 'One potential advance may be on the horizon. A solution being developed by Ravinn Novaeto's concern has had promising results in neutralizing the toxic gas arising from sinkholes. If the solution enters large-scale production, it could be sprayed in massive quantities.'"

Peter had picked up a second digest. "The *Weasel*, you'll no doubt be surprised to learn, has a different take," he said: "'An official with Supreme Leader Flammer's administration accused Ravinn Novaeto of developing a deadly poison that, under the guise of fighting the so-called damage from crystal mines, debunked as a phony story by the Supreme Leader, will be directed at communities where many True Believers reside.' The article goes on to say that Compactors are planning to introduce an act in the Grand Council to ban the solution."

"Banning something that could save lives," said Allie, shaking her head. "What a crazy place this is."

Winnie looked up from the *Current*, frowning. "Uh oh," she said, and read: "The MNAA has issued a bulletin that what it calls 'suspected Outbounders' are 'on the loose' near Bancara, and the agency is conducting searches in a wide area around the town.'" She put down the digest. "Allie was right—we need to keep to back roads."

As they prepared to set off from the inn, Eddie told them he'd looked at the map, and there were three roads aside from the East Highway that went into the mountains. He wasn't sure which they should take, but all at least appeared smaller than the highway. If there were any MNAA haulers or patrols in Candola, the voyagers might have to take whatever turns they could to avoid them, then figure out once out of town how to get to the closest of the back roads.

Eddie led them up the drive around the inn to the corner of the street. He peered around the corner, then pulled his skimmer back quickly, motioning the others back. "MNAA patrol!" he hissed. A few seconds later a red hauler with the black-and-white logo passed by. Eddie waited a minute longer, then went and looked around the corner again and waved them forward.

They turned onto the street in the opposite direction from the hauler. Sam felt his stomach tighten. Allie's grip around his waist was firmer than usual. They drove four or five blocks through a commercial district. Suddenly another red hauler came into view several blocks ahead as it turned onto the main street from a side one and headed toward them. Eddie immediately turned on the next street to the right, and the others followed. A man standing in front of the business on the corner glanced at the skimmers as they turned, then up the street toward the hauler. He waved both arms at them and pointed to a drive a few stores down. Eddie sped up and turned into the drive, and they all followed. It led to a parking lot behind the buildings. They jerked to a stop and shoved their skimmers against a wall and pressed against the wall themselves. The man who had gestured turned the corner and came toward them. He'd stepped only a few paces before the red hauler went down the street past the drive.

"You were clearly trying to avoid that hauler," the man said as he reached them. "The MNAA is hunting for Outbounders all over the place. Are you Outbounders?"

Sam didn't know what to say. *If he was going to turn us in, wouldn't he have flagged down the hauler?*

Winnie must have had the same thought. "We are Outbounders," she said. "We're not up to any mischief, I assure you." The man burst out laughing.

"I don't believe the preposterous Flammer propaganda, I assure *you*." He looked from one to the other. "You're dressed like proper Melencans, not like Outbounders—or should I say something else?" He chuckled. "Earthlings, perhaps?"

"You must have spoken with Beldan or Dalbin Falembo to know to call us that," said Winnie.

"Beldan Falembo, the alternate-techne merchant? No, I've never met him."

"Then how did you know . . ." said Peter, then, "Are *you* an Outbounder?"

"Or Earthling? Indeed I am."

"You sound American," said Allie, "though it's hard to tell since Melencans sound normal to us now."

"You're close. I'm Canadian—or I was. I've been here a number of years now. I'm Claude Sinclair." They introduced themselves, and told their story: how they'd come to Melenca, their search for Mentor Perroso and a possible portal, how they were now heading for Remora.

"Mentor Perroso is an Outbounder?" said Claude. "I didn't know that."

"And Tim Wooden?" said Allie.

"The artist? He is too? I know of him, though I'm not very familiar with his work." He told them he'd only met one other Outbounder after being caught up in the whirlwind while sailing his boat in the Caribbean, an old Englishman who had been in Melenca for years and made clear where he'd ended up and what the old man speculated had happened to them. "Now, I run this store," he said, pointing to the building they stood next to. "Have for years." He looked back toward the corner. "You're in a difficult spot. The area is crawling with MNAA patrols."

"We've been avoiding the East Highway," said Eddie. "We're planning to take back roads into the mountains. I see three routes on my map, but I'm not sure which one is best."

"Show me the map," said Claude, and Eddie spread it against the steering column of his skimmer. Claude pointed to a line on the map. "The Clinging Road. It's narrower than the other, and less likely to be watched." The road was outside Candola.

"I guess the challenge now is to make it to the road without raising suspicion," said Sam.

"Also, does this street lead to it?" asked Eddie. The map didn't show the streets in Candola.

"Not directly," said Claude. "You'd have to turn not far ahead, then turn again on the edge of town." He thought for a moment, then said, "Rather than you try to follow my directions, and maybe get lost avoiding an MNAA patrol—or have one catch you—I can fit you and your skimmers in my concern's hauler. I'll take you to the Clinging Road."

"We don't want to cause trouble for you," said Allie.

"I'm willing to take the chance. It's a small act to oppose the Flammer regime."

His hauler was against the opposite wall. After they were seated, Claude drove into the side street and continued down it to a smaller street parallel to the main one. Before long they reached the edge of Candola. They had passed two slowly cruising MNAA haulers. Claude drove into the countryside for another ten minutes, then turned onto a road and halted along a stretch without any houses. "The Clinging Road," he announced.

Amid their heartfelt thanks as they pulled out their skimmers, Allie said, "If—when—we find the portal, do you want us to send you a message? Or to someone in Canada when we're home?"

Claude smiled ruefully. "Thanks. I've been here too long, gotten established. I wouldn't know what to do if I went back. And no point in startling anyone after all these years." He asked Eddie for the map, and pointed farther up on the Clinging Road in the mountains. "The Branch Road at this intersection will take you back to the East Highway—you should be safe from the patrols that far up into the mountains. I doubt they'll consider that area a likely spot for Outbounders. Stay on the highway until you get to Lingora. The highway intersects the Mountain Trail there, and you follow that to the turnoff to Remora." He bade them farewell, and turned the hauler around toward Candola.

They headed due east again, and soon started the steep ascent into the Hazy Mountains. It was narrower than the East Highway, with more and sharper turns. The slopes were densely wooded, with firs, pines, and unfamiliar trees clinging to them, interspersed with bare rock face. The going was slow, as even at full acceleration the skimmers could not reach the speeds they had in the flatter areas. They passed almost no traffic, and no MNAA haulers. They found the Branch Road and then the East Highway without any trouble. In another forty minutes, they reached Lingora, which sat in a narrow valley.

They stopped in a park and Eddie studied the map again. He pointed to the left. The valley extended to the horizon in that direction. A ribbon of road was visible in the distance, threading between woods leading up to the mountains. Moving on they quickly found the intersection with the Mountain Trail. They followed it through a commercial area, then a residential area of modest houses. As they approached the edge of town, there was a crackling noise, then a rumble.

"What's that noise?" asked Allie.

"I'm not sure," said Sam. He listened intently. "It sounds just like what we heard in Kascara." As they approached another intersection, he heard a commotion to the right. A crowd mingled a few blocks down. Other people lined the street closer to the intersection, peering toward the crowd. Eddie stopped just past the intersection.

"Let's see what's going on," he said, dismounting from his skimmer.

"What's happening here?" Winnie asked two men and a woman standing nearby.

"Where have you been?" said one of the men.

"We're not from here—we're traveling, and we just reached Lingora this morning."

"Flammer Enterprises has been blasting in the mountains not far from here, to try to reach the crystals they say are there."

"There's been damage from the mine they're excavating, because of the blasting," said the woman. "Now it's here."

"Are they going to evacuate?" said Winnie.

"Can't," said the second man. "Leader of the District Council and the town administrator are there, and they won't let the constables in to try to evacuate."

"Let me guess," said Allie, "they're Compactors."

"They are—who else would be that crazy?" he replied.

"Not as crazy as Unifiers," said the first man hotly.

"I'll tell you what's crazy—refusing to petition the Flammer concern when the damage first appeared."

"What do you mean?" said Winnie.

"A lot of us were worried," said the woman. "We wanted to petition the concern to halt operations until they made sure they could proceed without causing any rockslides or quakes."

"But the leader of the District Council refused to let us submit the petition," said the second man. "I'm not sure he has that power, but he did it anyway—and the town administrator backed him up. Said stopping work on the mine would kill jobs around here that are going to open up when the mine does."

"And now those two are telling the crowd that sending in the constables to evacuate will make the mine officials look bad," said the woman. "Those officials have 'assured' them the damage is minor and they're containing it. Hah! We all have eyes."

Suddenly there was a loud roar, and the crowd retreated toward them. The three Melencans they were talking to hurried back onto the Mountain Trail. So did the voyagers.

We should get a move on, thought Sam. *We can't get caught in this disaster, and there's nothing we can do to help.* But he stood rooted there, curiosity getting the better of him. Most of the crowd stopped near the intersection, milling and muttering.

"You're destroying our homes!" someone shouted.

"We have to," called out a man with his back to them, clearly one of the two officials, "to protect the jobs that are coming. Besides, this damage isn't going to spread far."

"You're lying!" yelled someone else. "It's spreading the same as it has other places. It's spread like wildfire near the Cleft."

"Those stories are phony! I read the *Weasel*—I know these reports are not true."

There was a thunderous boom in the distance. Boulders were tumbling down one of the mountainsides, headed straight for the already afflicted neighborhood.

"No need to worry about jobs now," said the second man. "The workforce is vanishing." There was silence for a moment as the crowd processed what was occurring. Then as if a spell broke, people started running. Sam grabbed Allie's arm. The voyagers raced back to their skimmers and accelerated down the Mountain Trail. They could hear cracking and crashing behind them—likely boulders striking houses—and the hum of panicked voices yelling.

The noise diminished and then faded away as they rode down the valley, wooded and rocky slopes rising not far away on either side. The road was not as broad as the East Highway, but it was wider than the Clinging Road. They encountered no towns or farmhouses, only a few narrow roads turning off to the side. Sam felt exposed in this narrow valley. *If the MNAA is looking for us around here, there's nowhere for us to go.* Nonetheless, the ride was uneventful, and after two hours a wider road turned off to Remora. They soon climbed onto higher peaks. Within twenty minutes, they saw buildings in the distance, and soon they were driving into a residential area in Remora.

Sam suddenly felt deflated. They'd had their sights on Remora as the best chance to find Perroso, but that chance was gone. The odds that any of Perroso's associates would know anything about a portal seemed slim. *We can't just go blindly north in the Hazy Mountains, looking for the right valley. How would we know it was right?* The houses they passed were modest, neat, most of them built of mountain stone, with well-tended lawns and patches of roses and other, unfamiliar blue and yellow flowers. They soon passed into a commercial district, but it looked different from the typical Melencan one. The stores were small and a number advertised spiritual products or services. In addition, artisanal workshops were interspersed with the stores, whereas in most Melencan towns these were in a separate section. Some of them had signs denoting Ravinn's concern. In the middle of town, Eddie stopped next to a square, with a fountain in the center, that the road wrapped around. On the other side was a building that was clearly the Town Administration building.

"You going to ask for Perroso's HQ, Captain?" said Eddie. "I doubt there's a big sign that says 'Souls Saved' or 'Spirits Lifted' or whatever."

"He doesn't sound like the commercial type," said Peter.

"For God's sake, we don't have to go to the administration building," said Winnie. "Ask anyone."

After receiving directions at a nearby shop, they found Perroso's retreat center at the far edge of town. It was a two-story building with wings around a courtyard, set back from the road. Inside the central door was a large lobby, with a desk against the opposite wall. There were chairs scattered around, a few of them occupied. A disheveled young man sat behind the desk.

"We're looking for something Mentor Perroso has knowledge of," Sam told the young man. "Since he's missing, we wonder if there's someone here he might have confided in we could talk to."

"Talk about what?"

"It's not going to make any sense, except maybe to someone close to the mentor he might have said something to."

"No, you're not making any sense. I can't help you."

"It has to do with directions to a specific valley north of here," said Winnie.

"I don't know of anything like that. Besides, you might be here to cause harm."

"We're not rightcakes!" said Allie. "Or working for Flammer or Margan. We admire Mentor Perroso."

"So you say. But you would say that if you were any of those things. There's no one here to help you."

Suddenly a voice boomed behind them. "Well, well, if it isn't our Earthlings!" They turned around and there stood Ravinn.

21

— • —

A Surprise Meeting

"R avinn!" exclaimed several of them in unison.

"You know these people, Ravinn?" said the young man.

"Certainly I know them."

"I didn't know what to tell them."

"You handled it correctly. I'll talk to them." He looked back at the voyagers. "We can talk in the courtyard. Follow me." He led them back outside, to a cluster of benches.

"What are you doing here, Ravinn?" said Winnie. "What's going on?"

"Why I'm here will become apparent. You don't need to talk with any of Perroso's associates. You can speak with the mentor himself."

"What do you mean?" said Allie.

"He's here."

"Here! How is that?" said Sam.

"Why didn't that desk clerk let us talk to him?" said Peter.

"He was correct. You might have been rightcakes, or Margan's agents. And by 'here,' I don't mean in this building, I mean in this area."

"But again, how?" said Sam. "He'd been taken by rightcakes, or Margan."

"Rightcakes, yes, but led by some who were in contact with Margan after they seized the mentor. They were keeping him stashed away while Margan considered what to do with him."

"How did you find out all that?" said Winnie.

"Some of those rightcakes were in contact with Flammer's toadies as well." He looked at Sam. "Your suggestion about Arban Melroc turned out to be useful."

"His Flammer source."

"Arban managed to wheedle or bribe the information out of him. Once we knew the location, . . . I have resources. It took a few cracked skulls."

"But where is Mentor Perroso?" said Winnie.

"In a house nearby, where we can keep him safe, with some of my men guarding him. Miraban's the only other one who knows where. The mentor and I are discussing how he can continue to proclaim his message but remain safe."

"Can you take us to him?" said Sam.

"I did say you could speak with him, did I not? But all in good time. I'm hungry. There's a decent place down the street with good food—and drink, of course."

Can't it wait? I want to talk to Perroso. On the other hand, Sam *was* hungry, and it wouldn't do to spurn Ravinn's hospitality if he was going to lead them to their quarry. They soon found themselves in an outdoor café like the one they'd eaten at near the Academy in Mencara. Tables were filled with mostly young people, likely disciples of Perroso, Sam guessed. Ravinn drained his tankard fairly quickly and ordered another.

"So tell me, what have you been up to since leaving Pelora?" he said. "Managing to avoid trouble?" They took turns filling him in on their experiences. When they related the events with the commissars and the Correctness Patrol in Mencara, he snorted. "You've witnessed the lunacy on both extremes, then. You've had full value for your tour of Melenca." He took another hearty draft from his tankard.

"Do you know about the damage spreading from the new mines here in the mountains?" said Winnie.

"Careless blasting—no surprise, with one of Flammer's incompetent offspring in charge." He drank again. "But do *you* know that damage similar to that from the mines is occurring in the Hazy Mountains?"

"No!" said Allie. "We thought there wouldn't be any risk yet up here."

"The instability from the mines spread across the juncture of the Cleft with the Hazy Mountains. Crumbling has begun, and the valleys are being pummeled. It's heading this way."

"We saw articles in a couple of digests this morning about how you're working on a solution to counter the toxic gas," said Winnie. "Is that true?"

"My concern is. It's not my particular area. The Compactors are keeping my advocates busy, trying to ban it, but I think we'll prevail in the magistrates' chambers on this one too. We'll at least gain some time while the case works its way through the system." He put his tankard down for the last time. "I'll drive. Your skimmers and bags will be safe at the center."

At a building farther down the street, he told them to wait. A few minutes later a hauler came from behind the building and stopped next to them, and Ravinn, standing at the console, told them to board. He drove toward the commercial district but soon turned on a side street and followed it out of town. The road was bumpy but at least it was straight, which Sam was thankful for, because Ravinn drove faster than Dalbin or Katera had. After turning onto a winding road up the mountainside, he drove without decreasing speed. Fir trees clung to the mountainside, and boulders thrust out precariously. Several houses stood among the trees, and Ravinn turned into a drive leading to one such house and parked in front. As they got out, a man opened the front door and approached them. A slender cylinder was strapped to his waist.

Must be a firetube. Then Sam recognized the man: Ralkar Bodeno.

"Ravinn," said Ralbar. He looked over the voyagers. "And several men I remember from the DynaStream escapade." As they entered the house, several men sitting in the first room looked familiar, and Sam thought they must have been in Ravinn's contingent at DynaStream. All had slender tubes strapped on.

Ready for rightcakes, or Margan's agents. A fortyish man and a young woman stood apart at the back of the room. They did not look like they belonged with Ravinn's men.

"These people are here to speak with the mentor," Ravinn said to the couple as he moved toward them.

"He's in his time of study and meditation," said the man.

"We're going to interrupt his peaceful meditation. They have been seeking him for some time. The reason is urgent for them."

The man hesitated, glanced at the sturdy men and then at Ravinn, and nodded slowly. "I suppose it won't hurt to disrupt his schedule."

"Good you realize that. Now lead us to him."

The couple led them to a room down a hallway. The woman knocked on the door. "Pardon the interruption, Mentor," she said as she opened it. "Ravinn is here with some guests to see you."

Several straight-backed, armless wooden chairs were scattered about. Near the back wall was a table, with an apparatus and tools on it. In one chair sat the old man Sam had glimpsed from a distance in Calabra. He was wrinkled, with a headful of white hair, but he sat erect in the chair, his hands on his knees. He wore a plain gray tunic and beige pants of coarse cloth. The woman turned and left.

"My companions seek enlightenment from you, Mentor, but of a more prosaic sort than your usual seekers pester you for," said Ravinn. He had lowered his voice a little from its usual volume, but it was still loud in the chamber of study and meditation. "I'll leave them to it." He shut the door as he left.

"We've been searching for you for weeks, Mentor Perroso," said Sam. "We've been told you can help us."

"Or should we call you Captain Perroso?" said Winnie. "Or is it Major? I don't want to demote you."

The old man chuckled. "Captain Perroso disappeared to history many decades ago. I'm Mentor Perroso now." His voice was rich, and steady, Sam thought, not shaky like that of some older people he had known. Perroso pointed with an open palm to the chairs. "Please, be seated." As they accepted his invitation, he continued. "Are you all American?" Several nodded. "You've been sent to me for help. And you know about Miles Perroso. You've talked with Timothy Wooden, perhaps?"

"He told us you had made a study of a portal that might take us home," said Sam, "and thought you might be able to tell us how to find it."

"When I came to Melenca and realized what had happened, where I was, I thought that if there was a portal that brought us here, there must be one that would take us back—a reasonable hypothesis, I thought. But where? When my plane went into a tailspin in the whirlwind and then came out of it, I managed to climb for a while, but then the engine stalled, and I bailed out and landed on the beach, not far off. I thought it was in the Caribbean."

"That's what we encountered," said Eddie. "My plane crash-landed in the water."

"You must be a skilled pilot."

"Well, it was a seaplane—but yes."

"When I made it into a nearby town—Secora—everything was bizarre. It didn't take me long to realize that I had somehow been transported to a different world. And I soon met an old man, a German, who had been here for years who gave me a valuable primer on that new world. I wondered if there was a way back, and I thought at first that if the whirlwind was over the sea, a way to go back likely was too, so I wandered along the coast for a while. But I never spotted a whirlwind. Before long, I decided staying along the coast would be futile. So I took to wandering throughout Melenca—looking for any signs of another portal, though I wasn't sure what they would be—but also just curious about the land I found myself in."

"So you decided to stay, like Tim?" said Winnie.

"Eventually."

"You didn't have anyone at home, either?" said Allie.

He took a moment before answering. "I did have. I was married and had a young son."

"Yet you decided to stay?" said Peter. "I'm married and have two children. I want to get back to them—if it's possible."

"It was some years before I learned anything definite about the other portal, then more time before I found it, then more time before I was convinced it was in fact a portal—even then, I wasn't sure it would take me back to Earth. By then, my son would have been without a father for years. My wife and the rest of my family certainly would have assumed I died in the crash. She might have found someone else by then. Returning would have been awkward, even painful—not fair to them. And I had become fascinated by Melenca. What if the portal took me someplace besides Earth? I didn't want to have to start all over again."

"Someplace else?" said Sam. "What do you mean?"

"We're in a parallel universe to Earth's. Has it occurred to you that if there is one parallel universe, there may be more—perhaps many more?"

They were all silent for a moment. Then Peter said, "That might account for why Melenca is similar to Earth in many respects but different in others."

"Very possibly. There could be a spectrum of parallel worlds, ranging from very similar to what you know on Earth to wildly different, if still similar in some ways."

"So there's no guarantee the portal would take us back to Earth," said Sam. "It might take us to yet another parallel world?"

"You have to consider the possibility."

"But we can't go through this all over again—start from scratch on some strange world, strange in different ways from Melenca," said Allie, her voice breaking, a blend of anxiety and weariness in her tone.

"But isn't it likely that if the Caribbean portal takes us from Earth to Melenca, then a portal would return us?" said Sam. "After all, multiple people have come to Melenca from the Caribbean over many years."

"But has anyone on Earth ever stepped forward and said they've come back from Melenca?" asked Winnie.

"Would you have believed anyone who said that?" said Peter. "Maybe they thought it best to keep quiet."

"I believe it does lead back to Earth—but it's just a belief," said Perroso. "Still, I think you should be fully aware of all the potential outcomes."

"I for one am going to chance it," said Sam.

"Me too," said Allie.

"You're not leaving me behind," said Winnie.

"We're all in," said Eddie. "Right, Professor?" Peter nodded. "Hotshot?" Rafe hesitated for a couple of seconds, then shrugged.

What does that mean? thought Sam.

There was a knock on the door. "Come," said Perroso. When the door opened, the young woman stood there holding a tray with a teapot surrounded by small round cups.

"Ravinn thought you might like refreshment," she said as she entered. Perroso nodded, and she handed out cups and then set the teapot on the table before leaving.

"How did you end up becoming a guru?" said Peter.

"Please, a simple teacher." He laughed. "I majored in physics in college, but I studied a lot of philosophy as well. I'd always been interested in Asian philosophy, and Eastern religion. I grew up in northern California, and my father ran an import business. Among other things, he imported art from Asia, mostly China and Japan, so I developed an interest in the Orient early in my life."

"Did you become a Buddhist?" asked Allie.

"I studied Buddhist doctrines, but I didn't become a committed Buddhist. I was raised Catholic."

"So was I," said Peter.

"By the time I ended up in Melenca, though, I was a lapsed Catholic."

"So am I," said Peter.

"What do you think of Melencan religion, then?" said Allie.

"I may have left the Catholic Church, but I remained a believer. So I do believe in the Essence—as we call it in Melenca." He glanced back at Peter. "To answer your question, I had studied meditation, and I started offering instruction—really, for something to do besides study, and I could earn a little by teaching. Melencan religion didn't have any similar practice. So I gained adherents." His voice was mellifluous, and Sam understood how he could keep an audience of seekers enthralled.

"But the portal?" said Sam. "How did you find it?"

"I finally met an old woman who'd lived in the Hazy Mountains and liked to hike in her youth. She described a strange phenomenon she'd seen in a remote valley. It sounded like a portal. I searched in the area she mentioned, and finally I discovered the valley—and eventually observed the whirlwind, and then witnessed it more times."

"Then you can tell us how to find the portal?" said Sam.

"I can tell you how to reach the site where the portal appears."

"We're eager to learn that. Before you do, though, you should know that there's been a snag."

"Do you mean the spreading damage? Or interference from rightcakes?"

"I mean in the directions." Sam told him about their search for Guy Robinson and their conversation with him.

"He must have made a mistake in following the directions. They were clear."

"But that's not the only one." Sam told the mentor about tracking down Caruso's friend and the journal pages. He pulled the papers out of the pocket of his tunic. "Here."

Perroso read through the pages. "Something's changed, he says. Well, it *has* been a long time since I've been to the valley where the whirlwind appears. Still, I can't imagine a change that would prevent them from finding the valley."

"But he figured out, somehow, what had changed," said Allie. "He never came back from his last trip to the valley. We guess that he encountered the whirlwind."

"Our only choice, really, is to hunt for the valley and see what's changed in the directions," said Sam. "Then work out what Caruso did."

"If you want to return to Earth, it's the only means I'm aware of," said Perroso.

"There's one thing I wondered about. His friend told us that when Caruso went back the second time to check out his hunch, he said he was correct, but the timing wasn't right. Does that mean anything to you?"

"Simple. The whirlwind comes only in summer. Then it comes a number of times—but only then."

"And it's summer now, right?"

"You're in luck—if you can determine what has changed."

"You observed the whirlwind, you said," Winnie said. "How do you know it's connected to the one off Secora?"

"I experimented," Perroso replied. "I placed a bottle with a note in it instructing whoever found it to place it back in the sea, several such bottles over several years, without any results. Finally, though, one washed ashore near Secora." He paused for a few seconds, then resumed. "It's possible the portal transported it from the valley to the sea there—but none of the people I sent to the portal and who disappeared ever came ashore at Secora. I think someone found the bottle wherever the portal sent it and placed it back in the sea, and the whirlwind there found it."

"We knew from Wooden about the two Earthlings we tracked down. So there were others?"

"A handful, before Wooden's time as well as later."

"Is the valley far from here?" said Allie.

"Not far—two days' drive." He picked up the teapot and poured more tea into his cup, then invited them to partake.

"What are the directions?" Sam asked Perroso.

"You know the Mountain Trail? Follow it north from Remora. You'll reach a river that tumbles down from higher elevations. If you leave this afternoon it will likely take you until mid-afternoon tomorrow to reach that point."

"That means we have to spend the night somewhere," said Winnie. "Is there somewhere to stay? Or do we have to spread a blanket somewhere? Assuming we could find a blanket."

"Villages are few on the Mountain Trail, but there are some." He thought for a moment. "I'd say you should reach one, Velera, right around twilight. There's a small inn, with a passable common room."

"Show me," said Eddie, and he pulled the map out and spread it on a chair near Perroso. "Knowing where the landmarks are will help." The others gathered around the chair.

"I hope that's not how you navigated from the air." Perroso chuckled, looked at the map for a moment, then pointed to a small dot on the map with tiny lettering. "From here, you continue to follow the trail." He pointed to a line coming down into the valley from the mountains on the east side. "This is the Dilabel River." The line on the map continued toward the Mountain Trail for a short distance, then curved to the north.

"The river doesn't reach the trail on the map," said Winnie.

"You'll spot it, in the distance where it comes down, and then as it veers to the north and parallels the road." He pointed farther north on the map, to a space not marked with any letters or symbols, and moved his finger around slightly. "Somewhere in here stand two white birches twenty yards off the road, spaced a little apart, like a gateway. The Mountain Trail isn't heavily wooded where you'll be traveling, mostly small clumps of pines or firs—there aren't many birches, and most of the few you'll see are lone ones, among the pines and firs. There's a stone marker at the base of one of the trees with an arrow pointing due east."

"This sounds almost like they were put there to direct Outbounders like us," said Allie.

"They were—I planted the trees myself, and etched and erected the marker."

"'Like a gateway'—meaning we enter it?" said Winnie.

"Once through it, keep on that straight course until you reach the river, a couple of miles. There is an old wooden bridge across it. It may not look sturdy, but it will get you over the river safely."

"Did you build the bridge too?" said Allie.

"It was there when I first came to these parts. The valley is one long sparsely populated district. I doubt the district administration spent any resources on putting it there, in the middle of nowhere. Perhaps the Originals built it."

"Originals?" said Winnie.

"Groups of people who were here before the Melencans' ancestors arrived from the Lands Beyond. They're mostly gone now—a handful of their descendants live in the Darksome Wood, the Forest Order, they're called."

"Getting back to directions," said Eddie, "it looks like once we cross the river, we won't have far to go before we reach the side of the valley."

"A few miles. Then you'll find a narrow path leading up the mountainside. It's a strenuous climb. Eventually you'll reach a wide, level ledge, and a little way along it, a path leads down into a small valley, with wooded slopes on both sides."

Eddie frowned. "I don't see any valley on the map."

"It's too small, and the area is not well surveyed. There are no villages or farmsteads anywhere near, not once you leave the Mountain Trail."

"Beyond the gateway you mentioned, is there a road to the river?"

"Not even a path there, just the scrub-land."

"So we'll have to leave the skimmers?"

"It's rough ground. Once you reach the path up the mountain, they won't be any use to you, just a hindrance." He took a sip of tea. "Back to the small valley: follow the valley floor until you see two large bushes standing alone, like sentinels, off to the right. This time of year, they should be blooming with small yellow flowers. In the center of the valley, the whirlwind will find you."

"And if we get there and it doesn't magically show up, how long are we going to have to wait?" said Rafe.

"It's unpredictable. It doesn't come every day. But it appears often—usually a few times a week. If you have to wait overnight, between the bushes a hint of a path leads up the mountainside some two hundred feet. There you will find an opening, an entrance to a cave. Inside it's warm and dry."

"How will we know that the whirlwind is approaching?" said Sam.

"When it's calm and sunny, a strong wind will suddenly arise. Then there's a loud cracking."

"Cracking?" said Winnie. "How would we know it's not the damage? It's in the mountains now."

"There's always lightning—though there won't have been any clouds until just a moment before, and there's no rain. And then the wind will just as abruptly die down, and an eerie silence follows. And then suddenly the whirlwind materializes, and you're swept up in it."

"You've seen it? But you've never entered it—how do you know what happens?"

"When I first discovered where the whirlwind appears and observed it from a safe distance, back near the cave, I placed a stool in the center of the valley and waited. Two days later it came again, and when conditions calmed—after thirty or forty seconds—the stool was gone. The whirlwind was concentrated in that one spot, and as I said, it just materialized. So an object would not have been deposited farther down the valley."

"It sounds similar to when we were caught in the whirlwind to get here," said Allie. ""It was calm and sunny, and then it hit. Though there wasn't any lightning, or cracking sound."

"Or wind," said Eddie.

"I'm not sure why it's different in that regard in the valley. But then I didn't design the universe—any of them." He took another sip of tea. "I'm curious. How have you spent your time in Melenca?"

"Mostly looking for you," said Sam. He related some of their adventures briefly, supplemented by the others. Then he said, "What are you going to do from here on, Mentor? You've been freed, but you're still in danger, especially if you appear in public."

"I'm working that out with Ravinn and some of my closest associates. I can't just stay silent and hidden. The cause is too urgent." He sipped from his teacup. "I've tried to steer clear of politics in my teaching, particularly at the large public events, but it's no longer possible to disentangle political issues from philosophical, spiritual, and techne ones. The inaction or even counteractions of Flammer and his administrative team have caused great damage—as you've seen. Even more dire consequences lie ahead."

"It's interesting you mentioned techne with philosophy and religion in regard to politics," said Peter.

"Techne is not incompatible with religion and philosophy, as Technians argue, and Proclaimers argue as well but from the opposite viewpoint. In any case, Compactors have made techne a political issue."

"You seem to have found them compatible," said Sam. "That looks like an apparatus and tools on the table. So you explore nature from a scientific perspective as well?"

"When I arrived in Melenca, I began to inquire into techne. With my science background, I was fascinated by it. I've continued to tinker and experiment. Learning in various fields keeps me growing, spiritually and intellectually."

"I tinkered with tools too, especially when I was a kid," said Eddie, "though I never had any interest in religion or philosophy." He grinned. "Sorry. But I was interested in seeing what I could build—I built a radio in the garage when I was a kid."

"So did I."

"You had this knowledge of science, but you didn't ever try to introduce radio here, for instance?" said Winnie. "That would have been a real advance."

"Maybe—a Connecticut Yankee, so to speak? But I didn't want to interfere with Melencan techne and society to that extent."

"The Prime Directive."

"I beg your pardon?"

"Never mind—after your time."

Allie asked if he wanted to be brought up to date on events on Earth since he left. He shook his head.

"One world at a time is enough for me to worry about."

"No offense, but after we leave here, I hope we won't see you again, Mentor," she said.

"Unless you want to go with us," said Winnie. "You could assume a fake identity back on Earth so your family wouldn't know you were back."

Perroso laughed. "I've been here too long—building a life, a purpose. I can accomplish more here than there. I'll live out the rest of my days here."

"But if the damage reaches your center here?" said Allie.

"It most likely will. Still, I've thrown in my lot with Melencans, and I'll keep speaking out. Then, whatever happens, I'll be content that I at least tried."

"If we make it back to America safely, we'll drink a beer in your name," said Eddie.

"I'd be honored. Summon Dorenda for me, if you would."

Allie opened the door and called. The young woman quickly reappeared, and Perroso motioned her over and said something in a low voice. She went back and before long Ravinn came in, followed by Dorenda. She carried a large jar, with a thin ceramic top and bottom and a glass middle with a rod in the center.

"Who wants to carry it?" said Perroso.

"What is it?" said Sam.

"It's a lantern. You'll need it if you stay in the cave, and perhaps it might come in handy before that as well."

"I'll take it."

Dorenda handed it to him.

"We better get going if we want to reach Velera before dark," said Eddie.

"You've got more worries than the dark," said Ravinn. "Since the mentor's base is in Remora, MNAA patrols are searching throughout the area. From what you told me, they've got descriptions of some of you."

"Where we're headed, north, is sparsely populated, it sounds like," said Sam. "Will they likely be searching there?"

"They're nasty buggers, but they're not stupid. They'll think it likely we'll stash the mentor in such an area. That's one reason we're this close to Remora—they'll likely assume we'll be in the Hazy Mountains, since they're remote and with plenty of places to hide, caves for example, but won't be right at Remora."

"We'll just have to keep a sharp lookout and be ready to hightail it," said Eddie.

22

— · —

IN SEARCH OF THE VALLEY

As they retrieved their skimmers in Remora to set off once again on their own, Allie said, "I feel bad that we'll have to abandon the skimmers Lirea loaned us and won't be able to return them."

Ravinn snorted. "Bah! They own Dorwin Wines—they're not hurting for cash. With all you have to worry about, knock that off your list. Good luck with the other items on it!"

They thanked Ravinn profusely. He waved off their comments. "You need to get on the road—and watch constantly for the patrols."

Then they were back on the Mountain Trail. There wasn't much traffic. If they did encounter any MNAA patrols they'd stand out. There wasn't much cover, either, just the occasional small stand of trees off the road. To avoid notice as much as possible, they spread out: Sam and Allie together in the lead, Winnie and Eddie following a hundred yards behind, then Peter and Rafe another hundred yards behind them. Judging where they were or how far they had come was difficult since there were few landmarks, either in the landscape or on the map. Mountains soared on both sides of the valley, fir trees clinging to the higher slopes, pines and a few birches mixed in on the slightly lower elevations to the west. On both sides of the road lay uneven ground with small bushes mixed with wild grasses and occasional trees, mostly pines.

They'd been traveling for an hour when Allie said, "What's that up ahead?" Sam peered ahead and realized what was moving slowly along the road.

"MNAA hauler," he said. After another minute, he said, "We're gaining on it—it's probably looking for something."

"Likely us."

"Or Perroso. In any case, we need to pull off the road and give them some time to advance, then cut our speed."

"And hope they don't turn around and head back this way."

Not far ahead was a copse. They left the road and bumped over rough ground into the trees. Winnie and Eddie soon joined them, then Peter and Rafe. Sam told them what he had seen.

"And if they do turn around?" said Winnie.

"Not much we can do except keep going and hope they don't stop us. If they do, we'll have to bluff."

"How?"

"I'll try to think of something. The rest of you do the same."

"I'm not going to just stand there and get caught again," said Rafe. "There are six of us—we can overpower them."

"Don't be absurd, Rafe," said Winnie. "How do you know there won't be more of them? Besides, they have firetubes."

"They won't take me without a fight."

"Great plan, hotshot," said Eddie. "Yes, you distract them with your fists, and cover for us while we all escape."

"Make sure he behaves, Peter," said Sam. As soon as the patrol vehicle was no longer in sight, Sam said, "Let's go."

They returned to the road and drove more slowly. They did not encounter the hauler, or any other patrols. They reached Velera at twilight. A faint haze hung low on the horizon, an ominous sign: it fit the description of the toxic gas from the damage they had heard about in the north. It seemed distant, but still. . . .

There was something else unexpected on the outskirts of Velera: a number of tents in a field, with people milling about or sitting around campfires. They drove on into the village. The inn, the Golden Eagle, was on a square. It appeared decent enough, clean at least and well kept. As they checked in, Winnie asked the desk clerk about what was going on at the edge of town.

"Rightcakes," he said, "gathered here to search the area for Mentor Perroso."

"I thought he was missing, presumed kidnapped by the rightcakes themselves."

"He escaped, apparently. It's in the *Weasel* today." He pointed to a small pile of tabloids at the end of the counter. Copies of the *Current* and the *Vantage* were among them. "Most of them are camped out. We've got several of the leaders here. Not that we asked for them, you understand, but you can't turn down paying guests—that's no way to run an inn."

"What about that haze?" said Sam.

"Not sure. There have been reports of toxic gas spreading from the mining damage—you know about that? Whatever it is, it doesn't look like natural clouds."

"We better make sure we're on the road early in the morning," Eddie told his companions.

They ate supper in the common room. As Perroso said, it was passable, though nothing more. The MNAA was active in the area. Velera was crawling with rightcakes. Still, after the tension of the ride from Remora, Sam felt grateful for the opportunity to relax with a beer, if only for a few minutes snatched from their drive, their search, their evasion of patrols.

It was only a few minutes. Then Winnie held her finger to her lips and nodded toward a table a few feet away from where she sat. Four men sat there with beers, finishing their meal.

"We need to focus, sharp," said one, a burly, short-haired man around forty. "There's a lot of people out looking for Perroso. If we can nab that troublemaker, we'll win a lot of favor from the Supreme Leader."

"Well, he ain't the only one," said a second speaker, a thin man with thin hair. "There's Outbounders too. We'll get a lot of credit if we can catch them."

"Those rumors are all over the place," said Burly. "They could be anywhere. We need to use our noggins and zero in on Perroso. They most likely got him squirreled away up here in the Hazy Mountains. We just got to figure out where, before anyone else."

"It ain't just anywhere," said Thin Man. "I was talking to an MNAA agent. They're up here hunting Outbounders they ran into in the hill country around Delfera, had their hands on a couple, but they got away. Them Outbounders is as dangerous as Perroso."

"You're just going to confuse our boys if we send them off on different errands in all directions." They were interrupted by the landlord, who brought another round of beers.

"I've heard enough for now," said Allie in a low voice. "I'm going up to the room."

"I'll join you," said Sam. And he did.

They were up early, eating a hurried passable breakfast in the passable common room. Because they were traveling in sparsely populated country, they bought some bread and cheese to take for lunch and some ceramic water bottles at a nearby store. The haze was thicker and higher in the sky than it had been the day before—it was closer. They set off and had traveled for an hour when suddenly they saw ahead two skimmers and a hauler stopped just before a side road to the left. An MNAA hauler was parked on the side road at the intersection, and another to the side of the Mountain Trail just past it.

"An MNAA checkpoint!" said Allie. "What do we do?"

"We can't turn off the road—they'll see us and chase us," said Sam. "I have an idea." He kept going and pulled in behind the stopped vehicles. Winnie and Eddie soon reached them, then Peter and Rafe. "Listen to what I tell them and do what I do," he said.

When he reached the intersection, several black-clad agents stood there. "What's your business in this area?" said one.

"We just came from the camp of True Believers at Velera. We've been sent out to search the area where the Dilabel River flows down, us two and the four behind us. Our leaders reckon Mentor Perroso might be hiding around there."

"So they think they know more than the agency?"

"It won't hurt to have people searching," said another agent. "He could be anywhere in these parts."

The first agent stared at Allie. "A brown-eye among a group of True Believers?" Sam felt the tension in him rise.

"Not all brown-eyes oppose the Supreme Leader," said Allie indignantly. "Some of us have more sense."

"I *have* seen a few brown-eyes at his rallies," said the second agent.

The first agent stared at Allie suspiciously a moment longer, then nodded. "We've had reports of Outbounders in these parts too," he said. "Keep an eye out for anyone suspicious looking, and let us know of anyone. We've set up an outpost in Velera now."

"We'll be sure to," said Sam. "We heard the Supreme Leader's warnings."

"Right, on your way. Good hunting."

As they pulled away, Allie said, "That was brilliant."

"I wasn't sure it would work—it almost didn't, so that was quick thinking on your part. I didn't know what we'd do if it didn't work."

They rode for another hour. Sam was scanning the road ahead for the MNAA.

Suddenly, Allie exclaimed, "Hey! Is that the river?" Sam stopped and gazed east. Sure enough, a stream tumbled down from the mountains, flowing toward them for some distance before bending around gradually to the north and flowing on to the horizon.

"Hot damn!" said Winnie, as she halted beside him. "We're actually making progress."

His spirits rising, Sam set off again. They rode for another hour, the river paralleling their course in the distance. Another hour passed. Sam drove off the road into a copse of scraggly bushes, and the others followed.

"We've come pretty far," he said. "Shouldn't we have seen the birch gateway by now?"

"From where Perroso showed us on the map, I would guess yes," said Eddie. They had passed clusters of trees and lone trees, including a few white birches, but not two birches close together by themselves.

"I'd say go on a little farther to be sure," said Winnie. "Maybe distances are not to scale on the map, or maybe Perroso's memory was fuzzy about the exact whereabouts. After all, he said he hasn't been this way in a long time."

"I'm hungry," said Rafe. "I'm not going any farther until I have lunch."

"OK, but save some for tonight," said Sam. "We don't know when we'll find food again." So they ate some bread and cheese and drank some water, then were off on their skimmers again. The haze in the sky was thicker, and closer. They rode for half an hour, and then Sam spotted two birches close together to the right.

"Yes! There it is!" cried Allie.

"Let's go see." When they were parallel to the trees they turned onto the rough ground and drove across it, dodging scrub growth, to the trees.

"Where's the marker?" said Peter after they had all reached the trees. Eddie walked around the trees and poked among nearby bushes. He shook his head.

"Someone might have removed it," said Winnie.

"Why would anyone remove it?" said Rafe.

"How the fuck should I know? Why does anything happen the way it does in this place?"

"These are the only two birches together we've passed," said Allie. "We should go on to the river." They bumped over the ground until they reached the river. There was no bridge.

"Someone remove the bridge too, Winnie?" said Eddie.

"It doesn't make any sense," she said. "These things don't add up."

"Maybe this is why Guy Robinson couldn't find the valley," said Peter.

"But Dan Caruso did," said Sam. "He worked out what was wrong."

"If we can get across the river, we can at least see if there's a path and follow it," said Eddie.

"Maybe that's what Caruso meant," said Winnie. "There's only one way across the river—and this ain't it." The river flowed swiftly past them.

"That current is strong, and we don't know how deep it is. We can't chance swimming across."

"No way I'm doing that!" said Rafe.

"Do you understand English, hotshot? That's what I just said!"

"Does the map show any bridges on the river?" said Sam.

Eddie studied the map for a moment, then shook his head. "But Perroso said this area was sparsely populated, and the district wasn't likely to spend much money on it. We could walk for quite a while up the river and not find another bridge."

"So what do we do?" said Winnie.

Eddie looked back at the map. "There's another village on the Mountain Trail, not far ahead of where I estimate we are."

"So what?" said Rafe.

"If a couple of us go there, it's possible we could find a boat there, not too big, so two people could carry it across their skimmers."

"That sounds like a long shot," said Winnie.

"You got a better idea?"

"Even if there's no boat," said Sam, "we might find out if there is a bridge somewhere along the river and whether there are many. If they're few and far between, if we can find one, I'd bet that's the right one. I'll go."

"I'll go too," said Eddie.

"The others need you here in case anything happens to me. Rafe can go."

"Head into that haze?" said Rafe. "Are you crazy? I'm not going."

"Rafe's right, Sam," said Allie. "The road's headed right toward the haze, and you'd be putting yourself at risk."

"I doubt the damage has spread that far so quickly," he said. "It may be a long shot, but it's a chance worth taking. We're so close—I can feel it."

"If Rafe won't go," said Peter, "I guess I'll have to—against my better judgment."

"You're still recovering, Peter," said Winnie. "You're not at full strength."

"I'm pretty close. Enough to help load a small boat onto a skimmer."

So Sam and Peter dumped their duffels, turned their skimmers around, and bounced back to the Mountain Trail.

Twenty minutes later they were in the village. Haze clogged the sky. The air around them wasn't hard to breathe yet, and there were no signs of damage. In the small commercial area, Sam hailed a pedestrian approaching them. "Is there somewhere around here we can buy a boat?" The man stared curiously at him. "It's an odd question, I know," Sam added. "We need to get across the river."

The man shrugged. "Try Benero's Goods. Maybe they sell boats. There's not much call for one around here. It's over there, across the street." A storefront displayed a sign proclaiming "Benero's Goods: Everything You Need."

"Let's hope that's true," said Peter.

The store's front door was locked. A woman stood sweeping in front of a store half a block away. Sam walked over to her.

"Do you know when Benero's will open?" he said.

"Supposed to be open now. Benero went out to where we heard there was damage, to see what's going on, and how close it is."

"Where is that?"

She pointed up one of the side streets. "About a mile that way, maybe. Least that's what I heard."

He went back and told Peter what was going on. "I'm going to see if I can find Benero," he added. "You stay here, in case I miss him and he comes back. I'll be back as soon as I can."

"I don't know—that haze is close. Maybe we should just get back to the others now."

"I think we have a little time. We *have* to cross the river."

"Then hurry. That haze is going to reach us any minute. I won't wait long—and I don't want to have to tell the others I lost you. Especially Allie." Despite the anxiety in his voice, he smiled. "You two seem to be an item—being swept away into another universe has had its benefits for you."

"So it appears." *Are we an item? I feel that way, but I'm not sure what she thinks—or feels.* "That's one good thing to come out of all this."

"At least there's something good." Peter stared at the horizon. "Go. That haze is looking worse and worse."

Sam nodded and drove down the side street, past a few businesses and then houses. He was wondering if this was a false lead when he saw a small crowd gathered ahead, at the edge of a vacant patch of ground between two small clusters of houses. He parked and walked up to several men standing at the back of the crowd.

"What's going on?" he said.

One man pointed to the haze, not that far now. "That cloud is spreading the toxic gas the mine damage has unleashed. It's close, and they're trying to organize an evacuation."

"How long before it reaches us, do they think?"

"Not long, maybe an hour or so," said another man.

"But no actual damage here yet, no crevasses or anything?"

"Not yet," said the first man. "You're not from around here. What are you doing here?"

"I'm looking for Benero. Do you know if he's around?"

A large man with dark hair and a beard spoke. "You've found him. What do you want with him?"

"I need to buy a boat, a small one. I was told your store might have them for sale."

"You were told wrong. We used to carry a few boats, back some years. But sales were never that strong, and they tailed off. Why do you want a boat?"

"We need to cross the river, my friends and I. It's complicated, but we're looking for something on the other side. Is there any other place that would sell boats? Or do you know if there's a bridge anywhere near?"

"Don't know of any bridge. There's a store in the next village up that sells odds and ends, though I don't know about boats. But I don't know that you can get there—or want to." Benero pointed to a group standing beyond the crowd, perhaps twenty yards away across the vacant patch. "See that bunch? They've come from that village—there's been damage there. They're organizing rescue efforts here. They can tell you what conditions are like, whether you can even get there."

Sam made his way through the crowd and across the ground to the group. Several constables stood among them. At the house closest to the group, a man was leaning out of a second-story window yelling. "I'm not leaving!" he shouted at a constable and another man who stood a few feet from the house.

"That haze is poisonous!" yelled the constable.

"It's just fog. I know about the lies Unifiers are spreading—I read the *Weasel*, and I listen to the Supreme Leader."

"People have died in the next village from that fog, as you call it," said the man beside the constable loudly. "It'll be here soon. You need to get away as quickly as you can."

"Those are phony stories. No one's died from a cloud—that's ridiculous."

"Sam!"

He turned around, and there was Katera. She moved over and embraced him. He hugged her back. They clung together for a moment.

"I'm surprised to find you up here in the mountains," he said.

"Flammer has forbidden EmRes from helping people affected by the damage."

"*What!*"

"He says the agency is aiding Outbounders and Unifiers in their plots. So we're helping constables and volunteers wherever we can." She looked at him curiously. "And I'm surprised to find you here."

"It's a long story. We found Perroso."

"That's wonderful! I saw in the *Current* he'd escaped."

"He told us how to find a way back to our land. But we need to find a way to cross the river. I was hoping to find a boat, or if there's a bridge around here. Peter's here in the village. The others are back at the river."

"I doubt you'll find a boat. As for a bridge, Ermolo knows this area very well. We should ask him." She led Sam over to a man and told him what Sam wanted.

"There's a bridge eight or ten miles up the river," said Ermolo.

"Do you know if there are many others along the river?"

"A few, pretty far apart."

"There aren't any farms or villages across the river, are there?" said Katera. "Why are there bridges?"

"No one knows for sure. Most people think the Originals built them. There are ruins of old houses over on that side."

"You all were at the next village?" said Sam.

Katera nodded. "They've had injuries—and worse—from the toxic gas, and major damage from splitting land. We're trying to convince people here now to evacuate."

"We've just obtained some of the new solution that Ravinn Novaeto's concern developed," said Ermolo. "It's supposed to work on the gas, so we're going to spray it. But these people still need to evacuate—the cracks are spreading. And the solution is just a drop in the bucket." He gestured around him at the foggy sky.

Katera pointed toward the house where the resident, the constable, and the other man were still shouting. "It's the same old story. Some believe us and are preparing to move. But others refuse to believe us and won't budge. They've been told over and over by the *Weasel* and Flammer and a lot of other Compactors that it's all false, just a plot to take over their houses and land, and take their children as well. That's why we've had injuries and fatalities in the other village—people who refused to heed us and the local constables."

"This damage is spreading throughout large parts of Melenca, Katera," said Sam.

"What will you do? You and your family? It could threaten your area."

"What can we do? Just keep trying to minimize the harm. Keep trying to switch to the new techne, away from crystals. We can't quit trying."

"I hope we'll be going home soon, but I won't stop thinking of you and your family, and all the Melencans we've met, and worrying about you."

She took his arm. "Come over here with me, Sam." She led him away from the group. "I need to be open—I'm strongly attracted to you, Sam, more than I've ever been with a man. And you feel it too, I can tell. Stay here, Sam, with me."

He hesitated. *I didn't expect this. But she's right—I do feel it. What should I do?* He thought quickly. *How to make such a momentous decision on the spur of the moment.* But in a flash he knew.

"You're right, Katera, I am strongly attracted to you too. And I am strongly tempted to stay. But I belong in my land, Katera. People there depend on me. I need to return to my family, and my concern."

"But others from your land have stayed—Wooden chose to, and Perroso, and they've made good lives here. You like my family, Sam, and they're fond of you. You would fit in. Surely someone could take your place in your land."

"I love your family. And Wooden and Perroso made their decisions, for different reasons." He hesitated again. "But I have another reason to go back, as well."

She studied his face for a moment. Then she said, "Allie?"

"How did you know?"

"I could tell. But I wasn't sure how far it had gone."

"It's gone pretty far, Katera. I want to go back with her. If not, I might well stay."

She seemed lost for words for a moment. Then she said, "How do you know Allie feels the same about you?"

Good question. "I'm pretty sure she does."

"So you think—but you don't know. I'm telling you I do. And you do for me. If you stay here, we can build a good life together—you know for certain we would. Allie won't lack for someone to do the same with."

Am I positive? Is she right? Am I missing an opportunity? But he was sure of the answer. "I'm sorry, Katera. I've made up my mind."

"If you change it, you know where you can find me. I'll hope to see you. If I don't . . . well, I won't ever forget you."

"I won't forget you either."

She embraced him again, then kissed him, and he responded, and they held the kiss for a moment. Then she released him.

"Good-bye, Sam, and I'll pray to the Essence that everything goes well for you and your friends to return to your land. I don't understand how that will happen, but I'm confident Mentor Perroso understands."

"And I'll, uh, pray to the Essence for you and your family, and all of Melenca as well."

She touched his face, a forlorn expression on hers, then turned and walked back to the group.

Peter was pacing back and forth in front of Benero's Goods. There was relief on his face as Sam approached. "Finally. I was about to leave." He paused for a second, then said, "You don't have a boat—did you learn anything?"

He told Peter what he had learned about the bridge. He also told him that the toxic haze was closing on them, accompanied by splitting land. He didn't mention seeing Katera. He was trying not to think about her. A thought popped into his mind: *I never had this kind of feeling for a woman before, and I leave the universe and feel it for two women. Strange.*

"We need to get back," he said. "We have to stay ahead of that cloud and the damage. We don't have much time."

23

SORTING IT OUT

As Sam and Peter reached their companions back at the river, Allie rushed up to him and hugged him, and he held her tightly.

"This reunion is touching," said Winnie, "but I notice you're not accompanied by a boat."

"We don't need one," replied Sam, and he filled them in on what he had learned.

"We should have just kept going up the river to begin with," said Rafe. "We've wasted a bunch of time."

"Eddie was right," said Sam. "We didn't know there was a bridge—in fact it seemed unlikely."

"So let's not waste any more time," said Eddie. "That haze keeps spreading."

"Which way, though?" said Winnie. "Have we gone too far or not far enough?"

"We've only found the two birches once, and the bridge isn't that far up the river. I'd say continue that way."

"I don't know," said Peter. "From where Mentor Perroso showed us on the map, we're pretty far along that area."

"The area was vague. He didn't pinpoint a specific spot—just this area."

"If the bridge isn't that far, and we've only found the one pair of trees, going to the bridge makes sense," said Winnie. So they agreed to continue up the river.

Over the uneven ground next to the river, the going was slow. They rode for what seemed several hours before Eddie called out, "The bridge!" Sam felt his hopes rising. Once they crossed to the other side, they drove on to the foot of the mountain. They looked around.

"Does anyone see a path?" said Winnie. Sam couldn't see one. Fir trees clung to the rocky slope, with some scattered undergrowth as well. They searched among the trees and pushed aside small scraggly bushes. But there was no sign of any path.

Sam's spirits sank. *What's wrong with the directions? Something's changed, but what?*

"Where the hell's the path?" said Winnie.

"Mentor Perroso just said there was one," said Allie. "It should be obvious."

"Maybe it's visible higher up," said Sam. "Let's climb up and look, Eddie." They picked their way up slowly over the rock face, grasping for holds. About forty feet up they reached a narrow ledge. They could walk carefully, single file, one foot in front of the other. It wound up the mountainside, but did not widen, and no path branched off down, and there was no valley.

Twenty minutes later, Sam halted. "This isn't leading anywhere," he said. "There's nothing that looks like Perroso's description."

"But look at them down there like ants," said Eddie. "Take a look, Captain!" Sam did not like heights. He did not look. They turned around and slowly, carefully descended. Sam concentrated on the narrow ledge at his feet and willed himself not to look below. By the time they reached the others at the foot of the mountain, the sun was setting. After some discussion, they decided to spend the night there. They had no shelter, but driving in the dark countryside seemed a worse option than remaining in place.

"Where would we go?" said Winnie. "We haven't found anything that matches Perroso's directions, not completely. I don't know what to do now."

"It's frustrating," said Allie. "There has to be a way—Caruso realized what was wrong. Why can't we?"

They ate some bread and cheese and drank a little water, trying to save some for the next day. There wasn't much conversation. Sam was tired and dispirited, and that seemed the general disposition. In the quiet, he heard a distant sound: rocks splitting.

How are we ever going to get home if we can't find the valley? But if we're stranded here, how are we going to make it if the disasters—natural and political—keep spreading? There's an answer, but I can't find it. Maybe one of the others will. Suddenly, unbidden, the image of his mother seeing him off to the Caribbean sprang to mind. *"You can do this. . . . We have confidence in you, Sam. I have confidence in you." Think! Think! There's an answer.*

In the morning they agreed to save the last of their remaining food for later, Rafe being the only objector. No one seemed sure of what they should do. "Go along the river back the way we came?" said Winnie. "See if there's another bridge, with a path beyond it?"

"I don't see what else we can do," said Allie.

"That's slow going," said Eddie. "Look at the sky. That haze is closer."

"We can't get caught in it," said Peter. "Maybe we should retreat to Remora and regroup."

"We've already been on the Mountain Trail and haven't found anything," said Allie. "I say go back to where we turned off at the two birches yesterday, then follow the river that way at least for a little while to see if there's another bridge."

"No point in going along the road if we want to try to find the bridge," said Sam. "Allie's right. We need to—" He broke off as a sudden idea flashed into his mind. "No! Let's go back to the Mountain Trail. I think I may have it."

"And what the hell is *it*?" said Winnie.

"If I'm wrong . . . well, I am. But I don't think I am. Let's go—hurry."

They quickly went back to the road. The sounds of splitting and the booming of tumbling rocks behind them were louder. The sky was darker. They rode for several hours, passing the two birches, and then Sam turned off the road where a tall birch stood among a clump of bushes.

"Are you hungry?" said Allie. "We don't have much food left."

"The tree."

"But there's only one tree."

"Exactly. 'Only one—' I think that's what Caruso was saying—one birch. The other must have been cut down or toppled." They dismounted as the others pulled up. Sam told them his idea. "Look in these bushes for the marker." They pulled aside branches, but there was no sign of a marker.

"No doubt that disappeared too, eh, Captain?" said Eddie. "Along with the stump of the other tree."

Am I wrong? No, that has to be it! "I'll go look for a bridge," said Sam. "It was my idea." He rode to the river, but he knew before he got there that there was no bridge.

When he got back to the others and shook his head, Rafe said, "We could've gone all along the river checking for a bridge, but we took the road. Brilliant idea."

"There were maybe two or three other lone birches we passed going to Valera. We need to find the next one."

"And when we don't find anything there?" said Eddie.

"Go back to Remora," said Peter. "We need to escape that haze, before it catches us."

"Assess at that point," said Sam. "We—what's that noise?" They strained to hear.

"A vehicle—hauler by the sound of it," said Eddie. They quickly dragged their skimmers behind the tree and bushes and crouched. A minute later a red hauler drove slowly into view. Sam caught a glimpse of a black-clad man inside scanning back and forth. But the vehicle passed out of sight. They returned cautiously to the road.

They had driven for half an hour when they spotted ten or twelve people spread out ahead beside the road. Several stopped and stared as the skimmers passed.

"Rightcake searchers?" said Allie.

"I'd bet on it."

After another twenty minutes another white birch stood in a copse of bushes. They crossed to it. No one said anything as they pushed apart branches in the bushes. Then Sam's foot bumped up against something hard. He looked down. There was a wide stump. As he yelled triumphantly, Allie exclaimed, "Here it is! The marker!" They gathered around her and peered into the bush. A stone was wedged into the ground, writing chiseled into it.

"What does it say?" said Winnie.

"It says, 'Whirlwind Canyon,' with an arrow pointing up—toward the river," said Allie. "Wait, there's something smaller underneath." She laughed. "'New York' and then after a gap, a question mark and 'light years.'"

"The bush must have overgrown the marker," said Eddie.

They quickly remounted and bumped along to the river. An old bridge spanned it. They crossed and rode to the foot of the mountain. "Where's the path?" said Winnie. Sam didn't see one. Fir trees clung to the rocky slope, with some scattered undergrowth as well.

"Over there, maybe," said Eddie. He walked over to some bushes and spread them apart. Sure enough, after a closer look, Sam could see a narrow cleared area leading up the slope.

"You think that's it?" asked Peter doubtfully. "It looks pretty tight."

"No one's maintaining it," said Eddie. "But it leads up. We can walk on it, single file. There's nothing else that looks like a path."

"We'll have to abandon the skimmers now," said Sam. Without further conversation, everyone picked up their duffel and followed Eddie onto the path.

Sam was soon breathing hard, and after a while, he noticed Winnie and Peter were both moving more slowly, laboring. Despite his excitement and his anxiety, he thought about calling a halt so they could lay down their duffels and rest for a moment.

Suddenly, Eddie called back, "Here's the ledge!" Sam and Allie soon joined him on a wide, level projection from the side of the mountain. It stretched a little way ahead of them into a curve, from which a path led down a steep slope into a narrow valley. Several times one of them slipped and struggled for balance. No one fell, though, and they soon reached the valley floor. The slopes on both sides were wooded. There was no path, but the ground was easy to traverse, with tufts of grass poking through the dirt and here and there a small bush.

They had walked for several minutes when Allie cried, "Two bushes! With yellow flowers!" Sure enough, off to the side of the valley, two large bushes stood alone. They hurried over to them. On the other side, a narrow path led up the slope.

"So we look for the signs Perroso mentioned," said Peter.

"Calm and sunny—check," said Winnie. "But no strong wind. And we've heard cracking off and on for a long time. So we'll have to look for lightning."

"Wait here or find the cave and stay inside until we notice a strong wind and lightning?"

"We don't know how long after the lightning before the whirlwind comes," said Sam. "We can't chance running down from the cave when the whirlwind sweeps through." So they waited on the valley floor. And waited. Time passed, slowly. Sometimes they sat, sometimes stood. Eventually some paced a short way in one direction, then back in the other. No wind stirred. Occasionally they heard the sounds of rocks splitting or crashing down, but there was no lightning. Finally, the light began to dim.

"I'm tired of this," said Rafe. "How long are we going to sit here?"

"It's not bright and sunny anymore, and isn't going to be until tomorrow," said Winnie. "I think it's time to try out the cave."

They followed the path up as it wound among trees and outcroppings. Eddie had just maneuvered around a large rock, where the trail narrowed even more, when he said, "Here it is." Beyond the rock, an opening wide enough and just tall enough for two people led into the side of the mountain. It was dark inside. Sam retrieved the lantern Perroso had given them from his duffel and pushed a switch on the side. A bright light emanated from it, bright enough to illuminate the cave. It extended back about thirty feet, and the ceiling was about fifteen feet high. The rocky floor was fairly even.

"We're supposed to sleep on *that*?" said Rafe.

"Easy to fix, hotshot," said Eddie. "I'll collect some branches."

"What the hell for?"

"I'll help," said Sam. He knew what Eddie had in mind. They walked back down the slope, breaking off fir branches. It was dark, but they didn't have to go far before they had harvested armloads. When they returned to the cave, they spread these out along one wall.

"Better than bare rock," said Eddie.

They sat on that bare rock and ate a meager supper—several mouthfuls of bread and a few small pieces of cheese each. Sam was tired, but he knew they had several hours ahead of them before they could sleep. No one said anything for a few minutes after they ate. Everyone seemed lost in thought. Then Winnie said, "Anyone know any parlor games?" They laughed, but no one answered.

"How about campfire ghost stories," said Eddie, "anyone want to tell any?"

"Since we don't have a campfire, maybe we should skip that, or tell some other kind of stories."

"We do have a lantern," said Peter, "and we'll have to talk about something to pass the time. There's not much else to do."

"I can't stop thinking what if we end up in some different parallel universe," said Allie. "It worries me."

"If we do," said Eddie, "maybe I'll become a guru, now that I've seen how Perroso did it, and have my devoted followers wait on me."

"I have to believe we'll get back to Earth," said Sam.

"If the mother doesn't take us back," said Winnie, "maybe the next stop will at least have cigarettes, and coffee."

"We have to think about another possibility," said Sam. "The portal here is a long way from where we were deposited off the coast of Melenca. What if we do get back to Earth, but somewhere else—away from the Caribbean?"

"Compared to getting to Melenca in the first place and going back to some other parallel universe, I think that's a pretty piddly problem."

"Yeah, your credit cards should work, Captain," said Eddie. "You'll make sure we get home."

They talked about this possibility briefly, then Winnie said, "No one has mentioned the elephant in the room. What happens if the whirlwind doesn't appear?"

"If it doesn't appear tomorrow," said Sam, "that doesn't mean it isn't coming. Perroso said it doesn't appear every day. But he said it appears often. And he's sent people to it who never showed up again—including Caruso."

"We can't afford to wait long," said Allie. "The rockslides and gas cloud are getting closer."

"Don't run for it until we absolutely have to."

"We're assuming we're so remote we don't have to worry about the MNAA finding us," said Peter. "But we don't know how intensively they're searching the countryside. They appear motivated to hunt down Perroso, but they'd be glad to catch some Outbounders. So would the rightcakes we encountered."

"We have a good view from the ledge," said Eddie. "We can send a lookout periodically. If we see someone coming, we can hide in the cave."

"If someone does come into this area, they'll spot the skimmers," said Allie. "Then it won't take them long to find the valley."

"Let's hope we don't have to worry, and the whirlwind shows up soon," said Sam.

They fell silent again. Then Winnie said, "Let's talk instead about when we do get back. I am going to write about our travels in Melenca. But first things first—a pack of smokes."

"What we do first is going to depend on how much time has passed on Earth," said Sam. "Has the same amount of time gone by on Earth as on Melenca? If so, then the first thing to do is let our families know we're safe. And the world. For sure, we'll have been reported missing, and everyone will assume our plane went down somewhere in the Caribbean."

"Well, probably not," said Eddie. "We're pretty casual around the islands, at least with little charter services like mine. I don't file manifests with passenger lists. So I'm the only one who'll need to get in touch with the authorities—if anyone on Cabo Sereno was paying enough attention to notice my flight plan didn't work out."

"Then if not much time has passed on Earth, it won't be so urgent to notify people."

"Or if it's twenty years, it won't exactly be urgent either," said Winnie.

"Twenty years—maybe that pain-in-the-ass inspector on Lamora will be dead by then," said Eddie.

"Even if it's just a couple of days," said Allie, "I'll have to contact my friend, since I didn't show up at the resort where she's staying."

"What are you going to do, Eddie?" said Sam. "You lost your plane."

Eddie shrugged. "I've got insurance. If I buy a used plane, I'm good at fixing things mechanically—I can get it humming before long."

There was silence again for a while, then Peter said, "One thing we haven't talked about is what we've experienced on a deeper level. I mean traveling to a parallel universe. What does it all mean to go through this experience—to us as human beings?"

They thought about this question for a moment. Then Allie said, "I'm no philosopher, but I am a believer. There may be different universes, but they're all part of one creation,

I think." She paused for a moment. "I'm just thinking out loud, but it seems to me as different as our two universes are—and others, if there are others—there's still a lot in common between them. We were able to fit in, sort of, to some extent."

"People are people, you mean," said Peter. "Beldan, Dalbin, Lirea, Ravinn, all the rest. We felt a kinship with them." He paused. "I'm not a believer, but it seems to me there's a lot about the universe—or universes—we don't understand, and maybe never will."

"I don't worry about any of that deeper stuff," said Eddie. "To me, this was an adventure, and if I can disrupt the routine for a few weeks and get back safely, I'm all aboard."

"There's a lot of 'deeper stuff' to ponder," said Winnie. "But I'll leave that to you deeper thinkers. For me, immersing ourselves in a different world was fascinating. I could write a book. In fact, I think I will."

"What about you, Sam?" said Allie.

"I suppose I'm a believer. I don't go to church much. These deeper questions are fascinating, but I don't have any deep answers. What you said, Allie, makes sense, and what you said too, Peter. Now that I've been in Melenca, I'll probably think about these things off and on for the rest of my life. And also about the people we were involved with. I care about them."

"And you, Rafe?" said Winnie.

"There wasn't much I can use in starting companies. I mean, it was interesting and all that, especially seeing how the concerns work in Melenca, but I don't know how any of it helps me."

"But aside from work-related things, what did you find life-changing?" said Peter.

"Like I said, it was interesting. But I don't know if it will affect me in the long run. Sure, I'll remember it."

They talked more about what they would like to do with their lives once they were on Earth. Sam felt uneasy. He talked vaguely about making changes in the family business. He didn't talk about who he would spend that future with. Allie was vague too. *What is she thinking? What does she want? I'm still not sure.*

Finally it was late enough to turn in. Sam found the bed of fir branches comfortable enough, tired as he was, and he was asleep in a few minutes.

There was no food left. They drank the last of their water. *If the whirlwind doesn't show up soon, we'll have to go somewhere to get water. But we may have to run for it anyway.*

The morning dawned bright and clear overhead, but in the distance the haze filled the sky. Sounds of splitting and booming were increasing. It was dim in the cave, but light enough to see if they sat near the entrance.

Not long after waking up, Sam volunteered to climb to the ledge as a scout. He could see a long way from that vantage. No people or vehicles were visible as he scanned the horizon. He remained there for half an hour, as long as he dared—he didn't want to get caught up there if a strong wind suddenly whipped up—then returned to the cave. They waited, watching for any of the signs. And waited. After an hour, Eddie said he would take a watch at the ledge. When he came back into sight almost half an hour later, he was scrambling down the path from the ledge, and when he reached the valley he ran toward the path to the cave.

"I saw MNAA haulers, three of them, approaching the bridge," he said when he reached them. "Once they get across, it won't be long until they find the skimmers."

"How could they know to search this area?" said Winnie.

"As I said, they could have been intensively searching, area by area," said Peter.

Or did someone hear me ask Benaro about a bridge? Or Ermolo? And report it?

"What do we do?" said Winnie. "Stay here and hide? If the whirlwind doesn't appear before the MNAA does, we can't risk going down into the valley"

"Look at the bushes!" exclaimed Allie. "They're swaying in the wind. A strong wind."

"There wasn't any wind up on the ledge," said Eddie. Suddenly there was a clap of thunder and a bolt of lightning shot down across the valley, and the blue sky of a moment earlier was overcast. "Let's get the hell down into the valley!"

Instinctively, Sam reached into his duffel and grabbed his dead cell phone, wallet, and keys. He would soon need them. At least he hoped so.

"Good idea," said Winnie, as she reached into her own duffel, and the others followed her example. Then they hurried down the path into the valley.

On the opposite slope there was a loud crack and a rock face split and boulders tumbled down. The wind blew stronger. There was another loud peal and a lightning bolt flashed down. Winnie rubbed her eyes. "Dirt keeps blowing in," she said, her eyes red and watering.

The wind was fierce now. There was another loud crack, and a jagged streak of lightning shot down the valley across from them, then another peal of thunder and another vivid streak, this time on the side they'd come down from. Suddenly flames shot up on the mountainside across from them.

"Perroso didn't say anything about fire," yelled Rafe. There was another flash of lighting and then another and another. They all huddled together. And then suddenly the wind stopped. The sky remained dark, but it was still in the valley. There was no more lightning. There were no sounds.

"Wherever we end up, Allie, whatever happens to us," said Sam, "I want to be with you."

She looked at him. "So do I, Sam, with you," and she clasped his hand. Suddenly the valley was spinning around them, and they could see nothing outside the swirling air right around them, and Sam felt himself lifted, still holding onto Allie's hand.

24

— • —

GOING HOME?

The spinning abruptly stopped. Sam was lying on a beach. The surf rolled to a stop just below his feet. Straight ahead were woods at the edge of the beach—towering palm trees, as well as hibiscus and bougainvillea. A good sign. There was no wind. He propped himself up on his arms and looked to his left. Allie lay not far away. She shook her head and sat up. Beyond her lay Peter, and then farther, Winnie. He couldn't see anyone else in that direction and looked the other way. In the distance lay Rafe, and still farther away, Eddie. So they were all back—or wherever they had ended up. He hoped they were all OK. He scrambled up. Allie was standing too, and Winnie and Peter were both rising to their feet. In the other direction, Eddie was standing, and Rafe was kneeling.

Sam went to Allie. "Are you all right?" he said.

"A little shaken up, but OK."

Winnie joined them, then Peter. Eddie and Rafe were striding toward them. "Hallelujah, we're back on Earth!" exclaimed Winnie.

"Maybe," said Sam.

"Look at the palm trees, Sam. We didn't see any around Secora."

"Remember the possibilities. It could be that we've ended up on a parallel world that's closer to Earth in the range of possible worlds."

"Goddamnit, Sam, don't dash my dreams!"

"I'll bet we are back," said Allie. "Still, Sam's right, we do need to look for other signs, just to be sure."

"What kind of signs?" said Rafe.

"Familiar objects on Earth we didn't see in Melenca."

"If our phones work here, we can call our families," said Sam. "That should settle it."

"But what if it's a universe so close to us that it contains duplicates of the people we know?" said Peter.

"Then what would the difference be? What would it matter, if it was that close? If everyone in my family, and all my friends, are here, but there's no double of me anywhere, then I'll conclude I'm back on our Earth."

"At least can we agree that we're not in Melenca anymore?" said Winnie.

"We didn't see any palm trees along the coast there, and anyway we're for sure not in the Hazy Mountains anymore," said Eddie. "I doubt this portal, however it works, would be so inconsiderate as to dump us somewhere else in Melenca."

"As long as it doesn't have something else in store for us," said Sam.

"We're not going to find out standing here gabbing. Let's get a move on." Eddie looked around. "The question is, do we walk along the beach or head inland and look for a road?"

"If we are back in the Caribbean, we ought to run into a resort or a town if we stay on the beach," said Peter.

"Unless we're on a small, uninhabited island."

"That would be just our fucking luck," said Winnie, "make it all the way back to Earth and get stranded on a desert island."

"Let's walk along the beach," said Allie, "at least to start out. Even if we don't run into a town soon, or people, we might spot a clearing or a road or something off the beach, which we might not find if we go straight inland."

"Which way?" said Rafe.

"We ought to run into something either way," said Eddie.

They set off past where Peter had been lying. They walked for about ten minutes. Despite the initial positive signs, Sam felt uneasy. Then he heard a noise in the sky. A jet streamed lazily overhead. He stopped and watched it. So did the others.

"Look at that, Sam!" called Winnie. "Another sign! Convinced?"

"It's a good sign," he admitted. "Still, that doesn't change what I said earlier—we could be on a world that's just a little different."

"OK, how about if we come across any natives, we ask them who Babe Ruth is?"

"Very funny," said Allie.

They resumed walking. Another ten minutes went by. Then in the distance, Sam spotted two small figures, coming toward them. Eventually they resolved into two men, and as they got closer, Sam realized something else: one was black. The other had an olive complexion. Not like anyone they had encountered in Melenca. The men had on faded jeans and cloth work shirts, tucked in—not tunics down to their waists. As they approached closer, the two men suddenly stopped. They peered at the group in front of them.

"What kind of clothes are those?" said the black man in a Caribbean lilt.

"We've, uh, just been somewhere where they dress really differently," said Winnie.

"No kidding," said the olive man, with the same accent. "Are you part of a cult?"

"It's a long story," said Peter. "Tell me, what land is this?"

"Land?" said the black man.

"What island are we on?" said Allie.

"You don't know what island you're on?" said the olive man. "Are you on a drug trip?"

"I wish," said Winnie. "No, we're serious—we have a good reason for asking."

The men looked at each other. "You're on Cabo Sereno," said the black man.

Winnie looked at Sam. "Convinced?"

"I think so," he said, smiling. He looked back at the men. "Just to be sure, who's the president of the United States?"

The men looked at each other again. "Why, Joe Biden," said the olive man. "Everyone knows that."

"I think we're home," said Allie.

The men stared at them suspiciously when Peter thought to ask them what the date was. The answer: August 7. They looked even more suspicious when he asked the year as well.

"What was the date when we boarded Eddie's plane?" Peter asked his companions.

"August 4," said Sam. "Only three days have passed here!"

They got directions to the nearest town, which wasn't far down the beach. Eddie was familiar with San Felipe, which was large enough to find somewhere to buy clothes and phone chargers, and a good meal. They could catch buses there to wherever else on Cabo Sereno they needed to go.

They reached San Felipe in fifteen minutes. They were relaxed now, indeed exuberant. San Felipe had some old, small stores, as well as a few more modern, international chain stores. There were a couple of new modern hotels among old inns, and a few newer restaurants mixed between old hole-in-the wall eateries. People stopped and stared at them as they walked. *Our outlandish clothes!* Sam realized. At a municipal building, they waited while Eddie confirmed to the appropriate officials that he was in fact alive. It didn't take long.

"Did they believe you?" said Winnie.

"They didn't seem too concerned. They had sent out a plane over the water, but didn't spot any wreckage. I think they assumed I had gone off course to suit a charter passenger. There are lots of places I could have landed a seaplane."

He led them then to a large department store, one of the newer ones. "Wonder if they'll take Melencan coins," said Winnie.

"You go right ahead and try it if you want," said Eddie. "I'm not going to bail you out."

She used a credit card. They bought enough clothes for several days, and backpacks and phone chargers, and Eddie got a power strip. "Let's go get something to eat, and if I have to I'll bribe the waiter to plug in our power strip, and charge our phones," he said.

"Wait a minute," said Winnie, "one more thing." She wandered off. A few minutes later, she returned brandishing a carton of cigarettes. "Like I said, first things first."

"Before we go," said Peter, "our clothes." They found restrooms and changed into more conventional clothes for Earth. Back on the street, no one paid them any mind.

After waiting for Winnie to take a tobacco break, they were soon seated outdoors at a café, digging in hungrily to the first real meal they'd had since breakfast the previous day. It was early afternoon, they learned; several of them mentioned ordering coffee, since they had gone for so long without, but after returning safely to Earth, they all had beer or wine. They didn't stop at one.

"I don't have to contact my family. I don't have to look for a whirlwind," said Sam. "I'm good with sitting here all afternoon."

"I'm pretty sure we all feel that way," said Winnie. "But Allie's got to contact her friend, right? Though you seem pretty relaxed too for someone who's been missing for three days."

Allie laughed. "After what we've been through, having to explain why I didn't show up on time and where I've been in the meantime seems a pretty small problem. I've just got to decide whether to tell the truth or concoct some fanciful story."

"I think any story would come across as less fanciful than the truth. What about your family? What if she's contacted them?"

"She's a friend I used to work with. She doesn't know my family or how to contact them." She paused for a moment. "If she did dig around and find them, I'll just have to contact them too."

"The rest of us will have to get on with what we came here for at some point, I suppose. But I wouldn't mind another beer before we go."

As they enjoyed another round of drinks, Winnie said, "We'll soon have to go our separate ways, which will seem strange, since we've been voyaging together, as Eddie has it, for what seems eons now."

"Now I think we'll have to say we've been transportaling," said Eddie, "going through one portal, to a strange new world, and then back through another portal."

"OK, fellow transportalers, we can at least stay in touch. We can exchange contact info when we have our phones charged. Now, what next?"

"I'm supposed to meet a contact in the capital who's going to orient me to potential field research," said Peter. "I just said I'd be here this week and would get in touch. So I need to travel to Mantara."

"You'll have to take a bus," said Eddie. "I need to file a crash report and insurance claim and so on there. Stick with me, Professor."

"I planned to wing it once I got here," said Winnie. "I may just check into one of these hotels and get the lay of the land." She looked at Sam. "What about you, Sam?"

"I've had other things on my mind." He hesitated. Fresh from his adventures, and with his thoughts on Allie, focusing on the mundane was difficult. Returning mentally to the ordinary would take time. He shook his head to clear his mind. "I was traveling to Cabo Sereno to find out why a major supplier suddenly quit sending products and why the owner isn't responding." *And why we suddenly started getting bills for repayment of the loan my dad stood guarantor for.*

"So, Allie," said Winnie. "Are you going to tell your friend you're running off with a handsome stranger you met in a different universe?"

Allie blushed. "I need to contact her, as soon as my phone has enough charge."

"And you, Rafe?" said Winnie.

"I need to look into labor costs and tax incentives. I guess Mantara is the place to start."

After he finished his beer, Eddie went inside and gathered their phones and the power strip from the suitably motivated waiter who had put them to charge.

"I hope my friend hasn't given up on me," said Allie as she opened her home screen. "Here we go—I've got a text from her." She read it, then burst out laughing. "It's from the day I was supposed to arrive. She got called away by a family emergency and had to go back to the States. She apologizes for not being there, but the bungalow is paid for—she wouldn't let me chip in—so she hopes I don't mind, and can enjoy the place on my own." She looked at Sam. "I wouldn't mind a roommate this week."

"Oddly enough, I need a place to stay," he said.

Eddie told them her resort was one of several that had opened or were under construction along the coast, theirs about twenty-five miles away. They could take the bus, or might arrange a car and driver at a tourist office in town. After exchanging contact information and hugs and saying their good-byes to their constant companions in their adventure of the past few weeks, they parted in different directions, Winnie back down the way they'd come, toward one of the hotels they'd passed, and Eddie, Peter, and Rafe the opposite way, toward the bus station. Sam asked the waiter about a tourist office. It was not far.

There Sam and Allie arranged a car and driver and soon were on their way on the scenic coast road. At first the driver was talkative, but when they were reticent about what they'd been doing in the islands, he gave up. In about forty minutes they were at the resort: a good-sized central building with bungalows arrayed on both sides. There was a restaurant and bar off the lobby in the central building. Not far behind it was the beach.

As Allie checked in, Sam asked the woman at the desk for directions to the town where the supplier's workshop was. It was about twenty miles away. There was a bus.

They stopped at the bar and bought a bottle of wine, then found their bungalow. It was spacious, with a large living area opening onto a dining area and a well-equipped kitchen. A small hall led to two bedrooms. A balcony big enough for four wooden rocking chairs overlooked the sea. They were soon sitting on the balcony, glasses of wine in hand. Sam gazed out at the sea—the Caribbean, not the Boundless, which they were certainly beyond now—then looked at Allie.

"We both want to continue our relationship, Allie. How do we do that?"

She stared at the sea. "I'm not sure Sam. A long-distance relationship is complicated."

"Can we make it a short-range one, then?"

"Move, you mean. You can't—not with your position in your company. I'd have to change jobs, unless I could work remote. But I'd still have to uproot. That's a big decision. I do want to continue our relationship, but we haven't know each other that long. We can afford to take things deliberately."

"That time together has been pretty intense, though. We've grown to know each other as well as if we'd been going out for years under normal circumstances."

"I just need to be certain at each step. I don't want to make—well, you know. We talked earlier about my history."

"Don't compare me to your ex-husband."

She nodded. "It's not fair—I know. But I can't help going about such a big change cautiously."

He looked at her for a moment. "I understand. I'll wait for you to decide what you want to do."

"We've got the rest of the week."

Why can't she decide? She wants to be with me, and she knows I do with her. What's she waiting for? Maybe I should tell her I chose her over Katera, he thought. Then he thought better of it.

Allie rode with him on the bus the next morning. "Do you speak Spanish, Sam?" she'd asked. When he acknowledged he didn't, she said, "I took it in high school and college and spent a semester in Spain. You can use an interpreter." The bus was not an express. It stopped at several small towns. The ride took over an hour. "This factory you're going to stopped sending you products," she said. "Is that a big problem?"

"They're a big chunk of our business, especially since the pandemic started and the supply chain from Africa and Asia was cut. But it's more complicated. They came out of the pandemic with plans to expand, have the craftsmen they employ—and they're all men—take on apprentices to train, and produce more. So we've been gearing up to expand our offerings, reaching out to customers, hiring more staff, so on."

"Can't you replace this concern—firm—with another supplier in the Caribbean?"

"These craftsmen are renowned for their skill. But it's not just that. My dad guaranteed the loan—a big one—they took out to expand. Now we're getting billed by the bank. Apparently the loan isn't being repaid. And we're on the hook."

When they reached Dorengo, they soon found the factory. There was no sign of any activity. The door was padlocked. After questioning a few people nearby, Sam and Allie were soon sitting in an office in town. The lone official, Ricardo Caldera, told them the owner, Vicente Torrijo, once he received the loan, promptly closed the factory, laid off the artisans, and disappeared.

"You're not the only one wanting to know where he is," he said. "Those workers are mostly older, and this work is all they have—there's nothing else for them here." In response to Sam's question why the bank didn't foreclose on the factory, he said it was rented. "They auctioned off the tools, but that didn't amount to much."

Sam thought for a moment. "Who's the most skilled of the workers? Or the most experienced?" he said.

"Martín Portillo is both."

As they walked to Martín Portillo's house, Allie said, "Why talk with him? You've got something in mind?"

"An idea. We'll see."

Martín Portillo invited them into his small house when Sam introduced himself. "I liked your father," he said through Allie. "He valued our work. Understood the quality."

"So did our customers. If I can show you a way to start up again, your friends will join you, right? Can you hire and train apprentices, and make more of the items than you did before?"

"That was the plan, we thought. There are young men without employment in Dorengo, and we are skilled. We were ready to pass those skills on to a new generation. Now. . . ." He shrugged. "We lack the tools. And a facility. So I don't know what you can do."

"Let me talk with Ricardo Caldera, and some others. I will talk with you again soon."

As they stood up to leave, Allie said to Portillo, "That scarf on the chair—it's beautiful."

"My wife made it. She's a weaver, like many of the women here."

As they walked back to the development office, Allie said, "I'm with Martín. How are you going to help him, and the others?"

"If I can get the factory rented and reopened and the craftsmen back to work, replace the tools, then with a steady supply of products, they can pay the rent, and split the profits. I'll meet with bankers for a loan."

"Isn't that far afield from what your company does?"

"You've got to respond to changed circumstances. Melenca taught us that."

"But won't that take a lot of money? Wouldn't you be putting your company—and you—on the hook for its success?"

"It's a gamble, sure—a big one. Combined with what we're already paying on the defaulted loan, it's a lot of money. But I think it's a risk worth taking. If it works, it solves the disruption in our supplies here. Once they get on their feet, they can gradually pay us back for the loan."

She studied him for a moment. "It's more than just a business decision, though. Those men will be destitute without that work."

He nodded. "That's a concern, for sure. We can survive without their products, if I don't work the loan and so on. It will be a big blow, but we can survive—in some form.

I'll figure out how. They can't."

"You're not the only one with an idea. We know the men are artisans. The women are too—weavers. That was a beautiful scarf. What if you add that line to your business—and theirs? The women can work in their homes, at least at first—they already do."

He stopped and looked at her. "That's brilliant. You want a job as vice president of new development?" She laughed.

They were sitting on the balcony drinking wine. Sam was gazing out at the sea again. He felt a sense of accomplishment. *Mom was right. I can handle it.* He could return home with a sense of fulfillment. He'd made it safely through their adventures in Melenca and determined how to find the valley, and they'd returned safely. He'd resolved the problem in Cabo Sereno—at least he hoped so, and the situation looked promising. Still, there was one thing unsettled—something important. *Should I say something to Allie now or just wait until we're leaving?*

Before he could say anything, she spoke. "You asked if I wanted to work in your company. You were facetious, I assume. But I've been thinking. What you're starting is a big undertaking. I think I can contribute." She paused and sipped her wine. "Coordinating with those women, and then promoting their handicrafts on our end—I would find that a challenge, a fulfilling one. And I have worked in marketing."

He stared at her for a moment. "Does that mean . . . are you going to move?"

"I don't have any deep ties where I am now. My family's not there. When I took my current job, I moved to a new city. I've made some good friends—I don't have any trouble doing that."

"So we're going to be deliberate in close proximity?"

She laughed. "I guess so. But I haven't been thinking only about work. How you helped those Newcomers in Melenca, went to help Beldan at the DynaStream plant, and now how you're risking a lot to help these families in 'Dorengo—you're a good person, Sam. I don't have any doubt about that."

"Did you have doubts before today?"

"Not about that. But such big changes. . . ." She took a sip of wine. "After this morning, I suddenly realized I wasn't afraid to move ahead, take the next step."

"I'm glad we went to Dorengo, then, and glad the way things unfolded."

"And I'm glad we'll have to come back to Dorengo periodically, at least until this operation is firmly established. It will be good to come back to Cabo Sereno."

"There's just one thing I'll insist on, though."

"Insist on? Am I missing something?"

"We come straight to Cabo. No more transportaling."

ACKNOWLEDGMENTS

Most books are not completely solitary achievements, and this one is no different. Many people have helped me significantly in bringing it to publication. My readers for my first complete draft (well, second really: I revised the first one significantly after some reflection and some comments from family members who read it) gave me much valuable advice, and this version has changed considerably from the one I gave to my readers. So, many thanks to William Bolick, Michael Grimwood, John Holshoe, Lisa Stallings, and Linda Wootton, whose service was much appreciated and improved the book greatly. As is customary, I should add that any of their advice that I should have followed but didn't can be attributed to my stubbornness.

Thanks as well to Bill Nelson for the map of Melenca in the front matter, and to Praneeth Madushanks for the cover illustration and design, also very helpful services, also much appreciated.

And thanks to my family, both immediate and extended, for their support and interest.

About the Author

As the son of a career U.S. Air Force officer, Robert Milks grew up in many different places (all in this universe). By the time he left home for college at eighteen, he had spent half his life outside the continental United States. In this childhood, he witnessed cultures different from his own, but honestly, nothing prepared him for the America from 2016 on, so he felt compelled to make some of the types of people and the events of those years the object of satire (well, really, they suggested themselves), and placing them on a world in a parallel universe seemed a good way to proceed.

After working in writing and editing for forty-five years, in journalism, organizational communication, and publishing, he's mostly retired. He's taken lately to studying French, German, and Spanish, all of which he studied in his youth, in hopes of being able to communicate in them at home and abroad, but is finding now that remembering vocabulary and grammar is harder than it used to be—who knew? (When you're good at something when you're young, you should be good at it in your dotage, it seems to him. That only seems fair if you have a skill in life.) He's contemplated picking up his trumpet after more than forty-five years and relearning how to play it, but he's fairly confident his wife and their dog would not be pleased.

He lives in Cary, North Carolina, with his wife (and dog).